Dear Reader

Welcome to two books in one—and to two strong, sexy heroes brought to us by Janice Kay Johnson and Muriel Jensen. In the first story, meet gorgeous Chief of Police Ben McKinsey. He definitely doesn't intend to get involved with the family next door—but he ends up becoming a part of it. While our second hero, town sheriff Ethan Drum, finds himself duped into playing fiancé to a single mum—and loving it!

Happy reading,

The Editors

GW00402112

Harlequin, Harlequin Duets and Colophon are
trademarks used under licence.

First published in Great Britain 1999
by Harlequin Mills & Boon Limited,
Eton House, 18-24 Paradise Road, Richmond, Surrey TW9 1SR

THE FAMILY NEXT DOOR © Janice Kay Johnson 1998
THE LITTLE MATCHMAKER © Muriel Jensen 1997

ISBN 0 373 59715 0

20-9908

Printed and bound in Great Britain
by Caledonian International Book Manufacturing Ltd, Glasgow

The Family Next Door
JANICE KAY JOHNSON

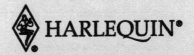

HARLEQUIN®

TORONTO • NEW YORK • LONDON
AMSTERDAM • PARIS • SYDNEY • HAMBURG
STOCKHOLM • ATHENS • TOKYO • MILAN • MADRID
PRAGUE • WARSAW • BUDAPEST • AUCKLAND

PROLOGUE

JUDITH KANE STARED at the television screen. Amid a wash of golden light and romantic music, a mother embraced her fair-haired daughter. Credits rolled down the increasingly misty picture.

With the suddenness of a blow, anguish gripped Judith, cramping her stomach, stealing her breath, momentarily paralyzing her. Oh, God, would it never get any easier?

She swallowed. Movement returned and she used the remote control to turn off the television set.

"Hey, I was watching!" her nine-year-old son complained.

"Tough," Judith said, her tone astonishingly normal, unsympathetic, motherly. He couldn't know how she suffered. At least she had him; she didn't want him ever to believe that he wasn't enough. "Time for you to do your homework."

Zach turned beseeching brown eyes on her. "All I have is spelling. Can't I do it tonight?"

"Nope," she said firmly. "Tonight we may decide we want to play a game or read for longer than usual. But we won't be able to if you have to do homework."

"Oh, okay," he agreed, disgruntled. When he

thought she wasn't looking, he scrunched his freckled nose at her.

She pretended not to see. As he got out his notebook at the kitchen table and she opened the dishwasher to unload it, Judith ran an internal check. The anguish had subsided, ebbing like a tide, leaving only a salty trace of its presence.

Would the time ever come when she could think of Sophie without that heavy, heart-wrenching pain? When she might go for days without a sudden reminder catching her unaware with the force of a blow and all but immobilizing her?

Did she *want* the image of Sophie's sweet face to leave her, even for a few minutes? The idea was terrifying. Nothing, she thought fiercely, would ever make her forget her small daughter.

Drawing a deep breath, she glanced toward Zach, to see that he was watching her anxiously. Judith managed to produce a reassuring smile for his benefit. After a moment, seeming satisfied, he bent his head over his work and began laboriously copying spelling words.

The dishwasher was empty; Judith scanned the kitchen, but counters, sink and floor were spotless. She hadn't always been such a compulsive housekeeper. Now she was constantly searching for something— anything—to keep her mind occupied.

When the telephone rang, her heart lurched. After two years, she still reacted the same every time. As if *this* call were the one, as if a voice would say, "Mrs. Kane, we have Sophie right here."

"Hello?" she said.

"Mrs. Kane?"

She knew the caller instantly, and her pulse leaped. Hope drained her strength and she sagged against the tiled edge of the counter. "Yes?" she said, with both eagerness and dread.

"This is Detective Edgekoski." The police officer didn't immediately go on.

In his hesitation she read bad news, the worst, and she stood frozen with her back to her son, her fingers squeezing the hard plastic of the phone until it creaked. She couldn't say a word. *Please, God,* she prayed, as she had prayed countless times these last two years. Always fruitlessly. But this time her prayer was different.... *Not dead. Please. Let her be alive. Healthy. Still my Sophie.*

"Mrs. Kane—" the policeman's voice was gentle "—we've found your daughter and your ex-husband."

A sobbing breath escaped her. "Is she...?"

"She's fine. She's in a receiving home waiting for you to come and get her. They were in Kansas City, Missouri. A mother at your daughter's preschool recognized Sophie from a photograph on the back of a local mailer. She called the police."

Judith couldn't think, could only feel. "Oh, thank God! I need to get a flight." Her mind jumped. "She's really waiting for me? Is she...is she anxious to come home?"

"I'm sorry, Mrs. Kane," he replied patiently, "they didn't say. She's undoubtedly scared. Why don't you let me know when you have a flight reservation, and then I'll alert the Kansas City police that you're coming."

"Yes. Fine." She scribbled his phone number down, as if she hadn't called him weekly for years, begging, pleading, nagging, bullying. A moment later, she hung up the receiver and turned to her son.

He was staring at her. "You're crying."

She touched her wet cheek in vague surprise. "They've found Sophie."

Zach's mouth worked, but he said nothing for the longest time. At last, he swallowed. "And...and Dad, too?"

"Yes." *May he burn in hell.* "Yes, the police found both of them."

"Are you sad?" he whispered, eyes saucer wide.

"No." Through her tears, a smile trembled, widened, blazed with joy and trepidation. "No, I'm gloriously happy!" She laughed and held out her arms. "Let me hug you. Then we have to get ready to go pick up your sister."

CHAPTER ONE

JUDITH PARKED at the curb behind the real estate agent's car and got out. The interior of her van was stifling but shadowy; now the direct heat of the sun struck her with a physical shock.

Zach had wanted to look at all the other houses, but the hundred-degree temperature had apparently enervated him, too, because this time he didn't say anything or make any move to follow her. In her booster seat in back, Sophie sat sucking her thumb, staring vacantly ahead. She was five years old and due to start kindergarten this fall, but either she was immature or she had regressed because of the trauma of losing her father. Was she ready for school? The psychologist she'd seen since her return thought she was, that kindergarten would be good for her. Judith wasn't so sure. Another worry to add to her list. She suppressed a sigh.

Lyle Strother, cool from his late-model air-conditioned Ford, stepped out and hoisted his pants. His belly immediately settled back over the waistband.

"Nice four-bedroom ranch," the real estate agent said. "Two and a half baths—something you'll appreciate with the kids there. Walking distance to the elementary school."

She turned to face the house. The lawn was patched with brown; the leaves on twin apple trees hung limp. The house itself was well cared for, clapboards painted white, black shutters, a big picture window in front.

"Air-conditioned," he added.

Longing seized her. Rylan *was* behind bars, after all, at least for the moment. Surely they were safe here, in such a small town. This was a good neighborhood. Zach would like being able to walk to school, to the town swimming pool, maybe to friends' houses eventually. She could walk to work. The house was empty, the agent had said; they could move right in.

And it was air-conditioned.

But what if a judge let Rylan go? She'd been warned he would probably be released on bail. And even after he came to trial... She'd heard so many horror stories about noncustodial fathers who'd stolen their children and barely been slapped on the wrist after they were caught. A policewoman in Kansas City had privately told her that when Sophie was torn from him, Judith's ex-husband had sworn he'd be back for her. "Tell that to your mother, the bitch!" he'd bellowed as they shoved him into a police car.

"I don't know," she said. "I'm used to living on acreage." That was a flat lie—she'd spent her entire life in Boston and never even had a real yard, much less a pasture. "Do you have anything farther out of town?"

Lyle looked at her as if she were crazy. Maybe he was right. "A single woman with kids, you're better off in town."

She gritted her teeth but figured she didn't dare

alienate him. Besides, hadn't she chosen a small community like this precisely because she knew people would stick their noses into each other's business? Now was no time to start resenting it!

When she said nothing, he hooked his thumbs in his belt and hoisted again, just as uselessly. Why did he bother? Judith wondered.

Sounding exasperated, he offered, "Now, I do have some places for sale...."

She wouldn't buy until she knew they were going to stay. Until she knew they were safe, that this could be home.

"I need to rent at first."

"You don't even want to look inside?" He jerked his head toward the house.

"Maybe I'll come back to this one."

He gave a noisy sigh. "I do know of a little place that's available out of town. Nothing near as nice as this. No air-conditioning. I don't even know if it has a dishwasher."

Judith pulled her shirt away from her sticky skin. "It's almost September. Surely it won't stay this hot much longer."

Lyle shrugged. "Don't know how good the furnace is, either."

Wonderful. Judith knew winters were cold here in Mad River, just on the east side of the Cascade Mountains in Washington State. Before she'd accepted the job here, teaching a fifth-grade class, she had gone to the library and read everything she could find about it, including temperature extremes.

She felt the sweat trickling down her back. Those

temperature readings had been pretty abstract when she was sitting in the cool, dimly lit Boston Public Library.

"May I see this other place?" she asked, struggling to stay pleasant. "If it doesn't suit, we can come back here."

The agent gave his balding head a disgusted shake. "Your decision. Just stick right behind me."

As if there were any traffic to make trailing him a challenge.

The town was so small they reached its outskirts in minutes. Judith didn't know whether they were still in the city limits or not when he turned off the paved road onto a dirt one. In his wake, a cloud of dust enveloped her car.

Zach roused from his trance. "Where are we going?"

"To look at another house."

"But nobody lives out here."

He was right, she thought uneasily. Woods that looked awfully dry to her New England eye clambered up a rocky ridge to one side of the lane; on the other, a bare trickle in an otherwise parched streambed meandered through the scant grass of a pasture bordered by a split-rail fence.

Living in town had its dangers, but she didn't want to be too isolated, either. There had to be neighbors nearby, somebody who would notice a stranger lurking around or trying to pull one of her children into a car.

The reluctant thought came: Sophie wouldn't need pulling; she'd go willingly. That was part of what terrified Judith. Rylan could take her back so easily.

"Well, if we don't like it…" she began.

"Horses."

At the one single word, Judith jerked her head up. "What?"

Glancing in the rearview mirror, she saw that Sophie had momentarily taken her thumb from her mouth and was—miracle of miracles—focusing on something outside the car. "Horses," she said again, almost eagerly.

It was true. A palomino and a brown horse stood motionless, heads hanging, in the meager shade of a dry pine tree.

"That's right," Judith said in that fake cheery voice she hated. "Maybe they'll be our neighbors."

Predictably, Zach piped up, "Can *we* have a horse?"

"Well, probably not for now."

"Why not?"

The car jolted into a rut and Judith's head struck the roof. She slowed still further and blinked grit from her eyes. "I wouldn't know how to take care of one," she admitted. And what if they had to move again? Would they haul a horse trailer with them? But she didn't want to tell the children that living here might not be permanent.

What good would it do to flee, anyway? her logical side demanded. It wasn't as if she were in hiding here; she'd taken a job under her own name, and her father and mother and Rylan's parents knew where she and the children were. A private investigator could find them with no trouble. To go into hiding, she would have to steal the children from their grandparents as

Rylan had with Sophie, and she couldn't do that to either of them. And how would she make a living if she couldn't use her teaching certificate? Waitressing wouldn't support the three of them very well.

But if Rylan came here, he'd stand out. She was counting on getting to know people and letting their neighborly eyes help keep her children safe.

Maybe he wouldn't even try, once he found she'd sold her town house and they had vanished. She was convinced he'd taken Sophie because he knew it was the best way to hurt her, Judith, not because he really wanted to be a single parent. He hadn't been such a good father back when she'd asked him to spend more time with their children.

The blue Ford ahead passed a two-story white farmhouse on the right, with a red barn behind it. Somebody did live here. They wouldn't be entirely alone. The lane narrowed further, and a few hundred yards beyond, it ended in the yard of a ramshackle house not old enough to have character but too old for air-conditioning.

It wasn't as bad as she'd imagined, Judith thought optimistically. Maybe it would do. It felt…safe here, so far off the main road. And the only way in and out required going by the other house first.

She put the van in park and turned off the engine. In the silence, she said, "You guys want to get out and look at this one?"

She braced herself for sullenness from Zach. To her surprise, he said, "Yeah, okay," and unbuckled his seat belt.

Cheeks flushed, Sophie stuck out her lower lip. "Can I go look at the horses?"

Feeling helpless, Judith said in that same false tone, "I'm afraid not, kiddo. What if they bite or kick or something? But if we rent this house, maybe their owner will let you pet them some time."

The five-year-old's mouth trembled. "I want to pet them now."

Oh, God. To make Sophie happy, wasn't it worth traipsing over to that split-rail fence to have a look at those poor hot horses, which were unlikely in this heat to do more than twitch an ear?

"Well...maybe after we've looked at the house," she said weakly.

Sophie gave her a measuring stare from gray eyes rather like Judith's own. "Okay," she said, and didn't protest when Judith climbed into the back and unfastened her seat belt.

Lyle was running a finger over the dusty hood of his formerly shiny blue car. The toothy smile that had greeted her at each of the previous houses was markedly absent. His gaze went past her to the drab, single-story house. "Not much to look at."

Beige paint was starting to peel, and the varying colors of roof shingles showed where patching had been done. The windows looked blank, covered only by cheap blinds, but the frames appeared solid and were made of wood.

"Well...it could use some work."

"Hasn't been anyone in it for eight months or so."

Which undoubtedly meant that gritty dirt had penetrated cupboards and closets, and spiderwebs would adorn corners. Well, she could clean, and school didn't start for two weeks.

"Is it owned by the people who live back in that farmhouse?" she asked, starting up the steps. The house did have an old-fashioned porch, at least, which she liked. And two big old lilac bushes, one on either side of the steps.

"Nah." Lyle was searching his heavy ring of keys for the right one. "Police chief lives there. Ben McKinsey. Not real sociable. He'd probably let this place fall to ruin if it was his."

"The police chief?" Judith turned to gaze consideringly back at the farmhouse. Sophie and Zach, sitting on the porch steps, did the same.

"Folks who own this place live over t'other side of the mountains. Issaquah. Bought this figuring they could keep it rented." His tone suggested they were fools. "There was talk about a ski area up here. Came to nothing."

She didn't care about ski areas or her future landlord, only her new neighbor. A policeman. How lucky could they get?

"Ah." The real estate agent had found the right key and inserted it into the lock.

The door gave way, and Judith, holding her breath, stepped across the threshold. Unless the interior was really, really terrible, this would be their new home.

The moment she saw the large living room and the neat brick fireplace, she let out a sigh of relief. Yes!

Zach was already thundering down the hall toward the bedrooms. Sophie, as usual, hung back. When Judith held out a hand, she shrank away. Though Judith knew she should be used to it, she still hurt every time her daughter rejected her.

She looked up to meet the agent's eyes. She'd seen him watching her with Sophie before, and by now puzzlement bordered closely on suspicion.

"She's tired," Judith said, forcing a smile. "We drove across the country in just five days, you know."

Only after a pointed pause did he nod and say expressionlessly, "Hadn't you better take a look at the kitchen?"

She bit her lip. "Yes. Of course."

Was there hardwood under the worn brown carpet? Judith was already making plans, mentally scrubbing the narrow sash windows until they shone, putting up new blinds, setting out her furniture once it arrived. If the rent was as low as she hoped, she wouldn't have to dip into the money she would use to buy a house once they were permanently settled.

Maybe here in Mad River; she didn't know. The name of the town reflected its oddity, or maybe her state of mind. This was an alien land, nothing like their old home, but for now it felt safe. Shielding her children from their father was all that counted.

THE POLICE RADIO crackled. Frowning, Ben McKinsey ignored it. Ahead of him, a kid who couldn't have been more than five or six years old was walking alongside the highway. The dirt shoulder wasn't very wide, and he flinched when a car whizzed by. Ben put on his flashers, slowed his squad car and eased to a stop behind him.

The boy gave a frightened look over his shoulder

but stopped walking when he saw the police officer get out of the car.

Ben didn't much like kids, but he'd look damned silly calling in backup to deal with this one. He headed toward the boy, hearing how forced his bantering tone sounded. "Hi, young man. You going somewhere special?"

Well, hell. A kid wouldn't recognize insincerity.

A short haircut didn't keep a cowlick from standing straight up on the crown of the boy's head. Skinny legs stuck out of blue soccer shorts. Dirty toes poked out of leather sandals.

Ben wondered if he had underestimated the kid. His eyes narrowed and he thought long and hard about whether he should answer any questions, but finally he said with dignity, "My mom's waiting for me. She works at the AM-PM."

The convenience store-gas station was another half mile away and across a busy intersecting road. What in tarnation was the kid doing out here alone?

Frowning, Ben asked, "Don't you have a baby-sitter who could have driven you or at least walked with you?"

"Lisa and her boyfriend were smooching." The boy made a horrible face. "I *told* her I wanted my mom, but she didn't listen. So I just left."

"Ah." If his mom didn't take care of the baby-sitter, Ben would. Hoping to be persuasive, he went with the favorite-uncle tone again. "Well, you just hop on in my car, and I'll take you to find your mom."

A semi thundered by, and the kid almost stumbled into the ditch. But still he hesitated, scuffing the dirt with one foot. "I'm not supposed to get in cars unless it's Mom's friend Janet or maybe my uncle John. I don't know you."

Why "maybe" Uncle John? Ben wondered. Okay, forget uncles, favorite or otherwise. "Has your mom ever talked to you about what to do if you get in trouble or you're lost? Who you should go to for help?"

His forehead puckered. "Yes. She said I should look for a policeman." His face cleared. "That's what you are, isn't it?"

"That's me." Ben raised an eyebrow. "I'd say you're in trouble right now. A highway is no place for a boy your age to be walking."

A pickup pulling a horse trailer passed next, the trailer swaying. The boy darted a scared look after it, then directed one at Ben. The frying pan and the fire. Smart kid.

"Okay," he finally decided. When Ben held open the passenger-side door, he scrambled in, looking curiously miniature inside the police car.

Once behind the wheel, Ben said, "I'm Chief McKinsey. What's your name?"

"I'm a muk, too."

In the act of pulling out onto the highway, he shot the kid a glance. "A muk?"

"My name," the little boy said precisely, "is Jonathan McDaniel. You know. *Mc.*"

Ben might not like kids, but he had to smile. "Gotcha."

He parked out front of the store, and he and Jonathan went in. Ben prayed that Mom really did work here and this was her shift. He didn't know what in hell he'd do with this kid if he couldn't find his mother. He sure wasn't going to leave him with the baby-sitter, but taking him to a receiving home seemed a little extreme. He was decently dressed and looked healthy enough. Dirty, but Ben seemed to remember that boys his age were always dirty.

The heavy gray-haired woman behind the cash register couldn't be the kid's mother. Jonathan glanced dismissively at her and rotated in place, scanning the store.

"Mommy!" he cried suddenly, and a young woman coming out of a back room hurried toward them.

"Jon! What are you doing here?" Crouching, she hugged her son protectively and looked up at Ben. "Is...is something wrong?"

He explained the circumstances; she chewed the kid out, but her eyes glittered dangerously when he told her about the baby-sitter being too busy smooching to notice Jonathan leaving.

"It'll have to be back to the day-care center, then," she said helplessly. "They charge so much, but I have to know Jon is safe."

The kid didn't look distressed by his mother's exasperation. Jonathan was bound to get in trouble again down the road, Ben suspected, but thank God he wasn't his problem anymore. With a tip of his hat, Ben uttered a terse goodbye and got back in his squad car. He fastidiously brushed dirt from the passenger seat where Jonathan's small rump had rested. Personally, he'd rather have a drunk in his car than a kid.

Back at the station, he dealt with some paperwork. His phone stayed silent, and according to the dispatcher, all was quiet in the little town of Mad River. Hell, the only crime he could imagine anyone committing in this heat was breaking into the grocery store freezer.

Ben wasn't in a half-bad mood when he turned onto his own road. He'd change to shorts, switch on the fans, indulge in a cold beer, maybe watch the Mariners game on TV.

Sherlock and Travis stood in the shade, using their tails to whisk away the flies. They didn't even lift their heads at the sound of his car, although normally they'd canter on over to the barn to demand alfalfa or oats. He'd wait until it cooled down some to feed them.

Movement caught Ben's eye and he swore under his breath. Someone was looking at the Weller place. He recognized Lyle Strother's blue Ford Taurus.

The last renter had been a reclusive fellow who hadn't bothered Ben much. He'd turned out to be a damned nuisance, though, when someone at the public utility noticed his excessive—and illicit—use of power. Hundreds of thousands of dollars' worth of marijuana plants had been reaching maturity in the bedrooms and living room. The guy had balls to set up business next door to a cop. Ben had kept to himself his regret at losing such an inoffensive neighbor.

The house wasn't exactly a desirable property, and lately real estate had been depressed around here. Nobody had even looked at the place for a long time. He'd hoped things would stay that way.

A woman was coming out of the house. Sunlight caught fiery sparks in her hair. Behind her—good God!—were two kids. They'd probably all climb in that red van and go back to town, find a rental near the school. But no, she was shaking Lyle's hand—not a good sign. And the kids were trotting down the lane toward Ben.

He debated whether or not to hide in the house, but he never had been a coward. He might as well find out the worst.

Now the woman was hurrying after the two kids, almost breaking into a run. They were probably hellions, and she didn't want them making a bad impression on him. Ben pulled his Stetson lower over his forehead and waited, arms crossed, focusing more on the kids than the mother. The father, if there was one, was nowhere to be seen.

The boy was skinny and freckled, hair a dark auburn. The little girl was a flat-out redhead, like her mother.

It was the boy who called, "Are those horses yours?"

"They're mine."

He stopped in front of Ben. "Can we pet 'em?" he asked eagerly. His sister, wearing shortalls and sandals, hid behind her brother.

"No." He didn't smile or make any apologies. "They're not children's ponies. You might get hurt."

"But we could just give 'em a carrot or something," the boy said mulishly.

His mother arrived, hand outstretched. "Hi, we've just rented the house next door. We'll be neighbors. I'm Judith Kane."

At the sight of her close up, he had the strangest reaction. Just a zap, as if he'd scuffed his feet on carpet and then touched something metal. Before he could analyze it further, her words penetrated. He thought an obscenity he didn't utter.

Reluctantly he took her hand, which proved to be small, slender, soft. She wasn't a countrywoman. "Ben McKinsey."

"My children seem to be enchanted with your horses." She said it apologetically, but with underlying teasing, as if she assumed he'd humor them just because they were children.

"I was just telling them to stay out of the pasture." He let go of her hand and flexed his fingers. "They might get kicked."

"Oh." She hesitated, as though expecting him to say more, maybe soften his refusal. When he didn't, her small chin went up a notch. "Certainly," she said crisply. "I'll make sure they don't go near them. Sophie, honey…" She reached out a hand, but the little girl edged away, keeping the brother between her and her mother.

"I want to pet the horsies."

"I'm sorry, sweetie…" Judith Kane sounded remarkably ineffectual. "This man will be our neighbor, but he says the horses aren't safe for you."

The kid howled, "But you *said* we could pet them!"

"I said maybe." Mom circled the boy to reach her daughter, grimly determined despite the half affronted, half apologetic glances she darted at Ben. "We have to go back to town now."

"I don't wanna!"

God almighty. Was he going to have to listen to

them screaming from here on out? Why did they have to choose this house? Why not one of the half-dozen places for rent in town? Was God paying him back for some sin?

Some sin, he thought ironically. If God was getting him, he knew what for.

Judith Kane chased the kid around and finally scooped her up. She carried her off kicking and screaming as if her toenails were being pulled out. Spoiled little brat.

Ben transferred his gaze to the boy, who hadn't moved.

"Hadn't you better go? You don't want your mom to leave you behind."

Something flickered in those dark eyes. "My mom wouldn't leave me."

The cop in Ben noticed two oddities about this simple statement. The first was the emphasis on "mom." So Dad *had* left them. The second was the uncertainty beneath his outward bravado. So maybe the kid was scared that Mom would desert him, too.

Ben gave an internal shrug. Divorce did ugly things to kids. Not that it was his problem, thank God.

"It wouldn't have hurt you to let her pet them," the boy said, and turned and ran off.

Ben didn't even flinch. If he humored them, they'd be over here all the time. If he'd wanted kids, by God he'd have had them.

Too bad Judith Kane came with such a burden, though, he reflected as he watched her stuff the little brat in the van and presumably buckle her in a car seat. She was a beauty despite the carrottop. He guessed that's why he'd felt that peculiar shock; he didn't often meet a woman he wanted on first sight.

Well, this one might have nice breasts, a cute butt and green-gray eyes with a hint of desperation in them, but she also had children.

What a waste.

CHAPTER TWO

ZACH HOVERED over Judith. Sophie peeked from behind him. "Mom," he said, "can't we just go *look* at the horses? We won't go inside the fence or anything."

Judith wiped a smudge of paint from the bare wood floor. She'd painted the living-room walls pale peach and now was doing the woodwork in white. The floor, stripped of the carpet, could have used refinishing, but after all, this was a rental.

"No," she repeated with eroding patience, "you may not. Chief McKinsey made it clear he wanted you guys to stay away from his horses." *And from him.*

"But I'm bored," Zach whined.

Sinking back on her heels, Judith sighed. "I know, hon. I wish you could help me with this part of the painting, but it takes practice. Besides—" she smiled encouragement at her daughter "—Sophie would be bored without you to keep her company."

"But she doesn't want to do anything." He paused, then added sulkily, "Not like there's anything to do anyway. It's too hot to run around, and our board games are boring. Besides, all she can play are dumb little kid ones."

Sophie's eyes widened and tears sparkled in them. "I'm good at games!"

His lip curled. "Yeah, right."

"Am!" she cried, and whirled and fled the living room.

"Zach, for Pete's sake..." Judith gritted her teeth. It wasn't his fault that his sister cried so easily. "She *is* a little kid. Now, go check to be sure she hasn't run out of the house."

"Gol," he mumbled, and shuffled off.

She couldn't blame him for being bored and impatient with having to watch his sister. He wasn't used to having a little sister. The one-hundred-plus degrees outside added to the misery. Judith could only pray it didn't stay this hot for the next month. From Zach's point of view, the worst part was that she was busy making the house livable and had no time to spend at the town swimming pool or playing games or making cookies with them. She had only a few days before it was time to report to Lincoln Elementary School and begin getting her classroom ready for the fifth graders who would arrive eagerly—and not so eagerly—on September 4.

Starting Monday, Zach and Sophie would be enrolled in a YWCA program for children that continued until the first day of school. Judith had been reluctant to put them in it sooner; the move was a big change, and Sophie already felt as if she had been wrenched from the familiar to live with strangers.

Pain tightened Judith's throat, and she briefly closed her eyes. She'd been so sure nothing would ever upset her again if only she had her child back. What she hadn't anticipated was that her own daughter would have forgotten her.

"Zach?" she called.

"She's in bed," he called back. "I think she's falling asleep."

It was naptime. Judith took advantage of the lull to paint as quickly as she could without being sloppy. Maybe Zach would find something to keep himself busy for a few minutes. Maybe he'd fall asleep, too.

If only there were kids next door....

My fault, she thought. She could have rented that house in town. Judith paused to wipe the sweat from her forehead and made a face. That *air-conditioned* house in town. The one that hadn't needed weeks of work to make it livable. Undoubtedly Zach would have found other boys to play with. Probably half the kids in town were at the local pool splashing one another and roughhousing.

But she couldn't afford the time to watch him. And even if he were willing to try to meet other boys on his own if she just dropped him off, she felt uncomfortable with the idea. She couldn't let him get in the habit of riding a bike to friends' houses or hanging out at the school. She had to keep him close. Besides, she needed him to help take care of Sophie.

Maybe that wasn't fair to him, but what alternative did she have? As she painted her way around the corner toward the fireplace, Judith's thoughts circled relentlessly in a rut already well-worn. Why not put Sophie in day care if she didn't have time to spend with her anyway? Zach would be happier—

"Mom."

Zach spoke from so close behind her Judith jumped. "Oh! You scared me."

"How come you're frowning?"

She managed to smile for his benefit—she'd had plenty of practice coming up with those smiles, no matter the turmoil she felt inside. "I was just wishing—" She stopped. "Oh, pooh. Let me finish the woodwork in here, and when Sophie wakes from her nap, we'll go swimming. How's that grab you?"

"Cool!" he said. "I thought you were going to paint the kitchen cabinets, too."

"Tomorrow," she decided. "Or maybe tonight, after it cools down and Sophie goes to bed. Want to help?"

"Do I have to be really, really careful?"

"Nah." Judith nudged him with her shoulder. "We'll lay newspapers on the floor and take the handles off. Just as long as you don't paint the hinges, you can slap it on." And she could go along behind him, smoothing out drips and wiping up messes. The job would undoubtedly be slower than if she did it herself, but the payoff was worth it.

"Cool," he said again. "I wish my Nintendo was here."

"Read," she said firmly.

Zach made a face but turned and left the living room. If he picked up a book at all, it would probably be horror, but reading was reading. Right?

She started on the fireplace surround and mantel, from which she'd earlier sanded flakes of olive green paint. Underneath might be beautiful wood, but she hadn't the time to strip it. Besides…this wasn't her house.

Her thoughts jumped back into the rut. If only the guy next door weren't such a jerk. She'd seen the thinly veiled irritation on his face. Either he didn't like kids, or hers had pushed the wrong button. If she hadn't already signed the papers, she might have changed her mind about renting this house, once she'd met Chief Ben McKinsey.

She could tell Lyle Strother didn't like him, either. What was it he'd said? *Not real sociable.* She snorted. If that wasn't the understatement of the year. Their new neighbor had been in his yard a couple of times when she passed, and his squad car had met her van in the long lane on one of her trips to town. She'd made herself smile and wave, even if she'd rather have snubbed him. The best he'd done in return was tip his hat or incline his head with cool civility.

Jerk. Judith still burned when she thought of the way he'd stood there, a monolith, not saying a single friendly word, not expressing the slightest regret to the kids about the horses, although he must have seen their disappointment. What had really gotten her was the assessing way he'd looked her over. He'd been summing her up as a woman even as he was stony cold to her children. A word for him leaped to mind that was more profane than *jerk* but expressed the same idea.

She had to keep reminding herself that she didn't need a best friend next door. She needed a guard, and she had a suspicion he'd be a dependable one. He'd struck her as a man who would do his duty, whatever his personal feelings for the victims. For her children. He'd looked competent enough: big and solid and intelligent, with a craggy face that missed handsome but would still flutter female hearts if his expression wasn't so grim.

Grim was good, Judith told herself, dipping the brush into the can of paint and ignoring the ache of little-used muscles in her upper arm and shoulder. Grim was an eight-foot-high stone wall around her children. Friendly might be sucked in by Rylan's charm. She pictured Ben McKinsey's square-jawed, expressionless face. No, he and Rylan were as dissimilar as they could be. They wouldn't like each other.

If Chief McKinsey didn't give pony rides to Zach and Sophie, so be it.

She finished the last stroke across the mantel and stepped back to admire her work. The effect was bright, clean, warm, even elegant. The kitchen could wait. She'd soak the brush, find her own bathing suit and spend some time with her children.

As if in response to her thoughts, Zach bounded into the living room. "Sophie's awake!"

Judith slapped the cover on the paint can. "Then let's get this show on the road."

"YOUR ROOM LOOKS terrific." Carol Galindez, the principal, leaned comfortably against Judith's desk. "I like the dinosaur posters and mobile."

Judith, too, gazed with satisfaction around her classroom, which had gone from bare and impersonal to comfortable and cheerful in record time. "I've always been interested in dinosaurs myself, and I've found that fifth graders are the perfect age to get excited about the subject. I've got some great books—I'll bring in some fossils...." She smiled. "Then I'll ask the kids to do projects and write reports. With luck, they'll still be enthusiastic."

"We're very fortunate to have found you with such short notice." The words hung in the air, not quite a question, but inquiring nonetheless.

Judith hesitated. The school district had been desperate for a teacher when the one she'd replaced resigned long after most of those looking for jobs had already signed contracts elsewhere. The relative isolation of the school kept down the number of applicants, the superintendent admitted. Instead of asking her to fly out, he, Carol Galindez and someone from personnel had interviewed Judith in a lengthy conference call. She knew they'd checked her references, and then they had promptly offered her the job. In the interview, she'd simply said that she needed a change. Now, she decided, the time had come for honesty.

"I'm the lucky one to find a position in a place that suited us so well, considering most jobs were filled by the time I decided I had to move," she admitted. "I felt we'd be better off in a small town. My ex-husband is currently awaiting trial for having taken our daughter and fled the state with her. I have no idea what kind of prison term he'll get. I'm afraid he'll try again. I want to live in the kind of community where people would notice a strange man talking to the kids or...oh, trying to take them from school." She let out a gusty sigh.

Carol Galindez was in her mid to late forties, a

plump but stylish woman with dark eyes, wavy brunette hair worn in a French roll and a taste for bright
colors. She'd straightened as Judith spoke, her expression aghast.

"He stole your daughter? Judith, how dreadful! Did
the police get her back right away?"

"It took two years," she admitted, those simple
bald words failing to disguise the agony they represented. "Sophie was only three. She's forgotten me.
It's...it's been very difficult."

The principal surprised her by saying fiercely,
"We'll guard her with our lives—I promise you that!"
She reached out and squeezed Judith's hand, her
brown eyes compassionate. "I take it your son isn't
his? I'm sure Zachary was your only comfort."

"Actually—" Judith's throat felt thick "—Rylan is
Zach's father, too. I've...only been married the once.
But Zach happened to have gone to a friend's instead
of to the day-care center after school the afternoon Ry
picked Sophie up. We assume he'd intended to take
Zach, too. I have no idea why he didn't wait and do
it another time. Part of me was grateful, and the other
part..." This was still hard to talk about. "I hated to
think of Sophie alone," Judith said starkly. "Zach was
so proud to be a big brother. He'd always...shielded
her."

"Oh, Judith," Carol said again. "I'm so sorry.
You've lived every mother's nightmare."

"Except that I'm lucky. I have Sophie back."

"We'll help in any way we can," the principal
promised.

"Thank you." Judith felt her smile twist. "I didn't

mean to get off on personal stuff. I just thought you ought to know.''

"Yes." Now Carol looked thoughtful. "We'll have to let the kids' teachers know the situation. In the staff meeting, I'll remind the aides that we have children in this school involved in custodial disputes. That way they can stay on their toes when they're supervising recess.''

"Thank you," Judith said again. She strove to make her tone professional. "Was there anything else we should discuss about the start of school?"

Carol blinked, shifting gears. "Did I tell you about the DARE program?"

"DARE?"

"Drug Abuse Resistance Education." The principal went on to explain about the program, in which a police officer came into the schools weekly for a semester to talk to kids about drugs, smoking, alcohol and peer pressure. "The DARE program has had great results, and I encourage you to support Chief McKinsey in any way you can."

"Chief McKinsey?" Judith repeated, unable to hide her astonishment.

"Yes, he's teaching it this year." Carol's perfectly plucked eyebrows rose. "You've met him?"

"We're…neighbors." She deliberately evaded the principal's gaze.

Carol asked bluntly, "Did you have a problem with him?"

"Heavens, no!" Judith lied. Well, half lied. "I just had the impression he wasn't crazy about kids. Maybe I hit him on a bad day.''

Carol was silent for a moment. Then she leaned forward and lowered her voice. "Just between you and me and the blackboard, I hear from the high-school principal that he can be pretty short with the teenagers. Which may not be a bad thing. He's probably trying to scare the kids when he's called out there for a fight or because drugs have been found in a locker." She grimaced. "I assume he wouldn't be planning to teach the DARE classes if he hated everybody under five feet tall."

Judith automatically straightened a transparency under the glass on the overhead projector. "Hasn't he done it before?"

"No. A young female officer has taught it the past several years. I hear she's having a difficult pregnancy and has taken some time off."

"Well…" What could she say? Maybe he'd turn out to be a wonder with children. Everyone's children but hers. "I'm sure it'll go fine. Does he start this first week?"

"Yes. We try to get the specialty schedule going immediately."

They talked a little more about the first few days of school before Judith locked her room and walked the principal back to her office.

It was stifling in the building, and through the windows ahead she could see the heat radiating off the pavement. "Do you send kids out to recess if it's still this hot?" she asked.

"I don't know if we've ever had to decide. This never lasts long," Carol assured her. "Days are getting shorter already—you've noticed, haven't you?—

and the thermometer ought to start dropping at night. By November, the sun beating down will be a pleasant dream.''

"Pleasant?" she echoed dubiously.

"Well, you're from Massachusetts, so you know what cold weather is like." Carol grinned as she turned into the school office. "Scared you yet?"

Judith laughed and headed out to the van, which was parked in the staff lot behind one wing of the L-shaped building. The school housed four classrooms at each grade level through sixth, and the middle school, right next door, encompassed seventh and eighth grades. The sports fields and playgrounds didn't abut each other, which she thought was just as well. Fifth and sixth graders already spent enough time thinking and talking about the opposite sex, makeup, popular music and how to look cool, without mixing with the older kids.

Sophie and Zach were safely ensconced in the YWCA program. Today the whole lot, brown-bag lunches in hand, had been loaded onto a rented school bus for a field trip to a lake where they could swim. Judith could go home for her own lunch and have several blissfully uninterrupted hours to continue unpacking her kitchen stuff now that she'd painted the cupboards.

The anticipation she felt at having some time without her children gave her a twinge of guilt, but she wouldn't let herself wallow in it. Everyone needed to be alone occasionally, and she couldn't remember the last time she'd been on her own. Sophie had alternately pushed her away and clung desperately these past two weeks, and probably she herself had needed to cling to her newfound daughter. But maybe now life would start getting back to normal. In the frantic haste of packing, selling their town house and moving, "normal" was the one thing she hadn't been able to give her small, frightened child. It could be that the familiarity of routine was what Sophie needed the most.

She liked the familiar, too, Judith realized as she drove a route she was already getting to know well. She idly noticed progress on a house being remodeled, how the river had dropped even further and the last of the grass had turned brown. She wasn't an adventurer by nature; she would be perfectly happy to live her entire life in a small town where she knew everyone.

Maybe Mad River. If only it would cool down. Rain. Clouds *were* gathering above the mountains. So far, distant thunderstorms hadn't brought the coveted rain, but maybe tonight.

As she rounded a curve, she suddenly realized how hard it was to hold on to the wheel. The van was pulling sharply to the left. It wasn't riding right, either. She braked carefully. As the van slowed, she felt and heard the bump, bump, bump of a flat tire. *Oh, hell,* she thought. Nobody got flat tires anymore!

She parked on the dusty verge of the road and watched a pickup roar past without stopping. She looked longingly after it. She'd never changed a tire in her life. No other cars appeared, and to each side were dry open woods. The nearest house was probably a quarter of a mile—and her own wasn't much farther. A mere stroll, were it not for the heat.

She was an intelligent woman, Judith told herself. She ought to be able to figure this out. She groped in the glove compartment for the driver's manual. At least in her old car she'd known where the spare was, but she'd traded in the trusty Toyota for this van, which had seemed more practical for the trip out here and their new life-style.

Per instructions, she opened the back hatch and leaned in. The floor panel lifted up, and sure enough, there was the tire. She hauled it out, letting it bounce onto the ground. In alarm, she noticed that there was something squishy about the way it landed. Judith leaned her weight onto it. The tire gave.

It was flat. She had a flat tire and a flat spare. Judith uttered a word she'd learned from one of her fifth graders.

She stared down the road and listened closely. Complete silence greeted her. Not a pine needle stirred. The heat was her only companion, pressing her down, singeing her skin.

Well, it wasn't that far home. She'd just have to walk. She could call a tow truck from there, then come back to meet it. A half mile more or less wouldn't kill her.

She'd gone about two hundred yards, the pavement burning the soles of her feet through her sandals with each step, when she heard the crunch of tires behind her. She glanced back to see a police car pulling onto the shoulder of the road. Surely not...

But yes, of course. She recognized him through the windshield. It had to be her new neighbor—Mr. Personality himself. Would he be grimly polite? She wondered if he knew he would be teaching in her class-room.

His car door slammed and he came toward her, even larger and more solid than she recalled. He touched the brim of his hat. "Ms. Kane."

Well, he remembered her name, at least. "Chief McKinsey," she said, inclining her head.

"Car break down?"

"Flat tire," Judith replied in the same tone, not letting herself crack a smile.

Under the shadow of the hat brim, his eyes swept over her. "Why don't I give you a hand changing it." His voice didn't rise to make it a question.

This expressionless stuff was killing her. She made a face. "The spare is flat, too."

"Ah. Well, I'll tell you what. I have a canister of that stuff we can use to inflate your tire. With luck, it'll hold until you get to the gas station."

She'd never heard of such a thing. She nodded knowledgeably and accepted his raised eyebrows as an invitation to return to her vehicle. But when she started to walk past his patrol car, Chief McKinsey said, "Why don't you get in. You look flushed. It's air-conditioned."

Oh, God, what she'd do for air-conditioning. He could lock her in the back behind that grille, just so long as it was cool.

"Thank you." Judith opened the door and sank into the blissful chill.

Ben McKinsey got in next to her and started the car. He turned toward her—uncomfortably close—to look over his shoulder as he backed his car up to hers, which was listing forlornly on the side of the road. She took the opportunity to snatch a good look at his face.

Heavy dark brows and spiky eyelashes surrounded his brown eyes, and deep lines were carved in his forehead and beside his mouth. There was a sprinkling of gray in his short dark hair, and his chin was stronger than it needed to be and just a little off center. He held his mouth so tightly she couldn't tell what it might look like relaxed into a smile.

He caught her gaze, but she whipped her head around before a staring match developed. And before he might conclude she was interested.

"Why don't you stay here," he suggested.

She blinked, realizing they'd come to a stop and he was already opening his door.

"Can I help...?"

"No." *Slam*.

Judith sighed. Did the man ever really and truly ask what someone wanted? Or did he use the question format only to issue orders?

Well, to heck with him. If he wanted to be dictatorial, let him. Her conscience niggled at that; after all, maybe he was trying to be chivalrous. Either way, she decided, she'd take him up on the offer.

She swiveled in the seat so that she could track him with the side mirror. He'd taken something out of the trunk that looked like a can of hair spray. No, whipping cream, she decided frivolously. Beside her right rear wheel, he sank to his haunches and began fiddling with her tire. She found herself fixated on the way his pants pulled tight over powerful thighs.

Catching herself, she lifted her shirt a few inches so cold air could find its way beneath. Jeez, what was wrong with her? This was not her kind of man, assuming she ever decided she wanted another man.

But somehow her eyes didn't stray from the mirror. He did have a nice body, she had to admit when he rose fluidly to his feet and strode toward her. Shoulders that could make a woman feel safe. Narrow hips. Long legs.

He stopped on her side of the squad car, and it took her a second to realize he was waiting for her to get out. The heat seemed even worse when she did.

"It's still a little low on air," McKinsey said, "but it ought to hold you long enough to get back to town. I'll follow you."

She shut his car door and made herself hold out a hand. "Thank you," she said.

His gaze touched her outstretched hand, and there was a discernible pause before he lifted his own and took hers. The grip was quick and hard; she felt the strength there, and an uneasy little quiver shinnied up her spine.

She scuttled toward her car like a mouse for its hole. Oh, yes, this man could more than stand up to Rylan.

All the way to town, she was aware of the police car right behind her, filling her rearview mirror. As she turned into the first full-service gas station, he sped up and passed her, lifting his hand in a choppy wave. She gave her horn a toot. He didn't even look back.

By the time they'd found the nail in her tire and fixed it, Judith was starved. At home, she was surprised to realize she'd only lost an hour, thanks to

Chief McKinsey—who had merely been doing his duty, not being neighborly, she reminded herself.

Judith unpacked and arranged a good part of her dishes and kitchen utensils before it was time to pick up the kids at the middle-school gymnasium where the YWCA camp was held. By then the air had a heavy, muggy feel to it, different from the usual dry heat. Black clouds climbed the ridges and peaks above town, making dusk seem closer. On the drive home, Zach chattered about his day and some boy named Chad who did a really great cannonball and could hold his breath underwater for three minutes.

Judith smiled over her shoulder. "Did you have fun, Sophie?"

Her thumb was firmly planted in her mouth, but after a moment she gave a shy nod. Her cheeks were flushed pink, but she didn't look sunburned. The leaders must be replenishing her sunblock frequently. Unlike Zach, whose skin had taken on a golden tan, Sophie would easily burn.

"Hey, it's raining!" Zach exclaimed.

Sure enough, scattered drops plopped on the windshield and kicked up puffs of dust on the roadside. Through Judith's open window came an odd metallic smell, as if the rain were creating a chemical reaction. "Let's hope it really pours," Judith said.

Thunder crawled overhead. Zach jumped, and Sophie shrank in her booster seat.

"It's okay," Judith said. "I didn't even see the lightning. I think it was miles away. Besides, we're safe in the car. We'll run into the house and watch the rain out the windows."

The horses were nowhere to be seen. They must have gone into the barn.

The light was eerie now, purplish and yellow at the same time. Judith felt the hair stand up on her arms. She parked as close to the front porch as she could, and after rolling up their windows, they all hurried inside.

It was dusky enough that she turned on every light switch she passed. After hurrying around to shut the kitchen and bedroom windows, she joined the children in the living room, where they stood in front of the picture window, which looked northwest at the mountains. Judith tentatively touched the top of Sophie's head, waiting for her to flinch or scoot to the other side of Zach, but instead her small hand crept into her mother's. Judith's heart gave a funny bump of pleasure. Progress.

Or perhaps any adult would do when Sophie was scared enough, Judith wryly admitted to herself. She laid her free hand on Zach's shoulder.

Lightning forked above, a shocking explosion of white light that imprinted itself on the inside of Judith's eyelids.

Sophie shivered. "I want Daddy."

It hurt every time. And what could Judith say? *If I can help it, you'll never see him again?*

"One thousand one," Judith counted, "one thousand two, one thousand three, one thousand four, one thousand—"

Thunder rumbled.

"Cool!" Zach exclaimed.

"A mile away. Did you know you can count to tell

how far away the lightning is?'' she asked Sophie. ''Five seconds for every mile. Next time, let's all count together.''

Lightning flared, and she and Zach recited aloud, ''One thousand one, one thousand two, one thousand—''

This time the thunder boomed and the windowpanes rattled. Sophie latched onto Judith, trembling so hard her leg vibrated. But when she suggested they read a story, the five-year-old shook her head hard.

Judith crouched down and wrapped Sophie securely in an embrace, which for once she accepted.

''You're right,'' she murmured, sitting down with her on the couch. ''It's less scary to watch the storm than it is to pretend it's not happening.''

Sophie nodded emphatically. Judith wondered if she was relating this fear to all she must feel about losing her father.

Still the lightning flung jagged rivers of cold white fury across the sky, which seemed to crack open from the force of the thunderclaps. The raindrops appeared weirdly large as they struck the window.

They quit counting; there wasn't time. The storm must be directly overhead. It was almost completely dark outside, although it couldn't be much past six. None of them said a word. They held one another on the couch and watched nature demonstrate her power.

Judith began counting again. Was the storm passing? A quarter of a mile. Half a mile. The windows no longer shook. The rain fell harder.

''Well,'' she said, feeling tension leaching out of her body, ''maybe we should think about dinner.''

White light flooded the sky again, thunder cracked—and the house was plunged into darkness.

Sophie shrieked, and even Zach pressed his body against his mother's. She took a breath, willing her voice not to betray her with a tremor. "Oh, darn. We lost our electricity. Cold sandwiches for us!"

"Will it…will it stay off long?" her son whispered.

"I have no idea," she admitted. "Let's find flashlights."

They only had three, and none was great. No candles; it hadn't occurred to her to buy any. Maybe she could start a fire in the fireplace—if she could find some matches.

Still holding Sophie's hand, Zach trailing her, Judith made her way to her bedroom. It wasn't completely dark, now that their eyes had adjusted; a glance at her watch told her it was seven o'clock. Thank goodness her flashlight was in the drawer in her bedside table. She was absurdly grateful for the small golden pool of light it cast on the wall.

She switched it off again. For now, they would save the battery.

"Let's go find yours," she said, and they trooped into Zach's room, which he was currently sharing with his sister, who didn't like to sleep alone.

The batteries on Zach's flashlight were dead. He probably read at night under his covers after she tucked him in. Sophie's was feeble. Judith briefly considered a quick trip to town—she could buy batteries and maybe hamburgers and French fries for dinner. But the electricity might well be off there, too, and with the way it was pouring… No. The house felt safe, snug. They'd manage. Sophie's flashlight would be adequate for the kids to make their way to the bathroom, assuming the electricity stayed off into the night.

"Do we have any more batteries?" Zach asked.

Another thing she'd meant to buy. All the staples she could have reached unhesitatingly for back home in Boston hadn't been worth shipping out here. She'd intended to stock up on necessities like lightbulbs and batteries. She would have. Eventually.

"Afraid not." She smiled cheerily. "Hungry?"

"Not really," her son said. "Can we…can you read a story or something?"

Sophie's head bobbed.

"Well, it's kind of dark for me to read, and I think we ought to save the flashlights for later. But how about if we play a game?"

They ended up snuggling on the couch, she and Zach playing a word game while Sophie clung to her, sucking her thumb. Rain continued to patter on the roof and window; the murkiness of a storm-clouded dusk settled into the darkness of night. At some point, Judith turned on her flashlight, knowing the children needed that comforting beacon.

"Mom." Zach squeezed more tightly against her. "Did you hear that?"

"Hear what?" It was ridiculous to whisper, but she did anyway.

"A…a bang."

This time she did hear it: a knock on the front door. "Someone's here," Judith said. How calm she sounded, considering her heart was drumming! "Remember, the doorbell doesn't work when the electricity's out.''

Judith lifted Sophie onto her hip. Her son stuck close to her as she went to the front door.

"Who's there?" she called.

The deep voice was muffled. "Ben McKinsey. Your neighbor."

"Oh." As quickly as she could with one hand, she unlocked the dead bolt and flung open the heavy door.

The large bulk of a man stood on their porch. For a moment, she couldn't make him out above the beam of his powerful flashlight, which he'd aimed at his feet. She directed her light toward his chest. The police chief had changed out of his uniform. The shoulders of his denim shirt were wet and he held his Stetson in one hand. Shadowed above the beam of her light, his face looked even grimmer.

"Just wanted to be sure you have everything you need to sit out the storm."

Pride made her want to claim they were fine. Which they were. Cold food and a little darkness never hurt anyone. But the children would be happier with some light, if he had candles or a lantern to spare.

"No," she admitted. "I…wasn't really prepared for this."

He grunted and shone his flashlight in the cardboard box he held in one arm. "Brought some things. Just in case."

Wonderingly, she looked. The beam picked out a camping lantern, candles and… Was that a pizza box in the bottom?

When she lifted her head, he shrugged. "Figured I could share my dinner."

It seemed he was neighborly after all. She had totally misjudged him.

On a rush of relief, Judith stepped back. "Please. Come in."

CHAPTER THREE

BEN FOLLOWED Judith Kane into her dark house, aware of the girl clinging to her like a limpet and the boy edging back just beyond the beam of the flashlight.

What the hell had gotten into him? He could have handed over the pizza, claimed he'd already eaten. Anything but come in.

He could excuse the impulse that had brought him over here; he liked to think he was a decent man. He'd grown up in a town where neighbors helped one another out. And he'd known for damn sure a city woman like her wouldn't be ready for power outages.

Ben remembered how terrified his little sister, Nora, had been when the electricity went out. Their mom had always been at work at night—she'd held down two jobs just to pay the rent and put food on the table. It had been left to Ben, the eldest, to comfort Nora. No matter how often he pointed out that once they went to bed, it would be dark anyway, she was still scared. She wanted to know she could turn on a light if she had to get up in the night. He guessed the little redheaded girl would feel the same.

"This is so kind of you," the children's mother was babbling. She was still wearing the shorts but had added a long-sleeved denim shirt over the sleeveless one. "I keep thinking of all the things we left behind when we moved—like candles and batteries. We didn't have anything like that camp lantern, though. The closest I ever came to camping was a picnic in the park. We're from Boston, you see."

He'd heard that New England accent in her voice. Why had a woman like her, with two children, moved all the way out from Boston, Massachusetts, to Mad River, the ass back of nowhere? And why rent a crappy little place like this when she was able to afford a top-of-the-line moving company to haul her stuff for her? That part he'd been wondering about ever since he'd seen that huge glossy moving van backed up to the house.

"Please, sit down."

Even in the shadows, he could tell that the living room had changed. His flashlight beam found a sofa— smooth, creamy leather. He settled on one end and lifted the lantern from the box. The boy perched on a chair.

"This is Sophie and Zach," she rattled on. "Did I already introduce them?" She laughed nervously. "I guess I did. Why don't you sit down, Chief McKinsey, and I'll just go get us some drinks from the refriger-ator. What would you like? We have all kinds of pop and, um…"

"Beer?" He felt like a fool the minute the word left his mouth. Of course she wouldn't have beer. Not un-less a man visited—which might be one reason she'd moved out here. He hadn't seen any other cars coming down the lane, though.

"I'm sorry. How about wine? What do you think, a good Cabernet Sauvignon with—what is it, pepperoni? Sausage? Everything but the kitchen sink?"

"Everything but the kitchen sink. That's okay. I'll take a cola." He turned the knob on the camp lantern one notch, waited two seconds and turned it the rest of the way. *Whoosh!* Bright white light filled the room.

"Cool!" the boy breathed.

Judith offered a smile as radiant as the lantern's glow. "Bless you. Here." She plopped Sophie on the couch next to him. "Honey, you stay with the police chief. I can't carry you and drinks and plates, too." She retreated through a dark doorway.

For an instant, all Ben could think about was how her bare leg, unnaturally pale in this light, had almost bumped him. He'd gotten a good look at those long, slim legs today when she'd walked ahead of him alongside the road. She had a hell of a body. And he must be desperate, he admitted, to get excited about a woman in shorts coming within a foot of him.

Then he stiffened, remembering the little girl. She sat so still beside him she might not have been breathing. Hell. She was scared of him. Or the darkness. Or maybe both.

"Mom doesn't have any matches," the boy piped up. "How come you didn't need one?"

Candles Ben could understand. But no matches?

"Modern technology. It's electronically sparked." He set the lantern safely in the middle of the table and leaned back slowly enough not to frighten the girl any further.

Out of the corner of his eye, Ben saw that her knees

were drawn up to her chest, her thumb was shoved in her mouth and she was staring unblinkingly at the lantern. Strange kid.

Cupboard doors banged somewhere in the house. Ben raised his voice. "You know you can't run water when the power is off."

She appeared like a shot, plates tucked under one arm, cans of pop under the other, that pitiful little flashlight gripped in her hand. "What?"

"Don't run the faucet. The well pump doesn't work without power," he said succinctly.

"Well?" she repeated, expression incredulous.

"Yeah. A big hole in the ground? We share a well. I maintain it. You pay me for water."

She digested that information. "Is the power off very often?"

"Fair amount." He lifted the pizza box out of the carton and set it on the coffee table, then saw the gleam of fine cherry wood and lifted it up. "What can I put this on?"

"Zach, will you help me?"

The kid took the plates from her, then helped her hand out the cans of pop without dropping any. She produced a magazine—some fancy one about decorating and architecture—and he put the pizza box back down on top of it.

"Oh, I forgot a knife," Judith Kane said suddenly.

"Who needs a knife?" Zach asked.

"And napkins."

"I can get 'em, Mom." The boy sprang to his feet.

"Take my flashlight." Ben handed it over.

The kid scooted off, the bright beam playing over

the walls—pink?—and an arrangement of pictures hung in the hall.

His mother came around and sat down on the other end of the couch. "This lantern is wonderful."

"You might want to buy yourself one." Surreptitiously, Ben watched the little girl, waiting for her to reattach herself to her mother. She didn't move.

"You've rescued me twice in one day."

"I wouldn't call this a rescue," he said dryly, opening the lid of the pizza box and starting to dish it out. The pizza wasn't as hot as it could be, but what the heck.

The girl—Sophie—took a plate from him but just stared at it.

"It's okay, honey," Judith Kane said gently. "If you don't like something, you can pick it off."

If you don't like something? Should he translate that as "I know you don't like anything on it"?

"What's that?" Sophie whispered.

Ben cocked his head. Beyond the circle of light came a hollow *thump, thump, thump,* followed by a clanking sound. *Thump, thump, thump, rattle.* It was getting closer. "Ooooh," said a ghostly voice from the darkness.

Judith snapped, "Zachary!" at the same moment the little girl scooted under Ben's arm and plastered herself to his side. He froze. What the hell—?

Laughing hysterically, the boy flung himself into his chair. "Did I scare you?"

Judith swiveled toward her daughter. "Sophie, honey…" Her voice sharpened as she turned back to her son. "Only your sister. That wasn't very nice. You tell her you're sorry."

"It was a joke!"

"You know she frightens easily. I've asked you to take special care of her." She sounded mad as hell, but her voice softened again when she leaned forward and held out her hands to her daughter. "Sweetie, come here."

Please, Ben thought. *Go to Mom.*

The little girl shook her head. Hard.

Ben's shoulder muscles were beginning to feel the strain from holding his arm away from her.

Judith stood, bringing a faint flowery scent with her, and started to pick up the kid anyway.

"No! I don't want to go with you!" Sophie screamed, and wrenched away, grabbing tighter hold of Ben. He automatically wrapped his arm around her.

Pain flashed across Judith Kane's face as she straightened. "Sweetheart, I was just trying to hold you. Chief McKinsey isn't used to having little girls on his lap."

The kid was frightened of her own mother? Against his side, he felt her little heart racing as quickly as a bird's. God. Was he going to have to report his new neighbor to Child Protective Services?

Her eyes met his, and he saw the desperation in them. "It's…she misses her father. I…I guess you've been elected as a substitute. I'm sorry."

"It's okay," he said, not meaning it, but the world wouldn't end if he had to cuddle a kindergartner for five minutes.

"Are you sure?"

"Yeah. I'm sure."

Looking tense, she settled back on the couch and picked up her plate. That was the moment the boy chose to turn on the flashlight. The beam skittered across the wall and then hit Ben straight in the eyes. He squeezed them shut for an instant, and when he opened them, the beam was drawing figure eights on the ceiling. Sophie had buried her face in his side.

"Can I use this to go to the bathroom?" Zach asked, too loudly. "It's better than mine. All Mom's bought me is a dumb kid one."

Ben was still seeing stars. He'd have given the kid hell except that he recognized the boy's general obnoxiousness as a bid for attention. Damned if he'd give it to him. "Yeah," Ben said shortly, "but don't flush."

The boy made a face. "Don't *flush?*"

At the same moment, Judith said, "Don't flush?"

Only the girl, slowly relaxing at his side, didn't seem to find the concept stunning. Ben felt as if he were dealing with travelers from the future who couldn't believe how primitive twentieth-century plumbing was. "You flush," he said, "water runs."

"But...but what if someone—"

Zach stopped dead. Thank God for small favors.

"I mean, I don't hafta... Not right now."

"Zachary," Judith said crisply, "we are eating."

Flushing—hey, a pun—the boy headed for the bathroom. An unpleasant thought struck Ben.

"How old is your son?"

"Nine. He's going into fourth grade." Her voice

gentled. "Sophie turned five in April, and she's starting kindergarten this year."

Ben made a noncommittal sound. Maybe he'd be sorry he *wasn't* teaching drug abuse education to kids the age of Zach Kane; he remembered his younger brothers turning into snotty little jackasses at some point. He hoped to God that wasn't at ten or eleven. He should have kept a diary.

"Do you have children?" Judith asked.

He barely stopped himself from coming out with a profane equivalent of "Are you kidding?" The little one attached to him was a fresh reminder of how children trapped you. But he didn't have to be rude. "No" was an adequate reply.

"We'll be working together, you know," she chattered on. "I'm a teacher. Fifth grade. Carol Galindez tells me you're handling the DARE program this year."

His worst nightmare. If he could have stuck it on anyone else in the department, he would have. But not a damned one of them was capable except for Julie Robinson, busy breeding her own future fifth grader. Ben didn't mind women cops; he just wished they wouldn't get pregnant.

"You're a teacher," he said. Brilliant.

She glanced at her son, who had returned and dropped to his knees, helping himself to pizza. "Mmm-hmm. That's why we moved here. I got offered the job at Lincoln. I'm excited to get started." She hesitated and set down her plate. "Sophie, honey, would you like to eat some pizza now? Or...or sit on my lap?"

The little girl shook her head.

"She's okay," Ben said again, meaning it more this time. It wasn't as if the kid were demanding anything from him. Her little body was warm and relaxed against his, bringing back some memories that weren't all unpleasant. "This your first teaching job?" he asked, to distract the child's mother.

Maybe she'd gone back to school after having kids. Despite her creamy skin and a pert nose that was cute as hell, his new neighbor had to be over thirty with a son in fourth grade.

"Heavens, no!" she exclaimed. "I've taught for seven years now. Fifth grade, sixth... The last couple of years I taught English to seventh and eighth graders. Now, there's an age to keep you on your toes!"

He had to agree with that assessment. The mini-criminals he considered middle schoolers. Pulling out their cigarettes before they'd cleared the school parking lot. Breaking windows with rocks. Lighting up joints behind the gym. Stealing a candy bar at the 7-Eleven. Taking Daddy's car for a joyride. Seemed like they all flirted with breaking the law, though he supposed that wasn't true. Maybe pretty Judith Kane had been so desperate to get back to teaching younger kids that she'd taken the first job she was offered.

"Why Mad River?" he asked.

"Oh... I wanted a small town." She studied the slice of pizza in her hand as though it held great fascination. "We needed a change. There was an opening here."

He'd been a cop too long not to notice the forced casualness in her tone, the way her body language had altered. Maybe she hadn't lied, but she was definitely being evasive.

None of his business, he told himself, as long as she didn't break the law. Her daughter's fear was enough to provoke him to run her through the computer, but hell, the school district must have done that. These days even volunteers got checked out by the state patrol. If it wasn't for the way the kid acted, he'd figure these folks were entitled to their privacy.

He just hoped a single mother and two kids allowed him his.

"Have you always lived here?" she asked.

"Last six years. Came from Seattle." After breaking up with Kelly, there was no way he could stay. And the kind of crime he'd seen as a detective in the Seattle PD was enough to make Mad River sound like heaven on earth. But he wasn't going to say any of that. He, too, could be evasive. "I grew up in a small town, though."

Up to this point, the boy had eaten in silence— pouting, Ben figured, after getting chewed out for scaring his sister. Hadn't seemed like much of an offense to Ben; he'd have thought it was funny when he was Zach's age, and his brothers had pulled that kind of stunt all the time. But clearly something unusual was going on here.

Now the nine-year-old piped up, "You ever shoot anybody?"

Yeah, he'd shot somebody, and still had nightmares about it. "No," he lied.

"Zach, what a thing to ask!" Judith said.

The boy ignored his mother's disapproval. "I wish *I* knew how to shoot a gun. Would you teach me?"

"Zach!"

"When you're a little older, the NRA offers classes in gun safety," Ben told him. "Around here, most everybody hunts."

"My father used to hunt." He gave his mother a sulky look. "Mom didn't like him to have a gun in the house."

"I'm with her on that. If you've got 'em in the house, they should be locked up. Too many accidents, otherwise."

"Mom's just scared of everything."

Ben watched Judith's spine stiffen. "That's enough, young man!" she reprimanded.

"I gotta go to the bafroom," said a little voice.

Ben lifted his arm from Sophie's shoulders. If she needed help, it wasn't coming from him.

"Do you want me to go with you, honey?" Judith asked gently.

Hesitation, then a small nod. The little girl wriggled to the edge of the couch and reached for her mother's hand, showing no sign of fear. They took Ben's flashlight and disappeared down the dark hall.

Conscious of a chill along his side where her warm body had been, Ben watched them go, frowning. Maybe the kid had just been looking for a substitute for the father she'd lost. He guessed he'd been that for his brothers and sister. They wouldn't have noticed any more than this girl had if they'd hurt their mother's feelings by turning to him first.

Still, Ben took the opportunity of being alone with

the boy to ask casually, "Your sister scared of your mom?"

His surprise looked legitimate. "Why would she be scared?"

"I don't know," Ben said truthfully. "You tell me."

The boy shrugged. "She misses our dad. That's all."

Ben opened his mouth to ask if his parents had just gotten a divorce, but he closed it again. Judith and Sophie were already coming back down the hall. The girl separated herself from her mother.

"Didn't hafta go," Sophie announced, and headed purposefully toward Ben.

He shot to his feet. "Listen, I'd better be off. I didn't let anyone at the station know where I was, and I should check in."

"Oh." For just an instant, Judith Kane sounded disappointed, even bereft. Then she produced a smile. "This was so nice of you. Let me get my flashlight and you can turn the lantern off."

"No, I'll leave it. I have another one. I'll trade you flashlights, too." He reached for hers. "I have some fresh batteries at home. We can exchange them tomorrow."

"Are you sure?"

"Yeah," he said roughly. "I'm sure." He crouched beside the lantern. "Zach, let me show you how to turn this off."

The boy listened solemnly to his explanation. "These are really cool," he declared. "We can get one, right, Mom?"

"Sounds like we'll have to, Zach," she agreed, "since Chief McKinsey says the power's often out."

"Why don't you make it 'Ben'?" he heard himself saying. He liked the way her kids' names came so softly and lovingly from her—except when she was annoyed at her son.

"Ben it is," she agreed with a quick smile. "Are you Benjamin?"

"Bennett."

He half expected to be ambushed by Sophie wanting a good-night kiss, but to his relief she clambered back onto the couch and stuck her thumb into her mouth again. Her whole body language was that of a child a hell of a lot younger than five, if Ben's memory served him right. Maybe she was mentally slow. That might explain the outburst and why her mother said the child frightened easily. He felt better with this explanation. Of course Judith wouldn't be anxious to tell every Tom, Dick or Harry that something was wrong with her kid.

"Good night," he said, nodding toward the little girl and then the boy. Only Zach responded.

Judith Kane thanked him six more times during the ten feet to the minuscule front entry. There was one awkward moment after he'd opened the door when they both hesitated, as if this had been a date and they weren't quite sure how to end it. The pale beam of the flashlight he held was aimed at the floor. A partial wall blocked the lantern and children from their view. He could just make out the pale oval of her face tilted up to him, and he remembered the one time they'd touched. Would he have the same strong reaction if he shook her hand again? Or—the thought came out of left field—what if he kissed her?

A woman with two young children? Was he nuts? Besides, she'd probably slug him. And with good reason.

Get the hell out of here, he ordered himself. Obeying the voice of wisdom, he nodded and settled his hat back on his head. "Good night."

"Good night," she echoed, so sweetly he almost raised the flashlight so he could see her face better, tell if she was wanting…

Oh, yeah, he jeered. She was hardly about to throw herself into the arms of a man just because he had fixed her flat tire and come bearing the gift of a camp lantern. The woman had a nice voice, just as she had nice legs. She made him think about things he hadn't thought about for a long time. It was a pretty good bet she wasn't thinking the same things.

Feeling like a fool, he nodded again and went down the porch steps into the rain, the inadequate beam of her light barely showing the way. Behind him, the door closed, shutting in any secrets the Kanes might have.

JUDITH DIDN'T ACTUALLY see her neighbor the next day; she heard the doorbell and the murmur of voices, and a moment later Zach reappeared in the kitchen with her flashlight in his hand.

"I gave him his," he said. "Look. Ours is really bright now." To demonstrate, he flicked it on and off, on and off.

Judith poured hot water over the tea bag in her mug. The warm glow of the stove burner had never looked so good. "Did you thank Chief McKinsey?"

"Sure." He frowned. "I guess."

She would have pursued the subject of his manners, but Sophie knocked over her glass of milk right then and began to cry. "I don't like milk!" she wailed. "Daddy didn't make me drink it!"

Daddy, it appeared, hadn't made her do anything she didn't want to do. Which might be true, Judith conceded; Rylan always had taken the easy road. On the other hand, she was beginning to suspect Sophie was using Daddy's name whenever it suited her purposes. Her stories about what Daddy had and hadn't let her do vacillated from day to day.

"But milk is good for you," Judith said gently, soaking up the spill with a sponge. "It makes your bones strong. And your teeth." She showed hers in a silly face and was rewarded by a tiny smile. "You want big shiny white teeth, don't you?"

"The better to eat you with!" Zach roared, and snapped his teeth shut just short of his sister's neck.

Sophie screamed, and tears flowed again. "I don't want big teeth! I want Daddy!"

Judith wheeled on her son in anger. "Zachary Kane, you go to your room this instant! What has gotten into you?"

She knew, of course. Several days later, she was still thinking about that incident and a couple of similar ones. Judith sat at her desk, facing an empty classroom. Guilt wouldn't let her concentrate on lesson plans.

She had overreacted. Zach wasn't doing anything any other boy his age wouldn't have done. But couldn't he understand that Sophie needed coddling? Judith had assumed that he would eagerly take over his role as protective big brother. But lately he seemed to be trying his hardest to upset Sophie with stunts like the one at the breakfast table.

Obviously he wanted Judith's undivided attention. She understood that he'd gotten used to having her to himself. But he wasn't an only child, and no matter how much extra attention she gave him, he acted as if it weren't enough.

He'd adjust, she told herself, sighing as she tried to turn her thoughts back to the American history unit she would be starting in only a few days. But thinking about school opening didn't distract her from her concerns about her children.

Once school started, Zach would be busier and away from Sophie all day. Before Judith knew it, their life would be back to the way it was before that terrible afternoon when she had gone to pick up Sophie at the day-care center, only to be told that she was already gone.

Panic shivered up Judith's spine, and she gave a little shudder. No! She wouldn't let herself relive the horror. She had Sophie back. She'd never lose her again.

Well... Judith smiled. Maybe she'd let Sophie go

off to college someday—when she was about thirty. But she'd have to come home summers.

"What are you smiling about?" Linda Mayfield, another fifth-grade teacher, appeared in the doorway.

"Oh..." Judith produced the only excuse that came to mind. "I was picturing our police chief teaching ten-year-olds how to handle peer pressure."

"Boggles the mind," Linda agreed. A thin, energetic woman with graying hair cut in a sleek cap, she smiled crookedly. "He almost arrested my son one time. Scared the pants off him." At Judith's look of inquiry, she grimaced. "Just the usual teenage pranks. But Ron was really toying with trouble that year, so I didn't mind. Still..."

The image of Ben McKinsey sitting on her couch, Sophie glued to his side, his arm held rigidly above her as though a hug would contaminate him, flashed before Judith's eyes. "Should be interesting," she said.

She might have actually been excited about having him in her classroom if he'd been friendlier since that night. She kept remembering the way he'd looked at her for a moment that had seemed to go on forever before he muttered a rough good-night. He hadn't once smiled that evening, yet she'd wanted him to kiss her. No, not wanted, exactly. Wondered what it would be like. Dreamed a little.

Oh, she'd been an idiot. Her kids had been right there in the dark house behind her. And she hardly even knew Ben McKinsey—and didn't like much of what she did know.

She'd baked banana bread the next day and taken it over to his house, but he hadn't been there, so she'd left the wrapped loaf propped inside his screen door with a note that said only "Thanks" and was signed with her name.

Any girlish dreams had withered the day after that, when their vehicles met in the lane and he barely tipped his hat at her as they passed. She'd seen him half a dozen times since then, and it was always the same thing. They were back to square one. Civil and incredibly distant. Not even neighborly.

Well, she would have enjoyed getting to know him, but so be it. She ought to tell him about her situation— about Rylan. The evening of the storm, she'd been thinking she would, as soon as she saw him without the kids. But now she couldn't bring herself to do it. Besides, Ry would be a stranger to him, and he wouldn't let a stranger take one of her children. Ben McKinsey might not be a friend, but he'd demonstrated that she could depend on him if she needed him. That was all that really mattered.

The weather had changed the past week, the air taking on a nip that spoke of autumn, the temperature dipping at night. The dry August had caused the leaves to turn color already, and vivid reds and yellows cloaked the foothills and tree-lined streets. Her co-workers hoped for rain and worried aloud about forest fires, a subject Judith was careful to keep from Sophie's ears.

The Sunday before school started, Judith called her parents and then Rylan's. Having the kids continue to feel close to their grandparents was important to her. Zach talked to Rylan's mother first; Sophie said a shy "Hi" and then thrust the phone at Judith.

"Sophie doesn't believe in long chats," Judith said lightly. "Maybe kindergarten will open her up a little."

If her mother-in-law responded, Judith didn't hear it over Zach's cackle.

"Yeah, like a clamshell! School will pry her open!" He drew out the word *pry,* pretending his hands were locked together and he was wrenching them apart.

Sophie's mouth trembled and she raced out of the kitchen. Still cackling, her brother chased after her.

Judith sighed into the receiver. "Zach *needs* school. *I* need him to go."

"I remember that feeling," Mary Kane agreed, but not in her usual easy way. The constraint in her voice had Judith tensing even before she heard her mother-in-law's heavy sigh. "Rylan is out on bail," Mary told her. "The judge called to let us know. Apparently he had a girlfriend in Kansas City who put up the money. You know we never would have."

Rylan was no longer behind bars. "Yes," Judith said slowly. "Yes, I know."

They talked a while more, but the only thing of importance had been said: Ry was free. He could show up here anytime.

Judith felt curiously numb. And why not? She'd expected this, prepared for it. The news wasn't a bolt out of the blue. Tonight, when she ought to be falling asleep, was when the fear would come. She would think then about how gladly Sophie would run to her father. She would worry about Zach's ambivalence and the fact that she couldn't watch them every minute.

But there was nothing more she could do. And she didn't dare tell the children their father was out of jail. The last thing she wanted was for them to be watching for him.

No, she could only wait.

CHAPTER FOUR

JUDITH WOULD HAVE thought it was her own stress level affecting Zach that first day of school, had he not been so obnoxious lately anyway. He was so wild during breakfast that she had to send him to his room. During the drive to school he was sulky, instead, which actually felt like an improvement.

For Judith, this first day of school was what opening night must be like for an actor—exciting, yet fraught with the possibility for disaster. What if the kids hated her? What if teachers out here did things differently than they did back East? This new anxiety almost—but never completely—overrode her worry about Rylan.

She'd made arrangements for Zach and Sophie to go to their new classrooms a little early. Both their teachers had been updated about the situation with Rylan. Judith walked each of them to the door and then stood back as they hesitantly entered. Zach's expression was defiant. Sophie for once didn't want Daddy; it was Mommy to whom she clung.

"I don't wanna…" she whispered, huge gray eyes pleading.

But Sandra Craig, the pretty young kindergarten teacher, was already holding out a hand to her and smiling. "Sophie Kane, thank goodness you're early! Could you possibly help me by passing out some construction paper and yarn for an art project? I don't think I'm going to have time before the bell rings."

With only a few anxious backward glances, Sophie went with her new teacher. Feeling reassured, Judith continued on to her own classroom.

She sat behind her desk and looked over her quiet, peaceful domain. She was ready. Her stomach was calm until the bell rang, and she suddenly felt as if she might throw up her breakfast.

The hall thundered as hundreds of children stampeded toward their rooms. Seas of them poured through her open door, and she smiled and rose to greet them. "Good morning," she said, over and over, as if she were composed and confident.

Laughing, talking, roughhousing, they hung or dropped their coats and lunches in the closet, found their names on the desks and sat down. A second bell rang. The room fell silent, and twenty-six pairs of eyes gazed expectantly at her.

She drew a deep breath, smiled again and began her performance. "Hello. I'm Mrs. Kane. I'm new to your school, but I have taught fifth grade before, as well as sixth and seventh." Just so they'd know she wasn't a rookie. "Let's spend this morning going over the rules—" she laughed at their groans "—most of which I'm sure you know already and always obey. But first we'll get to know each other. Let's start with the roll call." She moved unhurriedly behind her desk and picked up the list of names. "Erica Adams," she began, and a blond girl tentatively raised her hand.

Twenty minutes into the day, Judith had discovered that fifth graders in the great American West weren't any different from those in Boston. She'd already known that three of the boys in her classroom read at second-grade level or below. One of them was the class clown, one hid in the back and the other watched everything with such sharp eyes she suspected he would pick up most of what the other kids did even without the required reading skills. Of the girls, two wore more makeup than Judith did. A few were getting breasts; the rest were still sticklike or plump. Half a dozen of her twenty-six students were exceptionally bright; they would be pulled out for an enrichment program twice a week. Most of the rest could be good students, too, with some encouragement. She could hardly wait to begin coaxing the best from each one of them.

By the end of the day, she was awash in a glow of contentment that she knew wouldn't last for the entire school year. But it reminded her of how much she loved her job.

Grateful that the school district offered full-day kindergarten, she hurried to Sophie's classroom first, just in time to see her teacher hug Sophie goodbye. The little girl stood stiff in the embrace, but her cheeks turned pink. Judith wanted to hold out her arms and sweep her daughter up. Instead, she held out a hand. "Hi, sweetie. Good day?"

Sophie came readily to her and slipped her hand into her mother's. She nodded, eyes bright. "I made a big purple cat with yellow whiskers. Mrs. Craig hung it on the wall. I wanted to make a horse, but I don't know how to draw one.'' She looked up eagerly. ''Do you?''

She was talking. Really talking. Judith felt tears prick the backs of her eyes. ''I'm not an artist, but I can try. Shall we draw when we get home?''

They'd arrived in front of Zach's classroom. He came out when he saw them. Boys were walking away in pairs and groups, laughing and shoving one another. He was alone.

''How was your day?'' Judith asked.

He shrugged and looked down. ''Okay,'' he said flatly.

Her bubble of joy popped. Of course this would be hard for him. Everyone else already had friends.

She squeezed his shoulder. ''First day is scary, isn't it?''

He pulled away from her. ''It's just boring.''

Judith didn't argue. Instead, she chatted about her own day and rejoiced when Sophie joined in. Zach would come around, Judith told herself. Moving was harder on a child his age. But the other boys would soon accept him. In a couple of weeks, she'd be dragging him away from his gang and worrying that she couldn't keep him close to her.

Speed bumps required her to inch out of the parking lot. She turned left, past the middle school. Ahead of them, a police car was parked at the curb.

''There's Chief McKinsey,'' Zach said, displaying the first sign of animation since school let out. ''I bet he's going to arrest someone. Maybe a kid.'' He sounded pleased at the prospect.

Ben McKinsey was coming down the steps of the

middle school, but he was alone. No thirteen-year-old was being dragged off to juvenile detention. In the dark-blue uniform, the police chief looked even more forbidding. As she began to speed up, he turned his head, frowning, and looked directly at the van. He gave a short, sharp nod, frowned more fiercely and strode toward his squad car.

Judith resisted the temptation to stick out her tongue. Zach slumped back in his seat. She hoped he wasn't building their neighbor up to be some kind of father figure. Chief Ben McKinsey wasn't volunteering. She glanced in her rearview mirror to see that Sophie, too, had turned her head to look at him, but in contrast to her earlier eagerness, she had stuck her thumb in her mouth again, and her eyes were wide with alarm.

Oh, Lord, did he remind her of the deputies who'd torn her father away from her? But if that was the case, why had Sophie wanted to hold on to him the other night? He'd been out of uniform then; had she forgotten he was a policeman?

Judith's mouth tightened. If Ben McKinsey upset her children in any way, even if it was inadvertent, she'd break the lease and find another rental. One with neighbors who smiled.

PAPERWORK WAS STREWN over Ben's battered metal desk, but instead of concentrating on it, he scowled at the tall bookcase across from him, which was stuffed with law books and overflowing binders—and was damned ugly. He ought to do something to make his office more livable.

The bookcase wasn't any worse than the black metal filing cabinets below an interior window shuttered with venetian blinds that were bent and snapped off in places. If he hadn't hung any pretty pictures in the six years he'd occupied this office, he wasn't likely to start now.

And if he was going to distract himself, it ought to be with the report he was supposed to be writing, not the state of his office. But he kept frowning into space.

It wasn't as if he'd never talked to school classes before, although he shunted the task onto one of his deputies whenever he could manage it. Other adults told him that stepping into a classroom with its familiar smell of chalk and polished linoleum and lunchboxes with three-day-old leftovers made them feel like kids again, anxious because they'd forgotten to study for a test twenty years in the past. When Ben stepped inside that door, it wasn't his own school days he remembered so much as his brothers' and sister's. All those times he'd had to drop off brown-bag lunches forgotten on the kitchen counter, or pick up Nora or Eddie or John when they threw up at recess, or even attend parent-teacher conferences when his mother couldn't get off work. Once he himself had graduated from high school he'd even chaperoned a couple of field trips.

A muscle in his jaw jerked. He didn't let himself think about those days very often, and with good reason. How he'd resented playing Daddy when he could have been partying with his friends or playing football! Later, when those same buddies went off to college without him, he'd felt even worse. He'd made the sacrifices he had to, but not gladly.

Water under the bridge, he told himself impatiently. Ben rotated his shoulders a few times and bent his head to each side to loosen the stiffness. Then he forced himself to read what he'd already written on the form in front of him.

> Complainant says that the vehicle blocking an alley on the five-hundred block of Maple Street was left there during the night. Officer was unable to locate anyone in the immediate area who claimed knowledge of the vehicle. Registration checked. Officer attempted to contact owner.

He'd had to impound the station wagon just because that busybody Ruby Santoya took offense at anything slightly amiss within a ten-block radius of her home. Her browbeaten husband kept their lawn as beautiful as the greens at Pebble Beach Golf Course. The edges were razor sharp, the texture like velvet. Their car rarely sat in the driveway, never mind on the street. Windows sparkled, white paint shone. Ruby's roses won ribbons every year at the county fair, but as far as Ben was concerned, the bushes were ugly, perfectly spaced and pruned until they looked unnatural. Ruby used the excuse of walking her cocker spaniel to patrol the neighborhood for irregularities. Nobody even drove down the damn alley except the garbage truck, and pickup had been Monday. But what could Ben say? The car shouldn't have been left there.

He took up his pen again and wrote: "Failed to

locate owner. Vehicle impounded.'' Sometimes he wondered what he was doing in a place like Mad River, where every crime committed could be summed up in a short weekly column in the local paper. This week's offenses consisted of a chain-link fence cut by unknown vandals; a stolen purse—the woman had left it in plain sight in an unlocked car, which in his book meant somebody had accepted an invitation; two tires swiped from behind an auto body shop; and now this—an impounded vehicle. Hot damn.

On the other hand, there was something to be said for a community where the worst crime was some wire cutters taken to a chain-link fence. People kept an eye out for one another. That made a difference. In an era of budget cuts, the council still managed to find the funds to support the DARE program in the school. That was the kind of attitude that kept this town peaceful.

Ben grunted. He wished like hell the program had been cut as decisively as that chain-link fence now that he had to do it.

One of his officers rapped on the glass square of his door. His grin was just this side of malicious. ''Hey, Boss! It's almost two o'clock!''

As if Ben didn't know.

Ten minutes later, carrying an armload of workbooks, he stood in front of the elementary school. Lincoln was a hodgepodge of buildings from different eras. The fifth-grade classroom where he was headed occupied a one-story, plain brick building typical of school architecture in the 1970s. Nothing fancy, but functional.

He didn't want to go in.

He wished like hell Judith Kane's class wasn't the first on his schedule for the week. He'd have liked to get a little practice in before he had to do his thing in front of his pretty neighbor.

He snorted. What was it that his mother used to say? *If wishes were dollar bills, who'd ever do a lick of work?*

Ben squared his shoulders and strode up the walkway and into the building. After detouring into the office to greet the secretary and the principal, he marched down the hall, hardly aware of the occasional kid who shied out of his way. He scanned the room numbers as he passed the doors. L9 was what he wanted.

He found it. Ms. Kane had put the name of each child in the class on a cat-shaped cutout of bright construction paper. They pounced and lounged their way along the hall. On the door itself was a cheerful, enormous lemon yellow mouse that said, "Mrs. Kane."

Ben felt more like a small, helpless mouse being offered as lunch to a boa constrictor.

Firming his jaw, he opened the door and stepped inside. A book in hand, Ms. Kane sat on her desk, slim legs crossed, her posture perfectly ladylike. Her straight skirt might have looked prim, had it not outlined her shape so well. Her head wasn't the only one that turned at the sound of the door. The students all looked up at the same time from open notebooks. A few appeared grateful that his existence would rescue them from the dreaded task of putting words on paper;

others gaped stupidly, as if he were as out of place in their classroom as a Hereford steer.

Judith set down her book and smiled even as she scooted off the desk. Her back stayed elegantly straight, and his gaze lingered on the long, graceful line of her neck, where wisps of coppery hair softened her crisp teacher bun.

"Class, you may put away your journals now. Chief McKinsey is here to begin the fifth-grade DARE program. Why don't we welcome him?"

A ragged chorus of greetings rewarded her prodding.

"'Afternoon," he responded, nodding. Crunch time.

"They're all yours, Chief McKinsey," Judith said, gesturing toward the rows of students. Then she strolled off to the side of the classroom, where she stood with her back to the windows.

Ben couldn't decide if she was smiling encouragement at him or enjoying his discomfiture. The bright light formed a kind of halo behind her, hurting his eyes. After a microscopic pause, he went to the front of the room.

"Some of you have probably already heard about the DARE program from older brothers and sisters," he began. The ones who were lighting cigarettes by the time they hit the sidewalk in front of the middle school. Keeping the sardonic thought to himself, he went on to give a brief outline of the material they would be covering. He tried to scare them with a few stories about the effects of drugs: the violence that came in their wake, the damage to the heart, the hurt to parents.

He handed out the workbooks they'd be using over the next couple of months and then talked about the rules. They were to raise their hands so that only one person spoke at a time. They should be positive and respectful and answer only questions that were comfortable to them. When sharing a story about drug or alcohol use, they were to use the words *someone I know* instead of a name. That last one he regretted; he might have learned some interesting things if he'd been able to pick their brains.

By the time he'd covered some of the vocabulary that would be important—words like *assertiveness, consequences* and *abuse*—Ben could feel he was losing his audience. He talked briefly about self-esteem, while his own sank. The kids were thumbing through the workbooks and whispering. Damn it, this was how the instructions told him to start! He spoke more loudly, earning a few renewed glances, which quickly drifted away.

How the hell did he keep their attention, short of coming down hard on them? That was his usual technique with kids, but a big part of the idea behind the DARE program was to make police officers seem friendly and accessible. He was supposed to become their buddy.

His mouth refused to stretch into an ingratiating smile.

He fell silent. One by one, the kids did the same. Puzzled glances replaced vacant ones.

Now what? Ben refused to turn to their teacher for help. Instead, he tried desperately to remember suggested ways to engage his audience but came up blank.

Very casually, as if a deafening silence were normal in a fifth-grade class, Judith strolled back to the front of the room. He would have had to draw a gun to evoke their instant attention the way her gentle voice did, Ben thought. What did she have that he didn't?

"Chief McKinsey told me that after he went over the basics, he wanted you guys to do some role playing. Why don't we have a couple of volunteers. Let's see." She surveyed the forest of waving hands. "Jennifer and…Tony."

Role playing. Yeah. He grabbed the idea like a flashlight in a dark warehouse. They'd done some of that at the police academy, and the DARE teacher's manual had suggested it. He'd figured on doing it later…but he'd forgotten that kids weren't so good at waiting for later.

"All right," he said, trying to pretend the whole idea had been his. "Jennifer, Tony has just reached over and taken the best part of your lunch. Some cookies your mom made. He takes stuff from you all the time. Your pencil, a bookmark you really like, part of your lunch money. He just laughs when you say, 'Hey, that's mine.' You've decided to confront him. What are you going to say?"

"Um…" Jennifer, a cute dark-haired girl in denim overalls and a tight little shirt that looked like the ones the teenagers wore, turned to Tony. She squeezed her hands in front of her, which had the effect of hunching her shoulders. "I really don't like it when you take stuff like that. It's mean. I'm going to tell the teacher if you don't give those cookies back."

Ben's mouth twitched. She'd come through, illustrating his point perfectly. "Okay, class," he said, facing them. "What do you think? Is he going to give them back?"

He got a shouted response that, taken as a sum, added up to a big *no*.

"Why not?"

She didn't sound tough enough, they decided. She hung her head; she didn't look him in the eye; she didn't act as if she'd really go to the teacher.

"All right. Switch places," Ben said to the two kids.

Tony came through right on cue. He snatched an invisible object from her, leaned toward her with comic-book viciousness and snapped, "Don't touch my stuff again! I know where you live!"

Ben had to suppress a grin. With some coaxing, the class conceded that while Tony's approach might work, it had problems, too. Tony was making an enemy, both through verbal threats and body language.

They tried out some scenarios in which the wronged party calmly declared his—and her—rights and intentions by using eye contact, good posture and a tone that was neither aggressive nor wishy-washy.

At least he had the students looking thoughtful. Ben put them to work on a page in the workbook and then turned to Judith.

"Thanks," he said quietly. "I'm no teacher."

"You did fine," she assured him, also in a low voice. Her smile was as soft as he remembered it. "It'll get easier once you know the kids."

Oh, yeah. The fulfillment of a dream. He'd become intimately acquainted with a hundred ten-year-olds.

He frowned, thinking about the anger behind Tony's role-playing. Ben located him in the classroom and noticed that he was concentrating fiercely, although there was something clumsy about the way he held his pencil.

Ben's frown deepened. Maybe down the line he might find knowing these kids useful. If he had an idea of Tony's background, how his parents would react to a visit from the police, if required, whether the boy was a show-off or a bully, he might be able to head off trouble.

"Yeah," he said thoughtfully. The pupils' heads were all bent studiously over the open workbooks. Some of the kids chewed on their pencils or scribbled away in their books. Others sat frozen, pencil points poised above the ruled sheets. If he watched them long enough, even silently at work, he'd learn a fair amount about each one of them.

"That was a good exercise."

His attention snapped back. "Was it?"

"Mmm-hmm." Damn, that smile did something to his blood pressure. Her lips were pale, not pouty like a model's, but sweetly feminine. "I wish we could do more in the schools about relationships. Kids seem so blissfully unaware of how they come across to their peers. They trample on one another's feelings without even noticing."

Maybe they'd soak some grace up from her, Ben thought. "I'll bet you never have to raise your voice."

Her eyes, a clear gray-green, widened. "What?"

"Do you have any discipline problems?" He nodded toward the class, still hard at work.

"Well…not really." Her puzzlement showed.

"And I'll bet you don't accomplish it by yelling or threatening."

"No…"

He explained himself. "They'll learn from you."

She thought about it. "Maybe. Of course, every teacher hopes…" Then a hundred-watt smile blinked on. "Why, thank you."

Thank you? Understanding dawned. She'd taken it as a compliment. Well, he supposed it had been one. From what little he'd seen, Ben would be willing to bet she was a great teacher. He'd had one of those in sixth grade. Mrs. Lee. Sweet, strong willed, demanding, funny. He could still see her face clearly when those of other teachers had long since faded from his memory.

"Just an observation," he said uncomfortably. "By the way, uh, thanks for the banana bread. You didn't have to do that."

"You didn't have to come over when the electricity went off, either."

Her hand touched his, just a flutter of contact like a butterfly pausing between flowers. He felt it to the soles of his feet.

"I hadn't welcomed you." He looked toward the class, not her. "Figured your little girl might be scared."

What was wrong with him? He was *apologizing* because he didn't bake a casserole for every new resident of the crummy rental that happened to be down the lane from him? He'd be inviting her to tea next.

"She was."

He turned his head to see that hers was bowed, and her fingers were twisting together. The curiosity he'd tamped down sharpened again. Why did her five-year-old daughter make Judith Kane so anxious? He almost asked, "Is something wrong with her?" But that was a little blunt even for him. Besides, he didn't get a chance.

His pretty redheaded neighbor glanced up at the clock and straightened. "Class, time to put away your materials. But first, let's thank Chief McKinsey for coming."

The applause was more enthusiastic than he deserved, probably prompted by the kids' desire to please their teacher.

"See you next week," Ben told them, and nodded at Judith.

A wispy blond girl was already waving her hand for attention. "Mrs. Kane. Mrs. Kane!"

"Yes, Glenna?" Turning her head, Judith gave Ben an apologetic smile. "Thank you," she mouthed.

He nodded again and left. Students were already pouring out of classrooms, racing for the bus lines or, in the case of those who walked home, heading for the front doors. Twenty feet from Judith Kane's fifth-grade classroom, an alcove led to the gymnasium. Ben stepped around the corner before he got run down by the stampede.

"Ben! Crime broken out in our schools?" The stocky man who edged out of the flow of traffic was already completely gray although only in his midthirties. A plumbing contractor, Clay was a friend of Ben's. They did some cattle penning together.

"Just the rush hour," he said, nodding at the short bodies packing the hall. "What are you doing here?"

"Shari bulldozed me into picking up Sean for an orthodontist appointment. Braces," he added. "Four thousand bucks' worth of 'em."

Ben shook his head in sympathy. "I'm teaching the DARE program this year."

Over Clay's shoulder, he could just see Judith's door at an angle. He liked the way she said goodbye to each student individually, touching a shoulder here, smiling there, whispering a few words to earn a shy smile in return. He could tell when the last kid was gone, because she vanished. Probably she'd grade papers, or whatever else teachers did, while she waited for her own children.

But seconds later, she popped back out, purse over her shoulder. She came straight down the hall toward him, but she was hurrying too much to look to the right or left. Her anxiety was invisible, but he felt it coming from her like the stink from a skunk.

Curiosity nudged him. "Excuse me," he said to Clay, and stepped into the press of bodies to trail her. He hardly knew what was driving him; for God's sake, the woman probably had a dentist appointment! But something odd was going on with that small family, and he found he couldn't ignore the hints the way he had with the last renter.

Judith turned briskly into another wing of the school. Here the artwork on the walls got cruder and the elbows jabbing Ben were lower to the ground and sharper. Halfway down the hall, she stopped at a classroom door. The teacher there seemed to be waiting for her; Sophie must have been the last student out, because the moment she handed Judith's daughter over, the younger teacher waved goodbye and turned out her classroom lights. Holding her little girl's hand tightly, Judith rushed back the way she'd come.

Ben faded into a recessed area leading to the girl's bathroom. He almost fell over as the door opened behind him.

"Excuse me, mister," a small voice said. It belonged to a pink-cheeked, ponytailed cherub in green corduroy overalls.

"Sorry," he said, moving aside. Judith, towing her daughter and still oblivious to his presence, had already gone by him.

"It's Chief Muck!" another small voice cried in delight.

Ben turned his head. He had no trouble recognizing the boy, who carried a backpack big enough to topple him over. "Jonathan," Ben acknowledged. "Did your mom fire your baby-sitter?"

He nodded. "And Mom called her mother. Lisa was in big, fat trouble." He clearly relished the idea.

"She deserved it." Out of the corner of his eye, Ben saw Judith disappear around the corner. "Ah, excuse me," he said to the boy. Ben got his feet trampled on, but he made it to the corner in time to see her stop at another classroom door. In a replay of the scene with her daughter, her son was handed into her care.

Both kids with her, Judith slowed her pace. He guessed they were heading for the parking lot and decided to drop the tail.

Watching them go, Ben shook his head. It was the

strangest damn thing. He had the distinct impression that both teachers had waited for her, holding her kids until she came. Why didn't Sophie and Zach just make their way to her classroom? Why did she go collect them as if they weren't capable of finding her?

Something was wrong. Part of him didn't want to know what it was. But he was a cop, and he knew his duty.

No matter how pretty Judith Kane was, no matter how soft her smile, he had to find out what was going on with her and her kids.

CHAPTER FIVE

ONLY FOUR DAYS BACK at work, and Judith was already grateful for the weekend! She'd forgotten how hectic working and parenting and running a household could be.

If only she didn't have to live with uneasiness about Rylan prickling her nerves like the tension in the air before a storm. She and the kids had already done the grocery shopping this morning, she'd mowed the pitiful excuse for a lawn using the worthless piece of junk the real estate agent had called a mower and after lunch, while Sophie napped, she and Zach had tried phoning both sets of grandparents. Judith's parents had announced their intention of flying out here for Christmas, which had Zach excited. Ry's parents weren't home, which added to Judith's worries; she'd counted on them to give her updates. When, oh, when, would he finally stand trial? How had he managed all the continuances they'd reported? Why had the judge let him out on bail, when he'd threatened her the way he had during the arrest?

She straightened from scrubbing the bathtub. *Don't think about him,* she told herself. He wouldn't dare come after the kids now, not when he had to see his lawyer and make regular appearances in court. Rylan would be cocky; he'd be sure that he was going to get off, that the judge would sympathize with him, see how much he claimed to love his daughter and agree that his ex-wife should be blamed for making him unhappy. Rylan had always slid out from under every serious consequence in his life; he'd figure this one wouldn't be any exception.

He would bide his time.

She didn't have to worry. Not yet.

Somehow Judith failed to reassure herself.

She did succeed, however, in pulling herself back to the here and now. Thanks to her efforts, the old white porcelain bathtub gleamed everywhere it wasn't chipped. Satisfied, she turned to tackle the sink next, then she'd mop the bathroom and kitchen floors.

The bathroom door stood open, and she could hear canned laughter from the television in the living room. When she stopped cleaning to put dinner on, she'd suggest the kids dream up something more worthwhile to do, but for now, having them so easily occupied was a blessing.

She hummed as she washed the bathroom sink and counter and replaced the cap on Sophie's toothpaste. Sophie liked a different flavor from the one Judith and Zach used. Good thing, too. Sophie squished the tube in the middle and let the toothpaste overflow and then harden. Maybe it was genetic; Rylan had been a slob, also.

Sometimes it was hard for Judith to remember why she had thought she was in love with him at one time. Drying the faucet so it shone, she made a face in the shiny chrome. She'd been young and impressionable.

No, check that. Dumb and hormone ruled. Rylan Kane was dark haired, blue eyed, wiry and lithe. And that smile! His eyes would glow like the licks of blue deep in a hot fire. A dimple would form in one lean cheek when his white teeth flashed. Oh, yes, Ry was sexy. And he could make her laugh, even years later when she should have known better.

Judith sighed. Her own father was so…so *nice*. He wasn't a complicated man. What you saw was what you got: integrity, reliability, kindness. Not witty conversation or a wicked laugh or hints of devilment. Dad had been balding for as long as she could remember, and softening around the middle, too.

Maybe it was the contrast that had made Rylan so irresistible to Judith, who was fresh out of college and ready for a man who quickened her pulse and stole her breath away.

Well, she'd found him, all right. She'd just been too stupid to realize that he was also selfish, a little cruel and completely faithless. Or that he was capable of going to such lengths to hurt her, just because she'd grown up enough to see him for what he was.

There she went again. Why was she wasting time thinking about him? she asked herself, frowning. If she must picture Ry, it ought to be behind bars, where he would eventually end up. She hoped they made inmates at the county jail work. At least Rylan would get a taste of real life. She liked the idea of him with his hands deep in hot sudsy water, or dishing up two hundred plates of some sloppy casserole.

It was petty of her, but she took pleasure in fantasizing about Rylan suffering in small ways as well as large. But she didn't forget what was most important: he'd lost his children forever.

After hanging up fresh towels, Judith put away the cleaning supplies and headed toward the kitchen. On the way, she glanced into the living room. Slumped low on the couch, Zach stared unblinking at the screen, even though he'd seen the video playing a hundred times. Cable wasn't available this far out of town, and with the antenna, only two networks came in clearly.

Judith half smiled and shook her head. *Batman* was unlikely to have been Sophie's first choice. She leaned over the back of the big, overstuffed chair. "Honey, do you want to come cook dinner with—"

Sophie's most precious possession, a faded flannel crib blanket she'd somehow managed to cling to during all the moves with her father, was balled into one corner of the chair. Sophie herself was nowhere to be seen.

Judith looked up. Zach was still staring at the TV as if he hadn't even noticed his sister's presence, never mind her absence.

Bathroom… No, of course not. She'd just been cleaning it. A flutter of anxiety tickled in her chest. The kids' bedroom. Sophie had gotten bored with the movie and was playing with her doll or a puzzle. Judith had only half formed the thought before she was hurrying down the hall.

The bedroom door stood ajar. The light was off. No toys littered the floor. The bedcovers were still smooth from this morning's change of sheets.

"Sophie?"

Silence.

Judith whirled and opened the door to the spare bedroom that would be her daughter's when she felt brave enough to sleep alone. Maybe...

No. Furnished only with a bookshelf and an unused child's desk, this room was dim and empty.

Now the anxiety was mutating into panic. Sophie wouldn't have willingly gone far without her blanket. Besides, since they'd been here several weeks, she hadn't left the front porch on her own.

The kitchen. Would she have tried to get herself something to eat?

Deserted.

Judith rushed from window to window, searching desperately for her daughter's small figure. She could be crouched in the grass, watching a bug, or picking the purple asters in the weedy flower beds.

She wasn't doing either.

"Zach!" Judith punched the power button on the television set, turning it off.

"Hey!" He scowled. "I was watching!"

"Where is Sophie?"

"She's right..." His gaze failed to find his sister in the big chair. "She was there a minute ago."

"A minute?" Judith breathed deeply before she let herself say, "Zachary, think. When was the last time you saw your sister?"

He shrank back into the chair, his brown eyes not wanting to meet hers. "Not very long ago. I mean, it couldn't have been more than five or ten minutes."

"Or half an hour?"

"I wasn't paying attention!" he burst out. "Why

do I have to watch her all the time, anyway? It's not like Dad would want her back! He'd probably take me, instead.''

"What a horrible thing to say!" Judith's throat hurt. "We'll discuss it later. Now, get up and help me find Sophie. I've looked in the bedrooms already. You search more carefully in case she's hiding for fun. I'll go outside."

On the porch, she shaded her eyes against the setting sun. The lane was still, tan against the yellow brown of the dry grass.

"Sophie!" Rushing down the steps, Judith stumbled. "Honey," she called, "we're not playing hide-and-seek. Please come out!"

No sign of the five-year-old. Judith circled the house, panic winging into terror. Once she caught sight of Zach in the window; when he saw her, he shook his head. The flutter in her chest had grown into huge wings beating in fright, leaving her gasping for breath and screaming her daughter's name over and over.

She began running down the lane toward the police chief's house. Dear God, let him be home. He'd help her. If Rylan had taken Sophie…

"Sophie!" she screamed. Again and again.

Uniformed and hatless, Ben came running to meet her halfway between their houses. He gripped her arms and gave her a shake. "Calm down!" he snapped. "Tell me what's wrong."

He was right. She would be of no use if she was hysterical. Oh, God, she was shaking. *Please, please, please,* she prayed wordlessly.

"It's Sophie." Her voice broke. "She's…she's missing." Judith reached out and gripped his shirt-front. "I should have told you about my ex-husband. He might have taken her. He did before. Please. You've got to find her."

HE MIGHT HAVE ROOM for doubts later; he'd once been involved in an ugly case where a mother had sold her newborn baby and pretended he'd been kidnapped. She'd sobbed and clutched at him, also.

Judith Kane was hiding out from her ex-husband, afraid he'd steal the kids. No wonder she was so protective! In her spot, he'd have chosen a town like Mad River, too.

Ben gave her another shake, just enough to jolt her from the hysteria. "Was he arrested?"

Her wide, terror-filled eyes latched onto his. "Yes, but he's out on bail. He could have found us." Every word was ragged. "He…Sophie didn't even take her blanket. She never goes anywhere…" Her breath hitched on a sob.

Ben broke his own rules and hugged her—hard. "Maybe that just means she didn't go very far. Where have you looked?"

She quivered against him like a glass house in an earthquake. Right before it broke. Pulling away, she cried, "Everywhere!" Her eyes closed as she visibly tried to collect herself. When she opened them again, they were shimmering. "No. In the house. Zach's searching under beds and in closets right now in case…" She swallowed.

"In case she's hiding."

"Yes."

"All right." He released her and frowned, turning to survey the wooded hillside beyond and the field that separated their houses. "Is she brave enough to set off exploring?"

"I don't know!" Judith balled her hand against her mouth, holding back a sob. "I've only had her back three months. She was gone a long time. Years."

Another question answered. So that was why she didn't know her own daughter. If admitting the truth was such a torment, what must those empty years have been like?

He didn't let himself acknowledge the parallel that wasn't one, because unlike her he'd chosen the empty years. He hadn't wanted to be a father. Not then. Not now.

Ben's mind cleared and he began thinking like a cop. That bastard wasn't going to get away with stealing the little girl who had hugged Ben's side for reassurance in the dark. But chances were, the ex hadn't even tried. Ninety-nine times out of a hundred, missing children had wandered away or gone to friends' houses without telling their parents, or else they were sleeping somewhere nobody had thought to look.

"She wanted to meet my horses," he said.

Her sharp intake of breath told him the possibility was one she hadn't considered. "She *is* crazy about horses. Oh, no! You said they'd hurt her."

"Probably not," he admitted grudgingly. "If she doesn't spook them."

Judith whirled and hurried down the lane at a speed

his long strides barely matched. "If she went all that way by herself without asking me…"

"You'll wring her neck?"

"Yes!" She stepped in a pothole and would have gone down if Ben hadn't grabbed her arm. "No. Of course not. Oh, please. If only it's that simple. I won't even be mad. I promise. Oh, please."

She wasn't addressing him anymore. She was bargaining with God. He'd done that before himself, with mixed results.

His two-story house blocked their view of the pasture. He and Judith circled the back porch. She was running now, and only the fence stopped her. She gripped the top rail so hard her knuckles showed white, and she lifted herself on tiptoe, as if that would help.

"I don't see her!" She looked around frantically. "She's not there!"

His heart drummed. If the little girl wasn't here, he'd have no choice but to call up a manhunt.

"I don't see the horses, either," Ben said.

"No." With a sob, she flung herself away from the fence and raced for the barn.

He was at her heels. Barely inside the wide double doors, Ben heard singing.

Judith froze. "Sophie?" she whispered.

"'Twinkle, twinkle, little star, how I wonder what you are!'" The high voice was a tiny thread, almost lost in the cavernous interior of a barn built for fifty animals, not two.

"Sophie?" Judith moved forward again. "Sophie, honey! Where are you?"

The singing stopped abruptly. "I don't wanna go home."

Around the corner, past stacked bales of hay, were the two stalls open to the pasture. Sherlock, a sorrel, snoozed lazily on his side of the four-foot divider; Travis McGee, the palomino gelding, lipped hay from the girl's hand.

Her little butt was planted on the hard-packed dirt floor just outside the enclosure. One forearm and her chin rested on the lowest rail; with the other hand she tugged a few more strands of alfalfa from the nearest bale and offered them to Travis. The damn horse would probably have eaten himself into a major stomachache if Sophie had discovered the molasses-coated oats in the nearby barrel.

"Sophie." Judith crouched just behind her. "I was worried."

"The horses are nice."

"But look how big their feet are. And their teeth. They could hurt you by accident. That's why Ben asked you not to come over here."

The little girl still didn't turn her head. "His lips are really soft." She giggled. "See? He wouldn't bite me."

Judith's jaw firmed. "Sophie, stand up. We're going home now."

"Don't wanna." The kid grabbed the rail.

Ben felt stirrings of amusement. *Yeah, Mom,* he thought, *what are you going to do now?*

She must be really steamed, because all traces of her frantic worry were gone.

"Sophie Kane, you are in trouble. You know better

than to leave without telling me. Now, we *are* going home.'' She lifted her daughter, breaking her grip on the rail, and held her tight when she began drumming her heels, sobbing and trying to throw herself backward.

Judith raised her voice over the din. ''Thank you for your help. I'm sorry Sophie trespassed.''

''I'll walk you home.''

Over the kid's screaming, Judith asked, ''Are you sure?''

Who was she kidding? Did she think he'd quietly go away without finding out more about this exhusband who was likely to come around looking to steal her kids? Maybe she regretted telling him as much as she had.

Good God. Maybe the ex-husband had legal custody and *she* was the one on the lam.

No, he reflected, if that was the case, she wouldn't be able to hold a job as a teacher, where school officials would scrutinize her credentials and run a background check. Unless, Ben amended, the superintendent had hired her in such a hurry he hadn't done a proper investigation. Or unless she'd come up with a whole new identity.

''I'm sure. Want me to carry her?''

''No. I've got her.''

They walked side by side, not even trying to talk over the kid's unceasing screams. She had the lungs to grow up and be an opera singer. Her mother looked increasingly grim. Poor strategy on little Sophie's part. Pitiful whimpers would have gotten her further.

He should have been irritated. All that hysteria over

a five-year-old sneaking off to the barn to visit the horses. And now the caterwauling. Ben couldn't quite figure out why his sense of humor had kicked in, instead. That and his curiosity. He wanted to know more about these neighbors. He sure as hell wanted to know enough to keep the ex from snatching the kids.

Judith marched right in the house, past the boy, who held the screen door open. As he watched his mother take Sophie through the living room and turn out of sight, he had the oddest damn expression on his face. Maybe wistful. Maybe resentful. Or even a little of both.

Ben hoped the bedroom doors had a lock; if not, that obstinate little brat was going to shoot right back out of there the minute Judith put her down. Might be a good idea for him to stay here, blocking the front door.

Ben laid his hand on the boy's shoulder. "Were you worried about her?"

Zach started, as though he'd forgotten anyone else was there. "I…" His face closed. "Nah. I thought she was hiding or something. She does stuff like that."

Definitely resentment.

"Your mom has to watch her pretty carefully, huh?"

"*I* have to watch her, you mean. It's like I have this job." Zach let the screen door slam then went over to an Adirondack chair and slumped down in it. "Other guys don't have to take care of their little sister all the time." His voice held heartfelt loathing.

"I had to." The words just slipped out, shocking Ben.

The boy turned to look at him in surprise. "Really?"

"Yeah." Ben half sat on the porch railing, legs stretched out before him, and gazed at his booted feet. "Two little brothers and a sister. Our mom was always working."

"What was your dad doing?"

"He'd died."

"After...after he was gone, was it hard not having a father? I mean, did you mind it just being you guys and your mom?"

Had he minded? Ben searched back twenty-five years to when he was this boy's age.

"Yeah. Probably. Guess I didn't have time to dwell on it. He was killed when his tractor rolled onto him. I was nine then. Our mother didn't have any real job skills. She couldn't go to work as a teacher, like your mom, and make a decent living. We moved into town and she got a job as a clerk at the five-and-dime store daytimes, and when that didn't bring in enough to support us, she became a waitress, too, five nights a week. From then on, I had to take care of my brothers and sister."

"Jeez," Zach breathed. "You were my age."

"Yep."

The kid digested that. "Did you *like* your little brothers and sister?"

"Like 'em?" As if it would have made any difference. Ben thought about how to answer. "I got along better with them before Dad died. Afterward, even though I wasn't very old, I was supposed to boss them around. All of a sudden, Mom was ordering them to do what I told them to. That didn't go over very well.''

"But you could just, like, laze around and make them do everything, couldn't you?''

Ben grunted with amusement. "I was ten when Mom started working. My brothers were six and eight, my sister five. They weren't big enough to do 'everything.' I was the one who had to wait on them. The way your mom does on you. I made school lunches, cooked dinner, did the laundry....'' He shook his head. "I even helped with homework and science projects.''

"Jeez. And you didn't have just one little sister!''

"Nope.'' He hadn't been old enough to be a parent, not by any stretch. He'd hated tying shoelaces, slapping peanut butter and jam on bread, shoving little arms into coat sleeves, listening to spelling words and times tables. In comparison, this kid had it good. Ben hoped he realized that. "Your mom can't do everything,'' he said.

"I guess not,'' Zach agreed unhappily. He frowned at the screen door. "I liked it better with just Mom and me.''

Ben shrugged. "Most older kids do. Learning to share your parents is part of growing up.''

"I don't have a dad to share.'' His sullenness returned.

"Neither did I,'' Ben said with a decided lack of sympathy. "Neither do a lot of kids. You're luckier than some—you've got a great mother. Live with it.''

His curtness earned him a scowl. "Like you know everything,'' the boy said rudely. "At least your dad died.''

"And I did what I had to." Ben gave him a flat stare. "You're old enough to do the same."

"Why?" Zach's lip curled. "So I can be just like you?"

Ben would have been angrier but for the shock he felt. Was that what he sounded like? As if he thought he'd been noble?

He knew better. True nobility required generosity, a willing heart. Oh, he'd done what he had to do, all right, but he'd done it with the acid of resentment corroding what heart he had. And the scars it left had shaped his life, driven away the woman he thought he loved, left him an empty shell of a man living alone, policing a town where there wasn't enough passion to fuel real crime.

Noble? Oh, yeah. That was him. Sir Galahad himself.

"No," he said. "You don't want to be like me."

The boy started to say something, but he didn't have a chance. The screen door squeaked open and Judith stood framed in the doorway. Ben realized that only silence came from the house; he hadn't even noticed when Sophie quit screaming.

Judith's face was pale and set; dried tear tracks stained her cheeks. "Zach, please go in the house. You may watch your movie again for now, but we need to talk later."

"It's not my fault—"

"Later."

The boy's whole body quivered with outrage, but his mother won. After a moment, he stomped inside, letting the screen door slam so hard it bounced twice.

Judith closed her eyes and her shoulders sagged. Ben could see the effort it took her not to crumple into a chair and cry. She awakened his admiration by doing one better: she straightened her shoulders, opened her eyes and said forthrightly, "I'm sorry I made such a scene. I should have thought of the horses. I'm embarrassed that I didn't. I let my fears overwhelm me."

He didn't move from his comfortable perch on the porch rail. "Sounds like you have a good excuse for being afraid."

"Yes, but..."

"No buts. You have no reason to be embarrassed." Ben meant every word. "You did the right thing coming to me. If he'd had your daughter, it would have been important for us to act fast."

Her eyes filled with tears between one blink and the next, shimmering clear green and silver, like stones on the bottom of a mountain brook. "What am I going to do?" she whispered.

His hands itched to grasp her slender shoulders, squeeze comfortingly, maybe draw her into his arms. Instead, he rubbed his palms over his thighs. "Haven't you already done everything you can?"

"Yes. No." She bit her trembling lower lip. "I don't know! I thought I had, but he was in jail then." Her gaze clung to Ben's, beseeching. "I was so sure I could watch them every minute, but I can't, can I?"

"No," he said quietly, "and you shouldn't feel inadequate because you can't."

"The other teachers have been so good about this. And Carol—my principal—has been wonderful, but..." Judith crossed her arms tightly. "Basically,

I'm alone here. I should have stayed where I was. At least my parents were nearby.''

"Should you?"

For an instant, her eyes closed again and she hugged herself. ''No. No, it's easier here. I just wish I had someone else to rely on. Maybe my parents would come out for a while. At least until Rylan's trial.''

"If they can, it might not be a bad idea,'' Ben agreed.

Her thoughts were running as frantically as a trapped rat; he could see it in her eyes.

"No,'' she said. "Or...maybe they would, but I can't ask them. They had this trip planned, you see. They're meeting some old friends in Belize. Mom and Dad haven't seen them in ten years.''

"What's more important?''

She didn't answer directly. "They didn't want me to marry Rylan. They didn't like him.''

Ben understood. She felt guilty because they'd been right. The choice had been hers, and now she was determined to bear the consequences alone.

"I'll make a few phone calls,'' he said. "Find out where he is, whether anybody has a leash on him.''

"A leash?''

"Whether they're checking on him. Whether anyone will notice if he vanishes.''

"Oh.'' Now those beautiful eyes were great pools of hope. "Would you really do that?''

He would have checked out her story anyway, so it bothered him some for her to look at him as a savior. Why couldn't she see through him as easily as her kid had?

"Tomorrow." Ben pulled a notebook from his back pocket and had her give names and dates. The details he needed. "You know, chances are he's too worried about the prison term he faces to even think about hunting you down."

Her fingers twisted together. "When they caught up with him, he made threats."

"We've all made threats we never intend to carry out."

"That's true." She tried to smile, her lips curving wanly. "Thank you. You've been so nice."

Noble.

"Just doing my job," Ben said brusquely. Time to get out of here. He pushed himself away from the railing, wishing to God she didn't look so much like a woman who needed to be held.

Her fingers squeezed her upper arms. "I'm sorry," she said again. "I'm sure you're right. He won't come. We'll be fine."

"Don't apologize!"

She flinched, and he cursed himself.

"He's the bastard. You have no reason to take the blame."

His neighbor gave a jerky nod.

"I'll stop by tomorrow," Ben told her, "after I've made those phone calls. Let me give you my phone number, if you need me before then."

"I'm sure I won't…"

His expression stopped her. "Go write it down before you forget." He recited the numbers twice and made her repeat them. He left her then, although with every step he felt the pull to go back.

But he didn't dare. He'd end up taking her in his arms. She'd cry on his shoulder, wet his shirtfront. He'd make foolish promises to keep her and the kids safe. And then he'd kiss her, and he especially didn't dare do that.

Judith Kane and her two troubled children were a danger he might not be able to escape.

CHAPTER SIX

"DO YOU REALLY DISLIKE Sophie so much?" Sitting on the foot of her son's bed, Judith tried not to sound angry or judgmental.

Yesterday Zach had shocked her a little with his lack of concern when Sophie went missing, not to mention his sneering insistence that their father wouldn't want her anyway. But maybe, Judith had decided, she was overreacting. What kid didn't think his younger sister was a pain in the neck? And she *had* been expecting a lot of him since their move.

Zach's only response was to shrug and refuse to look up. No surprise, considering he was already mad at her.

Judith stifled a sigh. "Just remember, if you play your cards right, Sophie will be your number-one fan. Little sisters are famous for adoring their big brothers."

He turned his face away.

Let it go, she thought. They'd always been close as mother and son; once he got over his anger at being chewed out for not watching Sophie better, they could have a real talk.

"I know it's a drag, having to keep an eye on her all the time," she said. "But I need your help."

He didn't move.

Judith sighed again and walked out of his room. She peeked in her bedroom to see that Sophie was sound asleep, round cheek flushed and her thumb slipping from her mouth. Tiny coppery wisps of hair curled around her face and, damp from perspiration, stuck to her forehead and temple. Judith stood looking at her for the longest time, fear and a painful kind of love and awe squeezed together in her chest. All those empty years, and now she could watch her daughter sleep.

Her fingernails bit into her palms. Rylan would not get Sophie again. Whatever it took to ensure that, Judith would do it.

The doorbell chimed, and she left Sophie napping. Judith hurried through the living room to the front door, eagerness supplanting the bittersweet emotions she felt for her daughter. It must be Ben; he'd promised to make those phone calls today and let her know what he had found out.

He was half-turned away, head tilted back, when she opened the door. Above, a tiny bird harried a hawk that floated lazily on an air draft. The small drama in the sky didn't explain why Judith's heart gave a funny little lurch.

How could she not notice the breadth of Ben's shoulders beneath a gray T-shirt that molded to the long muscles of his upper arms and the planes of his chest? The faded, dusty jeans showed off lean hips and long, tautly muscled legs. In profile, his straight nose and square chin made his face seem less harsh than she thought of it, but still uncompromisingly male.

The faint sheen of gray threading through his dark hair suited him, somehow reflecting the inner grimness she sensed but didn't understand.

He was a sexy man. And she had to tear her gaze from his strong brown throat and hope she wasn't blushing when he faced her.

"I...hello. Will you come in?"

One dark brow lifted, but his voice gave away nothing. "Why don't we stay out here. I was just unloading hay. I might track in dirt."

Judith nodded and stepped outside, easing the screen door closed so that it didn't wake Sophie. A new tension made her forget her self-consciousness. "Did you...did you find out anything?"

"I talked to the detective in Boston who handled your daughter's disappearance. Edgekoski. You know him?"

"We must have talked a hundred times."

"Ah. Well, Edgekoski put a call in to Kane while I was waiting on the other line." Ben stood close enough to touch, big, solid and reassuring. "Your ex answered. He was in his motel room, right where he was supposed to be."

"Motel," Judith echoed. Brilliant. He was giving her the best possible news, and she sounded like a parrot. After yesterday's idiotic behavior, he must wonder about her.

She was more worried about the foolishness of her reaction to Ben McKinsey. She needed him to make her feel safe. Yet when she was aware of him as a man, he became a threat to her on some level she hardly understood.

"Yeah," he said patiently. "One of those places you rent by the week. Cheap but clean. Kitchenette. You know."

Judith tried and failed to picture Ry in a shabby little room with a lumpy bed, a kitchenette and a TV. Was that how he'd raised Sophie, moving from one sleazy motel to another?

"He's being cooperative. Even given the history, Edgekoski didn't see him as a risk to bolt."

Alarm flared. "They don't know him."

Ry would never accept responsibility for any wrongdoing. Oh, yes, he'd be cooperative, as long as he thought he could manipulate the system into letting him off. The moment he understood that he'd lost, that he *would* be going to prison, Rylan would vanish. Defeat wouldn't be acceptable.

What Judith feared was that Rylan wouldn't be satisfied by making his getaway; he would feel victorious only if he recovered Sophie. Only if he showed Judith that he was smarter than she was. That their daughter loved him more.

Ben waited until her eyes refocused. "Maybe you don't know him anymore, either," he suggested, voice gravelly.

"I know him." She sucked in a deep breath and let it out. "I'm sorry. Here I go again. After yesterday, the last thing you want to hear is—"

"Damn it." His hand shot out to grip her wrist. "Quit apologizing. The son of a bitch stole your kid. He threatened to do it again. You hate him and you're afraid of him. Why wouldn't you be upset?"

She stared at him, surprised as much by the anger

that glittered in his narrowed dark eyes as she was by what he'd said. Was the anger on her behalf?

"You…you don't think I'm being silly?"

He muttered a profanity. "No. I don't think you're being anything but cautious." He jerked his head toward the silent house. "Where are the kids?"

"In their rooms." She made a wry face to hide the painful emotions she felt. "I chewed out Zach. Now he's sulking." Knowing she was begging, she looked up at her neighbor's strong, blunt-featured face. Surely, surely, he'd give her the honesty she sought. "He's only nine. A child. Am I asking too much of him?"

"No," Ben said harshly. "That's plenty old to help you out and to understand how serious the threat is."

Surprised again by the force of his reaction, Judith said, "*I* see Rylan as a threat. Zach sees him as his father."

Ben grunted impatiently. "Does he even remember him as a father?"

"Yes. Well, more or less. I think…" She looked down at the porch floor; it was in need of new paint. "Truthfully, he sees his father through rose-colored glasses. Ry was never all that interested in the kids or their activities. He sure wasn't out there coaching T-ball or mother-goose soccer."

Muscles bunched in Ben's jaw. His tone was odd. "Not a devoted father."

She pressed her lips together. "No."

"Why your girl? Why not his son, too?"

She knew what he was asking and explained that

Zach hadn't been at the day-care center the day Rylan had taken Sophie.

Ben listened with frowning incredulity. "You're telling me the guy couldn't wait another day so he could have his son, too?"

"I don't know! I don't know why he did it that way!" Fiercely, she held back the tears that threatened. Zach and Sophie were safe; right this minute, she knew where Rylan was. And she had an ally. Judith struggled for control. "I have coffee made. Will you have a cup? It…it doesn't matter if you track a little dirt in. The floor sweeps up easily enough. Or I can bring it out here, if you'd rather."

A silent battle seemed to take place inside him; after a moment, he bent his head in assent. "Thank you."

When Judith opened the screen door and went in, Ben followed her, so close she smelled his sweat and…maleness. It put her on edge again, and she was glad to have her back to him as she took mugs from the cupboard, got out sugar and milk.

She poured him a cup and turned to find that Ben wasn't in the kitchen at all. The low sound of his voice came from the hall. Around the corner, she saw him immediately, standing in the doorway to Zach's bedroom. Part of her wanted to sidle close enough to hear what he was saying, but she would have felt as if she were spying.

Ben nodded and quietly pulled the bedroom door closed. He turned to see her in the archway to the kitchen. Something flickered in his eyes, but his face was expressionless when he came toward her.

She didn't question him, only handed him a steaming mug. "Sugar and milk on the counter."

He accepted the mug of coffee but didn't move past her. Without inflection, he said, "Your kids need to feel comfortable with me if I'm going to be keeping an eye on them."

Hope tightened her throat. "You believe me?"

That dark brow rose again. "You mean that your husband might still come after them?"

"Yes. Even though that police detective doesn't think so?"

A muscle twitched in his cheek when he looked down at her. "You know him better. He's done it once. Yeah, I believe you."

Relief weakened her knees. How easy it would be to sag against this man, rest her forehead on his shoulder, feel his arms come around her. But she remembered…oh, all sorts of things. She recalled how much faith she'd had in the police when Sophie first disappeared. And then as the weeks went by, she'd realized that they were busy with other cases, that a noncustodial parent taking a child didn't rate a huge number of man-hours. That if she didn't keep nagging and fighting and going on TV and distributing Sophie's picture herself, she might never see her daughter again.

And she remembered how confident she'd been that her parents were wrong, that Rylan was the man for her. That he would love her forever, and be a good father, and never deliberately hurt her.

Judith made herself stand straight. No matter how desperately she wanted to lean on Ben, she couldn't.

For the sake of her children, she couldn't afford to put all her faith in Ben McKinsey. In any man. It was up to her to keep Zach and Sophie safe, to keep them with her. She would be grateful for help but not depend on it being there unfailingly.

That kind of trust had been lost with Rylan's betrayal.

"Thank you," Judith said, her gaze holding Ben's. "It…helps to know you don't think I'm crazy."

"Even if I did," he said, "it's my job to give you the benefit of the doubt."

Somehow she'd retained a sense of humor, enough to let her laugh, if wryly, at his candor. "Hasn't anyone ever told you to quit while you're ahead?"

"Quit…?" The corner of his mouth twitched. "I, uh, didn't mean to imply that I *do* think you're wacko."

Her smile quivered into life again. "Thank you. I think." Judith touched his arm but quickly drew her hand back, startled by the heat of his skin and the way the muscle under her finger tips tightened instantly. She twined her fingers together and took a deep breath. "Ben, I'm sorry I dragged you into my troubles. I rented this house partly because the agent told me you'd be my neighbor. That wasn't fair."

The crease in one cheek deepened. "You did what you had to. And once you moved to my town, it became my job to protect you and your kids."

His job. Why was that not what she wanted to hear? Did she want him to feel like the knight in shining armor, galloping to the rescue of his ladylove out of pure chivalry?

"Thank you," she said again, her voice low.

His eyes seemed to darken. "Don't worry. I won't let the bastard—" He stopped.

"It's okay." Judith tried to smile. "You can call him anything you want."

"You don't have mixed feelings?"

Was it the cop inquiring, she wondered, or the man? Either way, the answer was easy. "No," she said simply. "I asked for the divorce. That's what he's trying to pay me back for. When I married him, I was a fool."

"We're all fools at some time or other." His dark eyes were steady. "Some of us most of the time."

"Have you ever been married?" she asked on impulse.

Between one blink and the next, the momentary closeness vanished. "No." He set down the mug of coffee, untasted, on the table. "I'd better be on my way."

"Oh?" She strove to sound uncaring. "Fine. I'll walk you to the door." As if he couldn't find his own way.

He nodded and strode ahead of her. Judith didn't follow him out. He let the screen door close, then turned to face her, its mesh blurring his features.

"If it's okay with you, I promised your son that someday this week after school, I'd put him and his sister up on the horses."

Dumbfounded, she could only repeat, "On the horses?"

"I'll lead them around. Unless the boy has ridden before."

"Zach."

"What?"

"Why do you always call him 'the boy'?" Judith asked, genuinely curious.

"He reminds me of one of my brothers."

Even more astonished, she wished she could make out his expression better. "What's his name?"

"Eddie." That giveaway muscle in his cheek twitched. "Ed now."

"Are you friends?"

"Haven't seen him in years." His mouth tightened. "The horseback ride okay?"

"I...if you have time. Is it safe?"

"We'll be careful."

She gave her head a bemused shake. "Fine. You know they'll love it. Any day."

"Tomorrow?"

"You're not working?"

"I'm taking a few days of vacation."

She wanted to ask why he wasn't going on a Caribbean cruise or climbing Mount Rainier or taking a fishing trip with friends instead of hanging around home alone, but considering how grateful she was to have him near, she figured it would be as well not to sound either nosy or critical.

"Thank you," Judith repeated for about the fiftieth time.

He nodded and left. Through the screen, she watched him cut across her lawn—such as it was—and turn onto the dusty lane. His strides were long but taut, controlled, balanced. This was not a man who sauntered.

Nor a man who did anything lightly. Protecting her children was his job, as he saw it, and he'd try his damnedest to do just that.

Why had he never married? she wondered. Some woman had missed a good prospect. Maybe he didn't smile or tease, and she doubted he'd bring a woman roses or write her poetry, but she'd be willing to bet that when he promised forever, by God he'd deliver. She thought maybe Ben McKinsey could be trusted. She'd take that over flowers or poetry any day.

But he hadn't offered her anything but police protection, and that was one thing she couldn't—didn't dare—trust. Not even when a man as steady as a rock offered it.

THAT EVENING, Ben phoned his sister. He'd stayed closest to her, in part because she was the youngest and had least resented his premature elevation to parenthood. He was her big brother, and Nora had worshipped him until she turned thirteen and he refused to let her date Brad Marcovich, a sixteen-year-old stud. At sixteen, she forgave Ben. He was a cop by the time she graduated from high school, so he was able to help pay her university tuition. Nora majored in—of all damn things—horticulture and was now a landscape designer in Portland, Oregon. Eddie and John had both married and had broods of their own; Nora, like Ben, was still single.

"Ben!" she cried when she heard his voice. "Is something wrong? What's up?"

Disconcerted, he said, "Does something have to be wrong? I just, uh, wanted to say hello."

"Really."

Slouched in his well-worn recliner, he frowned. "Is that a crime?"

"You don't call very often," his sister said with a hint of tartness, "and when you do, it's usually for a reason. I just figured we'd get family stuff out of the way first."

"There's no family stuff," he said shortly.

"Oh. Well then, how are you?"

Ben grunted. "I'm okay. You?"

She'd decided to strike out on her own, Nora announced; she was confident she'd built up enough of a reputation among local gardeners and horticulturists to make a living.

"New businesses take at least a couple of years to turn a profit," Ben noted. "Can you afford that?"

"Are you offering to invest in McKinsey Landscape Design?" she teased.

"If you need help..."

"I think I can pull it off," Nora said, her voice suddenly gone soft. "But thank you."

He mumbled something, then asked abruptly, "Have you talked to Eddie recently? How is he?"

There was a moment's pause. "Funny, he asked me about you the last time he called. Maybe you're both mellowing."

"I don't need to mellow. He's the one with the problem." The oldest next to Ben, Eddie had resented his brother's authority the most. An adult now in years if not maturity, he still held a grudge.

"A little mellowing wouldn't hurt you, either, dear brother." She didn't give him time to respond. "Eddie and his wife are having problems. He told me she walked out, but you know how he exaggerates. I think they'll work things out.''

"You always were an optimist.'' A wry smile kicked up one corner of Ben's mouth. "Everyone is always going to be okay.''

"I'm usually right.''

"Mom wasn't,'' Ben said harshly.

"No.'' The one word was as quiet as a breath released. "Maybe if she were alive…''

"We'd be one big happy family?''

"Well…you never know.''

For once, he didn't argue. Maybe if their mother had had medical insurance and gone to the doctor regularly, her breast cancer would have been discovered in time to save her. And maybe then her grown children wouldn't have drifted apart. They might be gathering for Thanksgiving feasts and on Christmas morning to watch the next generation of McKinseys tearing open their presents.

He shook his head to dispel the storybook images. Good God, he must be getting senile to imagine such scenes with anything but horror!

"So,'' Nora asked brightly, "what's new in your life?''

She always asked; "nothing special'' was his invariable response. The hell of it was, "nothing special'' was no lie. In Mad River, the greatest innovation was a novel flavor of ice cream at the café. Half to surprise Nora, he said, "I do have some new neighbors.''

"In that rental? The one the guy turned into a marijuana farm?"

"Yep. The walls inside are pink now."

"Pink?"

He shifted in his recliner. "Well... Kind of peachy. It actually doesn't look bad."

"It's probably gorgeous," his sister said reprovingly. "What's special about these neighbors?"

Ben told her about Judith and her troubles. "The boy reminds me of Eddie. Mouthy to cover up being unhappy."

"He has reason to be."

"Looks like he has it pretty good to me."

"He's a child, not a big tough guy like you."

"He's the same age I was when Dad died." He felt like a damn fool the minute the words were out; even he recognized that he'd come to the crux of his mixed feelings toward the kid. Ever since he and the boy had had that talk out on Judith's front porch, he'd been bugged by the parallels between Zach Kane and himself as a boy.

Back then, Ben had wanted to whine and pout and throw temper tantrums, too, but he hadn't, because who else could his mother turn to? Why should he look on this boy with anything but contempt?

Ben ended the conversation with his sister abruptly, wishing he could as easily cut off the self-examination. He knew damn well that his irritation with Zach Kane had roots more tangled than mere scorn. Maybe somewhere inside he was jealous. Maybe he even wondered if he'd *had* to turn himself into a martyr.

An uncomfortable thought nudged its way onto the

tail of the last one: maybe Eddie did have reason to dislike him. After all, Ben had been self-sacrificing beyond his years. Whatever poor Eddie did must have seemed childlike in comparison. If Ben hadn't been so determined to step into his dad's shoes, to do it all, he and his brothers could have been in it together, a team.

Yeah, at first Eddie and John had been pretty young, but with time they could have helped out more, taken more responsibility, made sacrifices just as he had. But no, by then he was the dictator, so wrapped up in his own bitterness it never occurred to him to loosen the reins even a fraction of an inch, much less hand them to anyone else.

And the whole damn time he'd begrudged every minute given to his siblings.

Ben swore and rubbed a hand over his face. He thought he'd put all that behind him, his resentment and his guilt. What the hell was making him dredge it up now?

Of course, he knew damn well what it was. The trigger was a kid named Zach Kane. The boy, his cute, sad little sister and his pretty mother, whose problems had begun to absorb more of Ben's time and thoughts than he liked to admit.

Ben hadn't told his sister this part—that he had offered to spend an hour or so leading a couple of kids around on his horses. If he had, she would have laughed, and Nora had a wicked laugh.

The next afternoon, as soon as he saw Judith's van turn onto their shared lane, he headed out to the barn to brush and saddle Travis, the more patient of his two quarter horses. The van passed his place without stopping, but the kids and their mother came streaming into his barn not two minutes later. No pause for milk and cookies there.

Sophie rose on tiptoe and stuck her hand through the rails without hesitation to clumsily pat Travis's muzzle. The horse winced with each whack but endured her affection without lifting his head out of reach. Zach hung back. And their mom...

Ben swallowed. "You're not dressed for riding."

She wore a mint-green, slim-fitting dress with sleeves that just covered the cap of her shoulders and a hemline that left bare long creamy legs, shapely enough to keep a man awake nights. The shorts had been bad enough. The dress was worse. If she didn't change to jeans right now, he wouldn't sleep tonight.

Her eyes widened at his suggestion. "Me? Oh, I can't ride."

"Why not?"

"I never have."

"Everyone around here rides," Ben told her. "Go on. I can take care of the kids. You go change."

Doubtfully, she looked from him to the horse, then at her kids and back to Ben. "Are you sure?"

"Yeah." He nodded toward the barn doors. "Scat."

Judith went with a few dozen backward glances.

The minute she was out of earshot, the boy swaggered forward. "I get to go first."

Ben lifted a brow. "Yeah? Why's that?"

"I'm the oldest..." He read Ben's expression correctly. "I mean, I ought to show Sophie how to do it, don't you think? Since she's so little?"

"I think maybe we'll start with both of you." Ben

backed the gelding out of the stall. "Can you two slip through those rails?"

Now Sophie was the hesitant one, looking a little wary as she inched out into the sunlight. She'd likely just realized how enormous the horses were without a fence separating her from them.

Ben bent and cupped his hands. "Zach, put your left foot right here and I'll toss you up."

The boy obeyed, swinging his other leg over the horse's back like a pro. Once up, he gripped the saddle horn and surveyed the world from on high. "Cool," he proclaimed.

Ben squatted in front of Sophie. "Okay, I'm going to lift you up. You'll fit in the saddle right behind your brother. You wrap your arms around his waist and you'll be safe as houses."

Wide, apprehensive eyes as lucid a gray as any he'd seen fastened on Ben. "Safe as houses?" she echoed in that high, piping voice.

"Yeah." He swiveled on his heels and pointed toward his farmhouse. "See how solid it is? It never slips off its foundation. You'll be that secure up on Travis. Besides—" he lowered his voice "—I think Travis likes you."

She giggled, and he had a flash of Nora giggling just like that. He'd always been softest on her.

Like a projector bringing up the next slide, he suddenly saw another little girl, this one dark haired. Did he have a daughter somewhere with eyes that wide and vulnerable? A child lifting her arms trustingly for someone else to boost her wherever she wanted to go?

He pinched the bridge of his nose hard enough to

hurt. Hell, he knew better than to let himself think like that! Besides, if he had a daughter, she'd be a lot older than Sophie Kane. More like six—no, seven years old now.

And she wasn't his, not in any way that counted.

Sophie was a featherweight. He swung her in an easy arc and settled her into the saddle. No boa constrictor could have grabbed a snugger hold.

Her brother gagged. "Sophie! Loosen up!"

Ben had to pry her small arms from their death grip on Zach's waist and reposition them. Travis shifted his weight just then. Her whole body quivered and her arms squeezed again.

"Easy," Ben soothed. "He won't do anything but walk. The first few steps will seem bouncy, but then you'll feel the rhythm. His back is nice and wide. You won't fall off."

"Promise?" she whispered.

"Word of honor."

She took a deep breath. "Okay."

"You doing all right?" Ben asked the boy.

His knuckles showed white around the saddle horn, but he said scornfully, "Of course I am! I'm not a baby like her."

"I'm not a baby!" Sophie cried.

"Are too!"

"Am not!"

This argument had a familiar ring to it. Ben ended it by the simple expedient of taking hold of the reins and starting Travis forward. The first rolling step brought two gasps and then silence but for the quiet thud of each hoof coming down. Ben turned his head to see two sets of saucer eyes.

As he led the quarter horse on a meandering path through the pasture, however, the kids loosened up. Zach let his body sway with the horse's rhythm and tried to look nonchalant. Sophie craned her neck to peek around each side of her brother, then twisted around to see the horse's big brown rump.

Both started when Sherlock trotted up, but when Travis did no more than stroll along, Sophie giggled. "Sherlock was lonesome."

"Yep," Ben agreed. "Horses are herd animals, you know. Pretty much like most people."

"I'm not a herd animal!" the boy protested.

"No? Before you moved here, what'd you like doing for fun? You a baseball player?"

"Yeah, and soccer. I was the striker," he boasted, then fell silent. "Well, just 'cuz they're team sports doesn't mean..."

"But we play team sports because that's what comes naturally." Ben patted Travis's neck. Despite the earlier grooming, dust rose. "A kid who'd rather stay in from recess is the oddball, right?"

"I guess," Zach agreed reluctantly.

"So you still want to argue?"

"*You* live alone."

He mostly worked alone, too. By choice. He'd always figured that after being crammed for all those years into that tiny house with three siblings, he needed solitude. He was comfortable with it.

Funny, then, that he was actually kind of enjoying

this ramble with the two kids, even the conversation. Maybe he *was* mellowing.

"When you're an adult, about the only way to have someone to live with is to get married, and that's a big step. You want to be sure you've chosen the right person. I guess I just haven't found her yet."

Sophie poked her head around her brother's side. "Mommy isn't married."

"Yeah, I know." Legs like that, and she wasn't married.

"I like horses," the little girl continued artlessly. "If you married Mommy, Zach and me could ride Travis and Sherlock lots, couldn't we?"

Ben had to laugh. At least she was straightforward. "Got it all figured out, don't you?"

Zach turned his head and burst out, "What about Dad? Have you forgotten him?"

Sophie blinked and looked confused. "No-o," she said doubtfully. "Not 'zactly. But...but I don't know where Daddy is!" Her voice rose and her face puckered.

Ben flicked a glance at the boy. "Way to go," he growled. "She's a little kid. She's just talking. Give her a break, why don't you?"

"Well, she shouldn't talk like that," Zach mumbled.

Ben dropped back to the gelding's side and laid a hand on Sophie's ankle. "Shall we go a little faster?"

Her distress vanished, replaced with delight. "You mean gallop?"

"Not quite. Just walk a little faster." He waited for the boy to respond.

Zach gave him a sulky look. "Big deal."

Ben returned to the horse's nose and urged him into a faster walk. After a while he looked back to see both kids grinning. On impulse, Ben said, "When we get back to the barn, I'll take you up with me, one at a time, and we'll canter. Would you like that?"

Yeah, they'd like that. Their mom, waiting at the water trough, wasn't so sure.

"I won't let them fall," Ben promised. Damn it, the jeans weren't an improvement. They fit her hips the way his hands would have liked to, and she'd paired them with a skinny little shirt in a shade of green close to that of her eyes. His quick survey told him that terrific as her legs were, they might take second place to a pair of high, round breasts. He shifted uncomfortably, hoping nobody noticed the way his jeans had tightened.

Behind him, Sophie said in her little-girl voice, "We'll be safe as houses."

Judith raised her eyebrows. Ben spread his hands and smiled disarmingly.

Something happened in that instant. Her smile trembled into life; her eyes softened, then shimmered as though tears had sprung into them. She looked at him as if he were the Sir Galahad she wanted to make him.

Ben felt short of air. He reached out a hand, then curled it into a fist and pulled it back to his side. "You okay?" he asked gruffly.

She gave her head a shake. "I...yes, of course. It's just..." Her eyes searched his. "You smiled. And...and Sophie trusts you."

"She can," he said quietly, then felt as if he'd been

kicked right in the gut. Who the hell was he to claim any kid could trust him, when he'd never even bothered to try to see his own?

"Yes." Judith pressed her hands to her chest. "I know." She smiled up at her children. "Who's going first?"

She believed him, just like that. Ben felt like scum. If she knew… But she didn't, and he wasn't going to tell her.

Anyway, his past didn't matter. Judith could trust him; he wouldn't let her down.

"Oldest first," Ben said, and turned to lift the little girl off the horse's back.

CHAPTER SEVEN

JUDITH HADN'T FELT so safe—and *happy*—since she couldn't remember when. The big brown horse ambled down the lane; she relaxed in the saddle with Sophie's round warm body squeezed in front of her; behind her was Zach, his skinny arms wrapped around her waist. Judith held the reins, but Ben strolled right by the horse's head.

Tiny puffs of dust rose with each hoofbeat; the pungent scent of ponderosa pine seemed part of the warm, late-afternoon sunshine. The larch trees, which Judith had assumed were evergreen when she first came, were turning to molten gold on the hillside.

Her gaze kept lingering on Ben's straight back and broad shoulders, his short dark hair with the strands of silver, his strong brown neck, the big, competent hand that patted his horse's shoulder. *He* was a part of her contentment, more so than she was comfortable admitting. He was here, rock solid, kind—if reluctantly so—to her children, a man who kept promises.

Reminding herself that she hardly knew him failed to do a thing to filter out the rosy color through which she seemed to be seeing the world today. And what was wrong with being happy? she asked herself defiantly. Why not enjoy a few hours of peace and…okay, dreams might be too strong a word. Hope. That was it. Hope that the time might come when she wouldn't have to worry about the kids, when Sophie would no longer beg for Daddy at bedtime and Zach wouldn't look at his sister with dark angry eyes, when Judith herself could fall in love, maybe trust a man again.

There was nothing wrong with hope, was there?

"Here we are." Ben grabbed the reins down by the horse's mouth. He'd stopped the gelding not two feet from Judith's front porch. Travis shook his head, jingling the bridle and making his mane flop.

Sophie stirred in front of Judith. "Can we ride again?" she asked hopefully.

"Yeah," Ben said, "we'll do it again." He reached up for Sophie, who tumbled willingly into his arms.

"Will you have dinner with us?" Judith asked as he set her daughter down on the porch steps. "I put on a stew this morning in the Crock-Pot." When he hesitated, she coaxed, "I make wonderful sourdough biscuits."

The way to a man's heart... Judith clamped off the thought. She was *not* trying to entice him; she was merely reciprocating his kindness.

He inclined his head in assent. "Can't resist an invitation like that. My stews are usually out of a can. Biscuits, too, come to think of it."

"Real men don't cook, right?" Zach said. "Mom tries to make me learn."

"If real men enjoy eating, they cook." Ben looked steadily up at her son. "I get lazy when all the effort is just for myself. 'Don't' doesn't mean 'can't.'"

"Oh."

Even without being able to see Zach's face, Judith felt the onset of sullenness. He needed a father, she thought, someone to ally himself with. What he had was a little sister who threatened his place with his mother. And a mother who was overwhelmed by the struggle to mend a family even as she had to stand guard. Although part of her wished Ben were the fatherly kind, she was glad he didn't cater to Zach too much; all she needed was a redneck neighbor who convinced her son that men didn't cook or clean house, that women were sissies and that his mom was overprotective.

But, oh, for a man who took Zach under his wing. Her fingers tightened on the reins. If only remarrying weren't the only sure way she knew to provide him with a daddy.

As if in answer to a prayer, Ben lifted a brow at her.

"Maybe Zach would like to ride back with me, help unsaddle Travis and feed the horses. I need to shower, but he could wait for me."

"Could I?" her son breathed.

"Sure." She smiled at the police chief. "If he wouldn't be a nuisance."

Something wry in his expression told her that yes, he expected Zach would be just that, but he shook his head. "Taking care of animals is part of owning them. Time he learned that."

"We don't *have* any animals," Zach grumbled. "Mom would never let me get a dog."

"We had no yard, and you were too young to walk one alone." *And I was too afraid to let you.*

"A dog might not be a bad idea now," Ben suggested. "Good early-warning system."

"Yeah!" Zach bounced behind her, and the horse's hindquarters bunched and shifted. "Could we?"

Judith grabbed the saddle horn. "I'll think about it."

Ben hid a smile without complete success. "You can get off anytime."

"Of course," she said with dignity. "Um…how?" She couldn't fall into his arms like a five-year-old or dismount the way you were supposed to, with Zach behind her. When she glanced down, the ground seemed awfully far below. Judith swallowed and looked back at Ben.

A grin deepened the slashes in his cheeks and the lines beside his eyes. "I'll catch you," he said softly.

"I don't *need* to be caught," she lied.

"All right, help you," he amended, still with that wicked gleam in his eyes.

Where had her grim neighbor gone? Judith wondered breathlessly.

"Bring your right leg over Travis's neck," Ben suggested. "It's awkward with the saddle horn, but you can do it. Like that," he said approvingly as she took her life in her hands and followed his orders. "Now, kick free from the stirrup and let yourself slide down."

"Slide…" Judith moaned, but Ben's hands had already closed around her waist, and he lifted her and swung her away from the horse.

"There." Ben deposited her with her feet on the grass. "That wasn't so bad, was it?"

He hadn't released her. She was so close she could

see individual bristles on his chin and dark spiky lashes around his eyes. Judith moistened her dry lips. "No," she squeaked.

Still his hands lingered. His gaze had moved to her mouth. *His* was incredibly sexy, even if the smile had faded. Her knees wanted to buckle, and she didn't think it was from the riding. Her heart raced, and she felt strange, as if everything around them had become misty, indistinct.

Ben's head bent, slowly, purposefully; Judith's lips parted.

"Mommy," said a small voice, "can't you stand up?"

Sophie. Judith jerked upright. Oh, dear Lord, Zach, too! She'd almost kissed a man right in front of her children!

Ben blinked and stepped back, his hands falling away from her waist. He looked as disoriented as she felt.

Long practice at hiding the most wrenching of emotions let her say, almost evenly, "I guess my legs are a little shaky. How about yours?"

"Uh-uh! Daddy says my legs are noodles. I can pract'ly do the splits. Wanna see?"

Judith didn't dare look at Ben. "Why don't you come take a shower with me, pumpkin," she suggested. "We'll wash the horsey smell off. You can show me in the bedroom."

"Okeydokey," her small daughter said cheerily, jumping up from the porch step.

Climbing the steps, Judith wasn't so sure it *was*

Ben's touch that had made her legs wobbly. They still felt very peculiar.

Behind her, he said, "A hot bath would be an even better idea. Otherwise, you may wake up sore in the morning."

"Sore?" Despite herself, she turned.

Ben was poised with one foot in the stirrup, about to swing himself up on the horse's back.

"Yeah, sore. Human legs aren't made to be spread so wide." He cleared his throat even as she blushed fiercely. The children remained oblivious to the unspoken "except" that had leaped to both adult minds. Hastily he said, "There's, uh, a reason old cowboys walk the way they do."

Without waiting for her to respond, Ben grabbed the saddle horn and pulled himself up easily. With a minimum of awkwardness, he swung his leg forward, over the saddle horn, and settled into the saddle. Pulling on the reins, he turned Travis away. Zach was getting so confident he didn't even grab hold.

By the time Judith ran a hot bath, her thigh muscles were stiffening and she wished she did have time for a long soak. The fragrant bubbles she'd added on a whim might not be medicinal, but they made her feel feminine. Of course, Sophie had to hop in, too, dumping a few quarts of water on the bathroom floor and mat, which squished under Judith's feet when she got out.

She dried her daughter's bare, wriggly body first, then herself. Sophie went off to choose her own clothes. Judith, for unnamed, unexamined reasons, did not reach for the sweatpants or jeans she would normally have worn on an evening at home; instead, she put on snug turquoise leggings and a loosely woven white sweater with a scooped neckline.

Sophie had combined an eye-popping ensemble: bright-red gathered skirt, lace-edged pink-and-purple knit shirt and green knee socks. Tactfully not commenting on her color coordination, Judith helped her turn the shirt around so at least the tag wasn't flopping under her chin.

Then she kissed Sophie's forehead. "All right! Let's go cook."

Listening to Sophie chatter as they mixed the dough, Judith felt another swell of happiness. The five-year-old was adjusting far quicker than Judith had dreamed she would. Their new home, comfortable routines and plenty of patience seemed to be the answer. Of course there'd be setbacks—there had to be—but Sophie had come so far.

The biscuits were in the oven by the time the front door crashed open. "We're home!" Zach bellowed.

Judith went to meet them, giving her son a once-over. Hair and dirt coated the insides of his pant legs and was sprinkled over his shirt. "You have time for a quick shower, if you hurry."

"I don't need..." He looked down at himself. "It's just horsehair, Mom." Seeing her expression, he made a face. "Oh, all right."

She'd been terribly conscious the whole while of Ben waiting right behind him. With Zach racing down the hall, Judith had no choice but to meet Ben's eyes. They were dark, quiet, deep. Watchful.

His hair was still damp, and he'd obviously shaved

for a second time that day in honor of her invitation. A long-sleeved white shirt, cuffs buttoned, was tucked into clean black jeans, which she guessed were meant for dress-up. Although unsmiling, he was handsome enough to set her heart to racing.

"Hi," she said breathlessly. "Thanks for taking him."

"No problem." One side of his mouth tilted up. "He's a talker."

"Motor mouth." The almost forgotten sobriquet popped out of her subconscious. "That's what Rylan called him. When Zach was four or five, I'd swear he woke up talking and was still murmuring to himself when he fell asleep at night. He's actually been a lot quieter lately. Having Sophie back—" Judith checked herself. The five-year-old was plopping silverware on the table within hearing distance. "Well… Come on in."

She felt Ben behind her as she went to the table. With the part of her mind that functioned automatically, she saw that Sophie had placed the silverware randomly.

"Honey, we each need one fork, one spoon and one knife." She made her voice light, teasing. "I'd look kind of silly buttering my roll with a fork, wouldn't I? And Ben might have a hard time stabbing cooked carrots with a knife."

Sophie giggled. "Okay," she said obligingly, and began rearranging the silverware, singing to herself as she circled the table over and over again.

Judith folded napkins and followed her around, placing one under the fork at each place. Sophie carefully set out the plates and bowls next, then glasses for water and milk. Finally done, she gazed expectantly at Ben, who had hovered in the background.

"It looks real pretty," he said, smiling down at Judith's daughter.

In an abortive gesture in which Judith read tenderness, he lifted a hand as though to touch Sophie's coppery curls but drew it back before the little girl noticed.

"You'll be a heck of a hostess when you grow up."

Sophie's eyes opened wide. "What's a 'hosess'?"

Taking the biscuits out of the oven, Judith left Ben to offer an explanation, although she wouldn't for the world have missed a word of it.

"A lady taking care of her guests," he said gravely. "A man with guests is the host."

"Oh." She frowned. "What's a 'heck' hosess?"

"A really terrific one."

"Oh," Sophie said again. She gave a pleased nod. "Okay. That's what I'll be when I grow up."

He gazed down at her with the oddest expression, as though this child, a mere kindergartner, fascinated and charmed and repelled him all at the same time. Finally he gave his head a shake.

"You'll be more than that." His voice sounded almost hoarse. "You'll be all kinds of things. A horsewoman, maybe a teacher like your mom, a wife and mother..." He gave a grunt that might have been a laugh. "Who knows? Maybe a gardener. An ambassador."

Sophie smiled radiantly. "A princess. I wanna be a princess."

He gave another grunt. "My sister did, too. That's what she dressed up as at Halloween every year."

"*Is* she a princess?" Sophie reached trustingly for his hand.

He froze, just for a second, then his fingers flexed and closed carefully around the small hand. "No." His head was bent as he looked down at Sophie. "No, instead she makes gardens beautiful enough for any princess."

"Can I see one?"

"Well, they're not around here. But maybe someday."

Beyond them, Zach asked, "Someday what? Can I do it, too?"

Ben straightened and let go of Sophie's hand. "Yeah, someday you can mow my lawn."

Zach blew a raspberry. "You think I'm dumb or something? I know that's not what you said."

How familial this felt, Judith thought with an odd clutch of pleasure as she called, "Dinner's ready. Everybody sit down."

Sophie ushered Ben to the spot at the table facing Judith's that had been empty until now. Then she scrambled up onto her own chair.

The dinner was more formal than usual. Everybody asked for dishes to be passed, kept elbows off the table, said please and thank-you. Judith was delighted by the children's manners, particularly Sophie's. When she'd first returned, the five-year-old had acted as if she'd never sat down to a properly set dinner table or been expected to ask nicely if she wanted something. But what gave Judith a lump in her throat was the way Ben listened gravely to her children, gave quick smiles or praise and raised an eyebrow to wordlessly chide. The whole while she sensed he, too, was on his best behavior, a little uncomfortable with the niceties of spreading a napkin on his lap and asking permission to take another biscuit.

A solitary man, but he knew how to be a father.

If she hadn't promised not to ask God for anything else, Judith might have sent up a small prayerful wish right then. But she had promised, and so she didn't. She only felt the ache beneath her breastbone and wondered if fate might be this kind to her.

Ben offered to help clean the kitchen, but Judith declined. It was Zach's bedtime and later than Sophie's usual one, so Judith had the kids clear the table and go brush their teeth.

"Zach," she called after them, "help Sophie with her nightie." To Ben, she asked, "Coffee? Tea?" *Or me?* Wasn't that how the saying went?

"Sure," he drawled. "Either."

She glanced at him to be sure he hadn't somehow read her mind and taken her up on an offer she hadn't—wouldn't—make, but his expression was bland.

By the time the water boiled, the kids were ready to be tucked in. Judith excused herself and went to kiss both good-night. Her lips lingered, first on Sophie's plump cheek, then on Zach's thinner, smooth one. She switched off the lamp and paused in the crack of golden light let in by the half-opened door. "I love you," she said softly. "Both of you."

"I love you," Zach murmured, the incantation a nightly one.

"Daddy loves me, too," offered Sophie in a sleepy voice.

The stab of pain was always unexpected, as if she'd been taken by surprise. The anger was more familiar. *That bastard had better love his daughter,* she thought, *or else what was his excuse?*

"'Night," she said again, and pulled the door to the precise correct position that she and Zach had agreed on after long bargaining sessions. Not wide open, not closed. A precise four inches kept the bedroom from darkness and let him know she would hear him if he called out. Now Sophie was the one who awakened with nightmares, sometimes finishing the night in her mother's bed, but the bargain held.

Ben had poured the coffee and was stirring a teaspoon of sugar into one mug when she returned to the kitchen. He added some cream, stirred and handed it to her. His own was still black.

"Thank you," she said, surprised. "You know how I drink my coffee."

"I notice things."

"Shall we go sit out in the living room? Or on the porch? It looks like a nice evening."

"Porch."

She hesitated but left the outside lights off. Ben was the one to ease the screen door closed. When she sat on the swing, he took up his usual position against the railing. Enough light fell through the windows to allow her to make out his features.

"Is it because you're a policeman?" she asked. "That you notice things?"

"Yeah. Probably. You get in the habit. Maybe not if you were always a small-town cop, but in a city for sure. People walk down the street totally oblivious to what's around them. Not a cop. You see that alley ahead, you quietly check out who's walking behind you, you notice the license plate on a car creeping by." He shrugged. "Habit."

"Did you always want to be a cop?"

"Truth?"

She nodded.

"Nah." His mouth had a wry twist. "I wanted to be a doctor. How the hell I thought my mother would pay for all those years of school, I don't have a clue."

"What happened?" Judith asked softly.

He pushed himself to his feet and turned to gaze out at the night. His voice became curt. "Real life. It's what happens."

His answer wasn't expansive, but she didn't have the sense he was shutting her out entirely as he had the other day. So she let her curiosity have its way.

"You couldn't afford medical school?"

"Didn't even make it to college, not out of high school." The way he stood now, his face was entirely shadowed. "I grew up in Puyallup. I stayed at home until I was in my early twenties. Worked at whatever I could find. Finally went to the community college, got a degree in criminal justice."

"Why?"

He turned his back on the darkness to look at her again, his head cocked. "Why what?"

"Why criminal justice?"

Ben didn't seem to mind her nosiness. "I put a new roof on a cop's house. He liked to have a beer and tell stories. He made his job sound exciting and...oh, hell, valiant. Honorable. You don't find out that you're going to spend your life with the scum of the earth until you're already on the job."

"But you don't if you police a town like this."

"Right." This smile was genuine. "But there isn't much excitement, either."

"I suppose not." Judith wanted to know more, so much more, but she had to frame her questions to sound casual, not as if this were an inquisition.

He beat her to it. "How about you? Why a teacher?"

She found herself talking about her own childhood, about her mother, who had started as a teacher at a prep school and eventually rose to be principal, and of her father, a midlevel executive in an insurance company.

"He always made more money than Mom," Judith said, "but he never liked his job. I wanted to find something I'd love doing. Of course, I never imagined it would be teaching. I remember telling myself *I* would never be like my mother! But I did some tutoring when I was in high school, and then I got a job as a summer counselor at a day camp and..." She spread her hands and smiled. "I loved figuring out ways to convince kids that they wanted to learn whatever I was going to teach. I enjoyed their questions, their silliness, their vulnerability. So here I am."

"Here you are," he echoed, studying her.

A silence grew, not awkward but not entirely comfortable, either. She set the swing to rocking and told herself to say something. Anything. Chat. But after the spate of background information she'd offered, her vocal cords seemed to have shut down. Or maybe that wasn't it. She just couldn't think of a single thing to say.

The sound of distant crickets or frogs, or possibly just brittle autumn leaves whispering in a breeze, came from the darkness beyond the porch. She still hadn't gotten used to how dark it was here, so far from city lights. And how many more stars she could see with cold white clarity if she just stepped off the porch and tilted her head back. But tonight, the light from the kitchen falling through the windows was like a circle of firelight, making a warm, safe place against the invisible terrors of the night beyond its reach.

Somehow Ben McKinsey had become the night *and* the security of her own front porch. He made her feel safe even as he scared her a little.

He hadn't moved, just kept looking at her.

"I've been wanting to kiss you."

His voice was the darkness, deep and mysterious and frightening.

Her breath almost stopped. Wildly she wondered what she was supposed to say to that. How about a bright, interested "Oh?"

"Any chance you've been hoping I would?"

Oh, Lord. He was asking her to declare herself. *Yes, you make my knees weak.* Or *No, sorry, not interested.* If she did agree to kiss him, she would have to take equal responsibility. She couldn't pretend to herself later that she hadn't really wanted his lips on hers.

"Is it that tough a decision?" he asked roughly.

"I...no." Her heart gave a funny thump when he made a sound and started to turn away. "No, I didn't mean— It isn't that tough. I..." Her voice faded to a whisper. "Yes. Yes, I've been hoping."

Ben stopped, and she saw that his hands were knotted into fists. Slowly his fingers uncurled and he rubbed his hands on his pant legs as he turned to face her. The expression on his face made her heart give a few more thumps as it swelled and filled her chest to the point of pain.

He didn't say another word. She rose to her feet and lifted trembling hands to flatten them against his chest. He was so warm, and Judith realized she'd begun to shiver.

"Thinking about pushing me away?" he asked.

"Oh! No!" She started to snatch her hands back.

His snaked up to grip her wrists. But instead of yanking her forward, Ben carefully splayed her fingers one at a time against his chest again. "I was kidding." His voice was low, gritty. "I like the way it feels. You touching me."

"I like the feel of you, too," she admitted, so quietly he had to bend his head to hear her.

He said something else, something quick and vehement, but she couldn't make it out. She didn't even try. His ragged breath was enough to let her know what was coming, and she lifted her mouth to meet his.

She hadn't expected tentativeness, not from this

man, and she didn't get it. He kissed her with the thoroughness of a longtime lover, but he was trembling as much as she was when his tongue stroked hers and his teeth closed on her lower lip.

She must have been starved for this, because her nervousness evaporated along with her ability to think. She just felt: his body, long and hard and muscular, flattened against hers; his big hands, one wrapped in her hair, the other gripping her hip; his tongue, hot and slick and evocative. Her arms encircled him now; he was groaning, and she was making little sobbing sounds as his mouth traveled down her throat, kissing and nibbling.

Ben pushed her sweater off one shoulder, her bra strap with it. In a thick voice, he said, "This has been driving me crazy all night. You're so delicate, so pretty…"

She let out a shuddering breath that he echoed.

"I think," he said hoarsely, "that I'd better quit while I can."

"Quit?" Judith whispered, not wanting to understand.

His hands brushed the sides of her breasts, wrapped around her upper arms. More kisses softly touched her collarbone and the hollow at the base of her throat. He groaned, then kissed her mouth again, but gently this time, with finality. With aching slowness, he stepped back and let her go.

"Ben?" she asked, still not comprehending.

"Do you want me to make love to you? Right here on the porch?"

"Make love…?" Judith looked around, awareness

returning. All he'd suggested was a kiss, and she'd been all over him. She'd never been so…so mindless before! She had kids in the house right behind her. They might not even be asleep yet. And she hardly knew this man. Certainly not well enough to…to…

"No." She swallowed. "Of course not! I'm sorry, I…"

His hands shot out again and gripped her shoulders. He kissed her again, quick and hard. "What's to be sorry for? It was a hell of a kiss. Let's do it again. When your kids are out of shouting distance."

"I…yes." Did she dare? It was scary, thinking she might be swallowed by passion. She'd always been able to think logically, even in the worst days following Sophie's kidnapping.

"Good night."

He seemed reluctant to let her go, or else why did his fingers uncurl so slowly from her arms? Why did his voice sound raw?

"Thanks for dinner."

He backed up a step, then another. At the top of the stairs, he took a long look at her, then turned and left, darkness into darkness, no longer part of the cozy world bounded by the porch railing and the reaches of the kitchen light.

Judith sank onto the swing and wrapped her arms around herself. She felt suddenly very alone.

He hadn't been gone two minutes, and already she missed him. Which gave her even more to be scared about. On a soft sound of distress, she closed her eyes and hugged herself against the loneliness and the night chill.

CHAPTER EIGHT

"OKAY." HANDS CLASPED behind his back, Ben strolled between desks in Judith's classroom, a meandering route that allowed him to look closely at each fifth grader. Things had changed; instead of whispering, they were all attentive. Heads turned as he walked.

"Jimmy heard some guys were going to gang up on him after school," Ben continued. "He's thinking about taking his dad's gun and sneaking it to school in his backpack to protect himself."

The students stirred; Ben felt their interest. From her quiet post at the side of the room, Judith smiled at him, a subtle little tweak to his ego.

"Let's talk about the consequences if he carries that through. Any good things that might happen? Bad things?"

Hands shot up.

"Bryan."

"He might get caught."

"True enough. Lauren."

"He might shoot somebody." Her eyes were wide at the very thought.

"Or else somebody else might have a gun, too, and

shoot *him*," Ian added with the relish of a typical ten-year-old boy.

Ben nodded his approval. "Anything good that could happen?"

Tony, the rebel, raised his hand. "Yeah, if he showed it around, the other kids would think he was cool."

The classroom erupted in agreement and protests. Ben picked out comments that went all the way from "*I* wouldn't think he was cool" to "Yeah, everybody would be scared of him. Even that gang."

He waited until they simmered down to ask, "Do you think the gang would bother him once they heard he had a gun?"

"Nah," Tony said. "They wouldn't be that stupid."

Ben was pleased when another boy interjected, "It might make them madder, though. If he doesn't bring the gun to school every day, they'd get him some day when he didn't have it."

"Well, he could bring it every day..." Tony began.

"But what if his dad noticed it was gone? Besides, *my* mom looks in my backpack sometimes," one of the girls said. "I bet most people's moms do."

Tony opened his mouth again, then shut it. Obviously, his mother or father did indeed mount an occasional search for school notices that hadn't been handed over or carrot sticks that might be decomposing in the bottom of the backpack.

They went on to talk about the risks of carrying a gun, whom Jimmy might talk to about whether this was the best way of protecting himself and what other choices he might make. The kids were so caught up in the discussion that Judith let them go until the bell rang. Within seconds, they'd put their chairs up on their desks, grabbed packs and were jostling one another out the door.

Almost as quickly, Judith dumped a load of papers into a briefcase. With another smile at Ben, she said, "You're getting good at this."

"Thanks." He studied her. Today she wore a simple white knit shirt and a flowery gathered skirt that swirled around her legs. Her fiery hair was braided in some complicated way that lay flat against her head and looked old-fashioned to him. Fresh and young in a way that had nothing to do with actual age, she made him think of spring, not fall, despite the color of her hair. She made him imagine he could start over.

"I've got to run and get the kids," she said, interrupting his reverie.

"I'll walk you."

She made a comical face. "Walk? You ought to see me racing down the halls."

Ben didn't want her to know that he had. "You take your life into your hands out there," he said, nodding toward the tumult in the hall. "I'll protect you."

"Now, there's an offer." Her quick, teasing smile made his blood sing.

"Will you have dinner with me?" he heard himself ask.

Now, where the hell had that come from? He hadn't consciously formulated the invitation, though he supposed it had been hovering in the back of his mind.

About to head out the door, Judith stopped. When

she turned, all kinds of emotions chased across her face. After a moment, she said slowly, "I'd love to, but I can't leave Zach and Sophie. Not with a teen-ager."

"Maybe I can think of someone."

She worried her bottom lip. "Well, normally… But right now, if I don't really know the baby-sitter…"

Oh, hell. Maybe he hadn't planned to ask her out, but now that he had, Ben realized how badly he wanted to be alone with her.

"Yeah, okay," he said. "I don't blame you. Maybe later, after Kane's been sent away."

Judith nodded, but her expression remained anxious. "I'm sorry," she murmured, then rose on tiptoe and kissed him, just a brush on the mouth, but affecting him more than an openmouthed kiss would from most women.

"Hey, don't apologize…" Ben began, but his eyes suddenly focused beyond her and he realized the school principal had appeared in the doorway. He nodded to her. "Ms. Galindez."

Judith whipped around. "Carol!"

"Judith. Chief McKinsey." The principal's brown eyes twinkled. "Romancing my staff?"

Pink blossomed on Judith's cheeks and she said in a flurry, "It was just a thank-you. But I apologize. I didn't consider what the kids might think if they saw me—"

"I was teasing." Carol Galindez came into the room. "Nobody saw. And you weren't exactly neck-ing, anyway."

Too bad, Ben thought.

"I couldn't help overhearing some of your conversation," Carol said. "And I have an idea. You have a minute, don't you?"

"I...I really need to collect the kids."

"I'll talk fast. My sister's bringing her family over tonight for a barbecue. Tim is in Zach's class, and Nadia is almost five—just missed the cutoff for kindergarten. With luck, they'll all hit it off and have such fun we adults won't have to listen to them whine about being bored."

"Oh, but..."

Carol strolled to the nearest bulletin board and scanned the student drawings hung on it. Over her shoulder, she said, "You could use a night to yourself. Assuming you want to turn down our revered police chief, you're welcome to come, too, but I'd be delighted to take Zach and Sophie if you want to kick up your heels a little." Her sly glance took in Ben, waiting quietly to the side.

Judith's mouth opened, then closed, then opened again in a pantomime of indecision. "Are you *sure?*"

"You bet." A woman didn't become a school administrator without knowing how to sound firm. "Why don't we go collect them right now and see what they think."

Judith turned a helpless gaze on Ben. "I guess you can't get out of that invitation now, can you?"

"Guess not," he said laconically. He winked at Carol, who laughed and went out the door. Then he took in Judith's flustered expression and frowned. "You've been pushed into this, haven't you? We don't have to do it."

"No. I want to." She didn't play coy. Her gaze was direct, her tone positive. "Really. You must have to go back to work. What time shall we make it?"

They decided on five-thirty. The Galindez barbecue presumably wouldn't last into the wee hours, even if it was Friday evening, so he figured they'd better enjoy what time they had.

Back at the station, Ben couldn't force himself to concentrate on the administrative stuff that made up too much of his job. He knew police chiefs who sat on their butts behind a desk all day, but he liked knowing what was going on out there. Since Julie Robinson had gone off on maternity leave, he'd taken extra shifts. Today wasn't one of them, but he figured having another cop on the street wouldn't hurt anything. Why not go?

He'd barely pulled out of the parking lot when his radio crackled. A break-in reported at a residence in the four-hundred block of Highland Street.

Ben grabbed his mike. "I'll take it."

The victim, a man in his twenties, met Ben at the door of the freshly painted 1930s-era bungalow. Clean-cut, the guy looked vaguely familiar. Ben searched his mental files. A checker at the supermarket? No, that didn't click. Hardware store? Nope.

"That was quick," the victim said, standing back. "Come on in."

Ben glanced around the living room. Hardwood floors, well cared for. Big-screen TV, a stack of expensive stereo equipment, two recliners and a leather couch. Two hundred or more CDs filled a wrought-iron rack on the wall above the oak stereo cabinet.

Okay, maybe the burglar hadn't taken the TV because it was too big. But why not the VCR or the tuner? Had this guy surprised him before he could make off with anything?

Taking out his notebook, Ben said, "When did you notice the house had been broken into?"

"Just now." The man held out a hand. "Josh Heyer. You're Chief McKinsey, aren't you?" Ben agreed that he was. "I just got home from work—I'm a pharmacist," Heyer continued. "Everything looked okay here." He gestured vaguely toward the audio-video equipment. "I went straight to my bedroom to change clothes. I was going to go for a run. My bedroom's…well, not a mess, but a couple of drawers and the closet doors were open, a roll of socks was on the floor…. Just little stuff. I thought maybe they were looking for money, but I don't keep any around, except for some small change."

"Jewelry?"

"Not really."

"So nothing was taken?" Ben doodled on his pad.

"Just clothes."

That got his attention. *"Clothes?"*

"Yeah. Pretty weird, huh?" Heyer nodded toward the bedroom. "You can look around if you want."

"Uh…sure." Clothes?

They passed the kitchen, where a juicer, a blender and an espresso machine stood at attention on tiled countertops. The door to a den was open. There a computer shared desk space with two printers and another piece of equipment that might have been a color scanner or a small copying machine. All untouched.

Considering the era of the house, the huge bedroom could only have been achieved by knocking down a wall. A king-size bed floated in the middle of three-inch-deep cream-colored carpeting. The doors on a bank of closets were ajar; the drawers on the pale wood dresser weren't.

Ben rocked on his heels and scanned the room. Another TV, twenty-seven-inch screen. Combination CD player-clock radio beside the bed.

"Are you single?" he asked.

"For six more weeks." Heyer had stayed in the doorway, as though reluctant to enter the bedroom again. At Ben's look of inquiry, he added, "I'm engaged."

"You had any teenagers here recently? Doing yardwork, whatever?"

No teenagers. Nobody but Heyer's cleaning lady, who had worked for him for three years now.

"Can you describe the clothes that are missing?" Ben held his pen poised.

Josh Heyer could. One dress shirt, pin-striped. Half a dozen white T-shirts. And his Grateful Dead shirt.

"I've had it since I was a teenager," he said, looking really fried for the first time. "I bought it when I went to see them play down in Oregon. Eugene. I don't suppose you went?"

Ben shook his head.

"Damn it, I liked that shirt! The rest of the stuff I can replace, but not that. The Dead T-shirts in catalogs now are so commercial looking. They're just not the same."

He described it in minute detail, down to the rip

near the hem, apparently sacred because he'd torn the shirt that same day in Eugene.

Ben didn't have any trouble figuring out how the intruder had entered the house. The screen had been removed from the kitchen window, which was wide open. Some branches had been broken off the rhododendron below the window, and footprints were visible in the flower bed but weren't clear enough to tell Ben much.

Heyer walked Ben to the front door, where he assured the pharmacist that they'd do everything they could, although he didn't hold out much hope. "Did you monogram your dress shirt?"

Heyer shook his head.

"Laundry marks?"

"I don't think so."

"Then there's probably no way to prove it's yours even if we spot someone walking around town in it. Same goes for the T-shirts. Still, I'd like to know why someone would break into a house just to steal clothes. And why just shirts? Once he was here, why not pants or socks? Why not a CD player or a VCR? At least those he could sell."

"*You'd* like to know? What about me?" Heyer grimaced. "It's damned kinky. And...oh, hell, I guess it makes me feel insecure. You know? I mean, I'll be more careful to lock windows, but still...."

Ben understood; the reaction was typical. Although this had hardly been a devastating break-in, the idea of someone poking through your drawers and trying on your clothes might hit you harder emotionally than the more impersonal burglary of a TV or stereo equipment. They shook hands, and Ben repeated his assurances.

By this time, it was after four. The radio was quiet, and Ben headed back to the station to write a report. By the time he'd finished, he had all at the station shaking their heads over the bizarre break-in.

Once he was home, Ben showered and changed with lightning speed. He hadn't been on a date in a while. A year, maybe? He wondered if it had occurred to Judith that, in a town this small, by tomorrow morning everyone would have heard that she'd had dinner with the police chief.

When he drove to her house she was ready. She wore a simple little dress the color of mint juleps, and all those auburn curls were gathered on top of her head in a snug knot, leaving her slender neck bare. He was glad she didn't wear much jewelry; he liked seeing her creamy skin unornamented. Hell, he'd like to see her in nothing *but* creamy skin and fiery curls.

On the drive back to town, Judith asked about his day, and he told her a thief was walking around town in someone else's Grateful Dead T-shirt.

"Damnedest thing," he said. "Why go to all that trouble for eight shirts, six of them plain white T-shirts?"

Tension crept into her voice. "What size were they?"

He shot her a glance. "You're thinking about your ex? Why the hell would he arrive in town desperately in need of eight shirts?"

"I can't imagine," she admitted. "Still..."

"Size fourteen neck. Small guy. Sleeves were only a thirty-two length."

"Oh." Her relief was obvious. "Ry wears a much larger size than that. It was a silly thought anyway. No, it's a silly crime! Do you think you'll ever find out why those shirts were stolen?"

"Probably not. There are a few cases I've spent years wondering about. This'll probably be one of 'em."

They speculated about the thief's motive. Perhaps he was in love with the victim or wanted to impersonate him. But why just shirts?

"Maybe the pharmacist's covering up a crime he committed himself," Judith suggested, eyes sparkling. "Let's see. He murdered someone and got blood all over his shirt. The dress shirt, that is, with one of the T-shirts beneath it. But it would sound funny if he reported only two shirts missing, so he threw in the others to be more convincing."

"He wouldn't need to report the shirts missing in the first place," Ben said. Though if the pharmacist's fiancée turned up missing, he thought wryly, he'd keep this bizarre episode—and Judith's farfetched explanation for it—in mind.

After some discussion they decided on a new restaurant in town, one that Ben privately figured wouldn't make it. This was cattle country, and folks liked a big slab of steak when they went out to dinner, cholesterol or no. This new place, called The French Invention, was just a little too fancy for the locals. The idea of having their chicken or steak wrapped inside a skinny pancake hadn't gone over so far. Ben happened to like crepes, and he wasn't surprised that Judith did, too.

Terra-cotta tile floors, wallpaper with tiny sprigs of lavender and white antique tables and chairs gave the place a feminine ambience that made Ben feel large and clumsy, but the hostess seated them at a booth in the nook formed by a bay window, where there was plenty of leg room. Only two other tables were occupied, neither of them close by; the room was romantically dark, with short fat candles flickering on the tables. Their light gave Judith a golden cast, as if she had stepped from a Renaissance painting.

Not a man given to compliments, he cleared his throat. "You're beautiful."

Her smile was soft and pleased. "Thank you. You should have seen me at eight years old, skinny and covered with freckles. Thank God, they seem to have faded away." She hesitated, then amended, "Mostly."

Was it his imagination, or had her cheeks pinkened? That made him wonder where she might have freckles, and the speculation had him shifting in his seat.

Fortunately, he was distracted by the necessity of ordering. He asked for the burgundy beef crepe, and Judith chose one with Swiss cheese and chicken and broccoli.

The waitress melted into the darkness.

"This is nice, Ben." Judith gestured gracefully with her small hand. "I haven't been out to dinner without at least Zach in…oh, ages. I've been too busy being Mommy."

"You have good kids."

"And you're wonderful with them. Why haven't you had your own?"

He usually found a way to avoid answering that one directly. But this time...oh, hell, he didn't know where this thing with her was going, but he knew that he, too, wanted to be honest.

Honest enough that she'd see right away that he wasn't stepdaddy material. Any more than he'd been daddy material, he thought grimly.

"For one thing, I've never married," he said. *Yeah,* his inner self mocked, *but if you were any kind of decent man, you would have.* He ignored that voice. "I have two younger brothers and a sister. After my father died, when I was Zach's age, I had to help raise all of them. My mother worked two jobs to support us. I did most everything else. By the time Nora, the youngest, made it safely to eighteen, I figured I'd done my part." He shrugged. "I've never wanted to do it all over again."

"I can see why you'd feel that way," Judith said with a solemn nod. "But, you know, it's not the same when the children are your own. It's..." Her brow crinkled as she sought the right word. "It's so *primal*—almost scary—how protective you feel. You know from that first moment that you'd do anything for this baby. Even die." She heard her own intensity and gave her head a shake. "I'm getting carried away, aren't I?"

Would she love a man as wholeheartedly? He steered away from the dangerous thought.

"Not everyone reacts to becoming a parent the same way," he remarked. "In my job, I see some parents who don't give a good goddamn. I don't want to become a father and find out I resent the obligations."

"But…" She stopped and with a visible effort made her face and tone expressionless. "No. I guess you're right."

"I may yet change my mind." The words came out unbidden, and he had no time to yank them back. He despised himself immediately; damn it, he was lying to her, giving her hope that he might be a man she could have a future with, when he wasn't.

Whoa! He didn't have a reason in the world to think she might want a future with him. This was a first date, for God's sake! Maybe he'd lied, maybe not; all he'd really done was soften his earlier statement. And a man never knew, did he? Famous last words were called that for a reason.

Lie or not, it worked. A smile reappeared on her lips and she said, "You'd be a great father."

Somewhere out there was a kid who'd dispute that. Judith Kane would despise him if she knew about that child.

There wasn't a damn reason she should ever find out.

"I can be pretty brusque with them."

"I thought so the first time I met you." Her wide, candid eyes searched his. "But you're so good with Sophie and Zach now that you know them. And I have to tell you, Tony Fiorentino has a bad case of hero worship for you."

"What?" Ben was genuinely startled. Trouble-in-the-making Tony?

"Mmm." He noticed the faintest hint of dimples when she smiled. He'd never noticed them before. "He's decided he wants to be a cop."

"So he can carry a gun," Ben said dryly.

"That could have something to do with it," Judith admitted. "But he also thinks it's so cool that people have to call you 'Chief.' And that even though you probably arrest *dozens* of people every day, you still come and talk to our class. He likes to imitate the way he's sure you throw a crook up against the wall. If he had a pair of handcuffs, he figures he could have them on a suspect in ten seconds flat."

"Good God," Ben muttered.

"Yes, I know, but it wouldn't hurt if you encouraged him. His dad is in the penitentiary in Walla Walla for armed robbery. His mother came home to live near her parents, who apparently make a habit of telling Tony he's just like his father. He's going to be a good-for-nothing, too, if he goes on the way he is, according to Grandma." Judith looked seriously steamed. "I heard the woman right out in the hall in front of my classroom!"

He imagined the scene. "Did you give her hell?"

"Darn right I did!" She made a face. "Of course, it didn't do any good at all. That poor boy. He's really sweet, you know." Her eyes beseeched him. "He just doesn't have a good role model."

Her words sank in. "Exactly what do you have in mind?"

"Well, if you could just take an interest in him."

Now she was treading delicately, apparently reading his stupefaction right.

"Maybe he could ride along with you in your police car someday. If I had him do a report about it…"

"Should I let him handcuff someone, too?"

"I was thinking more when you were off duty."

He could just picture the kid grabbing the radio, sticking his fingers through the grille, wanting to know if there were any bloodstains on the seat. He'd be a pain in the butt.

Reluctantly, Ben remembered thinking it would be a good idea to get to know kids like Tony, ones who seemed headed for trouble. He doubted he could have any lasting influence, but maybe if he got to know the boy well enough, he'd come to Ben before he did anything really stupid. Anyway, Tony would be sure to lose interest once he realized how dull Ben's job was. How rarely he handcuffed anyone, never mind slammed somebody up against a wall.

"Maybe," Ben said grudgingly.

"Oh, good." Judith smiled. "And here's dinner."

Over crepes they discussed life in general: baseball—neither cared about it; movies—most cop ones drove him crazy, while she admitted to liking them; and even Christmas—she went whole-hog, he ignored the entire season.

"But you have family!" Judith said, aghast. "Don't they invite you to join them?"

"Yeah." He sipped wine, partly to hide his discomfiture. The past few years, he'd known that if he went to the family get-together, Eddie wouldn't. It was more important that Eddie's kids know their relatives than Ben celebrate a holiday he didn't give a damn about with family who resented him. "Sometimes I go, sometimes not."

"But to spend the holidays alone when you have a choice…" She stopped, obviously astonished at the idea.

"I'm a loner."

"Oh."

She seemed to consider his words. He waited for her to decide optimistically that all he needed was a family of his own to cure him. To his surprise—and disappointment?—she only nodded and applied herself to her meal. She'd written him off, Ben speculated.

"Your kids want to ride again tomorrow, before the weather turns cold?"

Now what was he doing? he wondered. Talk about sending mixed messages! The honorable part of him was pushing her away, while the selfish part was afraid she'd agree that he was a lost cause.

She studied him with a perplexity he fully understood. After a long moment, she said, "Well, I suppose. If you mean it…"

"Sure." Incredibly, he did mean it.

Ben took a big gulp of red wine. If he didn't shut up, he'd find himself volunteering to take in foster kids or become a Big Brother. Something about this woman across the table from him had triggered an alarming shift in viewpoints that he'd thought were set in stone. Could you have a midlife crisis in your thirties? Ben wondered.

Over coffee, he asked Judith if she missed Boston. Mad River had been culture shock for him, and he'd grown up in a smallish town.

"You know," she said thoughtfully, "I really don't. Except for my parents. And even Rylan's, although that relationship is awkward. But the city itself...well, Boston is beautiful, and historic, and...*alive*. But I like the quiet here, and the lack of traffic, and I *hated* always hunting for parking places. Besides, I'm not that big on night life." She sipped her coffee, her expression far away. "The schools had problems we don't have here. More opportunities, too—better special services, for example—but classes were bigger, and even the elementary schools had more smoking and drug use and vandalism and kids who were really snotty to adults." Her eyes focused on him. "No. I'm actually a little surprised to discover that I like it here. What about you? Any second thoughts?"

"Aw, sometimes I miss having more challenges on the job. But I don't miss dealing with the pathetic excuses for humanity that we spent half our time arresting over and over, wasting time in court only to see them walk off or get probation." He shook his head. "No regrets."

"I don't suppose you liked the crowds."

Maybe that's what he'd hated about Seattle. All those people. But actually, he wasn't that antisocial; he got along fine with most of the folks he dealt with here on this side of the mountains.

"I like having the horses right here, not boarded an hour away from where I live." He took a last swallow of coffee and nodded at her cup. "More?"

"Oh, I don't think so. I should get the kids soon in case they're miserable."

"Shall we go pick them up now?" Ben signaled for the bill.

"But…why don't you just take me home? I can run back into town to get them."

"Why should you have to?"

What he really wanted to do was take her home and carry her up the stairs to his bedroom—or down the hall to hers—and hunt for the freckles that *weren't* on her nose. But he knew damn well she wouldn't go for a visit to either bedroom, not yet. And it would be just plain stupid for her to have to set out all over again in her own car. Besides, he'd only pace until he saw her returning headlights.

They argued about it for a minute, but he was adamant and she gave in at last.

He knew where Carol Galindez lived with her husband, who owned the town's one furniture store. The house was a nice place, cedar and glass, built into a rocky hillside among the larch and pine, with a driveway that wound up to it. By Mad River standards, Carol and Paul had money.

Cars lined the asphalt drive. Ben eased his pickup to a stop where he wouldn't be blocked in and cut the engine. Judith didn't hop out immediately. He rolled down the window. Muffled voices and laughter came from around the house, where the deck overlooked the valley. On this side, only a porch light and golden squares from a couple of smaller windows pierced the dusk, which was deeper here under the trees.

He turned to Judith and laid his arm across the back of her seat. "You would have enjoyed Carol's barbecue."

"She's nice. But I had fun with you."

"You're easy to talk to."

"So are you," she murmured.

His voice roughened as he touched her chin, tilted it up. "You're easy to kiss, too."

"Kissing you is...a little scary."

She said it so softly he hardly heard her. But her words stopped him dead. "Scary?"

"The way I feel. The way you make me feel."

She was admitting vulnerability. To him. His heart cramped. "Yeah," he admitted gruffly. "Maybe *easy* wasn't the right word." Maybe *earthshaking* was closer to the mark.

"I like it anyway," she said, even more quietly. "You kissing me."

Ben closed his eyes for an instant as powerful emotions buffeted him. When he could speak, he growled, "I like kissing you, too."

He made out her smile, the sweetest damn thing he'd ever seen, as she touched his cheek with her fingertips. Ben tunneled his fingers through her hair and took her mouth with a kind of ferocity that disguised what lay beneath it.

Kissing her didn't scare him. It terrified him. Because he'd just discovered that he wasn't suffering from a midlife crisis. He was falling in love.

CHAPTER NINE

JUDITH CLICKED OFF the lamp that stood on the bookcase separating the two beds in Zach's room. "Okay, it's late. I'm glad you guys had fun at Mrs. Galindez's. Now sleep."

"Mommy," Sophie said drowsily, "I don't remember how come Daddy is gone."

Judith stood rigid for a moment, her hand inches from the lamp switch. "What made you wonder, punkin?"

"Nadia was talking about her daddy. I told her my daddy is gonna come for me. That's what he said, anyhow. But he's been gone forever. Do you think he'll come?"

Sophie had cried for her father at first, and sometimes she still asked for him, but she'd never talked about what had happened when she was taken from him. Judith didn't know how much the five-year-old understood or should be made to understand.

She sat down on the edge of her daughter's mattress, conscious of Zach, quiet and listening, only a few feet away in his bed.

"Do you wish your dad would come for you?" she asked, striving for a tone of sympathy and warmth, hiding her own hurt.

Sophie tugged her thumb from her mouth. "Yeah," she murmured, even closer to sleep. "I guess."

"I'd miss you." Judith bent over to kiss her daughter's silky head.

"Can't Daddy live here, too?" asked the small voice.

"No, your daddy and I aren't married anymore. And I sure like having you with me." She almost lied and said, "Zach does, too," but what if he declared loudly that he didn't?

Sophie popped her thumb back in her mouth and sucked furiously for a moment. Then, around it, she said, "I don't think I want to go away."

"Good." Eyes stinging, Judith kissed her again. "'Night, sweetheart."

She rose and went to Zach's bed. She could just make him out, lying on his back, staring up at the ceiling, his sheet folded neatly over his covers. He could be messy and uncaring about many things, but his bed had to be just so for him to climb into it, and the door precisely ajar. Judith had long recognized his need to control important parts of his environment. The sight of him in bed, so still, as if he were afraid of movement, always made her sad.

"Good night," she whispered, bending over him.

"Mom?"

His voice was so quiet she doubted Sophie could hear him. "Yeah?" She sat beside him on the bed, close enough to allow her to smooth a hand through his hair.

"Dad's like the bad guys on TV, isn't he?"

She was torn, as she'd been a thousand times before.

Rylan had done the cruelest thing possible to her, short of killing one of the children. Yet she could never let herself forget that he was their father—their blood, their genes, an important presence in their early years. How could they grow up with healthy self-esteem if they'd been taught to hate a part of themselves?

She glanced toward Sophie. Her thumb had slipped from her mouth and she made a small grunt and burrowed beneath her covers.

Judith looked back at Zach. "No. Your dad's not a bad man," she said quietly, rumpling his hair again. "I loved him once, you know. He...was funny, and very handsome, and he could charm your socks off. People always like your dad when they meet him. Things went wrong between us, but it wasn't all his fault." Her fingers momentarily went still. "I don't understand how he could do such a terrible thing to us, taking Sophie the way he did. He's so angry it's as if he's gone a little crazy. He scares me now. But that doesn't mean he's a bad man, only that he's done bad things."

Zach lay silent, staring up at the dark ceiling. "Oh," he said finally, offhandedly. "I just wondered."

"When you're older, if you choose, you can get to know him again."

"Like he wants to know me."

"You were his favorite." Ironically, that was true. And it made Rylan's decision to leave with only Sophie all the more puzzling.

Zach made a jerky movement with his shoulders. "Yeah. Sure."

He sounded as if he didn't care. But he must. No child could be indifferent to a parent's rejection.

"Maybe," Judith said tentatively, "he didn't take you because he knew how hard it would be for you. Sophie was little. She'd have missed me, but she could get used to changes. You were seven. To get you to cooperate, he'd have had to tell you that I was dead." She pressed her lips together. "That…would have hurt. Maybe…"

"Right, Mom." His tone was scathing. "I don't need bedtime stories anymore."

"I wouldn't lie to you."

Zach turned his face away.

Judith tried again. "I'm only trying to make sense of things your dad did that I don't understand, either. I know he loved you. He didn't leave you because he didn't want you."

The nine-year-old didn't say anything.

Judith bent over and kissed his cheek. "You're all that saved me. I couldn't have stood it if you'd gone, too."

With startling speed, Zach rolled over and hugged her, his arms squeezing her rib cage so tightly it hurt.

"I love you, I love you, I love you," she murmured against the top of his head.

"I love you, too," he whispered, and let go of her just as suddenly, lying back against his pillow.

She hesitated a moment, but when Zach said nothing else, she rose to her feet. He immediately straightened and smoothed his covers anew before folding his arms on top of them.

Judith slipped out of the room, positioned the door and through the opening said softly, "Good night."

"'Night, Mom."

His voice drifted from the dark bedroom. Was he still upset? She couldn't tell.

Troubled, she made her way through the house, checking window latches and turning out lights. Why had she never realized before just how hurt Zach had been that Rylan hadn't wanted him? How could she comfort him when the only blessing she'd had was that Zach was still with her?

She hadn't seen Rylan in almost two and a half years, but she found fresh reason every day to hate him with a passion that frightened her.

Judith got ready for bed, then went back into the hall. At the children's bedroom, she whispered, "Zach?"

No answer.

She clicked off the hall light and went to bed, though she lay awake for another hour or more, worrying about her son, what Rylan's plans were and why she felt so much for Ben, who had made it all too clear he had no intention of being a father to anyone's children, including hers.

THE NEXT COUPLE OF weeks Ben was always around: taking Sophie and Zach riding, letting Zach help re-roof her garden shed, showing up with a pizza or sitting on her porch evenings. He was the perfect family man. After a while Judith convinced herself that Ben had been telling her how he *used* to feel about having children, before he met her. All he'd been doing, she decided, was explaining why he didn't yet have kids of his own. Otherwise he wouldn't be courting her children as patiently as he was courting her.

And he *was* patient. Judith and he never had a chance to be alone, except for stolen moments on her porch after she'd tucked the kids into bed. Those moments were sweet and intoxicating. Any sourness she'd felt toward men was washed away by Ben's kisses.

Having him around so much eased her worries about Rylan, too. Being alone, having no one to rely on, had heightened her fears. Now she wasn't alone; Ben was here.

She was cleaning out the flower bed along the front of the house with Sophie's help one Saturday. The previous weekend, when he'd roofed her shed, Ben had taken a long disapproving look at the lawn mower that came with the house. Today he was changing its oil and sharpening the blades and replacing the spark plug and probably half a dozen other things. Zach, of course, had eagerly asked if he could help. As usual, Ben gave one of his easy nods.

"Time you learned these things."

Now Zach was crouched beside Ben, who sat on his haunches with his back to her. The lawn mower lay on its side in the driveway. The whine of metal on metal suggested they were doing the blade sharpening right now. All Judith could see was Ben's broad back in a gray T-shirt, the muscles bunching in his upper arms as he honed the edges of the blades. Sweat darkened a patch on his back and under his arms, even though the air had an autumn nip to it.

Every so often, he'd let Zach take a turn. Zach was like a lion cub being initiated into hunting, its mock leaps and growls a perfect imitation of its mother's. From an occasional grunt to the safety glasses and the way he squatted over the mower, Zach was copying the big man beside him. Just as he would a father, if he had one. A real father.

In the act of gathering up a heap of withered leaves from the lilac bush, Judith stopped, watching them. The sight of Ben tutoring her son was all it took to bring a quick stab of happiness so sharp it hurt.

All of a sudden, her love for her son was all mixed up with what she felt for Ben McKinsey.

I love him. It came to her with the abruptness of a winter storm, and Judith wasn't sure the realization was any more welcome.

Well, why not? she asked herself. Was there a reason in the world she shouldn't fall in love? Some law that said she shouldn't be happy? And Ben showed every sign of returning her feelings, or else why was he here? Why was he bothering with her son?

But she sensed the danger in letting herself believe it would be that easy. How could she be sure Ben would be any different from Rylan? He *had* said he didn't want children.... *But look at him. He knows how to be a father. He's good at it. He's ready.*

She hoped. She prayed.

"Mommy," Sophie said, "the phone's ringing."

Judith blinked and turned her head. Sure enough, a muffled ring came from inside the house. Judith hurried up the porch steps, Sophie tagging along.

"Can I get a boxed juice?" she asked.

"Sure." Judith picked up the receiver. "Hello?"

"Hi, Judith? This is Susan Robb. We met at my sister Carol's the other night. I'm Nadia and Tim's mother."

"Oh, yes," Judith said warmly, remembering the dark-haired woman with merry brown eyes. "Tim's been including Zach in basketball games at recess since then. That's so nice of him."

"He likes Zach. In fact," Susan said with a rush, "that's why I'm calling. Carol explained your situation—I hope you don't mind. And…well, I wondered if your kids could come and sleep over tonight. Nadia and Tim are both excited about the idea. I'd take good care of them. And I figured you could use a break."

"Oh, but that's asking so much of you…."

"My kids have friends sleep over all the time. I order a pizza, rent some videos, maybe a Nintendo game for the boys, and they're all out of my hair for the evening. Nadia has a brand-new board game she's dying to share."

"You're sure?" She said that dismayingly often these days, Judith thought wryly. She seemed to have a bottomless need for reassurance.

"Are you kidding? I can beg if you want."

Judith had to chuckle. "That isn't necessary, I assure you. Let me ask them." She covered the phone. "Honey, do you remember Nadia, the girl at Mrs. Galindez's house? Her mom wants to know if you'd like to spend the night at her house."

Sophie's face lit up. "Can I?" Then the brightness dimmed and she edged closer to her mother. "Will Zach be there, too?"

"Yes, Tim invited him. Shall we go ask him?"

Her daughter nodded.

They went out on the porch. "Zach," Judith called, "Tim and Nadia want you and Sophie to spend the night. Would you like to go?"

"Cool!" he said, swiveling on his heels.

But it wasn't her son Judith was looking at. Ben straightened and turned at the same moment, a wrench dangling from one hand. The jeans and T-shirt clung to his big, lean body. Grease smeared his hands and one cheek; he wiped the sweat from beneath his eyes with his forearm. The whole time, his gaze didn't leave Judith. She remembered that night when he'd asked how she would feel about a kiss: the quiet, the darkness, the waiting reflected in his eyes. The same expression was there now, and her stomach somersaulted.

Judith heard her son—she even understood him—but still she looked only at Ben. "I...I'll tell Tim's mom," she said.

Ben was still waiting, but she didn't know the answer to his question. Was she ready? With her eyes, she begged him for time, for understanding, for more patience. *Maybe,* she said silently, and he gave a brief nod, as if she'd spoken out loud.

She was able then to tear herself away, to go back to the telephone lying on the kitchen counter. As if glued to her mother, Sophie went, too.

Judith brushed Sophie's hair back from her forehead before she picked up the receiver and said, "Yes. An emphatic yes."

"Oh, good. The troops will be happy. If I run over to get them, can they be ready in an hour?"

An hour. So soon. Her stomach took another tumble.

"I could drive them...."

"But then we'd just have to go back out to choose videos, so we may as well do it in one go. If we exchange directions, maybe you can pick them up tomorrow and we can have coffee and tell each other gory stories about the trials and tribulations of rearing children."

"Sounds like fun," Judith agreed, smiling. Susan's good humor was infectious. "Do you have a pencil?"

Judith gave directions, then wrote Susan's down. After hanging up the phone, Judith said, "Well, punkin, you need to get packed. What do you want to take with you?"

She went out on the porch and called Zach in to clean up and pack, too. Ben said something to him but stayed hunkered over the lawn mower. Judith left him to it and went to supervise Sophie's packing.

"Of course you can take your blanket!" she said. "I'll bet Nadia has one, too."

"What if I don't want to stay?" Sophie asked, clutching the blankie, her eyes newly fearful.

"Then you can phone me. In fact, I'll call and wish *you* good-night and sweet dreams. How would that be?"

Sophie nodded.

"You'll have a good time." Judith hugged her. "I'll bet you won't even miss me."

"She's a baby," Zach said from the other side of

the room, where he was stuffing clothes into a duffel bag. "*I* won't be homesick."

"It wasn't so long ago that I had to rescue you from a friend's house in the middle of the night," Judith reminded him.

"That was years ago!"

"Sophie is *years* younger than you." She smiled down at her daughter. "Just because he talks big doesn't mean he'd mind if you go wish him good-night, too."

Zach didn't say anything. Sophie smiled.

It seemed like only minutes before a car horn honked out front. Bag bumping on his back, Zach skidded down the hall and raced outside, screen door banging behind him. Sophie and Judith went out at a more civilized pace. By the time they reached the foot of the porch steps, Tim had already slung Zach's bag in the rear of the station wagon and the two boys were hopping in. Nadia came shyly to meet Sophie, who hung back.

In the act of wheeling the lawn mower into the shed, Ben stopped to exchange greetings with Susan. After a polite exchange, he disappeared into the small out-building.

"You've got our police chief working for you?" Susan asked, the hint of a smile dimpling her cheeks. "Good going."

"Strictly volunteer." Judith lifted her hands to proclaim her innocence. "He's bored without enough challenges on the job. He had to take us on to add some excitement to his life."

"Well, if he needed to raise his blood pressure, winterizing the lawn mower is the way to do it," Susan agreed cheerfully. "My husband always swears and throws a few tools when he does ours." She smiled at the girls, still eyeing each other from their mothers' sides. "You guys ready to pick out a movie?"

Sophie nodded.

Nadia said, "Do you like *Homeward Bound?* I think it's really funny."

Sophie nodded again but still clung to Judith's leg. Was she going to chicken out? Judith was ashamed to realize that she almost hoped Sophie did. That would postpone the decision she needed to make about Ben.

But Sophie gave a last squeeze to Judith's thigh and ran to the car. Nadia took her hand and the two girls climbed into the front seat. Judith watched as Susan buckled them in side by side.

"Have fun, guys!" she called as the station wagon pulled away. All four kids turned to wave.

Feeling absurdly bereft, Judith stood watching until they turned onto the main road and vanished. It was so quiet without them. So peaceful, she admitted guiltily.

She sensed more than heard Ben come up behind her. His voice was husky.

"We're alone."

"Yes." She drew in a deep breath and turned. Meeting his dark eyes, she saw what she'd expected: the banked desire. But his face gave away more: his vulnerability, the tension he tried to hide. "So," she said, "care to entertain a lonely lady this evening?"

"Yeah." His mouth curved into a smile that sent her heart into a tailspin. "I care."

"Good," she whispered.

Ben lifted his hands but stopped short of touching her. "I'm filthy. I don't want to get grease all over you."

"Shall I make us dinner? Or do you want to do the town?" she asked, the lightness in her tone disguising *her* nervousness. Dinner wasn't the kind of entertainment he had in mind.

"You'd probably like to go out, wouldn't you?"

The coward in her would. The mother wanted to stay home. The woman in love wanted the same.

"No," she admitted. "I'd rather have dinner here."

His brown eyes caressed her. "We haven't had much chance to be alone."

"No." Which was exactly why she was so nervous. In one way, she knew him well. But she knew him best as a neighbor and father figure for her kids, not as the man who kissed her as if she were his salvation.

"I'll go home and shower. What time do you want me?"

Anytime leaped to mind. *Now.* Judith swallowed. "Whenever you want to come back."

There was that word again. *Want.*

Ben read her mind. "Soon," he said roughly. "As quick as I can clean up." He backed away, one step, two. His eyes never left hers. When his feet hit the gravel lane, he stopped, took one last long, hungry look at her, then finally turned away. Ground-eating strides carried him toward his house.

Judith pressed her hands to her chest. Oh, he was beautiful! She'd never been a woman given to admiring the finer points of well-built men in jeans, but since meeting Ben, she hadn't been able to help herself. He moved with such effortless grace, muscles synchronized like finely tuned machinery. His biceps and thighs didn't bulge like a weight lifter's; instead he was long and lean. Even his rear end was taut. She imagined those muscles tensing as he lifted himself over her...

Judith's face heated and she wheeled around, making herself take the time to put away her rake and shovel before dashing—well, okay, stumbling—up the porch steps and into the house. For Pete's sake, if she didn't corral her thoughts, next thing she'd be staring at the part of his anatomy that *did* bulge and imagining herself easing down the zipper and...

Judith mumbled a word she wouldn't have said around the kids. Maybe being without them wasn't healthy. She never had thoughts like this! For all that she'd rebelled as a teenager, she'd been raised to be prim and proper, a girl from a good Bostonian family. Not a prude, but not a wanton, either.

Judith had to roll her eyes over that one. Honestly. A normal desire for sex with the man you'd already admitted you loved didn't mean you belonged on a street corner in hot pants. And maybe she and Ben wouldn't make love, anyway. She could say no. Ask him to wait.

But she knew she wouldn't, and that was why her hands were still shaking when she started dinner half an hour later. The shower hadn't relaxed her; the makeup hadn't given her confidence.

Footsteps on the front porch announced Ben's arrival even before he knocked. Heart pounding, Judith went to let him in. He wore his good black jeans and a white shirt again, cuffs buttoned. He'd shaved, she noticed. A tiny fleck of dried blood marred the smooth line of his jaw. Maybe his hands had been shaking, too.

She backed away. "Come on in. I was just putting dinner together." She was all too aware that her retreat into the kitchen resembled a fugitive fleeing the law more than a hostess gracefully welcoming a guest.

She'd been busy layering ingredients from half a dozen bowls and pans and jars on the counter into a casserole dish. "This is one of my favorites," she said brightly. "Except for the chopping, it's no work at all. It's called Chicken—"

"I'm not that hungry," Ben said.

Oh, Lord. She swallowed, unable to turn and face him. "I can...I can put it in the refrigerator for a while. Until you are."

"Why don't you do that," he agreed, his voice a rumble.

Feeling panicky, Judith slapped the last layers heedlessly together. She'd expected to have time to work up her nerve, to get in the mood, to have second and third thoughts, if necessary.

Why so scared? she scolded herself. If she didn't want to make love with him, all she had to do was say so. She was acting like a timid virgin, not a divorced mother of two. She'd done it before. She would insist Ben use a condom, so there wouldn't be any consequences if...well, if she realized she'd made a mistake. Or if *he* realized the same.

She looked down at the casserole and saw that it was ready to go in the oven.

"There!" How perky she sounded. Maybe she should have her own cooking show on TV: "How to Put Together the Perfect Dinner for the Postcoital Meal." Desperately, she said aloud, "It's all set. Just let me cover it with tin foil and pop it in the fridge. Would you like a glass of wine?"

He raised a dark eyebrow. "If you would."

She hesitated, then shook her head. She wouldn't let herself be that big a coward. If she was going to do something this reckless, she would be sober, in her right mind. "Um…shall we go sit down?"

Ben's mouth twitched. "Sure."

When they reached the living room, he took her hand and led her to the couch. As she sank down next to him, his arm came around her. For a moment she sat stiffly, but his warmth seeped through the thin fabric of her shirt and leggings, melting her resistance no matter how hard she tried to hold on to it. When his fingers began kneading her upper arm, she relaxed against his side and with a sigh laid her head on his shoulder.

"That's better," he said, his mouth against her hair. "Scared?"

"Petrified," Judith admitted.

"Of me? Or you?"

"Both. Everything. I'm afraid of making a fool of myself." She nibbled on her lower lip, glad she didn't have to look him in the eye when she made her confession. "I'm really not very experienced, you know."

His chuckle vibrated in his chest. "You've got two kids. How long were you married?"

"Eight years." She hesitated, then confessed in a rush, "Rylan was the only man I ever...you know. I was a virgin...well, not when we got married, but when we fell in love."

Ben tilted her chin up so she had to look at him. "Sex is pretty basic. Far as I know, I don't do it any differently from any other man."

"But...but it must be different."

A muscle in one cheek twitched. "Is that necessarily a bad thing?"

Startled, she examined the thought. "No. No, I guess not. I mean, Rylan did sour me on romance. So I suppose..."

Ben made a rough sound and captured her mouth with his. The kiss was hard and sure and more intoxicating than any glass of wine could have been. Her hands flattened on the muscled wall of his chest; his found her breasts, cupped them and massaged gently. He made a muffled sound, and she whimpered.

All that agonizing, and it was so easy. She no longer thought, only felt. Heat, thick and slow moving, flowed through her veins, starting in her belly and her chest, traveling out to her fingertips and her toes. His mouth did glorious things to her as it moved from her lips to her earlobe, down her throat to the hollow at its base, over the sensitized skin on her chest, until he ran up against the limits of her shirt. Judith lifted her arms willingly when he peeled it off. She stared down in fascination as his big brown hands wrapped around her breasts again, contrasting with the cream of her skin and the shimmery white satin of her bra.

"Lovely," he said, his voice hoarse.

With a sigh, she arched her back so he could unfasten her bra. When he had done so, he dropped to his knees in front of her to nuzzle her breasts, kiss them, tease them, suckle them. She curled her fingers in his thick dark hair and let out tiny gasps as he tugged awake unfamiliar sensations.

Rylan had thought her breasts too small; his caresses there had been perfunctory. But she seemed to be giving Ben as much pleasure as he gave her.

When he lifted his head to look at her, his eyes were hot and intense. Gaze never shifting, he unbuttoned first his cuffs, then the front of his shirt. Dark hair curled on the flat, muscular planes of his chest. Of their own volition, her hands reached out to him. The hair was silky, the nubs of his nipples as hard as her own. His heartbeat drummed under her palm, not steady at all, but frantic. She bent forward and kissed his neck, where his pulse beat. The skin was salty, feverishly warm. She moved lower, over the strong, jutting collarbone. When she closed her eyes and rubbed her cheek over his chest hair, Ben groaned and tangled his hands in her curls, lifting her face to meet his for a hungry kiss.

Her head was swimming by the time it ended. His fingers caught in her waistband and stilled.

"Your bedroom?" he asked thickly.

She tried to think. The children weren't home. It didn't matter.

He made the decision for her, rising to his feet in

one smooth motion that took her with him. Judith squealed and wrapped her legs around his waist.

Ben made a ragged sound and shifted his grip on her bottom, lowering her until she was wrapped around the hard ridge beneath the zipper of his jeans. Her shaky exhalation was close to a sob. Oh, he felt so good! She wanted...she wanted...

He muttered an obscenity. ''I could take you right now, right here.''

''Yes.''

Whatever else he said, she didn't hear. He strode down the hall and shouldered open her bedroom door. Three more steps and his legs bumped the bed. He began kissing her again, openmouthed, bold, tongue sliding over hers. He lowered her onto the coverlet, peeled off her leggings and panties, then yanked down his own pants without taking his mouth from hers. Judith arched her hips in a need so primeval it shocked her in the distant part of her brain that was still dimly conscious.

He laughed and touched her there, his hand so big, so *knowing*—another difference. He'd made her as bold as he was—she even reached up and stroked him, felt him quiver.

She opened her body to him and he entered her slowly, shaking with the strain of holding back. And then, suddenly, she felt how deep he was, buried in the center of her. She loved the way he filled her, and the way her body wrapped around him, squeezing him.

''No,'' she whispered when he started to withdraw. She clutched at his upper arms, sweat slick and knotted with hard muscles.

"I can't come back if you won't let me go."

She wanted him back, so she loosened her legs and arms and felt his agonizingly slow retreat, shivered with the power of his surging return. He did it over and over, giving her a pleasure so overwhelming she could only ride it helplessly, knowing that this time *was* different, and she was fiercely glad.

And finally it was too much. The pleasure coursed through her blood. She called Ben's name once, twice, again. He was thrusting hard and fast, growling her name in her ear, groaning, trembling, finally collapsing on top of her.

Judith smiled and kissed his damp skin. She could have laughed out loud with pure joy. If only she'd known making love could be like this!

And then a fugitive thought edged its way into her consciousness, a wisp of alarm. Had he used a condom? She couldn't remember.

For all her usual caution, she'd been as foolish as a teenage girl. What if he'd just made her pregnant?

The alarm evaporated. Delight almost as potent as her climax rippled in her belly and between her legs. He would be a magnificent father. She'd never even considered having more than two children, but with Ben... Judith smiled again, closed her eyes and rubbed her cheek against the smooth, cooling skin on his shoulder.

She wanted to have a baby. With Ben.

CHAPTER TEN

BEN SLIPPED OUT OF bed the next morning and left Judith sleeping, even though he really wanted to kiss her awake and slip his fingers between her legs and then wrap those legs around his waist as he eased into her. The sleepiness in her eyes would become a different kind of dreaminess. He'd like to see her face when she cried his name again. It made him feel ten feet tall. It made him feel like a good man.

Which was one thing he wasn't.

As he pulled on his pants, the questions rose unbidden. Did he intend to marry this woman? Raise her children as his own? And if not, what in hell was he doing in her bed?

He wouldn't steal out of the house; that would be too low, even for him. How would she feel when she woke up and found him gone? He knew the answer: used.

He could lie, leave a note saying he'd been called into work. But he'd have to face her sooner or later.

Not that she'd ask his intentions, but the question would be there in their minds. It wouldn't have to be spoken aloud.

And he didn't know the answer.

Ben took a last lingering look at her face, relaxed

in sleep. Her rosy cheeks and the pout of her lips almost drew him back to kiss her. In the morning light, he discovered new delights. Her closed eyelids were the creamy white of alabaster; her auburn lashes weren't straight and spiky like his, but actually curled naturally. That glorious coppery hair was everywhere, tangling over her pillow and cascading over her cheek and throat. Ben's hand rose to brush it away from her face, but he stopped. No. He'd wake her, and he needed some time to think.

He'd watched Judith cook enough to know where she kept most everything in the kitchen. He started with coffee. Just instant, but he needed the rich aroma and the acrid taste to get him going.

It was only seven-thirty in the morning. She might sleep for a couple more hours. Trying not to bang pans, he scrambled himself some eggs and buttered two slices of toast. While he ate at her kitchen table, morning sunlight pouring over him, Ben asked himself some hard questions without coming to any conclusions.

He liked Sophie and Zach; he even enjoyed the time he spent with them. Zach reminded him of Eddie, always wanting to help, wanting to know why, wanting to be a man even though he was a little boy. A kid himself, Ben had pushed Eddie away, hadn't taken the time with him that he should have. Sometimes, when Judith's son was dogging his footsteps, he'd turn his head and see Eddie there instead of Zach, hear his little brother's voice.

Ben wasn't sure whether the time he spent with the kid was for the boy's sake or his own. Did he think he could atone for past mistakes, win some kind of cosmic forgiveness? He gave a grunt of disgust and pushed his empty plate away.

"Hi," a voice said shyly from behind him.

He swung around, scraping the chair legs on the vinyl floor. Judith stood barefoot in the doorway, eyes still drowsy, wearing a prim cotton nightgown that was therefore all the more provocative. Just the sight of her made him hard. Ben cleared his throat. "Good morning."

No questions yet, just the shyness, as if she didn't know what to expect from him this morning. Maybe she understood him better than he realized, Ben thought on a wave of self-revulsion.

"That nightgown is made to be ripped off," he said roughly.

Her cheeks pinkened. "It's…it's not very sexy. Just warm."

He stood and went to her. There was plenty he should have said, starting with, *Last night was the best thing that ever happened to me. I love you* would be good, too. The first was true—he knew it was. But what about the second part? *I love you.* He thought he did. But was that love enough to encompass her children, too, and all the obligations they brought with them? He just didn't know.

So he didn't say a word. Instead, he kissed her.

Of course they ended up making love again, a slow, leisurely journey of pleasure and tenderness that frightened him some because it made him even more certain of his feelings for her. *I love you.* Every time the words rose in his throat, every time his lips started to shape them, he recalled his helpless rage at being stuck with responsibilities he didn't want. He made himself remember his resentment at the endless demands. Sleepless nights when one of the little ones was sick; the cooking, the cleaning, the hurrying home after school instead of playing football; the lessons in tying shoes, the homework, the whining. He couldn't let himself be seduced into forgetting. He couldn't let himself be trapped again. He'd done the unforgivable to avoid it.

Judith didn't seem to expect the words, for which he was grateful. Come to think of it, she didn't say *I love you,* either. He wondered if she did. Wasn't it a given, when she'd never had sex with any man besides her husband until now?

Maybe, he thought with a sinking feeling, she'd just decided her life needed a little excitement, and he was handy.

Or else she was trying to tie him to her so he'd stay close and defend her children from that scum Rylan Kane.

No. Ben rejected the second notion. That was too calculating for her.

They talked—just murmured words about this and that. He gave her a back rub, and she reciprocated. They made love again. He remembered she hadn't had breakfast and insisted on getting up to grill a couple of cheese sandwiches and make a salad. Then they took a shower together, which led to some more shenanigans. Personally, he could have gone on that way for the rest of the day and all night, too, but Judith insisted on calling to see how her kids were doing, and Sophie decided she was ready to come home.

To avoid questions, Ben didn't go with Judith. Instead, he tucked his shirt into his jeans, put on socks and boots, remembered his watch where he'd set it on her nightstand and kissed her goodbye.

She stood on tiptoe to reciprocate.

"I'll see you," he said gruffly.

He thought her smile was just a little uncertain, though her tone was light. "Can't seem to get away from us, can you?"

He could give her this much, at least. "I don't want to," Ben declared, kissed her again, quick and hard, and walked away.

He had just reached his own porch steps when she passed him in that cherry red van. He lifted a hand. She waved back. For the first time, it occurred to Ben that what they'd done together in bed hadn't changed anything. He couldn't be sleeping over there or kissing her in front of the kids. He was still just a neighbor. Last night might as well not have happened.

Except now that he'd had her, the wanting would be edgier, more urgent. It was just sex, Ben tried to tell himself. He'd had it before; he'd have it again. For God's sake, he wasn't being kept out of heaven if she wouldn't have him again!

But he couldn't fool himself with feigned indifference, because next thing he knew, he was trying to figure some way to get those kids out of the house again. He didn't know Carol Galindez or her sister well enough to beg them to extend further invitations, so he tried to remember who had kids more or less the same age as Judith's. Damn it, all his friends seemed to have older or younger ones or none at all.

Of course, he kept an eye out his kitchen window for the van's return. An hour went by, and he started to worry. She'd probably stayed to chat, Ben figured; two women, that's what happened. Another hour passed. He remembered she'd been low on milk. So, okay, a stop at the grocery store made sense. Two hours and fifteen minutes. Two and a half hours. He started to pace.

He had picked up the phone to call in and have the officers on duty keep an eye out for her, when the red van turned in and went on by his place without slowing. Ben looked at the clock. Almost three hours. Where in hell had she been? Why hadn't she told him she intended to dawdle all over town?

He went to his living-room window and pulled aside the lace curtains—they'd been on the windows when he moved in, and he never had liked them, he realized irritably. From here he could see Judith unloading children and then bags of groceries. Which still didn't explain three hours.

Among those rights he didn't have was the right to demand an explanation. He could go offer to help with the groceries, but he wasn't sure he was up to pretending in front of the kids that nothing had changed. Tomorrow, maybe, but not today.

He'd go for a ride, he decided. Ben changed shirts and went out and threw a saddle on Sherlock. Travis nipped his arm, just to show that he was put out at being left behind. Sherlock pranced a little as if to brag. Ben wondered if he married Judith, whether she'd enjoy leisurely trail rides or whether her interest in the horses went no further than keeping her kids happy.

Just across the highway, a well-worn track wound up the canyon, twice fording a small stream, near bone-dry at this time of year. Ben rode it often. The elevation didn't rise much, so snow didn't close the trail for more than a few months during the worst of the winter. Come spring and early summer, it ended up at a real pretty waterfall. He'd take Judith and her kids there once winter had replenished the streams.

His saddle creaked under him; Sherlock grunted when he had to scramble up a bank or jump a fallen log. They opened into a lope a few times but mostly jogged or walked. The air smelled like autumn: the musty scent of fallen leaves, the dryness, maybe a foretaste of winter storms. Bare branches silhouetted against the blue sky, which darkened as the afternoon wore on.

The ride cleared his mind but didn't resolve any of the issues churning in it. With no oncoming traffic, Ben sent the palomino clattering across the road. As soon as Judith's house came in sight, he checked for her van. Still there.

Irked at himself, Ben stripped the tack off Sherlock, rubbed down the gelding's golden coat and fed both the horses.

Once in the house, he did what he knew he had to. He got out his address book, flipped through the pages to the M's, picked up the phone and dialed Eddie's number.

His brother answered. "Yeah?"

Ben hunched his shoulders. He should have planned out what to say. "This is Ben."

Eddie didn't say anything. But he didn't hang up, either.

Ben grabbed for the first subject that came to mind. "I hear you and Anne are having problems."

"Called to set me straight?" Eddie asked, tone belligerent.

Ben rubbed the back of his neck. "No. My record in that department isn't too great." He hesitated. "I'm sorry."

"Sorry for what?" his brother asked, voice uncompromising.

For everything. "About you and Anne. Did she take the kids?"

"Yeah." Heavy breathing. Then, abruptly, Eddie said, "But we've been talking. I think she's coming back this week."

"Do you enjoy being a father?" The question was asked on pure impulse. He probably sounded like an idiot, but he really did want to know. Eddie had been seven when their dad died, so he probably had nothing but vague memories of him. The only other father he'd known was Ben, who'd let him down big-time. If he could overcome that and still like raising children of his own, anything was possible.

"Why are you asking?" Suspicion crackled like static.

If that didn't sound like the Eddie Ben knew and loved.

Ben massaged the back of his neck again. "I've been doing some thinking. Mostly about my mistakes." He let some irony sound in his voice. "Not surprising my thoughts turned to you."

After another pause, his brother gave a grunt that might have been laughter. "You're right about that."

"So? You going to answer my question?"

"Yeah," Eddie said. "The kids are the greatest. When I get home from work, they come running to meet me, and I feel like a king. They can be noisy— obnoxious sometimes—but I can't imagine being without them." He grunted again. "Check that. I know what it's like being without them. I call every night, but it's not the same."

Eddie, the Father of the Year. Ben closed his eyes and squeezed the bridge of his nose.

"I haven't seen them since they were babies. How old are they now?"

"Sheila is seven. Smart as a whip. Just tested into the school's gifted program. Jay's five. Started kindergarten this September. He already knows his letters and his numbers. Smart kid, too."

"I'm not surprised," Ben heard himself say. "You were a good student. I always told you that you could do anything in the world. If you'd wanted to be a lawyer, you could have done it."

"Well, probably a good thing I didn't. Who'd have paid for my tuition?"

"We'd have figured out a way."

"No one figured out a way for you to go on to school."

"I've done okay," Ben said. "I like my job."

"You never complained," Eddie said unexpectedly. "I used to wish you would."

"Why?"

"If you'd just once bitched, I could have listened, at least. I could have said, 'Well, why don't you let me help out?'"

It had only taken Ben twenty years to figure out that Eddie probably would have liked to shoulder part of the burden of keeping their family going. The fact that he hadn't been allowed to probably explained much of his resentment.

"Well, I wish I'd let you," Ben admitted. "I turned myself into a goddamned martyr. Got so I hated all of you, and Mom, and especially Dad...."

"You were a kid. Mom asked too much."

"Did she have a choice?"

"Yeah, she had a choice." His brother sounded angry. "Her trouble was, she had too much pride to accept charity. Wouldn't even take food stamps. Remember? She used to drum into us that you had to make your own way. Well, if she'd lowered her pride a little, you wouldn't have had to be a man when you were nine years old. You were the smartest one of us. You should have gone to college."

For the first time Ben could remember, Eddie had silenced him. He'd never thought of his mother's pride at getting by without welfare as selfish, but maybe her children would have been better off if she'd humbled herself some.

Or maybe not. What twisted in Ben's gut now was the fact that, even with all the bitterness between them, his brother was still willing to excuse him.

Ben opened his mouth to say again, "I did okay,"

but just in time he realized that Eddie would see it as a refusal to be honest. To share. To ask for help.

Yeah, he *had* done okay. Eventually. But at first, he'd believed his life had been ruined by having to raise two younger brothers and a sister.

So instead Ben asked Eddie if he remembered Pete Black, Ben's best friend in high school.

"Sure," Eddie said, sounding puzzled.

"He got a scholarship to Willamette University. The middle of the night after he left, I got out of bed and jogged a mile into the middle of the woods between us and Dellwing's dairy farm, and I screamed and cried and beat my hands against a tree trunk until they were bloody."

"And then you came home and pretended you didn't give a damn."

Ben grimaced. "That was *my* pride."

His brother growled an obscenity. "You know what? I turned sixteen that summer. What was John— thirteen, fourteen? Even Nora was almost a teenager. We'd have done okay. You weren't indispensable."

"Nobody told me that," Ben said simply, realizing how foolish that sounded but also how true it was. It had been beaten into him that he was needed, that he could keep the family together, that his mother couldn't do it alone. So he'd done what he had to, wearing blinders to prevent being tempted from the path of righteousness. He'd just plodded on like an old horse in harness, waiting for somebody to pull on the reins.

Ben guessed it was too late to get mad at his mother, but thinking back, he couldn't imagine why she hadn't said, "Go! You've been great with your brothers and sister, but they'll be okay now without you. Eddie can do what you've been doing. You apply to Willamette, too."

Maybe she'd been wearing blinders, as well, plodding along in her own rut. Maybe she'd hardly realized that her children were growing up. Or that her oldest was a kid, too.

Definitely too late for anger, Ben thought. She'd done her best. It was time he quit being mad.

"You shouldn't have needed to be told," Eddie grumbled. "I figured you were so used to playing God you didn't want to give it up."

"I'd have given my right arm to leave home."

Another long silence. "I wish you'd said something."

"I can't change what I did."

"Okay." Eddie's voice held a challenge. "You haven't said why you called."

Ben's mouth had been running away with him lately. Now was no exception. "I thought I'd have the family Christmas this year. I wanted to ask you first."

Silence sizzled like oil in a hot pan. Or maybe it was only in Ben's imagination, because his brother sounded downright amiable when he replied, "All right. It's your turn."

That easy.

Well, maybe not easy; the conversation hadn't been a comfortable one for Ben. And if he'd thrown this Christmas thing out first, Eddie would probably have told him where to go. The holidays hadn't been the point anyway; the conversation had been.

"Good," Ben said. "I'll ask the others, then. I hope you'll let me know when you work things out with Anne. I'd like to see your kids at Christmas."

"One way or another, they'll be with me," Eddie promised. He hesitated, adding awkwardly, "I'm glad you called."

"Yeah. I'm glad I did, too."

That was it. Something he'd put off for too long was done. One weight lifted from his shoulders, mostly thanks to Eddie's generosity. He'd been a good kid, as well as a smart one. Too bad Ben hadn't let himself appreciate his little brother then, when it would have done both of them a lot of good.

"RAT-A-TAT-CAT!" Judith announced triumphantly.

Zach groaned. "I get one more card."

"Me, too," Sophie chimed in.

"Yes, you do." Judith waited while they each drew again; Zach kept the new card and discarded an old one. Sophie's draw was a nine, illustrated with a sneering rat. She wrinkled her nose and put it down on the pile.

They all turned over their cards at the same time. Judith had won, although not by much.

"Let's play again," Zach pleaded.

"I've already won two out of three."

"Let's go for four out of seven," he suggested guilelessly.

Judith was in such a good mood she agreed. Watching him laboriously shuffle the deck of cards, she said on impulse, "I've been thinking. Remember how we talked about maybe getting a dog?"

His head shot up. "Can we?"

Sophie's eyes shone. "Can we get a puppy?"

"Probably not a puppy." She smiled at them. "There are always so many grown-up dogs that need homes—I'd rather take one of them. Puppies are cute, but they have to be house-trained and they chew stuff up and they whine at night and..." *They don't bark at intruders. Or bite them.* But she couldn't say that, not when it was their father she hoped the dog would attack.

"How come you know so much when you've never had a dog?" Zach asked.

"I checked out a book from the library," Judith admitted. "I read all about owning a dog and training it and what to feed it and all that."

"Oh." He fastened a hopeful look on her. "Can we go pick one out right now?"

"The shelter is closed on Sunday and Monday. To-morrow after school, we'll go to the store and buy food and bowls and a leash, then Tuesday we'll choose a dog."

"Hey, cool." He launched himself across the coffee table, tumbling her back on the couch. "Thanks, Mom!"

Sophie piled on. "Thank you, Mommy! Thank you!"

Judith tickled them both. They ended up in a wres-tling match that she lost, only partly on purpose.

"I give up!" she cried breathlessly.

Sophie bounced on her stomach. Zach gave one last tickle to the bottom of her bare foot. Then they helped their defeated mother up. The cards were scattered over the table and floor.

"Can we still play Rat-a-tat-cat?" Zach asked.

"Oh, let's go make dinner," Judith said. "I'm starved."

"We ate lots at Nadia's house," Sophie told her. "Nadia's mom made pancakes. Piles and piles and piles of 'em."

"Good for you." She didn't tell them she'd skipped breakfast and eaten only a scanty lunch, because they'd have wanted to know why.

Sooner or later, they'd catch on that something was happening between their mom and Ben, but Judith would just as soon go for the later. Or maybe never, if…well, if the whole thing fizzled out.

She opened the refrigerator door and scanned the contents without really seeing them. Instead she was remembering the way Ben looked at her as they made love: his face taut, eyes dark and glittering. Such hunger, but tenderness, too. And, oh, the pleasure, not just because the sex was so good. She had loved the feeling of contentment that came from holding him and being held by him, the joy she felt in knowing he wanted her.

Fizzle? How could feelings so incredible die?

"Mommy? Can we have pancakes again?"

Judith blinked and looked down at her daughter, who was peeking into the fridge, too.

"Again?"

"I like pancakes."

"I don't like 'em *that* much," Zach said. "I want lasagna."

"It's too late for lasagna. Let's see." She made herself concentrate for a moment. "How about...omelettes? We have cheese and ham and broccoli."

Her kids considered that for a moment. "Okay," Sophie said agreeably, and Zach shrugged his consent.

"They won't take long. You guys go wash up."

She set the carton of eggs on the counter and got out a bowl and the beater. But the moment Zach and Sophie left the kitchen, Judith looked out her window at Ben's house. His kitchen window showed light, too. Just knowing he was there, so close, made her heart squeeze. She had to shut her eyes.

She loved him. Forever and ever.

It wasn't *her* emotions that she feared. It was his. She could have sworn she saw love in his eyes, felt it in his touch, even heard it in the way he groaned her name. But he hadn't said a word about how he felt. No *I love you.* No *I can't live without you.* Not even *When can we be alone together again?* What was it he had said? "I'll see you"? Did that sound like a man in love?

Maybe he really didn't want to be a parent to Zach and Sophie. Maybe he was just attracted to her, and she'd made herself available, so he'd taken her up on it. *Want to entertain a lonely lady?* she'd asked him. How blatant could she have gotten?

Judith let out a soft sigh. *Don't jump to conclusions,* she told herself. *You always knew he wasn't a man given to poetry and bouquets of roses.*

At this point in her musings, the phone rang. Ben, she thought immediately. She picked up the receiver.

"Hello?"

Silence, then a slight rasping sound—an indrawn breath?

The hair on the back of Judith's neck prickled. "Hello?" she repeated. "Who is this?"

A soft click was the only answer. She slowly hung up, too.

Just a wrong number, Judith told herself. Nothing to feel uneasy about. Why would Rylan call? He had no reason.

The telephone rang again. Judith stared at it, her heartbeat accelerating. She picked it up as if it might bite. "Hello?"

"Hi."

At the sound of Ben's voice, reassuringly calm, Judith's anxiety vanished, and she felt silly to have reacted so strongly. "Hi," she said. "Did you try to call a minute ago?"

"No." His tone sharpened. "Why?"

"Oh…a wrong number, I guess." She shrugged, even though he couldn't see her. "It's just that I'd no sooner hung up than the phone rang again."

He accepted her explanation and they talked for a few minutes as she cooked. The conversation felt stilted, though. She wished he were here, instead, so she could see his face. She suggested he come for dinner the next night; he had a meeting.

"City council. We've had some vandalism of city property."

"They're not mad because you didn't prevent it, are they?"

"Nothing like that. I recommended a chain-link

fence and some barbed wire around the equipment yard, and tonight they're going to discuss paying for it."

"Speaking of preventative measures, I've decided to take your advice," Judith told him. "We're going to get a dog. Zach's thrilled."

"Good. I know some breeders if you want a pure-bred."

"I thought we'd just go look at the shelter. A mutt makes just as good a pet, doesn't it?"

"As long as you don't bring home something twelve inches high and yappy. Do you want me to come with you?"

Judith thought about it. She'd rather not get too dependent on him. And although she wanted a guard dog, she was hoping for an animal that would be a pet, too. A dog she and the kids would fall in love with. She was pretty sure Ben would scoff at such an emotional consideration.

"No," she decided. "We'll be fine."

"Okay. Listen, I'll talk to you later."

"Right." She bit her lip. "Goodbye."

"Yeah." She felt his hesitation, ached for him to say, "I miss you." But finally, almost brusquely, he added, "Bye," and hung up.

Judith stuck out her tongue at the telephone.

CHAPTER ELEVEN

JUDITH LINED UP the camouflage fabric and fed it under the needle of her sewing machine. Halloween was only a week away. They had found the perfect pink-spangled princess costume for Sophie at the town's one department store, thank goodness, but Zach insisted on being a dinosaur à la *Jurassic Park*. The coarse material—gray, green and brown—had struck Judith as most realistic. Now all she had to do was figure out how to give him stegosaurus plates that would stand upright.

She'd cut out the fabric before dinner, then set up the machine on the table as soon as the kids had cleared the dishes. Pinned pieces were laid in a logical order, waiting to be sewn together. The kids were off playing in the bedroom.

When the phone rang, she called, "Can one of you get that?"

"Yeah!" Zach yelled back.

She heard the thunder of feet, the crash of her bedroom door bouncing open, then the ring was cut off. Instead of him bellowing, "It's for you, Mom!" she heard only the murmur of his voice.

Her attention was snagged back to the sewing machine when the thread snapped. "Damn," she muttered, lifting her foot from the presser bar and reaching for the scissors.

She rethreaded the machine and finished the seam, then set aside the left leg of the costume. Who was Zach talking to? Even if one of his new friends had called, nine-year-old boys weren't given to chatting. What was up?

Her heels clicked on the wood floor; she arrived in her bedroom doorway just in time to hear Zach say, with some urgency, "I gotta go." Sprawled stomach-down on her bed, he spotted her and added hastily, "Okay," and hung up.

"Who was that?" she asked.

"Who?" Oddly, he looked flustered. "Oh. Um. It was just Tim."

"Big secrets?" she asked.

He sat up sharply, his expression accusing. "You were listening, weren't you?"

"No," she said, astonished. "Of course not."

"Then why'd you ask about secrets?" Zach demanded.

Her interest piqued, she sat down on the bed beside him. "Because you and Tim don't usually talk very long. You're action kids."

Apparently appeased, he relaxed. "Oh. Well, Tim just had stuff he wanted to tell me. We're making plans. For things we're going to do next time I spend the night at his house."

"That's fine," Judith said mildly. "I didn't mean to sound like I was conducting an inquisition."

He shrugged without looking at her.

Something was wrong, she thought. He could be a brat, but he was usually open about it.

The tinny sound of Sophie's tape player came from the kids' bedroom. The music from Disney's *Aladdin*. Sophie was currently enamored of it.

Looking down at Zach's bent head, Judith said tentatively, "There's something I've been wanting to talk to you about. Maybe this is a good time."

Although they weren't touching, she felt him stiffen. "Yeah?"

"About your father. It's important that you let me know if he ever tries to contact you. Especially if you see him, but even if he just calls and says he wants to talk."

Zach flung his head up. "You think that was him, don't you?" he cried, jerking away when she held her hand out. "I suppose you think I'm lying about it being Tim!"

"I didn't say that—"

"But you think it! I can tell." He leaped from the bed, quivering with outrage. "Why won't you just believe me?"

She stayed sitting in the hope of provoking him less. "I never said you were lying. The phone ringing just reminded me that I'd been wanting to talk to you about your father. That's all."

"*Now* you say that's all!" He sneered as if he were fifteen instead of nine going on ten. "Anyway, would it be so bad if I talked to my own father? Like that would hurt anything."

"It could. He's not in jail, you know." She pressed her lips together. "I'm afraid he'll try again—"

"You're always saying Dad wouldn't want me, right? It's precious Sophie he's after. So why are you worried he'd call me? Why don't you talk to *her?*"

She'd never realized he hurt so much. Or could hurt *her* so much. "I've never said that he'd only want Sophie," she explained quietly. "He's just as likely to come after you. I…" Judith had trouble finishing. "I don't want to lose you. Like I did her."

He stared at her, eyes wide and filled with an emotion she couldn't decipher. For an instant, she thought she'd gotten through, that he would fling himself at her for a hug, say he was sorry. But instead, in a hate-filled voice, he said, "Well, it was Tim. Not Dad. *I wish.*" And he left the room so precipitately she guessed he had begun to cry.

Judith sat on the edge of the bed, paralyzed. She was losing her son as surely as if Rylan had taken him. Losing him to resentment, because she was trying so hard to protect him.

No! She wouldn't let herself think that. He'd just reached a difficult age. She had sounded as if she were questioning his truthfulness. Well, all right, she *was* questioning his truthfulness. Of course he'd taken offense! He wasn't such a little kid anymore. He'd been wanting more privacy lately, was less chatty about what went on at school each day. That was normal at his age.

In the past, parents of her students had told her the same thing. All of a sudden, their son didn't come home chattering about his teacher and what they'd done in class and what Chad or Joey or Kyle had said. When asked how his day had been, their son would grunt, "Fine," and head for his room. They didn't know what to make of it. Now Judith understood their bewilderment and hurt feelings.

Zach was going through the same thing, she told herself. Maybe it was a little harder for him, and for her, because of the situation with Rylan. It didn't help that Zach had had to go from being an only child to sharing his mother with a little sister, too.

She was worrying too much, Judith decided. She'd better go check on his whereabouts, make sure he hadn't stomped off down the lane in a fit of temper, knowing that running away would upset her even more. Especially with it getting dark outside. But if he was around, she'd let the incident go. Work on his costume, have him come try it on as soon as she had enough sewn together. He might have an idea for the plates that would run down his back. By bedtime, this quarrel would be forgotten. Tomorrow they'd go pick out a dog, which would keep Zach busy for the foreseeable future. Everything would be fine.

With a sigh, she rose to her feet. Why couldn't life be simpler?

IN HIS OFFICE, the ratty blinds pulled down and his door firmly shut, Ben stared at the phone number he'd scrawled on a message pad.

Calling wouldn't achieve a damn thing. Kelly would not be delighted to hear from him, and Lord knows he had nothing to say to her. All he had were a few questions, and he wasn't altogether sure he wanted to be burdened with the answers.

What if he knew he had a daughter, blond and blue-eyed like her mother? Or dark like him? He'd start seeing her in every child's face, start wondering if she'd inherited his family's musical ability, which had skipped him for some reason, or his mother's and sister's love of flowers.

Worse yet, what if the child had the same tangled feelings Zach Kane had about his father? Then Ben would have to face up to his responsibilities, and wasn't that exactly what he had refused to do seven years ago when Kelly told him she was pregnant?

So why was he so damnably tempted to call?

He gave a gruff laugh. *Tempted* wasn't exactly the right word; *tormented* came closer. Sometimes, for months on end, he had almost buried his guilt and the simple curiosity that walked with it. But all it took was a glimpse of a pretty blonde who reminded him for a fleeting instant of Kelly, or maybe a child's wide-eyed stare in a grocery checkout line, and then he'd wonder. Had the birth gone all right? Was the kid healthy? Pretty? Homely? Smart? Did he—or she—have a temper like Nora's when she was little? Was the child loved?

He'd heard from a former neighbor that Kelly had gotten married. Pretty damn quick, too. Ben didn't know the guy, but Kelly had drummed him up from somewhere when she'd decided she needed a husband and a father for the baby Ben refused to acknowledge.

Actually, that wasn't quite true. He'd never denied his part. He'd been present and enthusiastic during some wild nights of sex. Maybe the pregnancy even had been an accident, as Kelly claimed, although he doubted it.

But she didn't want what he was willing to offer: money. She'd wanted him to be her dream husband and a father to her child. Ben had told himself that the decision to have a baby was hers; in offering to pay child support, he'd done all that he was obligated to do.

Goddamn it, he didn't want to be a father! And Kelly had damn well known that.

But somewhere out there a kid was growing up knowing that her own father hadn't wanted her. That sense of guilt had started small, just a drop now and then, easily ignored, but the drops were acid that corroded and weakened and ate their way through his defenses and justifications.

He hadn't taken a hard look at how full of holes they'd become until Judith and her children moved in next door. Now...

"Oh, hell," Ben muttered, and squeezed the bridge of his nose. Face it. He was the wrong man for Judith. He was a son of a bitch who wasn't good enough to be a father to his own kid, let alone someone else's.

When that even bigger SOB Rylan Kane was safely behind bars, Ben should gracefully let Judith go. Let her find a decent man. Wallow in his guilt without mucking up her life.

He crumpled the paper with the phone number in his fist and shoved his chair back. A DARE class was waiting; the fifth graders needed his moral guidance to grow into good citizens. Today, the irony was almost more than he could stomach.

In his present mood, he just thanked God the class wasn't Judith's.

BEN LEANED his forearms against the top rail of the stall and watched Travis lipping up hay from the full rack. To each side of Ben was a kid. Glancing at them, he saw that both were mimicking his posture, right down to the foot resting on the bottom rail.

It gave him the strangest feeling, seeing that. Sophie looked especially funny in this manly position dressed in her pink corduroy overalls and sparkling purple canvas shoes. How could he help feeling touched? What was that saying—something about imitation being the sincerest form of flattery?

Ben abruptly shoved himself away from the stall partition. God almighty, he didn't deserve their adoration.

The quick movement was enough to make the Kanes' new dog flinch. Some kind of collie and lab mix, the damn mutt was scared of his own shadow. Hell, he'd run with his tail between his legs if someone broke into the house in the middle of the night!

The kids both looked startled, too, but followed when he stalked out of the barn.

The boy clicked his tongue. "Come on, Hercules."

Out of the corner of his eye, Ben saw that the dog scooted along with them, his chin bumping Zach's heels. Hercules!

"Time to go home," Ben said curtly.

"You'll walk us, right?"

Sophie's trusting gaze was enough to drive the stake straight into his heart. How easily he'd been able to forget, to whitewash himself!

"Yeah." He started across the yard. The kids fell into step, the dog glued to Zach. After a moment, Sophie's small hand wormed into Ben's clasp. As always, he stiffened for an instant, but how could he reject her advances. After all she'd gone through?

Zach began talking about something or other to do with his friend Tim and heroics Hercules was going to perform. Ben tuned him out.

A week ago he'd loathed himself. He'd actually picked up the phone to call Kelly, before chickening out. But, hey, given a day or two, he'd had no trouble burying his guilt again and sliding back into his daily routines—which had mysteriously come to include Judith's children.

And Judith herself. Telling himself that she needed him right now, he could easily excuse the fact that he was probably leading her to believe marital bliss was in their near future.

The truth was, he was letting pure selfishness rule him. He wanted Judith, whether he was good for her or not.

She came right out on the porch to meet them, probably alerted by Zach's continuing chatter. The mutt instantly abandoned the kid for his goddess. When she bent to pet him, Hercules rolled over, dribbling pee. Ben made a sound of disgust.

Judith gave him a reproving look and murmured reassurances to the dog. But when she straightened, she'd apparently forgiven him. "Stay for dinner?"

How did a woman look so beautiful in plain chinos and a turtleneck? Her turtleneck was a warm brown that showed off the fire in her hair, which tumbled over her shoulders. That small dimple quivered at the edge of her mouth, as tantalizing as a lacy bra.

Noble as always, Ben surrendered without so much as a battle. "You sure you have enough?" he asked. "You don't have to always be feeding me."

"I like to feed you." Her smile deepened. "But we've got to hustle tonight. You're sure we won't get any trick-or-treaters here?"

"Positive."

"Go wash up," she told the kids.

When they raced inside, Hercules damn near knocked them over to make sure he got in the door, too. The dog had a self-esteem problem. Low self-confidence, Ben reflected, did not make for a powerful protector.

Judith lowered her voice. "Have you ever had any cases of candy being tampered with around here?"

"Worst thing about Halloween is cleaning up the eggs come morning. If you're nervous, though, the hospital x-rays the candy free." He kissed her, just because she was close enough. The sweetness of her lips always drowned out his conscience.

"Are you going to come with us?" Judith whispered.

He nuzzled her neck. "Can't. I have to get back to work. We do get a rash of calls about teenagers out kicking up a rumpus."

He'd always detested Halloween. Well, not always; as a kid, he'd had as much fun as everyone else. He and John and Eddie and Nora had had to come up with their own costumes, but they hadn't minded. An old white sheet had made Ben into a hell of a spooky ghost one year. They'd taken turns being hobos and hippies and clowns, whatever they could put together themselves. The annual gorging after Halloween was especially memorable since both shortness of money and their mother's convictions meant they hardly ever had candy in the house.

Of course, in time he'd wanted to drive around with his friends instead of walking his little sister from house to house, waiting with the parents out on the sidewalk. He did remember one fight with Eddie, who had wanted to go with his friends and refused to take Nora and John. Ben smiled wryly. He'd have to remind Eddie of that one.

But as a cop, Ben had come to think of Halloween as trouble with a capital T. What in hell possessed someone to put cocaine in a chocolate bar, he'd never know. But it happened. Not here in Mad River, although urban sickness tended to migrate here eventually. So far the problems were old-fashioned ones: teenagers throwing eggs, scaring little kids and vandalizing the high school. His nightmare was a kid in a dark costume getting hit by a car. Everyone on the force would be out tonight, slowing down speeders and patrolling the neighborhoods where most of the trick-or-treating took place.

Over dinner Zach talked nonstop, excitement fizzing inside him. He was like a can of soda someone had shaken up, Ben thought. God help the fool who opened it.

Sophie didn't know whether to be excited or a little scared. Apparently she'd never been trick-or-treating. Her brother launched into a story about a house back in their old neighborhood where the lady had dressed up as a witch to hand out candy. Weird music could be heard half a block away.

"But I didn't let it scare me," the boy boasted. "I just walked right up to the porch. I reached for the doorbell and—guess what?" His voice lowered and he leaned forward. "Out of the darkness came…"

Eyes saucer wide, Sophie breathed, "What? What came out of the darkness?"

"A bony hand!" he shouted, groping for her, his fingers writhing.

She squealed and shrank back in her chair. "Mommy, I don't want to tick-or-teat! I don't wanna!"

Judith opened her mouth.

Zach didn't even notice. He said cheerfully, "It's okay, Soph. The thing is, it was just a plastic hand. And that lady gave out practically whole *scoops* of candy. Most people are really stingy and give only one candy bar, or else they act like they're so generous when they give you two of these eensy teensy ones. She was cool." He stopped in remembered admiration.

"Oh," said Sophie.

"So you wanna go trick-or-treating, right, Soph?"

"Right," she decided.

"Well then." Judith looked around the table. "Let's get this show on the road!"

She hadn't let the kids put on their costumes before dinner, in case they spilled something on them. Ben hung around long enough to admire the princess and the stegosaurus, then headed for work while they loaded into their van for a night of trick-or-treating.

As Halloweens went, this one was a breeze. No hit-

and-runs, no poison or razor blades in candy, not even any broken windows. There were just the usual egg yolks and slimy whites dripping from car windshields and mailboxes, a few front yards strewn with toilet paper and—his personal favorite—the bejesus scared out of that busybody Ruby Santoya.

Quivering with fury, she'd snapped, "I almost had a heart attack! There I was, standing in the kitchen washing up the dishes, when this…this skeleton rises up out of my lawn! There was just enough light from the back porch for me to see it—shining white. *Oh!*" The last was an exclamation of rage. "Steven went right out there to check, and of course it was one of those silly plastic ones you can buy as a joke from mail-order catalogs, but it was rigged with strings going over the branches of the apple tree so they could make it move."

He suppressed a grin. "Which means they had to be sitting right under your kitchen window to pull the strings." And to hear her scream.

"They laughed!" she declared in outrage. "What a…a *mean* trick!"

The perps were long gone, of course. Ben figured this was a payback for one of a couple dozen phone calls Ruby had made to 911 reporting various misdeeds on the part of local teenagers. Ben thought the prank was actually funny, though he didn't say so.

It must have been midnight by the time he turned down his dirt road. The squad car bounced into a rut and he swore. He should have had the lane graded this fall. Monday morning, Ben told himself.

He slowed as he reached his house, but damned if

there weren't still lights on at Judith's. He kept right on going, rolling to a quiet stop in front.

Maybe Halloween made her nervous and she'd left a light on for security when she went to bed. But no, the kitchen was lit, too.

By this time he knew where every squeak on her porch steps was. Adrenaline pumping, he made his way carefully up them, his hand on the butt of his revolver. She was probably staying up to watch a late movie—tomorrow was Saturday. But the logical explanation didn't wash. She never stayed up late. She liked to get up when the kids did, even on the weekend. Right now, worrying about her ex the way she was, he couldn't imagine she would burn the midnight oil.

Instead of knocking, he eased over to the kitchen window and craned his neck. The dinner dishes had been cleaned up, but there was no sign of Judith.

Maybe one of the kids was sick. Probably throwing up after too much candy, Ben thought reminiscently. Judith would be holding Zach's head and bathing his sweaty forehead with damp washcloths.

He stepped back from the window and bumped the porch swing. The chains groaned as it swung away from him. From inside the house, barking erupted.

So Hercules was good for something after all.

Ben figured he might as well knock. He wasn't sneaking up on anyone, that was for sure.

Judith came to the door immediately. "Hi," she said shyly. Hercules the heroic stopped barking, peeked around her, then flopped to the floor.

She obviously wasn't upset about anything. Ben's

heartbeat might have settled back down if the sight of her in those snug jeans and turtleneck hadn't given him a new burst of adrenaline.

"You shouldn't open the door without knowing who's here. What if I'd been your ex?"

She smiled. "I could have taken great pleasure in telling him what a bastard he is."

"The kids…"

"Aren't home."

"Ah." With a surge of intense satisfaction, Ben stepped across the threshold. "So the blazing lights were like a flare?"

She blushed. "More of a welcome."

"I like feeling welcome." Deliberately, he shut the door and turned the lock. "Where are Zach and Sophie?"

"We trick-or-treated with their friends Nadia and Tim. Their mom suggested another sleepover. She followed me back here and they packed with lightning speed."

"How did Sophie make out tonight?"

"She had a lovely time. She couldn't believe all those people were just giving her candy."

"Yeah." A reluctant grin twitched his mouth. "I remember feeling pretty stunned, too. Our mother wasn't much for candy, and there I was with this huge grocery sack full, all mine."

"So you ate until you got sick."

"Right." He shot her another grin. "Brave woman to have a sleepover."

"Four kids with tummy aches instead of two."

Humor fled and he took that last step. "God, I need

you.'' Without giving her time to respond, he snatched her into his arms and captured her mouth with his.

She responded so naturally, body yielding, lips parting, that fierce pleasure filled him. The other night had been as good for her as it had for him; she'd summoned him tonight, waited up, melted into his arms. She must love him.

A part of him pulled back in alarm—what did love have to do with this?—but it failed to rein in his primal need to possess her, to claim her as his. She was his woman, and by God, he had to have her. Now.

He swept her into his arms and carried her down the hall, just as he had that first time. Blood was roaring in his ears, deafening him to anything but his need.

He tumbled her onto her bed, stripping her of clothes even as his mouth explored every inch of flesh he bared. She was gasping, clutching at him, murmuring his name. *My woman,* Ben thought with primitive masculine triumph, as though he were a caveman who'd snatched her from a rival tribe.

His own clothes disappeared with clumsy haste. Her arms were waiting to receive him when he came down on top of her, found the entrance to heaven and entered.

He'd never lost control like this, plundered instead of coaxed. But no woman had ever shaken him the way she did.

She convulsed around him, ripples of pleasure so intense he could only plunge once, twice, three times more before shuddering and calling out, ''Judith!'' in a voice so raw it couldn't possibly be his.

In the still eye of the storm, he lay on top of her

for long minutes, even though he knew his weight must be crushing her. At last he rolled to one side, taking her with him. Judith murmured something indistinct and nuzzled his neck.

The words "I love you" crowded his throat. He swallowed heavily and managed not to say them. Not yet. Not until...

Until what? Until he'd decided to become a family man?

A chill crawled up his spine. He stared blindly over Judith's head, still buried under his chin. God almighty. He hadn't used a condom.

He had one in his back pocket; he always did these days, just in case. But he'd been so damned horny he'd turned off his brain.

What if she was pregnant?

His eyes stayed open, but he no longer saw Judith's bedroom. In living color, Ben relived the scene when Kelly had told him she was pregnant.

She'd picked him up at work, insisting they go somewhere new, not to the sandwich shop around the corner where half the clientele were cops. She'd been subdued once they were seated in the small café.

Finally he had to know. "What's up?"

"I..." Her cornflower-blue eyes shimmered with tears. "I know what you've always said, but I hope you didn't really mean it. It's not as if I meant this to happen...."

He felt sick. "What to happen?"

Tears formed glittering diamonds on her lower lashes. She'd never been more beautiful. "I'm pregnant."

Her words ricocheted like a stray bullet. "Pregnant," he repeated without understanding.

"It was an accident!" Kelly cried. "You have to believe me! I know how you feel. But—"

"Pregnant."

"Yes! Is that so terrible?"

"Goddamn it, yes!" he roared, blundering up from his seat. A glass fell over, scattering ice cubes and sloshing cold water over the white tablecloth.

Her face was just as pale. "I love you," she whispered.

Ben had walked out.

Later, of course, they had talked. She insisted that it was an accident, but he remembered the packet of pills he'd seen recently in her bathroom drawer. It was the kind where you popped one out each day. Ben had noticed that it hadn't been touched and he'd wondered why. Vague disquiet hardened into angry suspicion. He'd made it clear he didn't want children. Ever. She'd pretended to understand, claimed she could live with that. Now, conveniently, she was pregnant and wanted him to marry her and settle down to cozy domesticity.

He declined with an offer of child support.

Her shock had metamorphosed into anger, maybe even hatred. It glittered in her eyes when she spit, "You don't want to be a father? Fine! You're not one. But I won't take your money. And changing your mind down the road isn't an option." Her voice was hard. "This baby will never be yours."

Kelly walked out. Ben had never heard from her again.

The movie played out, but no credits ran. What if Kelly *had* gotten pregnant by accident? Ben had wanted to believe it was deliberate, that she was trying to trap him. Maybe he'd wanted to believe it so bad he hadn't given her a chance.

She could be coy. She played little mind games. But she was basically honest. She probably figured that, like plenty of other men who weren't ready to have a family, he'd love his son or daughter once the baby was born.

She hadn't understood that his reasons were different from other men's, that he meant what he said.

And selfish bastard that he was, Ben hadn't thought about the kid at all. So what if Kelly had lied and schemed? It wasn't the baby's fault. A decent man would have seen that. He'd played the tune; he should have paid the piper.

Judith stirred in his arms. He ran a hand over the silken waves of copper that flowed over her shoulder and across his chest, mingling with the dark hairs that grew there. God, what if six weeks from now she told him she was pregnant?

Judith's sleepy, contented little wriggles abruptly ceased. He felt her stillness and lifted his head. She tilted hers back on his arm and gazed at him with fathomless gray-green eyes.

"We didn't use a condom tonight, did we?"

We. Both of them taking responsibility, not just him.

"No. I didn't."

"Oh." Her expression became thoughtful, and she nibbled on her lower lip. He doubted she realized how provocative that simple action was, small white teeth denting her lip, already swollen from his kisses. "You know," she said, "the first time we made love, I didn't see you put a condom on."

"You thought I didn't use one?"

Judith gave a small nod. "The thing is…" She hesitated, then finished in a rush, "I was glad. I'd like to have your baby."

The rush of intense pleasure that knifed through him shocked him as much as her words. It also scared the hell out of him.

Maybe that was his excuse. He shot up to a sitting position. "You know I don't want children."

The color leached out of her face.

"I didn't believe you." Judith sat up and reached for the sheet, tugging it up to cover her breasts. He'd made her feel naked.

He wasn't proud. "Why not?" he asked tightly. "How much clearer can I be?"

Spots of hot color appeared on her cheeks. In contrast, her voice was an icy shard. "You could stop spending half your time with my children. You could refrain from holding Sophie's hand or teaching Zach how to grow up and be just like you. You could convince them *not* to love you! That's how you can be clearer."

He'd done all those things. He knew he had. He'd wanted them to love him, just as he wanted her to. It didn't make any sense. He knew it didn't. Why did he want what he *didn't* want?

Ben shook his head, like a cornered bull, and stumbled to his feet. "I told you," he repeated, stubborn insistence overruling logic. "I didn't want you disappointed. Why the hell do women never listen? Why do they always think they can remake a man?''

Judith rose to her knees, clutching the sheet to her breasts with white-knuckled fists. ''What do you mean, women *never* listen? Am I just one of many?'' Temper sparked in her eyes. ''Do we all misunderstand you?''

It took him thirty seconds to find his goddamn pants. Like his underwear, they were inside out. He had to stand there buck naked, turning them right side out, while the woman he loved stared at him with eyes that burned with newfound hate.

She was just like Kelly, he told himself. She'd thought she could turn him into whatever she wanted him to be. Soften him up a little bit and he'd become Father of the Year.

''Do you all misunderstand me?'' he snarled. ''No. Just two of you.''

She actually flinched. If he hadn't been so full of rage and self-contempt and fear, he couldn't have finished saying what he had to.

But if he didn't drive her away, he was going to do what he'd sworn not to, and then he was going to let her and the kids down, just as he'd let down his brothers and sister.

''Yeah,'' he said cruelly, voice raw with self-disgust. ''Somewhere out there I already have a kid. But, damn it, I told Kelly not to get pregnant! I didn't want a kid, so she's not mine in any way that counts.''

Judith stared at him for the longest moment. His soul shriveled. Then she inched backward on the bed, as though his presence might contaminate her.

"Leave," she said clearly. "Please…" She clapped her hand over her mouth and her words came out muffled. "Please go now."

She leaped to her feet and ran from the room. The bathroom door slammed. The lock clicked.

Anguish ripped through Ben. He sank to his knees beside her bed, his mouth open in a silent howl.

CHAPTER TWELVE

JUDITH THOUGHT SHE might die. Back against the door, she slid to the bathroom floor, gripping the sheet as if it were her shroud. She had hurt worse only once in her life, when she knew she might never see her daughter again.

One of the worst parts of that day had been the knowledge that Rylan had done it to make her suffer. The realization that he could be that cruel.

She would have sworn Ben was everything Rylan wasn't. In her dreams, she'd endowed him with strength, unflinching integrity, kindness, compassion. She had believed with all her being that he would never hurt her or her children deliberately.

Tonight, he'd done just that. The idea of having a baby with her was apparently so horrifying he'd lashed out as viciously as Rylan at his worst. Was it so terrible that she'd let him see how she felt? Why had he found himself compelled to disillusion her so brutally?

And, dear Lord, why then? What a moment to tell her his darkest secret! Or maybe he'd created it out of whole cloth, she didn't know. Either way, the story made him a contemptible creature, a monster on a par with her ex-husband.

She was a fool to have let herself fall in love again.

With burning eyes, Judith stared at the bathroom cabinet without seeing it. She must have the world's worst taste in men. Was she one of those women who walked through life with a sign around their necks saying Kick Me?

What should she do? Where should she go? She had run away from Rylan, and she wanted even more desperately to run away from Ben, never to see him again.

"I hate you," she whispered, and buried her face in her arms when she felt the tears start. "I hate you." She would not scream it, however much she ached to; she wouldn't give him the satisfaction of knowing how badly he'd hurt her.

Judith cried for a long time, wrenching sobs that left her drained but not numb. She wished for numbness, but no matter how she tried to empty her mind, the tearing pain remained. Her legs began to cramp from the position, but she didn't move.

She dragged herself up and went to the sink, where she turned on the cold water. For a long time she stared down at the water splashing into the sink, unable to remember why it ran. At last she lifted her head and stared into the mirror.

The puffy, splotched face that stared back at her was unrecognizable. It couldn't be her. But whoever it was, she needed to blow her nose. Judith closed her eyes and took slow, deep breaths through her mouth.

As though she were a small child who had to figure out how to do the simplest thing, she took a tissue and blew her nose, splashed cold water on her face and then dried it. She even brushed her hair, with slow, mechanical motions.

What she saw in the mirror now was scarcely an improvement, but she didn't care. It didn't matter what she looked like. Zach and Sophie wouldn't see her. Thank God they weren't home.

Judith made herself think.

She and the children couldn't leave Mad River. She had to work, and she'd been lucky enough to get a job with such short notice in the fall. What were the chances of finding one mid-term?

Besides, she couldn't let Carol Galindez down. The principal had hired her, helped protect Zach and Sophie, become a friend.

But she couldn't live here. She'd find a rental in town. Yes, Judith thought, pouncing on the idea. Tomorrow. There'd been other places available. If they moved, she would scarcely have to see Ben.

Judith had no idea how much time had passed. Surely, surely, he would be gone. But still she opened the bathroom door cautiously, listening for any small sounds. Lying in the hall right outside the door, Hercules lifted his head. The tip of the dog's tail waved and his brown eyes were soft and sympathetic.

"Is he gone?" Judith whispered.

The dog rose to his feet.

"He is, isn't he?"

Hercules wagged his tail.

Even so, Judith crept down the hall, the sheet clutched around her, part of it trailing like the train on a wedding dress.

She would not think about wedding dresses. Ever.

The house was still and silent. She didn't want to

go back into her bedroom, but she couldn't wander around naked all night.

In the doorway she had to stop for a moment, frozen by the sight of tumbled sheets and strewn clothing and the scent of sex. Memories clawed at her. The way he'd torn her clothes off and fumbled with his own, the look in his eyes, the exquisite sensation of him filling her... And, oh, God, the pitiless tone of his voice when he said, "You know I don't want children."

Clapping her hands to her ears, Judith cried out in anguish. She would never understand him. Never trust herself to love a man again.

Judith scuttled into the bedroom and snatched a pair of panties and a nightgown from her drawer, fleeing then as if these walls harbored demons. She took a shower, scrubbing herself until the water grew cold. Armored by the flannel gown, she made the familiar rounds of the house, turning off lights and making sure windows were locked. The back door was just as she'd left it. She approached the front door reluctantly.

The knob didn't turn.

It was locked. He had locked it on his way out. Not the dead bolt—he couldn't—but the button on the knob. He had made sure that she wouldn't be left vulnerable. What did that mean?

She crept into the children's room, choosing Sophie's bed. The scent of bubble bath pervaded the sheets. Closing her eyes, burrowing her cheek into the pillow, Judith imagined that she held her daughter in her arms, soft, squirming, sweet scented. Miracles happened. She had Sophie back. She had survived one of the most terrible things that could happen to a parent. She would survive this.

If only she understood why he had done this to her.

HE GAVE IT his damnedest, but Ben couldn't quite convince himself that he'd done the right thing. His motive for telling Judith the ugly truth hadn't been to save her from himself. He'd done it out of panic. The fates closing in.

He muttered a profanity and bolted out of bed. The clock told him it was 4:00 a.m. The cold wood floor chilled the soles of his feet. Naked but for shorts, he didn't reach for jeans or a sweatshirt, even though he shivered. He deserved any discomfort he could serve up.

God. He remembered the moment when he'd felt the intense, purely masculine satisfaction at planting his seed in a woman's womb. Not *any* woman—his. She'd actually made him want children.

It wasn't anything she'd said that had scared the hell out of him. No, he'd done that all by himself.

He wanted her. He wanted to father her children. He wanted to *be* a father to Zach and Sophie.

There was nothing in the world he wanted less than to be a father.

Ben swore again and flattened his palms on the bedroom windowpane, resting his forehead against its smooth chill. Judith's rental house was a darker bulk against the night sky. He would never be welcome there again.

A harsh sound escaped his throat. He was the biggest fool in Mad River, and that was saying a lot. A good woman loved him, he loved her, he was even getting kind of attached to her kids—and he'd gone out of his way to make sure she discovered what a bastard he really was.

A man who deserted a woman pregnant with his child.

He could explain… *You mean excuse,* he mocked himself harshly. *Justify.* And what was his excuse? He was tired of bandaging skinned knees and turning on night-lights. He'd been there, done that, didn't want to do it again.

Fine excuse.

Eventually Ben went back to bed. He even slept, if the nightmarish images could count as dreams rather than memories and fears. The hatred staring out of Kelly's blue eyes suddenly switched to Judith's gray-green ones. A child taking his hand was first Sophie, then Eddie, then nobody he knew. And that small boy with the dark eyes—was that him an aeon ago?

Come morning, he fed the horses, ate a bowl of cereal, then sat around feeling hung over, waiting for a decent hour to make a phone call. One he should have made a long time ago.

When he finally dialed the number for directory assistance, it occurred to Ben that he must have written down that same number a dozen times over the years. Whatever scrap of paper he wrote it on always ended up in the wastebasket.

This time he dialed it.

The third ring was cut off. "Hello?" said a childish voice.

A noose closed around Ben's throat. He couldn't

breathe, couldn't swallow. The hand that held the phone receiver shook. He could not do this.

"Hello?" Now the child sounded uncertain. "Is somebody there?"

Ben hung up. Air rasped into his throat. He was goddamn crazy to think he could make any difference after all these years. Kelly would slam the phone down. He deserved to be haunted by unanswered questions. A man who sold his soul didn't go to hell; he spent an eternity in perdition.

Outside, a dog barked. Ben swung around. Unwillingly, he went to the kitchen window. The damn windows in this house were starting to feel like the bars of a prison cell. He could look longingly out, but never leave. He'd closed the cell door himself.

That pathetic excuse for a dog Judith had chosen was running in frenetic circles on her front lawn, barking the whole while. Wrapped in a white robe, Judith stood at the head of the porch, watching the dog. She held something, a cup of coffee, maybe. After a moment she leaned her head against the post, as if holding it up were too much effort.

Ben turned around, went straight back to the telephone and picked up the receiver. He didn't have to look at the number to dial it.

This time a woman answered. "Hello?" she said crisply, a hint of suspicion coloring the single word.

"Kelly." He squeezed the bridge of his nose. "This is Ben McKinsey."

He heard her shocked intake of breath, then silence. But she hadn't hung up.

"I'd like to talk to you."

"We have nothing to say."

"Maybe you don't, but I do."

"Oh?" she said sarcastically. "Do you have demands now? Or...let me think. You've had another child who needs a bone marrow transplant, so you're scraping the bottom of the barrel in search of a donor. Or maybe you just want me to absolve you, sprinkle your head with holy water."

He'd take number three. *Give me forgiveness.*

"I just...wondered...about her. Or him."

"What did you wonder?" There was no sympathy in her voice.

Exasperation swept him over the edge. "Goddamn, which is it? A boy or a girl?"

"Why do you want to know?" she asked uncompromisingly.

Why? He hardly knew himself. So his kid had a chance to deal with the son of a bitch who walked out on his mom? To make amends?

"I should have stood by you," he said.

"Yeah? Well, you didn't. It was too long ago, Ben. My daughter has a father." The finality in her voice warned him even before he heard the click as she hung up. She'd meant what she said all those years ago. The child would never be his.

But she'd told him something, at least. He had a daughter.

Ben knew he had to see her.

TOO BAD SHE COULDN'T use a glue gun to keep her smile in place, Judith thought grimly. She stood at the back of the classroom, doing her best to look attentive and pleasant as Police Chief Ben McKinsey talked about alcohol and drugs with her students.

Last week she'd felt an inner glow when he was in her classroom. She'd tried not to think about making love with him; it wouldn't do to have one of her students catch her blushing. She'd occupied herself by observing how far he'd come as a teacher and mentor for the kids. His body language was easy now, his dark stare compelling, his rare smile reward enough to have the children's hands waving eagerly when he asked a question or wanted a volunteer. He knew how to pace the flow of information, when to switch to role playing or ask them to come up with ideas. The other fifth-grade teachers had commented on how good he was. Previous years, they said, the kids were often bored and had less chance for input.

"Less chance to show off," Judith had said, laughing, and they agreed.

"But it's good for their self-esteem to have that chance," Linda Mayfield remarked, "and isn't that part of the purpose of the program?"

Today, all Judith wanted was for Chief McKinsey to get out of her classroom. It was bad enough that she had to pass his house twice a day, hear his car, know how close he was. She didn't understand why she'd put off looking for a rental in town. Maybe she feared the effect another move would have on the children, though it couldn't be anything but beneficial for Zach, she thought wryly.

How had her reliable, kindhearted, talkative son turned into a sullen, angry child? He'd been worse this week, defiant, mean to his sister, sulky. She knew why, of course; the reason stood at the front of her classroom. Zach had idolized Ben; no matter how often she explained that Ben's absence had nothing to do with him, it left Zach feeling rejected again.

She sensed Ben's gaze on her, knew the expression she would see if she let herself look at him. His mouth would be wry, his eyes troubled, his brow furrowed. A muscle in his cheek would jerk when their eyes met. She would swear he was silently asking her a question. Asking her *for* something.

Understanding? A chance to explain?

No! *How much clearer can I be?* he had asked. She was a fool to imagine he hadn't already said everything he wanted to say.

Don't think about him, she told herself. He was looking away now, sparring with Tony. The discussion was about what to do if you'd always wanted to belong to a popular group of kids and they finally asked you to a party, with the kicker that you had to bring a bottle of booze.

Judith returned to her brooding. Here she'd thought Sophie to be the problem child! Instead, it was worries about Zach that kept her awake nights. He hadn't been the same since the move. On one level, she blamed Ben. Hadn't he realized what he was doing, encouraging Zach to emulate him? But Zach's problems weren't all because of Ben. Her fight with Zach over the phone call the previous week had been the catalyst. Since then he had been...secretive. It was hard to relate that word to her son, but she couldn't deny that he seemed to be hiding something. Twice more she'd heard him talking on the phone, and both times he'd claimed the callers had the wrong number.

She wanted to believe he was telling the truth. But at least three times that week she'd answered the ringing phone, only to hear a click the moment she said hello. Five wrong numbers in a week?

Dread filled her. Was it Rylan calling?

No. Please let there be another explanation, she prayed. Maybe somebody at school was bullying Zach and he didn't want to tell her. But Judith had spoken with his teacher and she didn't know of anything like that. He was doing fine with his schoolwork and making friends, Becky Allen had assured her.

Apparently, Judith thought, his anger was all saved for her.

Maybe she *had* favored Sophie, the way he'd accused her. Probably it was true. Sophie was vulnerable. She had lost her father and was living with a family she barely remembered. The nightmares, the tears, the silence—all had demanded that Judith give her that extra time and attention. Having her daughter back with her gave special meaning to everything she did with Sophie. Somehow that must have made Zach feel she didn't want him as much as she did his little sister.

What could she do to show him how much she loved him? Was it too late?

"Ms. Kane?" Ben's deep voice cut through her troubling thoughts.

She snapped back to the present, no pasted smile on her face this time.

"Yes, Chief McKinsey?"

"They're all yours."

Twenty-six ten-year-olds stared at her. She could see the wheels turning. Why was Mrs. Kane acting so weird?

"Fine," she said with cool efficiency. "We'll see you next week, Chief McKinsey. Class, start cleaning up your desks."

Ben didn't leave. Instead he followed Tony, who went to the coat closet to retrieve his pack. Out of the corner of her eye, Judith saw Ben lay a hand on the boy's shoulder and bend his head to talk quietly to him.

What was he saying? Tony grinned and obviously agreed to something; Ben clapped him on the back, then with a furrow between his brows, he looked straight at Judith. A tight nod, and he was gone at last.

The bell rang and her students started streaming out. Judith waged a brief battle with herself and lost. She had a right to be curious, didn't she?

"Tony," she called. "Can you come here for a sec?"

He came, his brown cowlick as unruly as ever, his thin face wary.

"I really like the way you participate in the DARE program," she said, then smiled. "Now, if you'd just put as much enthusiasm into your spelling homework."

He screwed up his mouth, as though he'd bitten into raw onion. "Who cares about spelling?"

They'd had this discussion before. Rather than recap the many benefits of learning to fluently read, speak and write English, she settled for a simple "I do."

"You have to," he said impudently. "You're the teacher."

Judith laughed and rolled her eyes. "Get going or you'll miss your bus."

He slung his backpack over one shoulder. "See ya, Teach."

Judith let him get almost to the classroom door. "Tony?"

He turned his head.

"What did Chief McKinsey want?"

It was like turning on a light switch. Tony's brown eyes shone and his voice held wonder. "He said you told him that I'm gonna be a cop when I grow up, and he asked if I wanted a ride in his car. Like I'd say no!" He marveled at the very idea. "If I bring a note from Mom tomorrow, he's gonna drive me home."

"Lucky him," she teased.

"It's so cool!" Tony gave her a shy, almost sweet smile, devoid of his usual sarcasm. "Thanks, Mrs. Kane."

She smiled back. "You're welcome."

She needed to collect the kids, but once Tony was gone, she sat behind her desk, frowning at the empty doorway. What was Ben up to? If he so detested kids, why encourage first Zach and now Tony? A week ago, she'd have thought he was trying to please her. Obviously that wasn't the case.

And yet she'd have sworn he had made a point of talking to Tony where she was sure to see.

She gave her head a shake and reached for her purse. He was a hopelessly complex man, but she wouldn't be the one to untangle his motives. After all, she was fatally burdened with children.

He was a jerk, she told herself; she'd had a lucky escape.

Somehow, Judith didn't believe a word.

BEN STEPPED OUT OF the squad car and circled around to the passenger side. He'd pulled up to the curb right in front of the main entrance to Lincoln Elementary. His timing was flawless; the doors all popped open at once, as if a bomb had exploded inside, and the teeming masses spilled out.

Adopting a relaxed pose, Ben leaned against the car, arms crossed, and waited.

Maybe the kid's mother wouldn't have given her permission. With her husband in prison, she probably was no fan of cops. Ben wondered if Tony had told her what he wanted to be when he grew up.

Along with smiles and greetings from passing parents, he got plenty of stares from the shorter set. A few of them lingered.

"Hey, Mr. Policeman," a young boy was finally bold enough to ask, "are you going to arrest someone?"

Just then, Ben spotted Tony sauntering toward him. "Nope," Ben said. "Just giving a friend a ride home."

Tony struggled not to look too pleased. "Hi," he said.

"Tony." Ben nodded solemnly. "Got the note?"

The boy handed it over. By this time, twenty or thirty students had gathered to watch.

"Dear Chief McKinsey," it began in a round, childish script. "Tony says you want him to ride with you. That's okay with me. Just so he's not in trouble and that's why you want him." Signed, "Shelly Fiorentino."

"Looks good," Ben said, and held open the passenger door. "Shall we go?"

The crowd murmured as Tony, head held high, climbed in and Ben slammed the door. He tipped his hat at them and went around to his side. In the car, Tony sat with his back straight, hands on his legs, as if he were afraid to move. He was taking in everything, though, his gaze darting over the array of knobs and buttons.

Ben noticed belatedly that the boy was dressed a little better today than usual. Those were his best jeans, Ben guessed, less baggy than current style called for, and he actually wore a button-down shirt instead of an oversize T-shirt. A warm feeling enveloped Ben.

Annoyed with himself, he turned the key in the ignition. What kind of sap was he turning into, touched because a kid had made an effort to look decent for the occasion? Good God, his mother had probably made him!

"Seat belt?" Ben said.

"Oh, yeah." Tony scrambled to put it on.

Ben checked his mirrors and they pulled away from the curb. "Where to?" he asked.

"What?" The boy blushed. "Oh. You mean, where do I live. Um, over the other side of the highway. You know where those stockyards are? Past that."

Ben knew the area well. Thirty-year-old single-wide mobile homes sagged on cement-block foundations, the acre parcels they occupied defined by rusty, barbed-wire fences. Junk cars clustered around the houses like nursing babies. Any horses in the rocky pastures tended to be skinny, rib cages and backbones showing. Eighty percent of the domestic disturbance calls received by his department came from that small section of town farthest from the river.

The trip wouldn't take five minutes. Looking at the kid's big eyes, Ben gave an internal sigh. "You want to go straight home or ride along with me for a while?"

"Can I?" Tony breathed.

"Wouldn't have asked if I didn't mean it."

"Yeah! I mean, sure." His eyes widened. "Do you think you'll chase somebody?"

Ben glanced at him. "Well...you never know." Hell, if he saw someone going two miles over the speed limit, he'd pull 'em over, just to make the boy happy.

In no time at all, Tony warmed up enough to start asking questions. Ben showed him how the radio worked with the frequency selectors and the emergency channel and the microphones.

"How do you make the lights go on?" Tony's stubby fingers reverently caressed buttons without actually pushing any. "And the siren?"

Ben showed him how they worked, along with the radar unit and the CB radio. Tony happily rattled the cage and was disappointed to find out that a stain on the back seat wasn't blood.

"Let's just hunker down," Ben said, "and see if we can't catch a speeder."

He had a few favorite spots where success was damn near guaranteed. One was right behind some concrete bulwarks where the highway came into town. They'd no sooner aimed the radar than a red Mustang with a dent in the fender shot by going fifty-five in a thirty-five-mile-per-hour zone.

Ben pulled right out. "You turn on the lights," he said.

Tony was aglow. "Can we sound the siren, too?"

They'd probably scare the hell out of the driver, but what the heck. "Why not."

The car pulled over right away, much to Tony's disappointment. He'd apparently hoped for a high-speed chase. He was even more disappointed when Ben made him stay in the car. The pimply-faced driver, maybe twenty years old, sank into a funk when he saw what the ticket cost.

In contrast, Tony begged, "Can we do it again? That was cool!"

Despite his better judgment, Ben kept the boy with him for about an hour. He marvelled that he'd ever thought Zach Kane was a talker. Zach was a downright peaceful companion compared with Tony. Ben's ears were ringing and his throat was hoarse from answering questions by the time he parked the squad car in front of the rusting single-wide Tony said was his grandma's place.

Tony was still going at it. "Cops have to be really brave, right? So you can beat up bad guys and kick in doors and whip your gun out...." He gave a longing look at Ben's.

Ben turned off the engine and faced the boy. "Yeah, sometimes you have to be brave, but the most important thing a cop does is notice every little thing." His voice was dead serious. "For example, your mother is waiting right inside the door, I bet. I saw her take a peek out the window and then shy back. Now, if I were here to issue a warrant and I thought she might have a gun, that would be good to know. I can tell you what make and color the two cars we passed on your road were. I saw the mailbox that had been bashed in, and the greenhouse on your neighbor's place that looks too expensive to go with the house. I won't forget your grandma's taste in curtain fabric. That's what I mean by noticing."

He was a little surprised that Tony didn't seem disappointed that a cop's most important skill was observation, not martial arts. He only nodded, his brow puckering. "Does it take practice?"

"Yeah. You can start anytime."

"I will then," the boy said eagerly. He hesitated. "I guess I've got to go now."

Ben walked him to the door and said hello to Tony's mother, who looked about twenty-two, although she had to be older. She wore frayed jeans and a men's flannel shirt that hung on her skinny frame. Smoke curled from the cigarette in her hand.

But he was surprised again when she thanked him graciously and, after sending Tony inside, admitted that the boy's father was in prison and that she was happy to have her son dreaming about being a cop and not a felon.

"Tony's a nice boy," Ben said, realizing it was no lie. "He'll do fine. Uh, when's his father's release date?"

"Not for a couple of years." Desperation flitted over her face. "It's hard making it without him. I just lost my job. I was working at Dick's Burgers, but they're shutting down now, you know. They always do for the winter, but with that new burger place out on the highway, they're giving up. I don't know what I'll find next. We're lucky to be able to live with my parents."

He could tell she didn't feel lucky.

"You know how to work a cash register?" he asked.

Her head bobbed. "With my eyes closed."

"Seems to me I noticed a sign in the window saying that Food Mart on Tenth needs a checker. I know the manager. I'll put in a word for you."

"Would you?"

No one should have to look so incredulous at such a small favor, Ben thought with a twist of pity. But as he drove away, her renewed thanks chasing him like tumbleweed, he half regretted his promise. Hell, he didn't know if she was a good worker or a slacker!

Yeah, but maybe all she needed was a chance, his Good Samaritan side argued.

He swore out loud. He was starting to sound like a social worker, not a cop. And he knew who he could blame for the idiocy. Judith Kane. She just had a way of nudging him into…what?

Ben had to pull to the side of the road as the answer hit him harder than the windshield in a head-on collision.

She had a way of nudging him into caring, he thought with sudden comprehension. First for her. Then her kids. Then for his own brothers and sister. Now for Tony and his mother. Who knew where it would end?

Not to worry, he told himself bleakly. Without Judith around, he'd find her influence fading.

He'd better start getting used to it.

THE TELEPHONE HAD a way of bringing bad news. Ben sat in his office, receiver to his ear. "Rylan Kane has disappeared," he repeated, a cold knot in his belly. "You're sure?"

"No, I'm not sure," Detective Edgekoski said. "Maybe he rented a new room and just didn't bother to tell us. He isn't due in court until next week. All I'm saying is, I stopped by to check on him and he's gone."

"Car?"

"For sale at a used-car lot. He'd taken cash for it. Didn't buy a replacement."

Ben swore.

"If he flew out of here, it wasn't under his own name. I don't know what else to tell you right now."

"The bastard is on his way here."

"We can't say that for certain." Edgekoski sounded as if he were convincing himself. "Will you warn Ms. Kane, or should I?"

Ben snatched at the excuse. "I will."

His impulse was to surge to his feet and find the kids. Stand guard. But they ought to be safe enough at school for the day. He would be more usefully employed looking for Kane.

Ben left a message at the school office for Judith to call him about Rylan as soon as possible. He figured that would get her. As soon as he talked to her, he'd make the rounds of motels and bed-and-breakfasts to learn what he could about any lone male customers— and to ask the proprietors to let him know if anyone meeting Kane's description showed up.

His line rang. He picked it up. "McKinsey."

"It's Judith. Do you have news?" *You'd better,* her tone suggested.

"Yes." He kept his tone businesslike, although his gut churned. "Edgekoski just called. They've misplaced your ex-husband."

There was a pause. "Misplaced?" she echoed in disbelief.

"In other words, no confirmation that he's bolted, but he left his last place of residence without informing them, and he sold his car."

"Oh, God."

"We'd better assume he's on his way out here, if not already in town. We'll watch for him, but you need to be extra careful."

"Yes." She sounded dazed. "Yes, I will."

"Would the kids go with him willingly?"

"I…I have no idea." Judith let out a long, despairing sigh. "I hope not. I've talked to them about it, but he is their father. I just don't know."

"Okay. I'll come over this evening—"

"Please don't," she interrupted.

Hell. "About the other night..."

Her breath hitched. "Don't do that, either."

"That?"

"Don't say you're sorry or tell me we can talk about it or explain again that you warned me. Yes, you did. You were right. I didn't really listen." She noticed that her voice was rising and took a moment to collect herself. "Enough said. But I don't want you here, Ben. If we need the police, I'd prefer you send another officer."

Feeling as if a thousand-foot drop yawned beneath him and his fingers were slipping from the only possible handhold, he said stubbornly, "I'm the law in this town."

"You have an eight-member police force. I asked. Ben, I don't want to see you." Judith took a shaky breath, but her voice remained tremulous. "Please give me that much."

There had to be something he could say. He could only think of one possibility. "I'm going to try to see my daughter...become part of her life."

"I hope you do. That won't change the fact that we want different things out of life. Thank you for the warning, Ben. Now please stay away." A resounding *click* sounded in his ear.

Ben swore viciously. He was an even bigger bastard than he'd given himself credit for: he had made damn sure she couldn't trust him now that she really needed him.

CHAPTER THIRTEEN

CORDLESS PHONE TO her ear, Judith peered around her to be sure the kids were out of earshot. She hadn't hidden the fact that she was calling Grandma and Grandpa; she just didn't want them hearing the question she had to ask.

"Have you heard from Rylan lately?" She tried to phrase it casually. Why upset his parents unless something happened?

Something. The unthinkable. The unnameable.

She must not entirely have succeeded. Her mother-in-law's anxiety was audible.

"No, not for a week. I've been afraid—" She broke off, then added in a strained voice, "He loves the children so."

Was what he'd done to them "love"? Not in Judith's book. But Mary Kane had to excuse him. How else could she live with what her own son had become?

"Does he?" Judith strove for a noncommittal response. "Well, I doubt there's anything to worry about. I just like to know where he is."

"He complained about the room he was renting," her mother-in-law said. "He was paying an awful lot for it, and half the time there wasn't any hot water, and the tenant upstairs was terribly noisy, and the bed wasn't very comfortable....'' Her voice held less and less conviction, but, like Judith, she tried to sound as if she were convinced by what she was saying. ''I'm sure he just found a better place and hasn't let us know yet.''

''Oh, I imagine you're right,'' Judith agreed. They chatted briefly, but a minute after hanging up the phone, she couldn't have told anyone what either of them had spoken about. She was back to asking the same unproductive questions that had been hounding her for the past twenty-four hours.

Should she tell the children or not? She didn't want them living in fear—or looking for their father. Should she ask Carol Galindez for a couple of weeks off? The district could hire a substitute, and she and the children could flee again. Just temporarily. If Rylan didn't show up for court, there would be a warrant out for his arrest, and they'd get him sooner or later.

It was the possibility of ''later'' that frightened her.

It took them two years last time, an inner voice argued. *You'll lose your job. You have to keep it, unless you want to keep running.*

''No,'' she said softly, restoring the phone to its cradle. Rylan had done his best to ruin their lives. She wouldn't let him succeed.

She would go on doing just what she had been doing, only more obsessively: never let her kids out of her sight, except at bedtime and during school. Her glance strayed to Hercules, whose tail started to thump on the floor the moment he noticed her attention. He was definitely not an attack dog, but he did bark when he heard strange noises. He wouldn't let a man break into their house in the middle of the night unnoticed.

If only she could turn to Ben…

Judith opened the dishwasher with unnecessary force. She wouldn't let herself think that way. She was doing fine on her own. Just fine.

Later, she moved the dog's bed to the hall between the kids' bedroom and hers. When Zach asked why, Judith bent over to smooth Hercules's silken yellow ears between her fingers.

"He sleeps here anyway. Haven't you noticed? The wood floor must be awfully hard." It was true, but she couldn't swear that he stayed in the hall all night. Yesterday she'd gotten up from the couch and discovered she had dog hair all over her backside. Maybe that was where he spent the night. He did like his bed, though, so she hoped if it was near them, he'd use it. She wanted him as close as possible while she slept.

If Ben had been with them that day at the animal shelter, he would have wanted them to adopt the big German shepherd with a deep-throated woof that had scared Sophie, or maybe even the Doberman mix. But Judith didn't regret their choice. Hercules had crowded to the front of the cage, huge brown eyes beseeching, his whole bottom wagging along with his tail, and her heart had melted. When they opened the cage door, he'd erupted out and slobbered kisses on both kids' faces, squirming in pleasure at their tentative pats. He needed *them,* and he was a big dog. Big enough to be some protection.

Now Zach said, "Oh. Sure. *I* wouldn't want to sleep on the floor, either." He lay down experimentally on the rectangular dog cushion, which was stuffed with cedar. Making a face, he observed, "It's kinda lumpy."

Delighted at having someone down at his level, Hercules licked him. The pink, wet tongue worked Zach over from his neck to his ear. Zach laughed, the first time Judith had heard him do so in too long.

"He loves you."

He buried his face in the dog's ruff. "He loves you better."

"Oh, I don't know," she said lightly. "He's just smart enough to recognize the hand that wields the can opener."

"I feed him sometimes."

"But not as often."

He hugged Hercules with a fierceness he didn't seem to realize, still not looking at her. "Would he be just my dog if I was the only one who fed him?"

Judith's heart stilled. She crouched so that she could stroke first Hercules's head, then Zach's. "Why does he have to be just yours? Why not ours?"

"'Cuz then *she* gets him." He rolled violently away from the dog and jumped to his feet. "I can't even have my own bedroom!"

"I didn't know you wanted…" Judith began helplessly, but he had gone into his room—his *shared* room—and slammed the door. Apparently even his sister's company was better than hers.

What would he do, she wondered with dread, if his father asked him to go away with him, promising a special father-son bond that Zach seemed to need? He was only nine—impulsive, angry about the changes in his life, resentful of Sophie and the loss of part of his mother's attention. Rylan could be so charming, so…compelling.

She closed her eyes to shut out the chasm of fear that had opened before her. Zach wouldn't do that to her.

But children never thought about what they did to their parents; that was the nature of childhood. Zach was too young for empathy. He was so utterly wrapped up in his own problems right now he would be ripe for an approach from Ry.

Maternal fury rescued her from the feeling of hopelessness that threatened to overwhelm her.

Rylan wouldn't have that chance. He wouldn't get near either of their children, Judith vowed. She would die rather than let him take one of them again.

THE ONE PLACE SHE HAD always felt they were safe was at school. In her heightened state of fear, Judith no longer was so certain.

Her students hunched over a spelling test. She watched them write, waiting until enough faces looked up to move on to the next word.

''Messages,'' she said, speaking slowly and emphatically. Foreheads puckered and her students scribbled.

For the hundredth time today, her eyes strayed to the clock on the classroom wall. She knew to the minute when kindergarten and fourth-grade lunches and recesses were. Two grades went out at a time: eight classes in all. Close to two hundred kids. The aides couldn't possibly watch any one child all the time.

There were squabbles on the tetherball court to claim their attention, skinned knees, lost jewelry, swearing and insults. The handful of aides were fully occupied. Judith had seen parents strolling across the playground on their way to the office or a classroom. Nobody paid them any attention.

Zach and Sophie were most vulnerable then, among the crowds of other kids. And she couldn't do anything about it. If only the windows in her classroom looked out on the playground, she could at least reassure herself sometimes. But instead they looked out at the street.

Every day, she tensed when their recesses ended, waiting for a call from the office or a knock on the classroom door. "Zach didn't come in from recess," the secretary would say. "He's probably in the bathroom, but we thought you should know."

Judith shuddered, earning some curious stares. She shook off her dread. "Ready?" she asked.

"Wait!" cried several voices.

The minute hand on the clock clicked forward one notch. "Immerse," she said, strolling between desks.

Was Rylan really here in Mad River? Maybe watching their house with binoculars from the wooded hillside? Or even, this minute, sitting in a car across the street from the school, noting when bells rang, waiting for the moment when Zach or Sophie strayed close to an opening in the chain-link fence…. Ice seemed to fill her veins.

Her students were waiting. She had to pretend. "Imagine," she said, enunciating each syllable.

Tony waved his hand. "I gotta go to the bathroom."

"You can't wait?" she asked in exasperation.

"My stomach doesn't feel so good." He clutched it in graphic illustration.

"Do you need to go to the nurse?"

"Nah." He grinned cheekily at his friends. "I just gotta go. When you gotta go, you gotta—"

"Yes, yes," she said, interrupting both him and the general laughter. "Take a pass. Try to hurry."

They resumed the spelling test; she watched the clock. Zach's class was out right now. A quarter after two o'clock came. Tony strolled back in the door and went right to his desk. Another minute passed. Two minutes. The tension ebbed from her shoulder muscles. Afternoon recess was over. They'd be safe until tomorrow.

At the end of the day, she was collecting Zach and Sophie from their classrooms when she saw Ben down the hall. He was coming out of one of the other fifth-grade classrooms. When he turned in her direction, her breath stopped. Judith backed into the girls' bathroom, murmuring apologies as she bumped a girl on her way out.

Just as Ben went by in the hall, someone pushed open the door. Judith caught one good glimpse of his face. He looked weary, preoccupied, the lines carved from nose to mouth deeper than usual. A frown had settled as if it meant to stay between his dark brows. The harsh expression fit the man she had first met, not the one she'd come to know.

Which was he? she wondered on a wave of intense depression. Could his smiles, his kisses have been mirages?

He was gone by the time she stepped out in the hall again. Zach just shrugged when Judith asked how his day had gone; even Sophie was quieter than usual. It was similar to the day that thunderstorm struck, Judith thought; tension hung in the air like the electricity that presaged lightning.

On the drive home, her eyes strayed frequently to the rearview mirror, looking for a car that stayed behind her too long, but she didn't spot one. Rylan probably already knew where they lived.

Hercules was thrilled they were home. Zach ran around the yard with him, seeming his normal self. The boy chased the dog, then the dog the boy. Watching them, Judith was able momentarily to dismiss her secret fear that he would choose his father over her. Zach would be acting differently, wouldn't he, if he had already talked to his dad and planned to leave forever?

Their bedtime ritual seemed more precious than ever. Her lips lingered on Sophie's cheek, then Zach's. "I love you," she whispered, and he answered, "I love you, too," like always.

When she woke up in the morning, Zach was gone.

INSOMNIA HAD RULED the first hours of the night. Not until 3:00 a.m. did Judith fall into a heavy sleep. The shrill of the alarm clock at seven was not welcome. She groaned and turned it off, then stumbled into the bathroom. She showered every morning before waking the kids. Her preparations for the day always took longer than theirs, and this way, she got a head start.

Usually a hot shower swept away the cobwebs of sleep, but not this morning. She felt dull when she went into the kids' bedroom, a towel still wrapped around her head.

Zach's bed was empty and…well, not made, but neat. He was such a quiet sleeper. He must have gotten up while she was in the shower. Sophie slept soundly, her lips pursed and her knees drawn up to her tummy, so she formed a small round lump under the covers.

Judith started toward Sophie's bed to wake her, when a sense of disquiet penetrated her tiredness. The house was awfully silent, she realized uneasily. Zach usually came into the bathroom as soon as he got up. Where could he be?

And then something she should have noticed right away struck her. Hercules had not greeted her at her bedroom door. He lived for her to get up! Where was he? Her heart stumbled over a beat and she rushed out of the bedroom.

"Zach?" she called. "Hercules?"

Silence. The kitchen was dim and quiet; the living room the same. Back to the bedrooms. Her breath came in panicky gasps now. He wasn't in her room. The bathroom was just as she'd left it, the damp bath mat still on the floor. Sophie's Barbie dolls sprawled across the floor of the spare bedroom, most half-dressed, arms and legs poking up, naked torsos twisted. As always, Zach's toys were tidily ordered on shelves.

Mindless with fear now, Judith returned to the children's bedroom and peered under beds and in the closet. On her knees beside Zach's bed, she lifted his pillow with a shaking hand. His pajamas were neatly folded there. The same pajamas he'd worn last night.

Then he had gone deliberately.

She clapped a hand to her mouth to quell the rising nausea. No! She wouldn't believe that! He was outside; he had to be. He'd done something without thinking, like the time Sophie had wandered over to Ben's barn without telling anyone.

She found the front door unlocked. She knew she'd checked it before bedtime. So Zach had gone out. Please God, just to play or walk the dog.

But he was nowhere. She called and called without hearing an answering voice or bark. How could the dog have vanished, too? And so silently?

Think! she ordered herself. *What should I do?*

Judith ran back into the house and grabbed the phone. Her hands trembled so that she had to try twice before she succeeded in dialing Ben's number.

He answered on the first ring. "McKinsey."

"Ben." Her voice was high, shaky. "This is Judith. Is Zach there?"

"Not that I know of." He didn't hesitate a second. "I'll search the barn. Shouldn't he still be in bed?"

"Yes, but he's gone. His pajamas are folded under his pillow."

"The dog didn't bark?"

"He's...he's gone, too."

"I'll look here and be right over."

She could do nothing but stand beside the phone, quaking all over. *No. It couldn't be happening again. Not this. She couldn't endure it.*

Not more than two minutes passed before she heard footsteps bound up the porch steps. She met Ben at the door, hope and terror warring within her.

He shook his head. "I've reported him missing. We'll start hunting immediately. You have no idea when he went?"

Her teeth began to chatter. "Oh,God—oh, God…"

Ben grabbed her upper arms and gave her a shake. "Help me here, Judith. Don't fall apart."

She nodded, gritting her teeth to stop the chattering.

"When?" he repeated insistently.

"I don't know." She closed her eyes. "He went to bed at nine o'clock. No! Wait! I couldn't sleep. I was awake till three so he couldn't have crept out before then or I would have heard him."

"We'll find him."

Without warning, his arms closed around her, and for a few seconds, she let herself lean against his big, solid body, drawing strength. She straightened and he set her aside at the same moment.

"I'll make some more calls," he said.

Judith hurried back to check on Sophie, but her daughter still slept. For a moment she sat on Zach's bed, smoothing her hand over his pillow, touching the flannel of his pajamas. "Please come home," she whispered, and went back to the kitchen.

The day was as terrible as that other one she remembered too well. She had to call her in-laws first; they hadn't heard from Rylan and were clearly shattered by the news. Her parents were equally shocked and ready to rush to Mad River. Judith put them off for the moment. She didn't have the energy to reassure anyone else.

Uniformed police were everywhere; eventually search-and-rescue volunteers joined them. After studying the pictures of her son that she took from an album, they fanned out from her house in well-spaced lines, searching the dry hillside and pasture, crossing the highway to the hiking trail on the other side.

When they started out, Judith protested. "Rylan must have him! They won't be out in the woods! Can't you put up roadblocks or something?"

"The state patrol is watching for him," Ben said heavily, "but we can't do much when we don't know what kind of vehicle they're in. And we have to hunt here…just in case."

In case what? But Judith didn't want to think about the possibilities.

Sophie cried when she found out her brother was gone. Judith called Carol Galindez to tell her why she wouldn't be in; in an impossibly short time later, Susan showed up with Nadia.

After a quick hug, Susan said, "I'm home with Nadia anyway. I'll keep both the girls with me today—and tonight, if Zach hasn't been found. You need to concentrate."

Part of Judith wanted to cling to her remaining child. Another part knew how emotionally fragile she was. She'd only frighten Sophie. Besides, there had to be something she could do, some way of helping to find Zach.

So she nodded, hugged her daughter so hard that Sophie squeaked a protest, and watched with hot tears in her eyes as the station wagon drove away.

She turned to find Ben behind her. She felt him take in her distress with one glance. His own face showed a strain that echoed hers. "We'll find him. That bastard isn't going to get away with—" He bit off the end of his sentence.

On a trembling breath, Judith nodded. "Thank you for coming. Considering..."

He swore. "I'd be here no matter what. My God, Judith, you must know how I feel about you." A spasm worked down his jaw muscles. "All of you."

"You didn't want them." The words spilled out without volition, stark pain in her voice. Unreasonably, she felt the two things were connected: Ben had walked out because he didn't want children, and now she had lost her son. If Ben had been here...

Ben swallowed hard. "Did he miss me?"

She hurt too much to acknowledge that he hurt as well. "Do you care?" she asked bitterly.

His eyes darkened. "I care."

"Yes!" Judith cried. "Yes, he missed you! He didn't understand." Tears burned her eyes again and she turned away, hunching her shoulders. "He's been so mad at me. But he trusted you!"

Ben's fingers bit into her upper arms. She felt the steel, heard the raw agony in his voice. "I will find him if it's the last thing I ever do."

He disappeared again for a while. She made coffee for the searchers and numbly answered the questions they asked. Eventually Ben returned and had her go through Zach's drawers and closet to see what might be missing. She had to hunt through the dirty laundry, too, before she was certain: he wore a pair of jeans and a red-and-blue-striped T-shirt.

"And his basketball shoes." On her knees in front of his closet, she looked up at Ben, waiting in the doorway of the bedroom. "But he didn't take anything else. He loves his Boston Bruins jersey. He'd never leave that. He can't have packed anything!"

"Maybe he didn't intend to go far or be gone long," Ben said.

She felt stirrings of hope again. "Then where is he?"

"And where the hell is the dog?"

Her fingers twined together. "You don't think... Rylan would have..."

Ben spared her from putting the horror into words. "Killed the dog? Not if he wanted Zach to go willingly."

"That's true." More cause for hope.

Rylan had hated anything with hair. No pets, he'd insisted from the beginning. She hadn't argued; that was before she began to resent the fact that he always had to have his way. Rylan wouldn't like Hercules. He might hide his feelings for a few days, but eventually he would want things his way, and that wouldn't include the dog. Unlike Sophie, Zach was old enough to sneak away from his father when he got the chance. Judith had made sure he'd memorized their new phone number the first week.

Depression descended again like a thick fog, all the grayer because she'd momentarily glimpsed a light through the clouds. Even if Zach changed his mind, he might be afraid to call, convinced she'd be mad. Besides, he'd always been stubborn. He wouldn't want to admit he was wrong.

Earlier, Ben had asked Judith if she had a photograph of Rylan. She'd kept some for the kids' sake, so they could see their faces in his as they grew up. She handed him the best one. She overheard him talking with one of his officers about faxing it to the state patrol. After making a phone call in the late afternoon, he left again, Rylan's photograph in his hand. She watched him go without curiosity, so encapsulated in sorrow and fear that the activities around her seemed meaningless.

He came back swearing. At the sight of the anger tightening his face, Judith rose slowly to her feet, fright clutching at her. He had news. Oh, God, he had news. She pressed her hands to her chest, trying to hold back the sickness and the terror rising within her.

His eyes met hers and he came straight to her. "No, no, Judith." He drew her roughly into his arms. "We haven't found Zach. I did get confirmation that Kane was here in town, though."

She drew back and echoed numbly, "He was here."

"For the past four days. I checked all the motels, but I didn't go far enough. He rented a room for the week. The landlady IDed him from the photo." Ben swore viciously. "If I'd just checked the rooms for rent, too..."

"You didn't really believe he was coming, did you?"

He jerked his head to one side, as though his neck hurt. "Yeah," he said roughly. "I believed it. I was just so goddamned arrogant I told myself the son of a bitch couldn't snatch any kid out from under *my* nose."

A tiny arrow of understanding and compassion penetrated her grief. She reached a hand out to him. "Ben..."

"I screwed up big-time, didn't I?"

"No. It's not your fault." Angry as she had been at him, she had to make him see the truth. "Rylan's the bad guy, no one else."

His eyes showed his disbelief. "The worst thing is, the landlady never saw his car. He said he'd gotten off the Greyhound bus. In case that's true, we're checking used-car lots and ads from last week's paper, but we haven't come up with anything yet. So we're no further ahead than we were. And it's my goddamn fault."

Before she could protest again, he swung away to answer a question from one of the other police officers. She didn't know what she could have said, anyway.

Would it have made any difference if he had been around? Would Zach still have wanted his father? Judith had no way of knowing.

By nightfall, the search-and-rescue team had given up. Without any reason to believe Zach had set out on foot, they wouldn't expand their search radius.

Susan called, offering to keep Sophie. Judith agreed. She was exhausted, her strength sapped by the emotional roller coaster she'd been riding on all day. She couldn't be a parent to Sophie, not yet. It was an effort to hold the telephone, to get up to go to the bathroom, to thank the men and women who'd spent their day searching for her son. One by one, they touched her hand or paused in front of her to say a few kind words on their way out.

Eventually only Ben was left. "Are you hungry?" he asked.

"Hungry?" She had to force her sluggish thoughts to focus on the question. "No. No, I'm not hungry."

"Have you had anything to eat today?"

"Eat?" she repeated dully.

"I didn't think so." He left her sitting in the living room, her knees drawn up to her chest, her arms circling her legs. The closer she hunched within herself, the less she had to be aware of what happened around her. It was possible to float in limbo if only the world didn't keep intruding. Annoyingly determined not to let her withdraw, Ben returned with a mug full of a steaming liquid.

He set it on the coffee table in front of her. Soup. Noodles floated in the broth.

"I told you I wasn't—"

"You've got to eat. Just sip it."

Ben sat next to her, his large body curiously comforting. Too weary to argue, she followed the urgings of his strong hands and put her feet back on the floor and wrapped her fingers around the handle of the mug.

"Okay, now take a sip," he said gruffly.

Liquid heat flowed down her throat, bringing life with it. But life hurt terribly, and she whimpered a protest, trying to set down the mug of soup.

"No," he said in that tender, gravelly voice. "Come on, another sip. You've got to stay strong."

Why? she wanted to ask him. She couldn't do anything. Rylan had gotten to Zach despite her vows to protect her children. She was a failure as a mother;

otherwise this wouldn't be happening again. She wasn't strong—she couldn't be.

But she sipped because somehow the mug was at her lips, tilting toward her, and the soup was spilling into her mouth. Ben insisted she drink the entire cup, making a sound of satisfaction once she'd finished. Before she could curl again into her fetal position, he leaned back against the couch and drew her into an embrace so all-encompassing she felt as if she were part of him, his heat and strength enveloping her.

It was nothing like the times they'd made love, she knew; his gentle touch held no passion. With a sigh she rested her head on his chest. Her eyes closed, and she focused on the beat of his heart, steady and strong. The rhythm was something to cling to in the midst of her turmoil; every time disturbing, terrifying thoughts crept into her mind, she tugged herself back by listening to the beat of Ben's heart.

He kissed the top of her head and murmured something against her hair; she didn't even try to make it out. She must have slept, because she opened her eyes suddenly and was disoriented. Where was she?

She must have whimpered, struggled, because a voice the texture of velvet whispered, "Sh, sh," and a hand massaged her back, soothing her like a frightened animal that could only be calmed by a familiar kindly touch.

And the heartbeat was still steady beneath her ear, the vibration rocking the very wall of his chest. Ben.

Oh, God. *Zach.* The horror overwhelmed her. She cried out, "Zach, please be all right, please come home, oh, God, please," and the tender voice murmured comfort. Ben held her through racking sobs, then blew her nose, wiped her cheeks, kissed her wet eyes.

The night passed that way, although she was unconscious of time. She slept, woke, remembered, imagined the worst—*Rylan wasn't monster enough to kill his own son to pay her back, was he?*—cried hot tears and slept again. At one point Ben turned off all the lights, and terror rose in Judith's throat.

She struggled upright. "Zach likes some light! Please! If he comes back, the house can't be dark. Please," she begged.

Immediately Ben switched on a table lamp. Golden light spilled from it, and she sagged from the release of tension. "He likes his door open four inches," she explained, sensing she was being irrational but not caring. "That's enough to make him feel safe."

The knowledge that he hadn't been safe, that she hadn't kept him safe, was enough to bring tears again. Ben's shirt was damp from the last bout, but the weave of the cloth and every wrinkle were familiar now, her own security blanket.

Eventually she awoke to gray dawn coming through the windows. This time Judith knew where she was, and why. Ben's arms were heavy around her. His deep, slow breathing told her he slept. She drew back. His face was slack, his lashes thick and dark against his cheeks. His mouth softened in repose; the rigidity left those broad shoulders. She touched his hair, bemused by the sprinkles of gray. Were there more?

When Judith slipped away, Ben's arms fell to his sides, and though he shifted on the couch, he didn't awaken. The kitchen clock said it was seven-thirty, later than she'd thought. She went quietly to the front door, unlocked it and stepped out on the front porch. From a seat on the top step, she gazed toward the road, where Zach must have stolen in the early morning.

Yesterday. Only yesterday morning. It seemed like forever since she had discovered him missing. Could it really be so recently?

Had Rylan somehow signaled Zach that he was waiting? Or had they made an assignation? Surely, surely, Rylan wouldn't have asked a nine-year-old to walk alone in the darkness all the way to the main road! Emptiness yawned inside Judith. *Had her son wanted to go that much?*

The air held a bite and she wondered when the first real snowfall would come. The one dusting of white they'd had didn't count. Only days before, she and the kids had anticipated snowball fights and sledding, but now Judith couldn't bear the idea of snow blanketing the landscape. Not with Zach out there. If Rylan hadn't kidnapped him, if he'd…

She physically jerked from the picture that formed in her mind. No! Not that! That wasn't what she meant. She'd meant if they'd fled on foot. Yes, that was it. If they were trying to get away on foot and by hitchhiking, she dreaded the weather turning cold. Zach hadn't even taken a jacket.

Why hadn't he? Did he think his mother wouldn't want him to take his things? It made no sense that he hadn't packed even the duffel bag he'd taken to Tim's when he spent the night. Could Rylan have dragged him away?

But then she remembered the pajamas. No. He'd gone by choice. Still...

Had Rylan actually been in the house? Maybe looked down at Sophie and decided she'd be too much trouble this time?

Judith wrapped her arms around herself to stop the shaking. With a violence she hadn't known she harbored, she wanted to kill Rylan Kane. She should be shocked at herself, but she wasn't. He deserved it!

Still she sat there, unable to achieve yesterday's numbness, shivering because she *wanted* to suffer. How could she go about day-to-day life, eat breakfast, sip a cozy cup of tea, shower and dry her hair, when inside she was hollow, hurting, as if her heart were ulcerating?

A footstep sounded behind her, and the screen door opened. "'Morning."

At least he hadn't said *good* morning. She hunched her shoulders and didn't respond.

"What are you doing out here?"

She turned slowly to face Ben and saw the shock on his face before he succeeded in hiding it. She must look dreadful. She didn't care.

He spoke gently. "I'll make us something to eat—" The ring of the telephone interrupted him, and tension sharpened the lines of his face.

The sound quivered through her body like live wire. Was there news? Could they—*oh, God, please*—could they have found him? But how, when they didn't know where to look?

"I'll get it," Ben said, and vanished inside.

She froze, paralyzed by the need to follow him and her fear.of hearing the worst.

The conversation was short. He reappeared, an odd expression on his face. "That was Carol Galindez. I guess Tim told the other kids about Zach disappearing, and Tony came to the office and said he might know something."

CHAPTER FOURTEEN

BEN INSISTED THAT Judith shower, although she didn't want to waste precious minutes, but a glance in the mirror told her he was right; she couldn't appear at school like this. She didn't take the time for makeup or to dry her hair, just ran a comb through the wet strands and bundled them into a scrunchie.

Neither spoke on the drive to town, which was made in record time. Ben swerved to a stop at the red-painted curb right in front of the main entrance.

Carol waited in the doorway to the administrative offices, her brown eyes warm with compassion. Taking Judith's hands, she said, "I'm so sorry. You know we'll do anything, anything at all."

Thank God she hadn't asked how Judith was. The answer must be written on her face.

Judith nodded, the sting of tears in her eyes.

Seeing them, Carol said swiftly, "Come on in. Tony's waiting."

At the sight of them, he jumped up from the cushiony visitor's chair beside the principal's desk. When his gaze reached Judith, his eyes widened with the same shock she had seen in Ben's. So it hadn't been only tangled hair and puffy eyelids that had taken him aback. The horror inside her must show on the outside.

Carol stopped just inside the door, letting Ben take control. He wasted no time on niceties. "What do you know, Tony?"

"I…the other day when I went to the bathroom…" Tony faltered, his gaze sliding away from Judith. "See, the boys' bathroom is right by the doors going outside to the playground, you know. And I, well, I just kinda looked out."

Ben raised an eyebrow in disbelief. "All you did was look out."

"Well…maybe I went outside, just for a minute, see. We were having a spelling test, and I hurried…." Nobody said a word. He sounded desperate. "It really was just a minute. I swear!"

Judith wanted to scream, *I don't care what you did! What did you see?* Ben shot her a glance.

"Tony," he said, "we appreciate you coming to us like this. You won't be in trouble, no matter how long you were outside. I promise, no punishment."

"Oh." The boy stole a look at her. His Adam's apple bobbed. "Anyway, it was fourth-grade recess. And I noticed Mrs. Kane's son over by the fence, talking to a man outside. Zach had his back to the fence, and the guy was out on the sidewalk just kind of leaning against the building. Like he was waiting for something. You know? But I could see that even though they were pretending not to have anything to do with each other, really they were talking. And…and Chief McKinsey said I should notice things." Shyly, he added, "If I want to be a cop like him."

Ben gave an approving nod. "Sounds like you're already pretty observant."

Tony's cheeks flushed with pleasure.

Ben laid the photograph of Rylan down on the principal's desk. "Was this the man?"

"Yeah!" Excitement shot through his voice. "Yeah, that's him! Who is he?"

"Zach's father."

"Oh." Bewilderment clouded his face. "Then why were they pretending they didn't know each other like that?"

Judith heard herself say calmly, "Because he's not allowed to see Zach or Sophie. He…is not a good parent."

"Oh," the boy said again. He was thoughtful a moment. "Then why did Zach…?"

"He hasn't made up his mind how he feels about his father. I guess when it's your own dad, deciding not to love him anymore is hard."

Clearly, Tony understood that one. "Uh, I'm sorry, Mrs. Kane."

Tears in her eyes again. Through them, she said, "Thank you, Tony. And…and thank you for coming to us."

"I don't know if it helps," he said uncertainly, looking at Ben.

The police chief leaned against the desk. "The thing that would help most, Tony," he said almost casually, his intensity banked, "is if you saw the man leave. Maybe get in a car."

"Yeah. Sure I did." Tony looked from one to the other of them, as though he felt the instant electricity.

"I mean, they were acting weird, you know. I went outside because I saw them. The guy left after just a minute. That part was weird, too. I mean, there were lots of places he could have parked along the street right there, but he crossed and went, like, halfway down that other street...."

"You mean the cross street? Gilman?"

"Yeah, that one. And then he looked around real careful, like he wanted to make sure no one saw him, before he got in this car. It was blue and real shiny, like maybe he'd rented it. My grandma had to rent one once, and hers was the same car, except red. A Chevy Caprice. I remember it, because it was cooler than her real car—the one that was broken down when she had to rent," he explained.

Hope, real hope, swelled in Judith, glorious and intoxicating. They could find him now, couldn't they?

Ben gripped his shoulders and looked straight into his eyes. "A blue Chevrolet Caprice. You're absolutely sure?"

Tony nodded. "I even saw the license plate, 'cuz then he drove by." A frown crinkled his earnest expression. "I don't remember all of it, but the first two letters were UG. Like ugh, you know?"

"UG." Ben's teeth showed in a predatory smile. "Good boy. Now we'll get him."

"I did help?" Tony watched in bewilderment as the police chief strode out.

"Yes." Judith's smile trembled on her lips. "Bless you, Tony. You'll make a very fine police officer."

MORE WAITING, Judith realized. By the time Carol sent Tony back to class with a quiet word in his ear, Ben had already commandeered the office telephone to put out an all-points bulletin on a blue Chevy Caprice, license plate UG—the rest unknown.

After her first euphoria, Judith's optimism began to wane. Zach had disappeared more than twenty-four hours ago. If the car was a rental, Rylan could have turned it in and gotten a different one, or—if they no longer had Hercules—they could have taken a bus or train or even a plane. In that length of time, they could be two states away or more.

Once the essential calls were made, Ben suggested they get home, just in case Zach phoned. Judith went straight to the kitchen. No red light blinked on the answering machine. When the phone did ring, it was for Ben, just as all the calls that came in throughout the morning were.

Judith had to do something. Anything. She began cleaning windows, rubbing in furious circles as though every smear she obliterated was Rylan, or her fear, or every mistake she'd ever made.

At eleven, Judith heard a car door slam. She glanced in the kitchen, but Ben was on the phone again, a map spread out on the table. He seemed not to have heard the car out front.

Hesitantly she opened the door. Susan had parked her station wagon right in front of the steps. Sophie hopped out, Nadia right behind her.

Judith rushed out onto the porch. "Sophie?"

"Mommy!" Face alight with joy, Sophie dashed up the steps and flung herself into Judith's arms. "I mithed you," the five-year-old whispered from her mother's fierce embrace. "And Zachawy, too."

"Zacha…" Crouching to be at her daughter's level, Judith drew back, swiping at her tears. "You lost a tooth. No, two teeth!"

"Yeth." Sophie grinned proudly. "Nadia bumped me, and they both fell out!"

Susan smiled ruefully over Sophie's head. "The tooth fairy visited. How could she resist? I bet she doesn't get two in one trip very often."

Judith felt a surge of unreasonable jealousy. She'd missed so much because of Rylan. Now this, too!

She summoned up a big smile. "You look just like our Halloween jack-o'-lantern. If only you'd lost those teeth sooner, we wouldn't have had to dress you up to go trick-or-treating!"

"Mommy!" her daughter reproved.

The front door stood open as Judith had left it. Now Ben came out, letting the screen snap shut behind him.

Sophie went right to him. "Thee," she commanded, baring her teeth.

He cocked a dark eyebrow. "Thee?"

"Thee!" she repeated more emphatically, pointing at her mouth.

He crouched in front of her and inspected the evidence. "Where in tarnation did your teeth go?" He pretended to scowl. "Okay, who punched you?"

"Nobody!" Sophie trilled with laughter. "Nadia. But she didn't mean to." She smiled happily. "The tooth fairy came and brought me two whole dollars!"

"Thank you," Judith murmured to Susan. "You've been wonderful."

"Any news?"

''We…we know it was my ex-husband, and what car he was driving. Ben is hopeful now.''

Susan gave her a quick hug that said more than words.

Judith looked back at Ben in time to see Sophie wrap her arms around his neck and kiss his cheek. What had he said? She was more startled yet when he kissed her small daughter back on her round, soft cheek.

Satisfied, Sophie promptly whirled away. ''Let's go get some Barbies, like we said.''

Smiling shyly at the adults, Nadia followed her inside.

Ben swiveled to watch the girls go, his expression peculiar. The screen door banged and their chattering voices became more distant. He gave his head a shake, then rubbed his fingers under his eyes. When he turned to face Judith, his eyes were red. Tiredness, Judith couldn't help wondering, or an emotional reaction to Sophie's unbidden gesture of affection?

''More news,'' he said quietly, those dark eyes steady on Judith's face. ''The Seattle PD tracked down the seller of the Chevy Caprice. Private owner, had an ad in the *Seattle Times*. Now we have the full license-plate number. And since the car's not a rental, the likelihood is good that Kane is still driving it.''

''But he could have gotten so far already. He could be in California or Arizona or Montana.'' Judith hesitated, then put into words one of her worst fears. ''What if he took Zach into Canada or Mexico? Will I ever get him back?''

The desolation in her voice brought him across the

porch to grip her hands. Out of the corner of her eye, she saw Susan go quietly into the house.

"Chances are they're still in the U.S. Canadian and Mexican customs are supposed to check ID. If a child is with only one parent, they require a letter from the other parent giving permission for the child to leave the country. I know it's not foolproof," he admitted, forestalling her. "The letter can be forged, but your ex-husband wouldn't have any ID for Zach at all."

"That's true," she said hopefully.

"Besides—" Ben's jaw had a grim set "—we have to ask ourselves what Zach is doing and thinking right now. Is he a willing passenger? If not, his father won't dare approach a border crossing."

Pain crashed through her without warning. "You know Zach must have gone willingly, no matter what I want to think. The way he folded his pajamas… Rylan didn't drag him out."

"Those pajamas are the only evidence he went of his own volition. There is no evidence that he intended to be gone for any length of time. He didn't take anything of value to him."

Judith searched his face, longing to find certainty there, hungry to believe him. But she had to tell the truth. Not even to herself would she lie.

"That's…not true. He took Hercules. He…he didn't like sharing him. Especially with Sophie."

Ben didn't look impressed. "Did you have brothers or sisters?"

She frowned. "No. I'm an only child. Why?"

"I remember the way my brothers fought." He gave a grunt that might have been amusement. "Hell, one minute they were friends, the next Eddie would give John a black eye. Same thing with Nora. They'd let her tag along sometimes, no matter what their friends said, then the next day they'd torment her until she cried, and then laugh about it.'' His large hand cupped her cheek. ''That's what siblings do. I've seen Zach be nice to his sister. They play together, don't they? Just because he says rotten things sometimes doesn't mean a hell of a lot.''

Hardly aware she was doing it, Judith leaned her face against his hand. ''You think I've been worrying too much.''

''About that, yeah. Zach doesn't hate Sophie's guts. He's not running away because he won't share you with his sister. That's what you're afraid of, isn't it?''

The acute perception in Ben's brown eyes was unexpectedly comforting. He *knew* her. Right now she needed someone who did.

''Yes,'' she said on a sigh. ''I'm afraid that I've given Sophie too much attention and left him out. I know I didn't realize how hurt he was because his dad took her and not him. I think even he knows how perverse that is—he didn't *want* to go, not then—but it hurt anyway. Does that make sense?''

''Hell, yes.'' Ben gave a grunt of frustration. ''The damn phone's ringing again. I'll be back.''

Sophie packed clean clothes and Susan left with the girls again, insisting that she didn't mind, that Judith needed to focus on Zach. As the station wagon drove away, Sophie turned her head and was still looking back when Judith couldn't make out her face anymore. Fresh guilt clutched at her; did Sophie feel abandoned anew? Should they be clinging together, proof that their family couldn't be torn apart? But she reminded herself of how cheerful Sophie had been. How happily she'd collected the Barbies she wanted to take with her. No. It was better this way. She was young and needed to be cushioned from her mother's anguish.

While Judith was seeing her daughter off, Ben had slapped together sandwiches for lunch. He watched like a hawk while she ate, only nodding with approval when she swallowed the last bite.

After lunch, she sat at the table watching him as he got on the phone again. He seemed to be nagging, cajoling, reminding.

"He's out there somewhere," she heard him say sharply. "Goddamn it, we're going to find the bastard!"

Might-have-seen reports came in, too. Some Ben dismissed easily. Others were possible, he admitted, though unlikely. On the map before him, Ben put small *x*s where the possible sightings placed either the car or the man and boy. They were too scattered to all be true. If Ben had been hoping for a clear trail, it had yet to appear.

She stopped listening to the conversations until Ben picked up the phone after it rang yet again.

One word penetrated. "Eddie?"

Wasn't that Ben's brother? The one he'd said wouldn't come to a family Christmas celebration if he knew Ben would be there? Ben's office staff must have told his brother where Ben could be reached.

"Anne's back?" Ben listened. "Yeah, she's probably right. Counseling can't hurt. I wish I'd learned to speak my mind twenty-five years ago. Listening to other people wouldn't have hurt, either.''

What did he mean? Judith wondered distantly.

Back still to her, Ben grunted. ''Yeah, Christmas sounds good. I have horses.... Uh-huh, sure, the kids can ride.'' His shoulders hunched, as though the images of children astride his horses had punched through any momentary pleasure he'd felt in talking to his brother. ''I can't stay on the phone, Eddie. Something's happened.''

When he started telling his brother about Zach, she hung on every word, reliving each agonizing moment of the past day and a half. She was gasping by the end, when he said quietly, ''I'll get him back, Eddie,'' Ben said quietly. ''You'll meet him at Christmas.''

Please let it be true, Judith prayed, jumping to her feet and rushing to the bedroom. Laundry. There must be dirty clothes. She had to occupy herself.

Behind her, she heard Ben say in a husky voice, ''I've missed you, Eddie. Thanks for calling.''

He must have his family back. She was glad for him; she knew she would be—at another time—when her own pain hadn't worn her to numbness only thoughts of Zach could penetrate.

The afternoon stretched into forever. She ran out of things to do or the energy and purpose required to do them. Finally she sat on the porch swing, a magazine spread on her lap so that Ben would think she was still succeeding in distracting herself.

Zach and Rylan could be anywhere by now. What if they *had* left the country? It happened, she knew it did. Would it be possible to regain custody even if they were found?

The gray weight of despair settled over her. She stared unseeing at the barren lawn, the rutted lane, the dry grass in the pasture. The sun had disappeared behind the nearest ridge, and the night's chill crept along in the shadow of dusk.

Another night. Dear God, she couldn't bear another night. Or another, or another, or another. Yet she knew she must; she had done it before. But how? She didn't remember.

The phone was ringing again. She'd quit feeling a surge of hope every time it rang. It would be someone who remembered seeing a blue car in Bellevue or Boise or Reno. Places Rylan would probably never go.

The murmur of Ben's voice came through the screen door. She heard him thank someone. His footsteps approached; he came out onto the porch and sat beside her. She looked up dully, and her heart gave a bang, as if someone had shocked it into beating again.

The frustration and anger she'd become accustomed to seeing on Ben's lean, dark face were gone, replaced by something so intense, so triumphant, she could only whisper, "What?"

"We've found him." He didn't smile, not yet. "They're in Bend, Oregon. A resort near Mount Bachelor. Kane rented a cabin and parked behind it so the car couldn't be seen. But we got lucky. A state patrolman who'd been off duty the past two days remembered seeing the car pull in. The resort owner confirms the description, says the little boy didn't look very happy. They have a dog with them, a yellow lab, he thought.''

"Oh, my God," she breathed. "It is them."

"Deschutes County officers have gone out to make the arrest. They'll call as soon as it's over."

She didn't know what she felt. Emotions swirled and erupted as if they were some dangerous chemical compound being experimentally mixed. Terror and exultation, hurt and longing… A whimper escaped her. "I'll go down there. I'll leave right away." She looked around blindly, knowing she needed to find her purse and car keys, not remembering where they were or even where she was.

Ben's firm grip stopped her from rising to her feet. "Not until they call and we know they have Zach safe. Then *we'll* drive down there. Do you really think I'd let you go alone?"

He might as well have thrown a spark to the volatile mix.

"Let me? He's *my* son, not yours! And I managed to drive across the country to get here!" she flared, then closed her eyes, realizing how ungrateful she sounded. More quietly, Judith said, "You've done so much. I can't tell you how thankful I am, but…" Her anger was doused as quickly as it had been aroused. Releasing a shaky breath, she looked at him pleadingly. "I want this to be for us. My children and me."

Ben's face twisted and he rose abruptly from his seat beside her. He went over to the railing and braced his hands on it, his back to her as he stood looking out at the yard. His shoulders and neck were rigid.

"Yeah," he said without expression, "I said I didn't want them, didn't I?"

Anxiety and hope swirled within her. But then she recalled that the worst part for her hadn't been his rejection of Zach and Sophie; it was knowing he'd denied his own child. If he could do that...

"Yes, you did. Why should you want mine when you didn't even want your own?" She took a breath. "But that's your business. I should never have assumed, just because you were friendly..."

Ben swung in a violent motion to face her, his mouth a thin line. "You had every reason to assume. Good God, I'd been hanging around here like a homeless dog begging to stay! And the kids..." His voice thickened. "I just didn't see what was happening."

Judith gripped the edge of the porch swing so tightly that the texture of the wood imprinted itself on her fingertips. "You were good to Zach and Sophie. That didn't give us any right to think you were ready for a walk up the aisle. It was my inexperience that let me think making love with you meant forever."

Ben scrubbed his hand over his face. In doing so, he stripped away every ounce of pretense and reserve. Everything that saved a man's pride. At the sight of his vulnerability, Judith's heart swelled painfully.

"I told you one thing and I felt another." Ben's voice no longer sounded like his. His throat worked. "I was scared. So damned scared."

"Scared?" she whispered. "Of what?"

"That if I let myself love you, I'd feel trapped someday, and then I'd fail you, and especially the kids." A raw sound came from him. Maybe he'd meant to laugh. "I always told myself I hated being around children. I'd spent enough years hemmed in by them. But lately, thanks to you, I've realized it was more complicated than that. I didn't do so great a job, especially with one of my brothers. I'd told myself I was sacrificing everything for them, that I'd done my best. Scary thought, when one of my brothers ended up hating my guts. Not a very good report card. I must have screwed up with them, and I didn't want that to happen again."

Something he'd said flashed into her mind. "It wasn't true that you're always invited for Christmas, was it?"

"Oh, yeah, I'm invited. Trouble is, if I go, my brother Eddie and his family won't. I know damn well which one of us the rest would rather have there."

"I don't believe it," Judith said fiercely. "You raised them! You gave up so much. They must see that!"

"Funny footnote." Ben massaged the back of his neck. "Just a while ago, Eddie pointed out that I was so busy playing martyr I hung around longer than I was needed. I gave up things I didn't have to, then hated everyone else for making me do it. Nice irony, isn't it?"

Judith stood, although her knees quaked. "We've needed you, and you haven't failed us. I don't believe you ever would. Look at these last two days! You promised you'd get Zach back, and you have."

His mouth twisted again. "*I* didn't get him back. I didn't do anything another cop wouldn't have done."

"That isn't true." Judith found the courage to step

forward, to flatten her hands on his chest. "Don't forget, I've been through this before. The other time—" she made herself remember "—the police went through the motions. They didn't care. They didn't hold me when I cried. They didn't stay all night or make me eat. There was no breakthrough, because they hadn't taught a boy headed for trouble that he could be somebody worthwhile."

"Tony's part in this was just luck," Ben argued.

But his hands reached up to grip hers, and he wasn't pushing her away, which emboldened her.

"It was luck that Tony went to the bathroom at the right time. But the rest wasn't. You didn't fail Tony. And because of that, you didn't fail Zach."

"I almost did." He squeezed his eyes shut. "When you told me he was gone…"

"What?" she whispered, scarcely able to breathe…to hope.

Ben opened his eyes. They were rimmed with red and wet with tears he couldn't hide. "I discovered that I didn't just love you—I loved your kids, too." His chest rose as he sucked in a huge breath. "But I guess I was a little late figuring that out."

"No. Oh, no." Judith wrapped her arms around him and hugged until he did the same to her. "Never too late, Ben…"

"Too late for my own daughter."

"Oh, Ben," she whispered, "I should have listened to you. Will you tell me about her?"

"Are you sure you want…" he began raggedly, then cocked his head. "Hell. The telephone."

"Yes." Now her heart did leap.

He let his arms drop with obvious reluctance, but his eyes never left hers as he opened the screen door. "Coming?"

"Are you kidding?" From somewhere deep within her, a smile dawned. It felt stiff and unfamiliar but, oh, so good. *Zach, you can come home now,* she thought. *This man will be the kind of father worth having.*

"Yeah?" Ben was saying into the phone. His dark eyes never wavered from Judith's. "You've got him." Some of the tension eased from his shoulders. "It went okay?" He listened again, then said, "The boy's mother is standing right here. Can she talk to him?"

Judith's heart threatened to break her rib cage. She reached out slowly and took the phone.

"Zach?"

For a moment she heard only the static of a cell phone. Then a small voice said, "Mom?"

"Zach." Her own voice broke. "You're all right?"

A distinct sniff came across the line. "I'm...I'm okay. Are you mad at me?"

"No. Oh, no!" Tears wet her cheeks. "I've been scared, and I've missed you terribly, but how could I be mad? I love you so much!"

Ben reached out and wrapped his hand around the back of her neck, massaging gently, letting her know without words that he was there for her.

"You never told Dad he could take me skiing, did you?" Zach asked bleakly.

"Skiing?" What on earth...?

"We were only going to breakfast." He spoke in a rush. "I just wanted to see him, and I knew you wouldn't let me. But then he drove all the way to Ellensburg before we stopped, and Dad made a phone call, and then he told me he had a surprise for me. He said he'd always wanted to learn how to ski, and that you'd given permission for me to go, too. He told me things you'd said, like making him promise to buy me a really warm parka, and saying to be careful, and it sounded like you, so I thought…'' His voice died. ''I was really dumb, wasn't I?''

''Zachary Kane,'' she said, putting all the love she could summon into her voice, ''you're nine years old. You aren't supposed to be able to tell when an adult is lying. Especially when that adult is your own father.''

''Yeah, but…''

''No buts. You shouldn't have sneaked out without telling me, but the rest of it wasn't your fault.''

Zach sniffled again. ''He didn't even really want to ski! He lied about that, too! It was just an excuse! I wouldn't have gone with him otherwise. I could tell he didn't like Hercules. He was just faking when he said he did!''

''I'm sorry,'' she said helplessly, wanting to hold him, feeling his tears even though she couldn't see them.

''It's okay, Mom.''

''Was it scary seeing him arrested?'' She'd imagined Sophie having to be physically wrenched from her father, sobbing, reaching out, seeing him handcuffed and led away…. Sophie was young enough that those memories were already blurring. Zach wouldn't forget so easily.

"He tried to get away." Zach let out a hiccuping sob. "He was really nervous and he kept looking out the window, so he saw them before they got all around the cabin. I told him I wouldn't go with him, but he dragged me out anyway. We went out the back door 'cuz the car was right there. But when he tried to push me in, I kicked and screamed, and Hercules bit him. Really hard. He let me go." Satisfaction sounded in his voice, despite the tears. "Dad was bleeding, and he's going to have to have stitches and everything."

"Hercules bit your father?" Judith echoed in astonishment.

Ben mimed disbelief.

"Yeah. He saved me." Zach blew his nose; somebody must have handed him a tissue. Either that, or he was using the hem of his T-shirt, which wouldn't be the first time. "Can we buy him a steak or something?"

"We can buy him a diamond-studded collar if you want." She smiled through her tears. "Kiss him for me, will you?"

"Sure." He sounded suddenly very young. "Mom, how am I going to get home?"

"We're coming to get you," she said firmly. "I'll bet somebody will take you home with them, just for tonight. But Sophie and Ben and I will be on our way as soon as we can. We'll be there sometime tomorrow."

Chief Bennett McKinsey gave her neck a last squeeze and backed up, leaning against the kitchen table, his eyes still lingering on her face.

"Ben, too?" her son questioned.

"Ben, too." She gave the subject of the conversation a saucy smile. "I think you'll be seeing quite a bit of him."

Sounding like his normal self, Zach demanded, "You're not going to marry him, are you?"

Her smile faded. "Would you mind?"

"Heck, no! That would be so cool!" He hesitated. "I mean, if he didn't mind Soph and me. He doesn't, does he?"

"What do you think?"

"He never acted like he did," Zach said doubtfully. "But sometimes he doesn't say what he means."

I told you one thing and I felt another. Had Zach known...? "What do you mean?" she asked cautiously.

"Like, he called Hercules a useless mutt and said he was good for nothing, but then he sneaked him a dog biscuit and scratched him right where Hercules likes it."

Judith smiled. "Ben just doesn't want to admit what a softie he is. I guess we can judge best by what somebody does, though, not what he says."

"Yeah, yeah." She knew he'd scrunched up his nose. "'Actions speak louder than words,'" he mimicked. "Ben doesn't say much, but sometimes I can tell he thinks I did good."

This was not the moment for a grammar lesson. "And it makes you just about burst with pride, doesn't it?"

"Yeah," he said thoughtfully. "I don't know why, but...yeah."

"Well—" she smiled at the man standing with his

arms crossed not three feet away "—Ben's next action is going to be driving me all the way to central Oregon to pick up my son." Without warning, tears sprang to her eyes again. "Zachary Kane," she said fiercely, "I love you. Don't you ever doubt it!"

Then her son gave her a gift greater than pearls. "Why would I doubt it?" he asked, obviously surprised.

Seeing her weeping, Ben handed her a paper towel. Her turn to blow her nose. He took the phone from her. "Hey, Zach, how do you like Oregon?" A crooked smile softened his harsh face. "Yeah, okay. We'll see you tomorrow. Do you want to put Lieutenant Beck back on?"

As they talked, Judith sobbed a little more, but happily. She saw that Ben was writing down the addresses and phone numbers they needed to collect Zach tomorrow. Surely, surely, this time it would all be over. Rylan had truly lost his son now; he'd destroyed any chance of ever building a relationship between them. She would never understand the self-destructive choices he'd made. Despite their divorce, he could still have been a real father to his children. Now, please God, they were beyond his reach forever.

What's more, if Ben had meant what she hoped and prayed he had, Sophie and Zach would soon have the father they needed. The father they already loved.

And *she* would have the man she loved.

BEN HUNG UP THE PHONE and cautiously studied Judith. Though she was still mopping up her tears, he didn't miss the glow of happiness that shone from within her. It made him think of that night when she'd left all the house lights on to call him to her. To welcome him, she'd said. He couldn't believe she was really welcoming him now, not the way he wanted her to mean.

That disbelief lent a harshness to his voice. "We still have things to talk about."

"Nothing that can't wait." Her eyes were bright above her tear-stained cheeks. "Oh, Ben, is it really over?"

"You mean Zach's disappearance?" Hell, he was being selfish again. She wasn't happy because of him; it was the fact that her son had been found that had her beaming. "Yeah. It's over. He's safe."

Something in his tone brought a crinkle to her forehead. "You don't mind driving to Oregon?"

He snorted. "I was the one who wasn't going to let you go by yourself, remember? Hell, no, I don't mind. What I would mind is staying here worrying about you."

"I am capable..."

"I know you are." He moved his shoulders uneasily. "I'd go crazy if I had to stay here."

"Ben." Those clear eyes fastened on his, insisting on truth. "Do you love me?"

"God, yes! But there's something we haven't talked about yet."

Her eyes widened. "Something new?"

"Not something new, damn it!" he growled. "The fact that I walked away from a woman I'd made pregnant. The fact that, until a few weeks ago, I never even made any effort to find out whether the baby was a girl or a boy.''

Her voice softened. ''You need to tell me about it, don't you?''

''I need you to know the truth.'' He rubbed his hands over his thighs, scared to death now that the crunch had come. ''You think I'm going to have excuses that make it all right, don't you? But I don't have any. None. You need to decide whether you can live with a man who did something that ugly.''

The crinkles back on her forehead, Judith searched his face. ''Why did you?''

He swore. ''I don't know! I never even considered doing the right thing and marrying her. It just wasn't an option. I told her I didn't want to have children, and she said fine, and the next thing I know she's got tears in her eyes and she's telling me she's pregnant.'' Ben's chest heaved as if he'd run two miles and tackled a bad guy. Himself. He guessed in a way he was tackling himself. ''I...hell. I just panicked. And I really believed she'd done it on purpose. I saw the birth control pills in her bathroom, and a month later that package was still lying there without any more of those little pills punched out. But that's not an excuse,'' he added grimly. ''The little girl Kelly had shouldn't have to suffer because her mother figured wrong about a man.''

''Marrying her wasn't the only thing you could have done,'' Judith said tentatively, taking a step toward him. ''You could have taken responsibility in other ways.''

''I offered money.'' He despised himself for how

glad he was to be able to say that much. "I would have paid child support. Kelly wouldn't take it."

Concern still puckered Judith's forehead. "What did she do?"

"Married someone else. She tells me my daughter has a daddy, thank you very much."

"So maybe she's not suffering."

"No thanks to me," he said from between clenched teeth.

"You said you'd called this...Kelly. What did she say?"

He tried hard to see what Judith was thinking. She wasn't flinching, the way she had that night when he'd told her. On the other hand, she hadn't said, *It doesn't matter. I love you anyway.*

He wasn't even sure he wanted her to. Because it did matter.

"Same thing," Ben said tersely. "'We're doing fine. You didn't want her, so don't bother calling again.'"

She mulled that over, head cocked. She looked absurdly pretty, considering what she'd been through. A few blotches hadn't faded yet from her pale skin, and her hair was falling out of the cloth rubber-band thing that was supposed to be holding it, but the news that Zach was safe had returned the serenity to her face. Nothing he'd told her so far had shaken it.

A terrible thought came to him. Maybe he *couldn't* shake her serenity, because he didn't matter enough to her. Not the way her son did.

She was contemplating him again with an unnervingly thoughtful gaze. "So, what are you going to do?"

"I want to see her." The words were torn from him. "Just once, so I know what she looks like. And then…" He shook his head. "I did what I did. I can't storm into their lives insisting I get visitation rights or anything like that. For all I know, Kelly has gotten a court order terminating my rights. Maybe her husband has even adopted my daughter." He had to swallow at that one. *His* daughter, bearing someone else's name.

"That's true," Judith said, as if she were agreeing with a casual observation. But then she waited.

Ben swore and thrust his hands through his hair. "I figure all I can do is get Kelly to promise that if our daughter ever asks about me, she'll tell her that I want to meet her. We could go from there, but I want her to know that I wish I'd done things differently. That I'd still like to be a father to her, if she needs one."

Judith considered what he'd said, and she kept searching his face as if looking for…what? Insincerity? He endured her scrutiny, feeling as if she were performing open-heart surgery while he was yet conscious.

Finally Ben couldn't stand another minute. "Say something," he said hoarsely. "Tell me what you're thinking."

She pressed her lips together, then smiled tremulously. "I'm thinking that I love you so much it hurts. That I wish that little girl would someday call you 'Daddy.'"

He broke then. Crying like a baby, he took those

couple of steps to go into Judith's arms. And they
closed around him with the kind of welcome and comfort and love a man could waste a lifetime wishing
for. She cradled his head and kissed his cheek and told
him that a man who cared about any wrongs he'd done
and tried to atone for them was one in a million.

When he finally got a grip on himself, Ben lifted
his head and roughly wiped his face on his shirtsleeve.
Judith smiled at him with such love she was luminous.
She made him think of dawn, when the sun had just
risen and painted the sky with colors he couldn't even
name. There'd been times he'd been so awed by the
sight of the sun rising he'd known that anything in the
world was worth enduring for this.

She was his dawn.

"Will you marry me?" he asked, knowing he could
make anything right if she only said yes. He could
give her children what he hadn't known how to give
when he was only a child himself.

She laughed softly, and tears shimmered in her eyes
again. "Yes. Oh, yes, Ben McKinsey. I'll marry you."

He let free the breath he'd been holding. Cupping
her face in his hands, he bent his head, but he didn't
kiss her. He couldn't seem to quit feasting on the sight
of her face. She was giving him heaven, no matter
what kind of sinner he was. He swore then that he
would never let her regret her decision.

"Did you mean it?" he asked abruptly. "When you
said you'd like to have my baby?"

"More than anything." She tensed under his hands.
"Which is lucky, because I'm a few days late. It might
mean nothing, but…"

"You might be pregnant."

"Yes."

He had to grit his teeth against the most powerful stab of sexual hunger he'd ever felt. Pregnant. With his baby. Why did knowing her body might be ripening with his seed make him want to rip her clothes off and take her again, as if he had to claim her?

Later, he promised himself. Right now, she needed to get to her son.

"I love you," he said in a voice that couldn't be his. "Shall we head for Bend, Oregon?"

"Yes." Her lips touched his. "Soon," she whispered. "But not yet. We have...unfinished business."

Elation roared through him. The desire ripped free and he captured her mouth with desperate ferocity. "Soon," he agreed as he lifted her into his arms.

The Little Matchmaker
MURIEL JENSEN

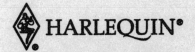

HARLEQUIN®

TORONTO • NEW YORK • LONDON
AMSTERDAM • PARIS • SYDNEY • HAMBURG
STOCKHOLM • ATHENS • TOKYO • MILAN • MADRID
PRAGUE • WARSAW • BUDAPEST • AUCKLAND

CHAPTER ONE

SHERIFF ETHAN DRUM swept his flashlight in a wide arc in front of him, willing the missing little boy to appear out of the rainy darkness. The three-hour search had become desperate and very personal. As a parent himself, he didn't have to guess at the anguish of the mother who waited at home; he knew it all too well.

His daughter had once disappeared at a family picnic, and he could still remember how the unthinkable possibilities had driven him and Diana to the brink of madness. Then a Search and Rescue volunteer had walked out of the woods with her, and Ethan's heart had almost stalled with relief.

He wanted to bring that same relief to this boy's mother. It wasn't that he wanted to be a hero. He'd been the sheriff of Butler County long enough to know that the job wasn't about heroics, but about maintaining peace and order in a little corner of Oregon, where the Columbia River met the ocean.

Generally people weren't the problem here; nature was. The pine, fir and cedar woods that ran along the beach could hide a boy in their dense undergrowth so that a man could walk right by him in daylight and not see him.

Tonight there was no moonlight, and a steady soaking rain served to blot out any remaining visibility.

At least the temperature was on his side—a reasonably moderate midforties rather than the just-above-freezing levels usual for early February.

And nothing was impossible. Ethan's ancestry was Portuguese, French-Canadian and, somewhere way back, Mohawk, which was as hardheaded an ethnicity as could be created in any gene pool. It meant he liked to have his way and was willing to go to any lengths to see that he did. He was damned if he was going to be deprived of delivering this boy alive and well, home to his mother.

He flipped the switch on the shoulder mike connected to the radio at his belt and called the office. "500," he said, indicating his call number.

"500," a woman's voice answered. "Go ahead."

"Ebbie, it's Ethan."

"You found him?" she asked hopefully.

"No," he replied. "I was just checking to see if he'd turned up at home."

Evelyn Browning, secretary and reliable source of gossip both in and out of the office, sighed audibly. "No. His mother left a friend waiting at home and came into the office. She, ah…she'd like to borrow a car."

Ebbie's tone suggested that the mother was standing within earshot. He frowned at the darkness as rain dripped off the brim of his hat and into his jacket. "What?" he asked.

"Well…you know…she wants to help. But she doesn't have a car."

Ethan could imagine Ebbie smiling reassuringly at the woman as she spoke to him.

"She was thinking," Ebbie went on, "that she could go up the dump road while you're—"

"No."

"She says she's an excellent driver."

"No! I don't care if she's Michael Andretti. Do *not* give her a car. I know she's upset, but it's an abso—"

"Sheriff Drum." This was a different voice—younger, deeper. "This is Bethany Richards. I know the idea might sound foolish to you, but your assistant here tells me that Search and Rescue is all tied up looking for a group of missing campers and you're searching for Jason alone. We could cover twice as much ground if I was searching, too. And please don't tell me the county's insurance wouldn't cover me. I don't care. I'll sign a waiver."

He'd been about to bring up the safety rules governing county vehicles until he'd heard the fear and the end-of-her-rope torment in her voice. To mention such practical matters in the face of that seemed insulting.

"Mrs. Richards," he said patiently, "I'm going to find your son. You've got to have faith."

"I've *got* faith!" she said, her voice rising as she lost the calm with which she'd come on the line. "What I want are wheels!"

"You don't need wheels, Mrs. Richards," he said firmly. "You need to stay right where you are so that when I bring Jason back, I can put him right into your arms. I don't want to have to tell him when he's cold and scared that you're driving around somewhere and we don't know where *you* are."

He heard an inrush of air—a swallowed sob, he guessed. "But you *aren't* finding him, Sheriff," she disputed hoarsely. "And he's only seven—he'll be eight tomorrow—"

"But I *will* find him," he insisted. "You told us

that Forest Beach is one of his favorite places. I've walked the beach and checked the woods. He must be on the hill.'' The road at the top of the gradual thickly wooded slope behind the woods was a favorite parking spot of teenagers because of the seclusion it provided. He prayed that was where Jason Richards had gone to hide.

There was a moment of silence. "What if he isn't?'' she asked finally. The question had an edge of despair. The mile of darkness and woods that separated him from the voice on the radio disappeared, and Ethan knew exactly what she was feeling.

"I thought you had faith,'' he chided gently, rubbing the chest of his bulky jacket with a gloved hand. Inside him, frustration was burning a hole.

He heard that sound again, the little inrush of air.

"What time is it?'' he asked her.

She hesitated. He imagined her looking up at the ancient round clock on the wall over Ebbie's desk. "Ah…five minutes after ten.''

"All right,'' he said, knowing this was risky but unable to stop himself. "You watch that clock, and by five minutes after eleven, I'll have Jason back to you.''

He heard her sigh of acceptance. He knew it didn't mean she believed him; it just meant she'd give him the hour because she had nothing *else* to believe in.

He switched off the radio and headed for the hill, sweeping the beam of his flashlight methodically from side to side.

"YOU JUST SIT right there.'' The plump middle-aged woman in the beige-and-brown county uniform, whose gold badge was inscribed with "E. Browning,'' pointed Beth to a chair. Beth had avoided it since she'd walked into the office an hour earlier, because she'd been afraid that if she sat down it would be an indication she was prepared to wait—and she wasn't. She wanted Jason back now!

The woman pressed a steaming mug of coffee into her hands. ''Drink this and watch that clock just like Ethan told you. If he said he'd be back with your boy in an hour, he will be. Ethan Drum is a man of his word.''

Beth wanted to believe that, but it was a night out of a horror movie. Jason, just a day short of turning eight, had been frightened and angry when he'd left; if he wasn't already unconscious from hypothermia, he might hide from the sheriff rather than be brought back home to face the risk of being taken away by his grandparents.

Beth took a long sip of the coffee. Her eyes widened when the generous dose of brandy in it hit her tastebuds.

The sheriff's staff assistant had gone back to her desk and now turned to wink at her. ''Nothing like a good medicinal cup of coffee.''

Medicinal, indeed. There was enough alcohol in the cup to pickle her for posterity! Still, the warmth of the brandy brought a measure of relaxation to muscles that had been clenched in terror ever since darkness had fallen. Ever since she'd realized that Jason had followed through on his threat to run away.

Beth had explained to him over and over that her mother-in-law's threats to take her to court for custody of Jason were a bluff, and that nothing and no one would ever separate them.

She and Jason had moved here to Cobbler's

Crossing three months ago. Some bully at the school, who'd overheard Jason expressing his fears to a friend, had been teasing and tormenting him. And all her assurances that his grandparents had no legal cause to take him from her hadn't comforted him. She imagined that when a boy's father died, his sense of security died, also, leaving him to feel that everything else he held dear could be taken, too.

Beth looked at the clock. Ten-fifteen. She took another sip of the coffee-cum-brandy, or rather, the brandy-cum-coffee, leaned her head back against the wall and closed her eyes, remembering the man she'd been married to for thirteen years.

They'd met in high school. Steve Richards had been of average height, with a handsome face and muscular build. She'd admired his drive to achieve and accomplish, especially when other boys seemed to spend much of their time avoiding homework and skipping classes. It was in wood shop that they'd become fast friends; they were the class misfits—she, because she was the only girl, and he, because he had no skill for carpentry.

Her parents had died in an automobile accident when she was six, and she was raised in a Seattle suburb by a grandmother who was loving and supportive, but possessed slender financial means. Steve's parents were indulgent but overbearing, and he'd been anxious to strike out on his own.

And so Steve and Bethany had married right out of high school. He'd gone to work at a furniture store, part of a retail chain, while she'd worked in the office at the community college—which enabled her to take art classes without charge.

For two years they were very happy. She'd produced painted wooden art and worked every craft show in the area, and he'd worked long hours at the store, eager to get ahead.

Beth became pregnant with Jason at the same time Steve was put in charge of the chain's newest and largest store, in downtown Seattle. And then everything changed.

By working night and day, catering to all his customers' needs and demands, and keeping costs down by serving as both clerk and manager, Steve put the store in the black the first year.

Over the next two years he made enough in bonuses and stock options to strike out on his own. Though Beth knew he loved her and Jason, she also accepted that he put them second to his career. What had once seemed such an admirable trait had become, in her eyes, an insatiable and obsessive drive to succeed at any cost.

In search of some adult contact, she'd joined a co-op of artists that required each member tend the small neighborhood shop several mornings or afternoons every week. But many of Steve's contacts called him at home, and he resented their having to deal with an answering machine rather than a person. He wanted Beth there.

"Steve, the co-op is important to me," she'd tried to explain.

He'd made a sweeping gesture with one hand that encompassed the vaulted ceiling and floor-to-ceiling windows of their new house on Puget Sound and said, "The store means this house and the way we live. If I land the deal to furnish the redecorating of the convalescent home on Markham Road, it's going to mean two weeks in the Caymans for us."

She'd sighed, tired of the argument. "If you don't slow down, Steve," she'd warned, "you're going to land *in* the convalescent home on Markham Road."

"That's what it takes to build a business, Beth," he'd said. "You have to work at it all the time."

It had been on the tip of her tongue to tell him that what built a business could also destroy a marriage, but Jason adored his father and she'd made a vow. She'd looked around—at the oversize sofa with its distressed-velvet slipcovers, the Scandinavian pine dining table under the iron rope chandelier—and decided that she was caught in a very elegant trap.

So she'd left the co-op and worked on her art at home, unwilling to discard the time and emotion she'd invested in her marriage or to dismiss the love Jason felt for his father.

Then one day a little more than a year ago she'd received a telephone call from a client with whom Steve had a lunch meeting. He told her Steve had collapsed as they were leaving the restaurant and had been taken by ambulance to the hospital.

She'd left Jason with a neighbor, and by the time she'd arrived at the emergency room, her thirty-two-year-old husband was dead of a heart attack.

She'd grieved for months over the loss of the man that driving ambition had robbed of his potential as a husband and father. The bank holding Steve's loans took everything, including most of the money Beth made by selling the house, which, thank God, had been paid off by mortgage insurance.

When she'd signed the check over to the bank and was given only a small fraction of it back, she'd stood on the sidewalk in front of the bank with Jason beside her. A curiously quiet happiness stole over her.

She was free.

For the first time in years she was free of Steve's crippling need to do more, to have more. Free of the terrifying debt that resulted. Free of all the pressures that suppressed who she really was and who she really wanted to be.

She'd called Kelly Braxton, one of her co-op friends who'd moved to the Oregon coast and with whom she'd kept in contact. Kelly had sent her the newspaper from Cobbler's Crossing, population two thousand, and Beth had seen the picture of the old cannery that was for sale at the end of a pier on the waterfront.

Kelly had checked it out with the Realtor for Beth. She reported that a previous owner had tried to put shops into the old building, and that some of the interior had been painted; plumbing and wiring had been installed, along with a furnace. Then the small-town entrepreneur had run out of money.

"But the rest of it's pretty primitive," Kelly had warned over the phone. "The walls to break it into shops are up, but they're not painted. There's flooring, but the roof leaks on the river side. The dock would probably also have to be checked for safety before you could allow any commercial traffic."

Beth had looked at the photo of the cannery and seen everything she'd always wanted—space for a studio combined with living space so that she had only one set of expenses. And if she was willing to work hard, the place had income potential as a location for rental studios. Artists were always looking for big inexpensive spaces.

She put a down payment on it sight unseen and moved with Jason to Oregon, sure it would be a fresh start for both of them. But Steve's parents, who adored their grandson but only tolerated Beth, had come to visit two weeks after she and Jason moved into the cannery. They'd been appalled by the general condition of the building, by its location at the end of a pier and by the tiny living area, which was the size of a very small apartment.

Beth took them through the rest of the building in an attempt to show them its possibilities. But all they'd seen were the ceiling and walls stained with water from the leaky roof, and the stark bareness of the building, not the happy little art community she envisioned.

Joanne, her imposing, haughty mother-in-law, had met Beth's eyes and said ominously, "We can't let Jason live like this. Steven would be appalled. We'll see you again when we've looked into our options."

Beth had swung her gaze from Joanne to Zachary, her father-in-law. "You have no options, Jo," she said. "Steve let you intrude on our lives, but I won't. I want Jason to be able to see you, but don't think for one moment I will let you take him from me. Jason is *my* son, and he's not going to replace Steve in your lives."

Her in-laws had left in a huff, Zachary making threats of suing her for custody.

Beth hadn't know Jason had been listening until they'd slammed the door behind them and she'd turned to find him in the doorway to his tiny bedroom, his eyes wide with fear.

She'd done her best to reassure him, but he'd been convinced that, since his grandfather was a judge, he'd be able to carry out his threat. When Zachary had called yesterday to tell Beth that he and Joanne were coming to Cobbler's Crossing for Jason's birthday tomorrow, Jason had been sure they were coming to take him away.

Now Beth was wondering if indulging her dream had been selfish and irresponsible. It was one thing for an adult to leave family and friends and flirt with poverty to fulfill an ambition, but had it been right to uproot her son? At this moment she wasn't sure. She'd gladly go back to life in Seattle if it meant the sheriff would walk through the office door right now with Jason by the hand.

THE GRASSY HILL was slick with rain and difficult to negotiate, but the muddy trail was worse. So Ethan tacked across the face of the hill, swinging his light in wide arcs, careful not to miss anything.

"Jason!" he shouted. "Jason, are you here?"

For the first time in hours of searching, he thought he heard a faint response. His heart lurched and he swung the beam of his flashlight up the hill in the direction of the sound.

But the wind was howling and the rain was noisy; he couldn't be absolutely sure. The light revealed nothing.

He waited for a lull in the wind, then shouted again. "Jason! Where are you?"

So weak he wondered if he'd imagined it came, "Over here!"

"Where?"

The answer was a little louder. "In the tree at the top of the hill!"

Relief surged through Ethan as he pressed on up the slope. He knew precisely what tree Jason meant.

The lone mangled fir that leaned east from a lifetime of being buffeted by the wind.

He stopped under the tree and shone his flashlight beam upward. About fifteen feet above his head he saw a small sturdy figure in jeans and a red waterproof parka. The boy was straddling a branch and holding on to the trunk with both hands. He was crying.

"Hi," Ethan said, propping the flashlight in the fork of a branch so that its beam remained on the boy. "I'm Sheriff Drum."

"Yeah," the boy replied, his voice shaking. "I know."

Ethan reached for a branch above the one in which he'd propped the light. He pulled himself up, then bracing himself against the trunk with his feet, reached for the next branch.

"You mean we've met," Ethan said when he was only a few feet below the boy, "and you'd make me come out on a night like this to find you?"

"You...you came to school to talk to us," Jason said haltingly. "And the other kids told me all about you...."

"Ah." Ethan's head was now level with Jason's feet. He could see that the tree had kept the boy reasonably dry. "Okay, just hold the branch above your head and swing your leg over the branch you're sitting on."

Instructing the boy step by step, cautioning him to always keep a hold on the branch above, Ethan soon had him down to his level and clinging to his neck.

"Well done," Ethan said, pleased. "You okay?"

Jason, teeth chattering, wailed, "I want my mom."

"Right. I know." Ethan was afraid to risk freeing

a hand to comfort him, so he had to use his voice, instead. He spoke quietly and with confidence. "She's waiting for you in my office. All we have to do is get down this tree."

"I'm okay," Jason said after a moment, tightening his grip on Ethan's neck and wrapping his legs around his waist. "I'm ready."

Ethan smiled into the darkness. At fourteen his daughter was fiercely independent and resisted all his efforts to help or counsel her. And though she never said so directly, he suspected she considered him generally useless and unable to function competently in her world. So having a child willingly depend upon him was a treat he hadn't experienced for a while.

"Here we go. Hold on tight." Ethan moved slowly, the boy's sixty or so pounds a challenge to his balance. Still, he reached the bottom branches without incident.

"Okay," he said into Jason's ear. The boy's cheek was pressed so tightly against his that conversation was easy. "Now I need you to let go of me and hold on to this branch so I can jump down and catch you."

"No," the boy said adamantly, fearfully.

"Jason," Ethan explained, "if I jump holding on to you, we'll get hurt."

"I don't want to let go!"

"It'll only be for a minute. If I bring you back to your mom with a broken bone, she'll be really mad at me."

The boy apparently considered that something to think about. "She's gonna be really mad at *me*."

"I talked to her on the radio," Ethan said. "She sounded much more worried than angry."

"Yeah, but after she doesn't have to be worried anymore, she'll be mad."

Probably true, Ethan thought. "Well, running away isn't the best way to handle whatever the problem is."

"But *he's* coming for me."

"Who's 'he'?"

"Grandpa Richards. And Grandma. He's a judge and he's gonna take me away." Jason began to cry again.

Ethan decided it was time to be firm. "Look. I want to hear about this, but you're going to tell me about it in the car after we get out of this tree and down the hill. So listen to me."

Jason sniffed. "Okay."

"Take your right arm from around my neck and hold the branch that's over our heads."

"I don't want to!"

"I know, but you have to. Just do as I say, and this'll be over in a minute."

Still whimpering, Jason freed one hand, reached up and grasped the branch just above his head. The pudgy face now visible in the light from below was pinched and pale, and the blue eyes were wide with fear.

"Good," Ethan said. "Now reach up with the other hand and catch the other branch." Jason complied.

Ethan's neck was free, but the sturdy legs around his waist felt riveted to him. "Great." Ethan uncoiled one of Jason's legs and placed that foot on a branch.

"Feel that?" he said.

"Yeah," Jason replied thinly. "It's wobbly."

"It only has to hold you for a minute."

He did the same with the other leg, and before the

boy could realize what he was doing and complain about it, he jumped backward to the ground.

"Hey!" Jason shouted.

Ethan clapped his hands and reached up for him, bracing himself to take his weight. "Come on. Just—" Before he could complete the command, the boy fell into his arms. Ethan, his hat dislodged and rolling away, landed on his back on the wet grass with the boy on top of him.

"We did it!" Jason said exultantly, sitting up on Ethan's stomach. "And I didn't even get a broken bone! Did you?"

"No," Ethan replied with a half laugh. "I'm squished. You want to get off me so we can radio your mom that you're all right?"

"Oh. Yeah." Jason scrambled to his feet, found Ethan's hat in the process and handed it to him.

Ethan drew the boy back under the shelter of the tree and called Ebbie.

"You found him?" she demanded.

It gave Ethan great pleasure to be able to say yes. "Put Mrs. Richards on," he said. "Here's Jason."

Ethan disconnected the mike from his shoulder and held it to the boy's mouth. "Mom?" Jason said, then he whispered to Ethan, "Am I s'posed to say, 'Over'?"

Ethan bit back a grin. "No. Just talk."

"Mom? Hi. It's me."

Ethan heard the voice he'd spoken to half an hour ago laughing and crying at the same time. "Jase, are you okay? Where are you?"

"I was in a tree, Mom, only I couldn't get down 'cause it was too slippy, but Sheriff Drum came up and got me. He jumped down at the bottom and then he caught me. It was really cool!''

Cool, Ethan considered, shaking his head. That's not what *he'd* have called it.

Jason's voice lowered and he asked gravely, ''Mom, are you mad?''

''Jase, right now I'm just happy and grateful you're alive and all right,'' she answered. ''But by tomorrow I'm going to be mad. It doesn't mean I don't love you, it just means…'' There was a sigh. ''But we won't talk about that until tomorrow.''

''Tell her we'll be there in twenty minutes,'' Ethan prompted.

Jason repeated the information.

''I'm waiting for you, sweetie. I love you.'' Her voice was a comforting sound in the roaring blackness. Then she added softly, ''Tell Sheriff Drum that I love him, too.''

Jason handed the mike back to Ethan. ''She said—''

''Yeah.'' Ethan had to cope with a weird sensation in the pit of his stomach. ''I heard her.''

It had been five long years since a woman had said those words to him—his wife, Diana, only days before she'd died of ovarian cancer. And this time, of course, the words were simply an exaggerated expression of gratitude. All the same he found them touching.

CHAPTER TWO

ETHAN LED THE WAY down the muddy trail, one hand holding Jason's, the other holding the flashlight. They slipped and slid and finally arrived at the small parking lot, which was empty except for the brown-and-white patrol car.

Ethan put Jason in the front seat, retrieved blankets from the trunk, then took the boy's jacket off and wrapped him in one of the blankets. He pulled the seat belt over him, then covered him with another blanket, unmindful of the mud that caked him from foot to thigh. At last he climbed in behind the wheel, cranked up the heat and turned the car toward the road.

The wipers beat hard against the rain sheeting the windshield.

"Warm enough?" Ethan asked. When Jason didn't answer, Ethan glanced over to find the boy staring at him.

"Yeah," Jason said finally. Then he fell quiet, but continued to stare at him.

"How'd you get this far from home?" Ethan asked.

"On my bike," Jason answered. "But I crashed on the trail when it started to rain and bent my front wheel. Then my bike fell down the hill."

Ethan turned his full attention back to the road.

They were approaching a long series of hairpin turns that led to the state highway. Ethan could still feel the boy's eyes on him.

"What?" he asked. "You worried about your mom coming down on you when you get home?"

Jason sighed. "No. Well, yeah, but that's not what I'm thinking about."

"What are you thinking about?"

"I was thinking," Jason said hopefully, "that you could maybe…arrest me."

Ethan glanced at him again. The blue eyes looked serious. "If it was up to me," he replied, "I *would* put you in jail for scaring your mom like that. Unfortunately the law doesn't consider running away criminal."

"But you're the sheriff." The boy shifted in his seat, turning toward him, his voice going to a higher pitch as he warmed to the idea. "You can do whatever you want."

"No, I can't," Ethan corrected. "I can only do what the law tells me."

"Well…you could say I resisted arrest. I'd tell everybody that I really did."

"But you're not *under* arrest. You haven't committed a crime."

"You could say I stole something."

Ethan shook his head. "Now, how do you think your mom would feel if I told her that?"

"She'll feel worse if Grandma and Grandpa take me away! And if I'm in jail, they can't get me, right?"

Ethan heard the very real anguish in the boy's voice. "What makes you think your grandparents want to take you away?" he asked.

"They told Mom it's 'cause of the cannery."

"What cannery?"

"Mom's an artist," Jason said, wiping rain off his cheek with an edge of the blanket. "We bought the old cannery out on the pier."

Ethan nodded, remembering his brother mentioning that some gullible out-of-towner had bought the old Baldwin Cannery building.

"We're gonna make an art mall out of it," Jason went on excitedly. "And when it's all rented, we'll make enough money to send me to college. But right now it looks pretty awful. And just one little part of the building's fixed up, and that's where we'll live till Mom gets the rest of it done. Grandma said my dad would be *appalled.*" He gave the word dramatic emphasis.

"Pretty strong word."

"Yeah, well. Grandma doesn't like a lot of stuff. She doesn't like artists, so she doesn't like Mom."

"Your mom and dad are divorced?"

"No. My dad had a heart attack and died." Jason's voice became very faint.

Ethan turned to the boy and was encouraged to see that he looked sad but not destroyed. He reached over to pat his knee. "I'm sorry. It's hard to lose a dad."

"He wasn't home that much, but when he was, I really liked him. My mom says he loved me a lot."

"That's a good memory to have."

"Yeah."

Ethan heard the lack of conviction in Jason's reply and realized that a memory, especially to a little boy, was a poor substitute for the real thing.

"I bet you miss him a lot."

"Yeah." Jason heaved a sigh. "I used to miss him

a lot *before* he died, too.'' He shifted in his seat, then asked, ''Where do *you* live?''

''In a big old house in town. In fact, you can see it from the cannery. It's gray with green shutters.''

''That one?'' Jason's voice was reverent. ''Wow! It has that tower thing?''

''That's the one.''

Jason sighed again. ''I wish I lived there.''

''Oh, I don't think your grandmother would like it any more than she likes the cannery. It's not very fancy, just comfortable.'' Jason grinned at the boy. ''You warm enough?''

Jason nodded, then sat straighter. ''Hey. Maybe you could arrest my *grandpa!*''

The boy definitely had a future in law enforcement, Ethan thought. He was determined to have someone arrested—anyone. ''But he hasn't done anything against the law.''

''If he tries to take me, wouldn't that be stealing?''

''Ah…that would be kidnapping,'' Ethan said. ''And if your grandfather's a judge, I'm sure he wouldn't try to take you away without first getting a judgment from the court. And to do that, he'd have to prove that your mother wasn't doing a good job of being your mother.''

''She does a great job,'' Jason said staunchly.

Ethan could believe it. From the way she'd sounded on the radio, it was clear she was very caring.

''Then you probably don't have as big a problem as you think you have.''

''Yeah, I do.'' Jason's voice was anxious again. ''Taylor Bridges's dad is a lawyer, and he says my house is awful enough to prove my mom's a bad mother.''

"Taylor said, or his father said?''

"Well, Taylor.''

Ethan sighed as he turned off the highway and down the road into Cobbler's Crossing. "Think about it, Jason. What does an eight-year-old kid know about it, even if his father *is* a lawyer?''

"Taylor's nine.'' Jason seemed to think that was significant. "He's in the fourth grade.''

"Well, I don't think you learn much about the law in the fourth grade. He probably just likes to rattle you.''

Jason looked at him in surprise. "That's what Mom says. How did *you* know that?''

"Evreybody's got somebody like that in his life. You just have to let them talk, but you can ignore it and hold to what you know to be true.'' Ethan turned into the parking lot of the small complex that held the sheriff's office and the jail. "If your mom's a good mom, you don't have to worry about what Taylor Bridges says.''

"I wish Grandma and Grandpa weren't coming for my birthday,'' Jason said plaintively. "Then I could have a pizza party like the other kids have. With balloons and video games.''

Ethan brought the car to a stop directly in front of the office's back door. "I'm sure your grandparents love you a lot and just want to help you celebrate.''

"Uh-oh,'' Jason said. His voice had a despairing note.

Ethan turned off the engine and unbuckled his seat belt. "What?''

Jason pointed to the white Cadillac two spaces over. "That's Grandma and Grandpa's car."

Ethan removed the blanket he'd put over the boy and unfastened his seat belt; Jason was wrapped too tightly in the other blanket to do it himself. "When your mom came to the office tonight, she left a friend at your house in case you came home. Your grandparents probably got there, heard you'd run away and came down to the office because they were worried about you."

Jason shook his head adamantly. "But don't you see? Now they're really gonna think Mom's bad!"

"We'll explain everything," Ethan promised. He reached for his door handle and found his neck caught in Jason's death grip.

"Let me stay with you," the boy pleaded. "Just till Grandma and Grandpa are gone. You can tell them you had to arrest me, even though it isn't true. And I'll wash your car and sweep out the jail. I can paint, too. I helped my mom paint the bathroom. Please?"

Ethan held the boy close and let him absorb the comfort he seemed to need so desperately. But he had to be honest. "Jase, if I had a way to help you, I would. But your mom's been worried to death about you, and we can't keep you away from her any longer. Now let's go in there and explain what happened."

Jason groaned and clung to his neck.

Ethan backed out of the car, holding the boy to him, and ran the few short steps to the door. Once inside the vestibule, he grinned at the still-clinging Jason and said, "You can stand now." But the boy only wrapped his arms and legs around him even more tightly.

Loud voices from the office filtered back to them.

"Yes. Well." The two simple words were spoken perfunctorily and in a high disdainful voice. "You can make all the claims to good motherhood you want, but the fact remains your eight-year-old son has been missing for hours in a raging storm and the police had to be called out to find him."

"That's Grandma," Jason whispered.

"We're the sheriff's office, ma'am," Ebbie said in the no-nonsense tone she used on drunks and attorneys, "not the police. Search and Rescue is a county function. Though we do have a very small police force and we often back them up."

"Moving here was irresponsible, Bethany," a man's pompous voice accused. "You should never have taken Jason from Seattle."

"Grandpa," Jason whispered to Ethan.

"Steve always said you had no sense of what's important in life," the man went on. "You snatch a child away from all that's familiar less than a year after his father's death and drag him to this godforsaken place. You make him live in a hovel where he can't even play outside for fear of falling in the river!"

"The sheriff found Jason," Ethan heard the beleaguered Bethany reply mildly. "I'm sure it was frightening for you to arrive to such confusion, but he let me talk to Jason and he sounded fine. They'll be back anytime now."

Ethan waited for her to tell them that they were the reason Jason had run away. But she didn't.

He felt a sense of outrage he couldn't have explained, except that in the dark stormy night he'd made a connection with that voice on his radio and knew with a certainty born of long experience that she hadn't been careless about the boy he now held in his arms.

And he felt guilty about trying to minimize the boy's fears about his grandparents. They did indeed sound like people to be feared.

Jason clung to his neck. "Can't you tell them you lost me again?"

Ethan smiled grimly, then settled Jason on his hip and pushed his way through the door into the office.

A young woman ran at him instantly, a blur of red coat and dark hair pulled back in a disheveled ponytail. For a moment, he had a second pair of arms around him, crying and clinging.

"Jason! Oh, Jase." The woman buried her face in the boy's hair, then looked up at Ethan, her head just topping his shoulder. Her eyes were enormous in a face that was pale with worry. "Is he okay? Is he hurt?"

"Just a little scared," Ethan replied, having to think about words with those blue eyes so like her son's, on him. "He had a warm coat and the good sense to take shelter in a tree."

Jason looped an arm around her, but his other arm remained securely fastened to Ethan's neck. "Yeah, Mom," he said, "I'm okay."

"Sheriff, thank you!" A portly balding man in glasses and a raincoat came forward to clap Ethan on the shoulder. "I can't tell you how grateful we are. Jason. Come see your gramps."

The man tried to pull Jason out of Ethan's arms, but the boy held on to Ethan with one arm while retaining his hold on his mother with the other. "Hi, Grandpa," he said.

Jason turned his gaze to Ethan and looked him in the eye. Ethan recognized it as a man-to-man communication. He and the boy had shared a lot tonight, and something in Jason's eyes told him he was going to test their developing friendship.

A tall full-figured woman in a silky lavender raincoat came near, her features hard—until she put a hand on the boy's back. Then the contours of her face softened.

"Jason," she said in a gentle, yet wheedling tone, "why did you run away? You can tell Grandma. Are you tired of living in that awful cannery place?"

Jason stiffened. "No. I ran away because I thought you and Grandpa were gonna try to take me away from Mom, but Ethan says you can't."

The older woman looked momentarily horrified. Then the horror dissolved into confusion followed immediately by suspicion. "Oh, really?" she asked. "And who is Ethan?"

Jason pointed in the vicinity of Ethan's nose. "This is Ethan. The sheriff."

The woman assessed Ethan haughtily. "I have rights as a grandmother," she said, then redirected her gaze to Jason. "And it's not that I want to take you away. It's that I want to make sure you're well taken care of."

"I am," Jason insisted. He looked at Ethan, and Ethan couldn't fail to notice the strange plea in his eyes. Then the boy said, "And now that Ethan and Mom are getting married, I'll have a dad to take care of me, too. So now there's no problem, right?"

For the tick of ten seconds there was absolute silence. Through his own shock, Ethan felt the woman in his arm clutch at the back of his jacket.

So that's what Jason's man-to-man look had meant—*Watch it, buddy. I'm about to shaft you.*

"He has a neat house on the hill where you can see the cannery," Jason went on, undeterred. "We live there now."

While Ethan tried to decide how best to cope with the situation without denying Jason's claim and humiliating him in front of his pompous grandparents, Bethany Richards looked up at him, her eyes stunned.

The press of bodies around Jason had forced her right into Ethan's arms. Jason's grandfather took a step back and looked at them in shock. The grandmother made a strangled sound.

"So you don't have to worry anymore," Jason said, adding to his little fiction. "We have a dad now and a great house."

Jason's mother looked from man to boy, and Ethan saw understanding dawn in her eyes. She knew what her son was doing. The eyes she fixed on Ethan were suddenly sad and apologetic.

At last she turned to her in-laws, apparently prepared to refute Jason's claim, but Ethan interrupted her to introduce himself.

"Ethan Drum," he said, offering his hand to the older man. "How are you, Mr. Richards? I'm sorry it's been such a harrowing night for you."

He had no idea what in the hell he was doing. He was an agent of the law, for God's sake! He couldn't make up stories to deceive people. But he also couldn't shatter Jason's story or let this woman admit to her bullying in-laws that her son had lied.

Jason's mother was staring at him. He evaded her by tipping the brim of his hat at the grandmother.

"Mrs. Richards. Did my assistant, Ebbie, give you some coffee?"

"I don't believe it!" the woman said, drawing herself up like some kind of dangerous blowfish. "I don't believe it for a minute!" She turned accusing eyes on her daughter-in-law. "You never said a thing about seeing anyone. You never even *hinted* you were getting married. This is just a trick to try to stop us from getting custody of Jason."

Before Bethany Richards could speak, Ebbie got to her feet from the other side of the counter. "Oh, it's true, Mrs. Richards," she said with a smiling glance at Ethan and Beth. "In fact, the wedding's taking place at my house."

Joanne Richards's expression tightened.

"Next Saturday," Ebbie added.

"I don't believe it," the woman repeated.

Beth Richards stared at Ebbie as though she'd lost her mind. Then she turned to her mother-in-law. "Jo—" she began.

"Guess you'll have to come and see for yourself, won't you?" Ebbie interrupted.

Ethan hadn't a clue what his staff assistant was doing, either. He only knew she was everyone's self-appointed mother, and she must have taken a real liking to Bethany Richards.

Jason's grandmother turned to her husband, who shrugged helplessly. Then she spun toward Ethan, who still had Jason on his hip and Bethany in his arm, and said adamantly, "No. You're all lying. And just to prove it, Zachary and I will stay and attend...the wedding." She spoke the last two words with scornful disbelief.

"Great." Ethan decided, now that he'd been drawn

into Jason's scheme, the only way to play it out was with all sincerity in the hope that the Richardses finally believed them and—God willing—remembered some previous appointment that conflicted with the wedding day. "Meanwhile," he said, "you'll want to come to Jason's birthday party tomorrow. We're having it at Dinosaur Pizza."

Jason's eyes ignited with pleasure and he tightened his grip on Ethan. "All the kids have their parties there!" he said.

Bethany Richards frowned at her son. But before she could speak, Jason grinned convincingly. "At three-thirty," he said. "Right after school."

Bethany gasped.

Ebbie smiled at the grandparents. "I'll add two more to the reservations."

Joanne Richards studied the staff assistant closely, obviously suspecting collusion. But Ebbie met her eyes with that same friendly smile. The other woman finally turned away.

"We'll be there," she said. Then she turned her attention to her grandson. "Jason, are you sure you're all right? Where are your shoes?"

"They were muddy and wet and Ethan pulled 'em off me." He strangled Ethan with a hug. "'Cause he's gonna be my dad."

Ethan was treated to that disbelieving stare again, then the woman began to button her coat. "Dads don't usually lose track of their children."

"I sneaked away," Jason said quickly. "It wasn't his fault. He's prob'ly gonna spank me. Aren't ya?"

Ethan tried to back him up. "No. I don't spank. But I do yell and take away privileges."

Jason looked pleased and relieved. "That's what

Mom does. Only she doesn't yell. She talks like a
queen.''

Ethan couldn't quite interpret that. ''Like a
queen?''

Jason lifted his chin and assumed an expression of
royal displeasure. '''Jason Peter Richards,''' he said
in a deeper adult tone, '''I've warned you about that
before. This time I have to take action.''' He relaxed
and assumed his own voice again. ''And then I can't
watch TV or go out and play.''

Joanne Richards put her purse over her arm and
pulled up the collar of her coat. ''I'm happy you've
agreed on parenting techniques,'' she said with a disdainful lift of an eyebrow, ''but I think they'll have
to improve considerably before we're convinced
they're good enough for our grandson. We'll see you
at your party, Jason.''

''We're gonna have a cake from the bakery!'' Jason called after them, thespian skills at full throttle.

Ebbie exchanged a grinning glance with Ethan.

At the door Zachary turned to add, ''We're staying
at the Coast Motel if you need us, Jason.'' Then he
slammed the door behind him.

Beth took her first full breath in hours. She ex-
tracted Jason from the sheriff's arms and let him slide
through her hands to his feet. The blanket puddled on
the floor.

She pulled it up over the boy again and gave him
a little shake. ''Jason Richards, what do you think
you're doing?'' she demanded. ''You've been lying
like Pinocchio since you came through that door!''

The anguish of this interminable night was still
very clear in her mind, and added to this incredible
little drama her son had just performed—with the help

of the sheriff and Ebbie—she felt as though she'd lost complete control of her life.

"Grandpa won't take me away," Jason replied simply, somewhat subdued in the face of her displeasure, "if he thinks I have the sheriff for a dad."

She pulled her son close for a moment, in sympathy with his fears of being taken away. Over his head, she met the eyes of the wet and muddy sheriff, who was the lead in Jason's drama. He seemed to be studying her.

He was a big man, with a good solid look about him. And he'd rescued Jason—possibly even saved his life. She understood his appeal for her son, because at the moment she'd like nothing better than to run into a pair of arms like his and let him deal with her in-laws and all her other troubles, too. But unlike her son, she was a grown-up and understood that real life had to be dealt with in a real way.

She held Jason at arm's length and looked into his eyes. "Jase, I understand why you ran away, because I would rather die than be separated from you." She swallowed hard, as emotion and the strain she'd been under threatened her composure. "But I promise you that isn't going to happen. Your grandparents are just making threats. But we can't involve the sheriff in a lie to make those threats go away."

Jason shrugged. The blanket slipped and he caught it and pulled it tightly around himself again. "Why can't we just make believe he's gonna be my dad until Grandma and Grandpa go home?" He turned to look up at the sheriff. "Why can't we?"

Beth caught the boy's chin in her hand and turned him back to face her. "Jason, because of what you told Grandma and Grandpa, they're not going home until *after* the wedding." She shook her head. "But there's not going to be a wedding. So they'll know you lied and then they'll really think I'm a terrible mother."

Jason smiled cautiously. "Then let's have a wedding."

"My house is too small," Ebbie said, "but my garden is available."

Ethan frowned at her. "It's February."

"So I'll borrow the Ladies of Law Enforcement's tent. We use it at the Winter Festival and everyone stays dry."

Beth turned condemning eyes on the sheriff's staff assistant. "And you, Ebbie, *what* were you thinking?"

The woman smiled, obviously unaware she'd probably just blown a hole right in the middle of Beth's life. "That you needed a little help against a pair of bullies, however well-meaning they are."

"But you told them I was getting married." Beth was trying to sound reasonable. Difficult when you were on the verge of panic. "What do you think they'll do when I *don't* get married? They'll tell one of Zachary's judge friends that I'm delusional and a liar, and they'll get custody of my son!"

Ebbie folded her arms, looking concerned at last. She unfolded them, frowned at the sheriff and sighed penitently at Beth. "I'm afraid I didn't think that far ahead. In the time I've spent with you, I got to sympathize with you and wanted to help."

Beth reminded herself that this woman had come back into the office after a full day's work to man the radio and keep in touch with the sheriff while he searched for her son. Anger seemed out of place.

She moved to the counter and put a hand on Ebbie's. "Thank you. I know you meant to help."

Ebbie placed her other hand atop Beth's and patted it. "Don't worry. The sheriff's always got a solution. When the county cut our budget, he found a way to keep me on. When the van died and we didn't have money to replace it, he bought one at an auction and got his brother to overhaul it. He shut down the drug house near the middle school when the police department claimed they didn't have enough manpower to do it. We only had four people in the department at the time."

Those accomplishments enumerated, she looked up at the sheriff expectantly. "So, how about it, boss? How do we get Beth and Jason out of this mess?"

Beth turned to him, too, hoping against hope that Ebbie was right and he would have a solution. He looked capable of it. He pulled off his muddy jacket to reveal a muscular chest and broad shoulders. But in his dark eyes and the thoughtful lines of his mouth were a wit and intelligence that said he wasn't just another set of pretty pecs.

He tossed the jacket at a chair, removed his hat and flung it atop the jacket. His dark hair was a little too long and curled just above his ears and at his neck. It was still wet from his hours outdoors.

Beth watched him run a hand through it and was surprised to find herself wondering if it was as coarse and thick to the touch as it looked.

She pushed the thought away, equilibrium held on to by a thread. She focused her attention on the sheriff's face as he smiled. Thank God! He had a solution.

"I guess," he said, "we have a wedding."

CHAPTER THREE

JASON THRUST a fist in the air. *"Yes!"*

Beth's heart began to thump wildly, not with joy and excitement, but thanks to a surge of adrenaline brought on by her body's "fight or flight" reaction.

An index finger raised in protest, she began, "Ah—"

"You come with me." The sheriff caught Jason by one arm, then pushed open the gate in the counter with the toe of his boot and urged him through. "You, too," he said to Beth. "We have to get this guy into some dry clothes and then we have to talk." He glanced at Ebbie. "You can go home, Eb," he said firmly.

"But I want to know what's happening," she said, then added righteously, "After all, I'm hosting the wedding."

When his response was a darkening of his expression, she reached for her purse. "Fine. I'm out of here. But don't worry about the cake for the party tomorrow. I'll pick it up."

The sheriff's inner office was a small beige room furnished with a plain oak desk littered with paperwork, four gray metal file drawers and two old ladderback chairs. A venetian blind covered the room's only window, and there were certificates, maps and a wildlife calendar on the wall.

The sheriff pointed Beth and Jason to the chairs and opened one of two doors. A small closet was revealed.

Beth sat, but Jason stayed glued to the man's side and peered into the closet with him. She watched the sheriff pull a brown sweatshirt off a shelf and turn, prepared to walk toward the chairs with it, only to find himself nearly tripping over the boy.

With a look of amused exasperation, he pushed the blanket off Jason's shoulders and dropped to one knee to pull the sweatshirt on him. Its hem fell almost to the boy's knees. Then he cuffed the sleeves back until they were inches thick around her son's small wrists.

She felt an almost physical pain at the sight of them together. Jason glowing with the attention and a full-blown case of hero worship, and the sheriff a seemingly perfect male specimen who obviously re-lated to children, this one particularly.

The sheriff rose to his feet, reached into the closet again, snatched another pile of fleece and turned, only to find once again the boy standing squarely in front of him.

"You know, you're like a wart on my knee," he said to Jason with a grin, handing him what turned out to be a pair of sweatpants. He pointed to the door beside the closet. "Bathroom. Put those on, tie them as tight as you can around your waist—see the string?—and roll up the cuffs."

"Cool," Jason said. "These yours?"

"Yes. I get muddy a lot in the line of duty. I usu-ally have a change of clothes here."

Jason walked into the bathroom, carrying the brown sweatpants as if they were royal robes.

The minute the door closed behind her son, Beth

got to her feet and confronted the sheriff. "I appreciate your willingness to help me and Jason," she said to his back as he reached into the closet for another sweatshirt. "But there's no way out of this mess." She moved a little closer, afraid he hadn't heard her. "The only thing I can do at this point is explain to my in-laws why Jason told such a tale and pray they'll understand."

He turned suddenly in the doorway of the closet and had to catch himself from tripping over her, just as he'd done with Jason. For one protracted moment her nose was a fraction of an inch from his second shirt button.

She could smell the outdoors on him, the rain in his hair. She could feel the warmth emanating from his big body.

She took two quick steps back and said flatly, succinctly, "It'll never work, so thank you for all you've done, but I'll just take Jason home and get on wi—"

"How?" he asked. He walked past her, the sweatshirt thrown over his shoulder as he unbuttoned his flannel shirt.

"How what?" she asked, a little impatient with him because this evening had been all too frightening and then weird, and he didn't seem to notice.

"How will you take Jason home?" The shirt unbuttoned, he pulled it off, revealing a rock-hard torso tightly clothed in simple white cotton.

Beth saw the jut of his chest and the concavity of his stomach, which disappeared under his belt. "My friend…at the cannery. She'll come and get us."

He pulled the sweatshirt over his head and yanked it into place. "You go home to the cannery," he warned, "and you'll make a liar out of Jason in front of his grandparents."

"Well, he *did* lie." She walked around the office, arms folded. "That's the problem here. And anyway, they've gone back to the motel. In the morning I'll—"

"No, they haven't," he said. He threw the flannel shirt at the bottom of the closet. "I just saw the white Caddy turn into the trees across the road. They've doused the headlights."

Beth frowned. "What do you mean?"

He caught her wrist as she started toward the window. "I saw the car through the blinds when we walked in here. I imagine they decided that a little simple spying might tell them something and get specific evidence on you, so they thought they'd hang around and watch us leave. *Don't* turn around. Relax."

It was just a touch, a hand on her wrist, but it claimed control of the situation.

It wasn't that she wanted to give over control of her life for any length of time, but it would be delicious to let someone else be in charge for a little while. After an absolutely hideous year, she'd been trying against overwhelming odds to rebuild her life in a simpler, cleaner pattern. Then her in-laws had intruded, casting a pall over her newfound happiness and, worse, stealing Jason's comfort in his new surroundings.

Now there seemed to be more wrong with her life than she could ever fix.

"If you can see them," she said, the emotional knot inside her tightening, "they can see us."

He drew her toward his desk and sat on a corner

of it, retaining his grip on her wrist. "That's my point. Your taking comfort in the arms of a loving fiancé will only lend believability to Jason's story. And you look as though you're going to dissolve into a puddle any minute."

"I don't need comfort," she denied as he drew her closer. Everything in her was trembling now.

"What *do* you need?" he asked quietly. He was watching her with gentle dark eyes that moved over her face feature by feature. There was no judgment in them, no demand, no criticism. It seemed forever since she'd looked into a man's eyes and found simple interest there.

Her composure unraveled. She had no idea why this man should even ask the question, much less care about the answer. "Why does it matter to you?" she asked. Instinct told her to pull away from him, the warm serenity he represented had never been her destiny. All her life she'd moved from one demanding, unsatisfying situation to another. A tempting taste of comfort and security would only remind her of what life *could* be like, but wasn't.

As though sensing her need to pull away, he put his free hand to the middle of her back and used it to draw her between his knees. "This is my county," he replied. "Everyone in it matters. You can cry if you want to. I think that's what you need."

She sniffed resolutely. "Thank you, but I'm fine. Maybe you could just…walk over and close the blinds."

He ignored her suggestion. "My daughter was lost once for a couple of hours," he said, rubbing gently between her shoulder blades. "When she was finally found and my wife and I took her home and put her to bed, we cried for hours. The fear of what could have been just sits in your gut if you don't.''

Yes, Beth thought. She could feel it there, hot and heavy, with barbed edges that continued to hurt even though the danger was over.

Ethan had never seen a woman—or a man, for that matter—under such tight control yet with an urgent need for release in her eyes. And he guessed it had to do with more than just this night.

The rigidity in her back had to be tension of very long standing. His father had been gone a lot, Jason had told him, and then he'd died.

Had she gotten what she needed from her husband? he wondered. If she had, he knew from personal experience that the death of a spouse was like a fresh wound every day for years.

If she hadn't, that was a different kind of tragedy. Either way, he couldn't imagine having to cope with grief and then having to deal with the threat of someone trying to take your child away.

"Jason's safe now," he said. Her fists were clenched between her breasts and she'd closed her eyes. There was a frown line between her eyebrows that seemed to deepen as he rubbed gently up and down her spine. "And we can deal with the issue of his grandparents."

"How?" she whispered.

"I don't know. We can talk that over, explore the options. But if you're going to stand up to it, you have to do two things."

"What?"

"You have to let this tension go and let yourself be human." She opened her eyes to look at him, the anguish there so great he swore he could see sparks.

"And you have to trust someone to help you. It looks like I'm it."

He felt something snap in her. She lifted a hand to cover her eyes, and below it her mouth contorted on a sob. "All I want," she said in a high desperate voice, "is to be left alone to make a life with Jason. That's all! Is that so much to ask? Is it?"

He knew he didn't have to answer. He simply pulled her the rest of the way into his arms. She wrapped hers around his neck with a strength that might have surprised him if he hadn't seen the intensity in her eyes close up.

She clung to him and sobbed and he held on, sure the Richardses were watching. The way they operated, he'd probably be brought up on charges of sexual harassment if they weren't convinced that he and this woman had a relationship.

He couldn't believe the bizarre turn the missing-child call had taken tonight. He'd been able to relate to Jason and hadn't wanted to make a liar of him when he'd made those outrageous claims in front of his grandparents. And then he'd looked into Beth Richards's blue eyes and known he had to help. He wasn't sure why, except that he cared about everyone in his jurisdiction, and she'd touched the same chord in him Jason had. What could he say? He was the paternal type. That was what had led him to law enforcement in the first place. It hadn't been the excitement of high-speed chases or pistol-drawn stand-offs. It had been the simple desire to keep safe the people and the place where he'd grown up.

But when Beth Richards drew back from his shoulder and shifted her weight, her hip brushing the inside

of his thigh, he experienced a reaction that was decidedly not paternal.

He absorbed the startling impact of it for an instant,
then cleared his expression when she sniffed and
looked into his eyes. Her own were like a turbulent
sea, her eyelashes wet and spiky against her pale skin.

"Are they still there?" she asked.

"Who?"

She frowned at him. "My in-laws. Are they still
watching?"

He pulled himself together. "Ah...yeah, I think so.
The car hasn't moved."

"So what do we do now?"

"I guess," Ethan answered, thinking it was going
to be interesting explaining this to Nikkie, "we go
home."

The bathroom door burst open and Jason came out,
his muddy jeans over his arm and more of the sweat-
pant legs rolled up than not. In spite of his ordeal, he
looked pink-cheeked and clear-eyed.

Until he noticed that his mother had been crying.
He crossed to her. "What's the matter, Mom?"

She took him in her arms and held him, resting her
cheek on top of his still-damp curly hair. "Nothing,"
she replied, putting her concerns aside to reassure
him. "I'm just very glad you're all right."

"I'm sorry I scared you." He gripped her tightly
around the waist. "I was just gonna hide out till
Grandma and Grandpa were gone, but then it got rain-
ing so hard." He leaned away from her to smile at
Ethan. "I was really glad when you came to find me.
Are you gonna take us home with you?"

Ethan suspected the little devil's penitence
stretched only so far. Jason was getting what he

wanted, at least temporarily, and he was unashamedly pleased about that. Well, hell. What lonely little kid didn't deserve to pretend he had a father who cared about him?

And what lonely frightened woman didn't deserve a buffer between herself and the bullies in her world?

"Yes, I am," Ethan said, getting to his feet. "Then tomorrow, while you're in school, your mom and I are going to decide what to do about all the fibs you've told." Ethan gave him back the blanket he'd been wrapped in earlier. "Put that around you. We'll get your jacket washed tomorrow."

Jason did as he was told, then said, "Ebbie fibbed, too."

Ethan took a clean jacket out of his closet for himself. "I know. And I didn't bother to correct either one of you. I'm not saying it's all your fault. I'm just saying it's going to take some doing to straighten it out."

"Why do we have to?" Jason asked, watching Ethan as he put on his hat.

"Because they're lies, Jason," Beth said.

"But the sheriff doesn't have a wife," the boy said reasonably. "And you don't have a husband. Why don't we just have a wedding? He's got that house on the hill with the cup thing. Grandma would like that."

Beth looked at Ethan in surprise. "The cupola? That's your house?"

She smiled. He'd seen enormous relief and gratitude on her face when he'd walked into the office with Jason. But he hadn't seen pleasure there before. "That's a wonderful house," she said. "Jason and I used to imagine who lived there. We thought maybe the mayor.''

"Nope." Ethan caught her arm and drew her with him to the front office. Jason followed. "Just the sheriff. You want to call your friend and tell her where you'll be? You might want to invite her to Jason's birthday party so we can get some bodies in the pizza place to make our story look good.''

She made a wry face but finally seemed resigned to going home with him. "This is all so unreal," she said, dialing the number while Ethan put a clean pair of big tube socks on Jason's feet.

Her friend Kelly did not understand the simple explanation Beth gave.

"What do you mean, you're going home with the sheriff?" she asked. "You mean he's…holding you or something? Your in-laws have filed charges?''

"No," Beth said. "Jason sort of told them that…that we're…"

"Yeah?''

"Getting married," she said in a rush, watching the sheriff cuff the long socks on her son's ankles.

"Who?" Kelly demanded.

Beth turned away and lowered her voice. "Me," she replied, "and the sheriff. Jase told my in-laws we were getting married, and they didn't believe him. They think he did it just to make them leave me alone—which he did—so they're hanging around outside waiting for me to go home.''

There was silence on the other end of the line. "So you're really going home…with the sheriff?''

"Yes.''

"I see." There was a note of interested speculation in Kelly's voice.

"No, you don't," Beth said. "It's just a stopgap measure until we can talk it over and figure out what to do."

Kelly cleared her throat. "It's odd that telling the truth hasn't occurred to anybody."

That was true. And it was something Beth didn't care to give much thought to because, in retrospect, she realized she should have firmly denied her son's claims at the time.

But Jason had seemed so thrilled with his solution to the problem of his grandparents, and frankly, she'd rather enjoyed their shocked surprise. Throughout her married life they'd cajoled and coerced Steve into doing what they wanted rather than what *she* wanted, and since she'd moved here they'd bedeviled her with their threats of taking Jason away.

It had been thrilling to see them outsmarted, if only for the moment.

She sighed. "I'm sure it'll have to come to that, probably tomorrow at Jason's birthday party. Oh. You have to come. Okay? Dinosaur Pizza at three-thirty."

"Ah…sure. But I didn't know you were planning a party."

"I wasn't. It was all rather impromptu. Kelly, listen." Beth wished she had her friend in front of her to give her a hug. In the blackness of her despair when she'd realized Jason was gone, she'd had no one to turn to but Kelly, who'd hurried to help. "Thank you so much for coming over and for staying so late. I owe you big. Go into the gallery on your way out and take that welcome sign you've been admiring."

"No, I—"

"Kelly, please. Take it." Beth glanced over her

shoulder and saw the sheriff sitting in a chair by the back-vestibule door, her son in his lap. "I've got to go. See you tomorrow for pizza?"

"I'll be there. Beth?"

"Yeah?"

"You know…be careful. The sheriff's a hunk and all, but this is all kind of…sticky."

"I know. Don't worry."

The ride to the sheriff's house took less than ten minutes. Ethan checked the rearview mirror and grinned without looking away from the road. "Guess what?"

Beth played the game. "We're being followed by a white Cadillac?"

"Yep. And they're coming with us up the hill."

The neighborhood was old and comprised of beautiful turn-of-the-century homes. The old sidewalks were broken by the roots of oaks and cedar trees that had probably been there when the town was settled 150 years before.

It was now almost midnight, most porch lights were off, and only the occasional light glowed in an upstairs window. Ethan's house was dark as he pulled up in front of it. He checked the rearview mirror again.

"Are they still with us?" Beth asked.

"They're maybe two hundred feet back. Just turned off their lights."

Beth held the car door open while Ethan pulled Jason out of the vehicle and into his arms. "I hope we don't wake your daughter," she said. "You must worry about her when you have to leave her alone at night."

When he looked surprised that she knew about his

daughter and that the girl was alone, she explained. "Ebbie told me that your wife died and you live alone with your fourteen-year-old daughter."

He shook his head. "It's a good thing Ebbie works for me and not the CIA," he said. "National security would be a thing of the past."

"It was a long wait," she said in Ebbie's defense. "We exchanged confidences."

"To her that's like oxygen. No wonder she offered her garden for our wedding. Follow me."

Beth trailed Ethan up the porch steps and waited while he held Jason with one arm and fitted his key in the lock with his free hand. "My brother lives next door," he said, indicating a large Craftsman-style house on the neighboring lot. "He watches out for her."

The door open, Ethan set the boy on his feet just inside and flipped on a light.

Beth saw a short-haired calico cat race down the stairway to the right, then stop abruptly at the sight of strangers, big green eyes peering at them through the balusters.

Ethan went to the stairway and reached a long arm up to scratch the cat between the ears. "This is Cindy Crawford," he said with a light laugh.

Beth noticed the small black spot above the cat's mouth. It did indeed look like a glamorous mole.

Jason went forward to get acquainted, but Cindy meowed once and darted upstairs.

"My daughter's a cat lover." Ethan led the way up and beckoned them to follow. "She also has a big gray Persian named Simba, but he's usually too lazy to investigate visitors after he's gone to bed. Cindy, on the other hand, has to know everything."

Beth noticed the subtle green-and-yellow-flowered wallpaper and dark woodwork as she and Jason followed Ethan. They proceeded down a corridor softly lit by a night-light in a bathroom, and Ethan paused to look behind a partially open door. His daughter's room, Beth guessed.

Apparently satisfied that all was well, he continued to the end of the hallway where he pushed open a door and reached inside to flip on a light. He ushered Beth and Jason inside.

The room was fairly large, despite a sloping wall under the eaves. The walls were white, the curtains blue-and-white gingham, and a pair of maple bunk beds had red-white-and-blue bandana-print coverlets.

Jason launched himself gleefully at the ladder. "I get the top one!" he declared.

Beth shushed him, aware of the sleeping girl down the hall and the major inconvenience their presence in the house had to be to the sheriff.

"It's not ideal," Ethan said, indicating the bunks, "but it should do for tonight. I'll get you some pajamas. You saw the bathroom?"

"Yes, thanks."

Ethan disappeared and Beth looked around, experiencing a strange sense of distance from the situation. She felt as though she was watching her son move around on a stage as he shed his blanket and crawled, still wearing the oversize brown sweats, under the blankets of the top bunk.

"Isn't this cool?" he demanded in an exaggerated whisper. "Bunk beds!"

Beth looked at the narrow bottom bunk and decided that even a king-size water bed could not have been more inviting at the moment. She was exhausted.

"Every woman's dream," she said, pulling off her jacket. She opened a door under the eave and found a garment rod, several empty hangers dangling from it. She hung up her jacket, feeling as though she was establishing at least a modicum of order to the chaotic jumble her life had become.

She picked up the blanket Jason had draped over the ladder and folded it at the foot of the top bunk. She turned to find Ethan standing behind her, a pair of gray pajamas in his hand.

"Nikkie could probably lend you something more suitable," he said, "but I hate to wake her."

"Of course." Beth took them from him. "These'll be fine."

"There's a fourth bedroom, but at the moment there's no bedding in it and not much furniture."

"The bunk will be fine. Thank you, Sheriff. I—"

"If you call me Sheriff in front of your in-laws," he interrupted, "it's not going to help sell our story."

"Right." She held the pajamas to her, feeling suddenly as though she needed a shield. Ethan looked comfortable and relaxed in his home environment, and she felt as though she'd landed on an alien planet. Not an unfriendly one certainly, but far removed from where she'd thought she'd be spending the night when she'd awakened that morning.

She felt compelled to chatter. "Of course. Ethan, thank you for spending hours in the cold and rain looking for Jason. And thank you for trying to help him with his grandparents. I know you've put yourself out on a limb and probably turned your household upside down. I'm very sorry we got you into all this."

"I'm not," Jason said, chin resting on his folded arms on his pillow. "This is gonna be fun!"

Beth turned to her son in complete exasperation. "Jason—"

Ethan chuckled. "He's not going to see it your way, so don't even try. Just sleep well and we'll sort it all out in the morning."

She couldn't imagine how they could sort it all out without either admitting the truth to Zachary and Joanne or staging a wedding. But she was too tired to think about that now.

"All right. In the morning."

Ethan turned to Jason. "You have everything you need?"

"Yeah." Jason reached out and caught Ethan around the neck. "Thanks. Are Grandma and Grandpa still watching from outside?"

Ethan shook his head. "I checked out my bedroom window when I got the pajamas. They're gone."

Jason freed Ethan and grinned broadly. "So they're probably thinkin' right now that everything's going to be okay with Mom and me."

Ethan imagined they were thinking they were going to hang around and see how this all played out on the supposed wedding day. But Beth didn't look as though she could deal with that right now, so he said nothing.

"Do you think I could have Buzz Lightyear on my birthday cake?" Jason asked. He fell back against his pillow. Ethan stepped forward to pull up his blankets and tuck him in.

"Sure. Who's he?"

"A space hero in *Toy Story*," Beth explained.

When Ethan still looked puzzled, she added, "The Disney movie."

Ethan nodded. "We'll see what we can do. I'll call Ebbie in the morning."

Jason kicked his feet under the covers as though his delight with the prospect of his birthday party couldn't be contained. "Thanks. This is gonna be so cool!"

Ethan turned away from the bunk to find Beth standing behind him, the pajamas still clutched to her chest. She looked uncomfortable.

"I'll pay for the party," she said.

He took her by the arm and pulled her with him to the doorway. "Good night, Jase," he called, flipping off the light.

"Night, Ethan," Jason called back.

Ethan drew Beth into the hallway and said quietly, "We'll work that all out later, all right? Why don't you just change into the pajamas and try to get some sleep."

"But I don't want you to—"

"I do pretty much as I please," he said mildly, pointing to the bathroom. "You're welcome to shower if you want to, take a bath, whatever. Just try to relax and don't sweat the details."

"Life, Ethan," she said, a little prudishly, he thought, "is all about details."

He folded his arms and shook his head. "No, I don't buy that. Life is about the big picture and not getting all hung up on the details. And right now the big picture is seeing that Jason has a great birthday."

She folded her arms, too, over the pajamas. "I agree, but I just want to make it clear that I'm the only family Jason has. Therefore I will pay for the party.''

''I'm afraid I don't buy that, either.'' He watched her sigh and firm her jaw, as though intending to resist whatever he was about to say. He found something challenging, even stimulating, about that. ''Jason and I developed a friendship tonight. I know from what he told me about you that you've done your best this past year to be everything to him. But he's coming to a point in his life where he needs more than you can give him. Maybe you're going to have to share him a little. So let's not worry about who pays for the party.''

Her eyes widened in the shadowy hallway. ''Did he say he's unhappy? I mean, besides the worry about his grandfather?''

''No,'' Ethan assured her quickly. ''He seems to understand and accept his situation. And he was proud to tell me about the cannery and all you intend to do with it. But he said he missed his father. In fact, he said he used to miss him even *before* he died.''

Beth heard those words and felt the impact of them right in the middle of her chest. So much of her grief over Steve's death was because they'd had so little of him the last few years he was alive.

''His father loved Jason very much,'' Beth said gravely. ''But he failed him.''

Ethan spread both hands in an expansive gesture. ''So let's indulge the kid a little. Let him have his fantasy for a while. We'll do his party up big and between us, try to convince the grandparents we're making a cozy home for him.''

''That sounds reasonable,'' she said on a sigh, ''but if you carry that plan to the conclusion my in-laws

will demand, you may very well find yourself married
to me.''

He leaned a shoulder against the wall and grinned.
''Are you suggesting I might find that unpleasant?''

Beth did her level best to quell the spark of excitement those words generated in her. For the last five
or six years of her marriage, she'd wondered what it
would be like to live intimately with someone who
was aware she was there.

And she had the feeling the sheriff was always
sharply conscious of who was around him and what
went on.

''I'm an artist,'' she said, thinking she could erase
that grin from his face, ''and not very domestic. I'm
a marginal cook and I often forget things like laundry
and shopping.'' She let her eyes run lazily over the
attractive length of his body. ''I imagine a man like
you pictures the perfect wife as a cross between Mar-
tha Stewart and a Playboy bunny.''

He laughed softly. ''I had a perfect wife,'' he said,
''and she was nothing like that. She often forgot to
do laundry, too, though she was a lawyer and not an
artist. She was loving and funny and forgiving.'' He
sighed, his voice taking on a moody quality. ''And I
had her for only twelve years—she died five years
ago. I miss her often, but it's never her domestic skills
I think of, only the warmth and laughter she brought
to my life.''

Beth felt small for having tried to force him to a
distance by suggesting he was in any way typical.

''I'm sorry,'' she said. ''I guess it's because I
haven't been appreciated as anything but a business
prop for a very long time. It sounds as though you
had a wonderful marriage.''

"I did. I'm sorry you didn't."

She shrugged, having long ago accepted that domestic bliss would never be hers. "It was good in the beginning, I learned to live with what it became, and now it's over. Art and marriage aren't compatible, anyway."

Now he shrugged. "A lot of people think law enforcement and marriage are incompatible because the job comes first." He grinned again. "So that makes cops and artists compatible, doesn't it?"

She blinked. "I believe that's a flawed equation," she said. "I think it means neither of us should get into a relationship. Anyway—" she squared her shoulders and cleared her throat "—thank you again for finding my son. And for being his friend. I...I do appreciate your concern for him. I just don't think it has to extend to me and my problems with my in-laws." She smiled at him hesitantly. "So, good night. We'll organize the party and the...the problem in the morning. Okay?"

It was a moment before he nodded. She got the distinct impression he was simply humoring her. "Okay," he said. "Sleep well."

"Thank you. You, too."

She stepped into the bathroom. She'd change into the pajamas and shower in the morning. As she closed the door and stood in the dark, her heartbeat skipped erratically. She attempted to analyze her feelings and finally concluded that they didn't appear to be caused by worry or fear.

Her racing pulse was caused by excitement. She groaned, knowing that suggested big trouble.

CHAPTER FOUR

BETH TURNED OFF the shower and stood for a moment in the warm steamy space, pulling her arguments together. After a good night's sleep and in the sunny sanity-restoring light of day, she felt in control again.

Her in-laws were forceful and demanding and single-minded, but she was sure she could make them see reason if she was calm and logical. That was certainly a more acceptable solution to her problems than marrying the sheriff.

She reached beyond the shower curtain surrounding the old tub, caught a towel off the rack and wrapped it around herself, wondering what had happened to her that she'd even considered such an outrageous scheme.

Actually the answer was simple. Her son had been missing for hours in rain-filled darkness, and when he'd finally been restored to her, she'd have done anything to ensure she'd never be parted from him again.

But such dramatics weren't necessary. Last night the storm had heightened the dangers of her situation. But this morning she was thinking more clearly. She would thank the sheriff for his help and be on her way.

Wrapped in a fluffy green towel, she pushed the shower curtain aside—and found herself face-to-face with a girl in a red chenille bathrobe with tabby-cat faces embroidered on its big patch pockets.

The girl was probably as tall as she was. Her long curly mass of dark hair was disheveled, and the expression in her dark eyes as she stared at Beth was one of complete disbelief.

Beth stared back, searching her mind for some brief and reasonable explanation to give the girl for her presence there.

The girl smiled suddenly. "Hi," she said in a voice still groggy with sleep. "I'm Tanika. But nobody calls me that. It's Nikkie." She laughed a little nervously, then indicated Beth's towel. "So. You stayed the night?"

"Ah...yes," Beth replied. Then realizing what the girl was suggesting, corrected her quickly. "Oh. No, no. Not like that. I mean...my son was missing and your father searched for him for hours. Then...well, he brought us home because—"

"Hi!" Jason burst into the little room, still wearing the brown sweats. His thick dark hair stood up in spikes, and his blue eyes were as filled with excitement as they'd been the night before when he'd discovered the bunk beds.

Nikkie's friendly smile turned to confusion.

"Nikkie," Beth said, stepping out of the tub, "this is my son, Jason. Jase, this is Ethan's daughter, Tanika."

Jason looked at her as though assessing her worthiness to associate with his hero. "Weird name," he said.

"It's American Indian," the girl replied somewhat stiffly. "My mother liked it." She looked from Jason to Beth and asked, "What are you doing here?"

Beth opened her mouth to explain, but before she could form the words, Jason said with considerable pride, "The sheriff's going to be my dad!"

Nikkie stared at him for a full ten seconds, then demanded in an over-my-dead-body tone of voice, "What? *What?*"

"Hey." A quiet male voice spoke from the doorway of the crowded little room. "I see you've all met. Who needs a family room when you've got a bathroom? Good morning, Nik."

He was already showered, Beth noticed, and dressed in a beige shirt with all the brass buttons and pins of his office, a brown tie and brown slacks.

"Daddy." Nikkie turned to her father, a formidable picture of indignation not at all diminished by the kitty faces on her bathrobe. "I want to know what's going on. *Now.*"

Beth clutched the towel closely, feeling her cheeks redden as Ethan's eyes ran over her. "Good morning," he said, his attention diverted from his daughter. "Sleep well?"

"Yes, thank you," Beth replied awkwardly, feeling apologetic that his daughter was upset, wishing desperately that she was anywhere but this tiny packed room. "I, ah, was hoping to be out before Nikkie got up, but—"

"The kid says you're going to be his father!" Nikkie indicated Jason with a disparaging wave of her hand. "Is he delusional or was I left out of the loop on something important?"

Jason threw his arms possessively around Ethan's waist. "Tell her," he said, wrinkling his nose at Nikkie. "Tell her about you and Mom getting married."

"What?" Nikkie shrieked.

"We are *not* getting married!" Beth told Nikkie, hoping to defuse what was rapidly becoming a little war. The source of the dispute, she accepted wryly, was the sheriff. Nikkie felt he belonged to her, and while she might have been willing to share him with a woman who'd spent the night in his bed, that generosity didn't extend to another child.

And Jason, who didn't want anyone or anything to endanger the flimsy hold he had on security, was also staking his claim on Ethan.

Beth couldn't help but feel left out. She was the only one in the room with no claim on the sheriff, and her own son didn't even seem to notice her presence in his determination to make sure that Ethan noticed *him.*

Ethan put a hand to Jason's back, then extended his free arm to Nikkie. "Jason, why don't you get ready for school while I catch Nikkie up on what's going on," he said. "Beth?"

"Yes?" She looked up, a little surprised to be noticed after all, even if it wasn't by her son.

"Brodie'll make you breakfast."

"Brodie?"

"My brother comes over every morning to eat. Don't let him scare you. He's all talk."

And with that he patted Jason's shoulder and left the room with Nikkie.

Jason stared after them longingly. "You don't think he'll change his mind, do you?" he asked, his voice small and pitiful.

Beth, her early-morning confidence shaken by the volatile confrontation, found that she could neither reassure him that Ethan wouldn't change his mind, nor explain to him that it would probably be better all around if he did. At the moment she wasn't sure of anything.

And there'd been something friendly, even… needy, in Nikkie's eyes when she'd introduced herself to Beth. As though a woman in her life might be welcome.

But that tentative extension of friendship had been shattered when she'd thought Beth—and particularly Jason—might be intruding on her life with her father.

Beth closed her eyes for a moment, wondering how things could possibly get more complicated. She quickly dismissed the thought, afraid maybe they would.

"Take your shower," she said briskly to Jason, "and remember, when you're a guest in someone's home, it isn't polite to tell them you think their name is weird."

Jason sank onto the closed lid of the toilet. "She doesn't like me. Do you think Ethan'll change his mind because she doesn't like me?"

"I don't know what will happen, Jase," she said frankly. "Take your shower and get ready for school, and I'll try to figure everything out today."

He looked at her doubtfully. "You'll tell Grandma and Grandpa the truth because you won't want to lie. Then…then it'll all be over."

She took his face in her hands and leaned over to kiss the tip of his nose. "Sweetie, it never began. The sheriff is *not* your father, even though you'd like that very much. And you can't make it happen, just because you want it. He belongs to Nikkie, not to us."

Jason's eyes brimmed with tears. "Well…how come we don't get a dad?"

"We had one," she reminded gently. "Remember?"

A tear spilled over onto Jason's cheek. "Not very much. Mostly it's just been you and me. I love you and all, Mom. But he's...he's got muscles."

Beth wrapped her arms around her son and hugged him. "The heart's a muscle, too, Jason. And mine works just for you."

He returned her hug and giggled. "It's funny to think of a heart being bulgy."

Now she laughed, relieved to hear the humor in his voice. "At my age, Jason, everything gets bulgy, only not in a good way. Now hurry up and get showered and dressed so you can have breakfast before you go."

"Okay." Momentarily distracted from his problems, Jason pulled off the brown sweatshirt as Beth hurried to the bedroom to put on the undies, old jeans and sweater she'd been wearing last night before this whole drama had begun.

ETHAN SAT on the blue-and-yellow coverlet on the edge of his daughter's bed and watched her pace in front of him, much as he'd seen her mother do during opening or closing arguments in court. He felt a bittersweet pang in his chest.

"I thought we were in this together," she said with an air of injured pride as she marched past him. Her cats watched her movements with interest, one on each of her two pillows. "That's what you're always saying when you want to learn something from me. 'Nikkie,'" she quoted him, "'we're in this together. There isn't anything you can't tell me or ask me.'" She gave him an angry glance as she went past him again, headed in the other direction. "I thought that applied to you, too."

He caught her arm and pulled her down beside him onto the bed. "It does apply to me, too." He put an arm around her shoulders. "But I just explained what happened. Jase was a little kid in trouble, and Beth looked like she was at the end of her rope last night. And while I imagine the grandparents have the boy's best interests at heart, they were terrifying. I had to do something."

"So you brought them home." Nikkie sighed with exaggerated patience. "Fine. But what's this stuff about you becoming the little twerp's father? You're not going to do that, are you? Marry her just so the grandparents won't go to court to get the kid?"

Ethan rubbed his forehead. He hated starting the day with a headache. "I don't know what I'm going to do. I thought I'd wait till the birthday party this afternoon and see how the grandparents react."

Nikkie played with the belt of her robe, knotting and unknotting the ends. "You always wanted to have a boy, didn't you?" she asked moodily. "Only, Mom died before you could do it."

"No," he replied honestly, pulling her closer. "We never talked about having another baby. You were great and your mom had a busy career. You were enough for us."

"But you always took me fishing with you and out to cut wood and to football games at the park."

"I thought you liked coming with me."

"I did. I do. But it'd be more fun for you with a son. All your friends bring their boys and you just have me."

He wasn't sure where this was coming from and

he tried to tread carefully. "You're a good sport. They all like you. It's never been a problem, has it?"

"No," she replied with a certain lack of conviction. "But I'm getting older now. Worms are losing their thrill for me, and I hate having to go to the bathroom in the woods."

He laughed. "Your mom did, too. But the point is, you never gripe and that makes you one of the guys."

She leaned into him and put her arms around him. He knew he had her sympathy if not her understanding. "I think it'd be a little scary around here if you got married—even if it wasn't for real. I mean, they'd have to *live* here, right?"

"Beth and I are going to talk about that later." He squeezed her to him and kissed the top of her head. "But you must know you're the most important person in my life and I'd never do anything to hurt you."

"I know. But you have to fall in love again *some*-time. I mean, you're still a young man." She said the words seriously and with some surprise.

He bit back a laugh. "Thank you."

"But it'll be hard for me to share you. What if she doesn't want to go to Bailey's for breakfast on Sunday mornings and read the paper while we eat? What if she doesn't like 'NYPD Blue' and wants to rent some mushy movie?" She sat up, her eyes wide and horror-filled. "What if she doesn't like cats?"

"Then," he said with a theatrical sigh, "I guess you'll have to make pancakes on Sunday mornings, sit through *Love Story* on Tuesday nights and…I don't know, give the cats to some lab-animal bounty hunter who—"

That earned him a doubled fist to the chest and an indignant "Da-ad!"

He laughed and dodged a second punch, catching her wrist. "Come on. You know I'd never let anyone deprive you of your cats. And the rest of the stuff is something all families have to deal with. Sometimes you give up something to get something else. It's life."

"I like *this* life," she said petulantly.

"I know." He grew serious. "I do, too. And I promise not to do anything that'll change it too radically. Trust me, okay?"

She appeared to consider that. "I always trust you. But I never got up to take a shower and found a woman wrapped in a towel in the bathroom before."

Yes, he thought with a slight quickening of his pulse. That had been quite a sight. Soft breasts pressed under the enveloping edge of the towel and two long shapely legs visible below. He'd had to force himself to focus on Nikkie and Jason.

"Right. But everything happened too suddenly last night, and too late for me to explain it to you. I thought I might get to you before you got up this morning, but apparently Beth's an early riser."

"So." Nikkie went to a dresser drawer and pulled out a pink sweater. "Her name's Elizabeth."

"No." He stood. "Bethany. Bethany Richards. She's an artist. She bought that old cannery on the waterfront."

Nikkie pulled a pair of jeans out of the closet and turned to frown at him. "An artist? You mean, paintings and stuff?"

"Yeah, I guess. I'm not sure." He went toward the door, then turned as he opened it and asked, "What are you doing after school?"

"The drama club's meeting to decide what play to

do for the Winter Festival weekend.'' She retrieved a pair of fat-heeled boots from the bottom of her closet. They were the ugliest things he'd ever seen, and he remembered paying a fortune for them. "Why?"

"We're having a birthday party for Jason at three-thirty at Dinosaur Pizza. If you have time to come, it'd help his story in front of his grandparents."

She rolled her eyes. "You want me to come to an eight-year-old's birthday party?" Then she huffed impatiently. "And how come *you're* giving him a party? You just met him last night."

Ethan nodded. His daughter definitely had some of her mother's gift for argument. "He happened to mention when I was returning him to his mother that he wished he could have a birthday party like all the other kids have, rather than one where his grandparents come to bully his mother. So when he started telling his story about me becoming his father, I backed him up by inviting them to the party—which hadn't really been planned but which Ebbie's supposed to put together this morning."

Nikkie tossed her boots at the bed, then yanked open a drawer and pulled out a pair of thick flowered socks. "And it'd help your story if I show up and act like a big sister."

"You don't have to act like anything. But it'd be great if you could come. And pizza will likely be dinner tonight."

She tossed the socks after the boots and moved toward him. "The meeting'll probably break up too late for me to make the party," she said with little visible sign of regret. "But maybe you could bring me home a couple of pieces of pizza. Sausage, pepperoni and onion—no olives."

"Right." He leaned down to kiss her cheek. "Have a good day."

She hugged him briefly. "You, too. And, Daddy?"

He stopped in the hallway and leaned back into the room. "Yeah?"

She hesitated, as though considering what she was about to say, then blurted, "Did you and...Beth have sex last night?"

It always startled him when his daughter brought up the subject of sex. He understood that she was no longer his *little* girl and that it was far healthier for her to bring him her questions than talk about them to someone else, but the subject was so important it unnerved him.

He was always tempted to tell her horror stories about how sex at too young an age ruined lives and futures, but that wasn't smart. He didn't want to frighten her into never discussing sex with him again. Still she was pretty and shapely already, and he knew that several of her classmates were experimenting. The prospect that she might terrified him.

"I prefer the term 'making love,'" he said, trying not to betray his fears. "But no, we didn't."

"You'd only known her a few hours." Nikkie studied him gravely. "You couldn't possibly have learned to love her in that amount of time. So you couldn't have made love to her. But you could have had sex. People have recreational sex all the time."

Dear God! He leaned a shoulder against the wall as much for support as to appear casual. "*I* don't. Sex is for love...and for communication and procreation, but not recreation."

"She's very pretty," Nikkie persisted. "And you've been celibate a long time."

He closed his eyes briefly. He certainly could never be considered guilty of having stifled his child's curiosity. "Like I said, love's important. I had it with your mom, and that's made it impossible for me to ever use sex just for fun. Though it certainly can be."

She sighed, apparently satisfied. "I sure would like to know what it's all about," she admitted wistfully.

He found relief in her admission that she didn't know. "It's all about things that are just too big to deal with at fourteen," he said, leaning down to kiss her again. "Even for a fourteen-year-old as smart as you are."

She gave him a rueful and knowing look. "But someday I'll be ready. Right now, though, there's enough going on in my life."

"Amen to that," he said. "See you tonight."

He went into his room to retrieve his utility belt and jacket, praying he would be much older and wiser by the time she *was* ready.

BREAKFAST BRODIE-STYLE was bacon, eggs and hash browns with onions and garlic. Beth considered herself lucky that she had a preference for onions and garlic, because Ethan's brother had been generous with them. She poured coffee while he brought their plates to the table.

Brodie Drum was a little taller and leaner than his brother, but had the same rich dark hair and eyes. He wore a blue-and-white-striped shirt with a large sewn-on patch on the back embroidered with "Drum's Garage." His name was on the front pocket.

He exuded energy and a confident sexuality that Beth concluded was the reason for Ethan's warning, but he was friendly and welcoming. She guessed he was four or five years younger than Ethan.

They sat across from each other at the small table in the middle of the sunny yellow kitchen. Ethan had explained her presence to his brother earlier, and Brodie had commiserated with her while he cooked.

"So what we have to do now," he said, sounding eager, "is convince your in-laws you're marrying into a solid loving family. I'll come to the birthday party."

"Thank you," she said, shaking salt and pepper on her egg and potatoes. "I'd like that, but we're not sure what we're going to do about the...the wedding thing."

Brodie seemed surprised. "But what other solution is there? And you can't do better than Ethan, even if it's just a temporary thing. He's a solid citizen, good provider, and he knows all that—" he waved his fork over his plate "—all that sensitive stuff. He shouts only when he's exhausted every other option, and he's willing to lend a hand to people everybody else has given up on."

Brodie's eyes softened. "His wife, Diana, I know, was very happy with him. And he's great with Nikkie. She's a good kid and he's raised her by himself the last five years."

"Hi!" Jason burst into the kitchen, jacket held by its collar and dragging on the floor. Someone had laundered it already. It was easy to guess who.

He came to Beth's side and smiled at Ethan's brother.

Brodie pushed his chair back and reached across the table to shake Jason's hand. "Hi, Jase," he said, pulling a chair out for him. "I'm going to be your uncle. Sit down. I'll get your breakfast."

Beth opened her mouth, prepared to remind him that the wedding issue was undecided. But Jason followed him to the stove and said excitedly, "Wow! I never had an uncle before."

"Well, you're going to like it," Brodie replied, carrying the warm plate to the table with a hot pad. Then he went to the refrigerator and poured a glass of milk. "Uncles spoil you. They let you do things your father won't. Want some chocolate in that milk?"

"Yeah!"

Jason sat in the chair at a right angle to Beth and dug into his breakfast while Brodie poured a generous amount of syrup into a dessert spoon, then stirred it into the milk.

"I'm coming to your party this afternoon." Brodie resumed his chair. "What'll I bring?"

"What do you mean?"

"For a present."

"Oh! You know those *Toy Story*..." Jason began a complicated description of the movie's action figures, then caught Beth's reprimanding eye and stopped. "You don't have to bring me anything." The denial was offered with a smile but lacked conviction. "I'd just like you to come so I can introduce you to Grandma and Grandpa."

"I'll be there," Brodie promised.

Beth had difficulty taking issue with her son's ear-to-ear grin of delight. Brodie was as comfortable to be with as Ethan was and just as indulgent with Jason. But he also seemed as bent as his brother on believing that marriage to Ethan was the solution to her in-law problems. She'd tried to stop him from letting Jason think that was going to happen, but he hadn't seemed to notice her protests.

"Hi!" Jason said when Ethan entered the room.

The concern that Ethan would no longer like him because Nikkie didn't showed clearly in his expression. But Ethan touched Jason's shoulder as he passed him, and the expression evaporated.

Ethan went to a far corner of the kitchen where a large bag of cat food was tucked away. He lifted it easily and shook food into two bowls.

Cindy and a gray ball of fur Beth presumed to be Simba ran into the room and began to eat. Ethan stroked each down-bent head, then crossed to the oven to retrieve his plate.

He poured a cup of coffee and brought it and his plate to the table. He grinned at Jason as he sat opposite him. "Mm," he said. "Smell those onions and garlic."

He picked up his cup without using the handle and took a sip, smiling at Beth over the rim. "Did Brodie ask you to run away with him to the Seychelles yet?"

"I was saving that for after she gets to know me." Brodie winked at Beth. "Think you could take to island living?"

"Easily," she replied. "I like the thought of warm beaches and blue water."

"But Gauguin already did the island thing in his paintings," Ethan said. "Don't you want to do something else?"

Beth laughed. "I wouldn't complain about where I was if I had the time to paint." She chewed and swallowed a bit of crisp bacon. "But I don't, at least not right now. All my dreams of being a real artist—you know, doing oils on canvas—have to take second place to paying the rent, so to speak. I make signs, plaques, decorative boxes, children's chairs, stuff like that."

"In the Seychelles, you could make those little figures you see made out of shells in tourist shops." Brodie drew a picture in the air with his fork.

Beth made a face. "I don't think so. But we could make our living pearl-diving or something. Maybe you could open a garage there."

Now Brodie made a face. "No. When I make it to the Seychelles, the only thing I'm doing is beach-combing. No more squeaks you can't find, brakes that don't act up when I'm test-driving them, no customers unwilling to pay for the time it takes to repair a transmission…"

"You mean you'd be expecting monthly checks from me," Ethan said, clarifying his brother's day-dreams. "Or Beth would have to support you."

Brodie chewed thoughtfully on a mouthful of potatoes, then shook his head. "No, I don't want Beth to have to lift a finger. And you owe me for all the times you beat me up when we were kids."

Ethan made a scornful sound. "You deserved it. You were such a whiner, always running to Mom over every little thing. Like the time I gave you a little tap on the nose in the grocery store."

Brodie sat up indignantly. "That wasn't a tap. It was a punch! My nose was bleeding all over the candy aisle!"

"You tried to steal a package of bubble gum."

"It might have had a trading card in it that would have made me a rich man today!"

Ethan shook his head at Beth. "I wouldn't go anywhere with him if I were you. No matter how inviting he makes island living sound."

"Me, either." Jason grinned from brother to brother, happy to be part of their banter. Then he said staunchly to Ethan, "I'm staying with you."

"Well," Brodie said, pretending to be affronted, "Forget getting any *Toy Story* character for your birthday."

The three of them laughed and Beth forced a smile, but she felt a mild resentment over how quickly her son's allegiance was switching from her to Ethan.

Nikkie flew through the kitchen calling goodbye to her father and her uncle as she reached into a cupboard, snatched a granola bar and headed for the door. To Beth and Jason she threw a polite smile and a casual "See ya."

The door closed behind her just as a school bus pulled up in front of the house.

Brodie pushed his empty plate away and made a conciliatory face at Jason as the boy downed his last swallow of milk. "My shop's a couple of blocks from your school. Do you want to come with me or do you want to wait for Ethan to drive you?" He turned to Beth. "Is it all right?"

"Of course." She smiled gratefully. "I'd appreciate that."

"Good." Brodie stood and carried his plate to the counter. "Then I'll pick him up after school and bring him to the party."

Jason followed his example with his own plate. "Even though I won't go to the seashells with you?"

"The *Sey*chelles," Brodie corrected. "And I'm sure you'll eventually come to your senses. I'm a much nicer guy than Ethan."

Jason cast an adoring look at Ethan. "Nobody's nicer than Ethan."

Ethan gave him a thumbs-up. "You're okay, Jase," he said.

CHAPTER FIVE

"YOU LOOK RESTED," Ethan said as he got up to get the coffeepot off the warmer and bring it to the table. His gaze skimmed Beth's face and lingered on her hair before he topped up her coffee mug and then his own. "If you can sleep in a bottom bunk with a squirmy kid over your head, you can sleep anywhere."

She added cream to her coffee, then pushed the small jug toward him, resisting the impulse to touch her hair. She'd combed it and left it swinging free this morning because she had no idea what happened to the pins and fastener she'd had in it the day before. "You've had the experience?"

"Brodie and I had bunks," he said over his shoulder as he returned the coffeepot to the counter. "He sleeps with the same energy he displays when he's awake. And he makes great hash browns."

"That he does." She kept her eyes on her plate, wondering how best to explain to Ethan what was on her mind.

"So, do you want to talk about the birthday party and the problem with your in-laws?" he asked between forkfuls of food.

She put her own fork down and squared her shoulders, his direct question reminding her that the only way to deal with this man was with the same direct-ness.

"Yes," she said, "but *I'm* going to talk and you're going to listen." She waited for him to object. When he didn't, she was surprised into silence for another moment.

He pretended to cock his ear. "I don't hear any-thing."

"I expected an argument," she admitted.

He raised an eyebrow. "Arguments are generally two-sided. 'I'm going to talk and you're going to lis-ten' doesn't really encourage that."

She felt her shoulders sag a little. "True. But you saved my son's life and I'm a guest in your home and at your table. I...I guess I'm having second thoughts about the way I phrased that."

He grinned at her. "I'm not that delicate, Beth. If I want to argue, I'll argue, whether or not you try to stop me. Speak. I'm listening."

She collected her thoughts, the corner of her mind not occupied with her son and his grandparents think-ing that this man would be interesting company if her circumstances were different. And if she didn't mind always being in a dither. But they weren't. And she did.

"All right." She pushed her plate away and leaned toward him on folded arms. "I could never repay you for all you've done. I can't tell you what my son means to me, but I don't suppose I have to because I can see how much you and Nikkie care for each other." She smiled, despite her determination to make her point. "She's lovely, by the way. Before Jason managed to annoy her, she was very warm and polite to me."

He smiled, too, the gesture filled with pride and amusement. "Thank you. That was because she thought you'd spent the night." He gave the phrase significant emphasis.

Her smile widened. "I know. And then Jason flew into your arms and she became Warrior Woman, protecting her home."

"I'm sorry."

"Don't apologize. It's a quality that admits her to our sisterhood—even at fourteen." Beth's expression sobered. "But that's not what I wanted to talk about."

"I'm still listening," he said, then took another sip of coffee and leaned back in his chair.

"I wish it was possible for me to let Jason go on thinking he can have you for a father," she said quickly before she could lose track of her arguments. Ethan's quiet dark eyes were focused on her, and she found their intensity unsettling. "But let's face it. Getting married to keep my in-laws out of my hair would be ridiculous."

"Why?" he asked. "Or is it my turn to talk yet?"

She sputtered, wondering how he could possibly ask such a question. "What do you mean, why? Because you don't love me and I don't love you. We don't even know each other. And even if we did it just to appease them for now, Joanne and Zachary will be a threat to me until Jason's an adult. You'd have to be married to me for at least ten years!"

Ethan watched the fire in her eyes, saw the color tinge her creamy cheeks, saw her eyebrows disappear under rich brown bangs as she strained to make him understand her position. He remembered how her voice had sounded over the radio when her son was lost and she wanted to take one of the county's cars and go look for him herself.

He was beginning to think she was wrong in believing he didn't love her.

Well, maybe *love* was too strong a word. Maybe it wasn't love at all. But he had feelings for her. A very powerful...*like*. And that seemed a pretty good basis for a relationship.

"Fifty percent of the marriages supposedly based on love," he said calmly, "end in divorce. And many of the couples who stay married do so out of laziness. Even *you* said you'd simply gotten used to what yours had become."

"That's right!" she said fervently. "And that's precisely why I've sworn I'll never get married again."

"Maybe something more reliable than love should be the reason for marriage. Like a mutual need."

"I'm thirty-two years old, I'm finally free to do what I want to do with my life, and I'm determined that no one is going to get in the way of that."

"What makes you think I would?"

She looked heavenward in supplication. "You would. I'm sure it would upset you if I didn't cook and forgot to do laundry and stayed up all night finishing a project for a craft show."

"I can cook," he replied reasonably. "Nikkie does our laundry, my uniforms go to the cleaners, and I wouldn't care how late you stayed up if you finally came home to me."

She stared at him in disbelief, opening and then closing her mouth several times as she apparently considered, then discarded one argument after another.

"Are you forgetting the kids?" she asked finally, her voice high and a little desperate. "Do you think it'd be good for them to know we married to perpetrate a hoax?"

"I think," he said, "that Jason really likes the idea of having me for a father."

"But Nikkie," she argued, "*doesn't* like the idea of sharing you, which is perfectly understandable. And I seriously doubt it would be good for a fourteen-year-old girl to have her life upended like that."

"Nikkie's been without a mother for five years." He leaned his elbows on the table, cupped one hand over the other and looked at her, his eyes reflecting that he, too, had been without someone he loved. "That was an important time for her. I did my best to be there for her and I think we've held our own, but I know she's lost out on some things because I can't be what Diana could have been to her. And now I'm looking at an even more critical time in her life. A time when she should have a woman to turn to."

Beth felt her arguments growing fuzzy in the face of his emotional honesty, but she struggled to clear them. "Ethan, I can't be what Diana could have been to her, either. I'm me, and unfortunately I'm not at all a typical mother. And, anyway, if you married me, I think she'd see me as a threat, rather than someone to turn to and confide in."

"Maybe in the beginning," he agreed, "but she's a smart kid. She'd see how much you have to give to our lives."

Beth shook her head in disbelief. "Why do you *say* that? I just told you—"

"I know. You don't cook, you forget to do laundry, and you hang out in your studio all night." He sighed, lowered his arms and leaned toward her. "I guess because your husband resented the artist in you, you have trouble understanding that when a man really loves a woman, he wants her to be who she really is. Whatever inconvenience that brings him is tolerable—particularly if she loves him back."

"But you don't *love* me!" she said emphatically, slapping both hands on the table so hard the crockery shook.

He didn't even blink. He smiled, instead, and that completely unsettled her. "I like you a hell of a lot, though. And you like me."

She closed her eyes and put a hand over them. "What I really like," she said with quiet exasperation, "is a man who listens to me when I'm talking."

He laughed softly. "I've heard every word. I think what you mean is that you like a man who listens, then does what you want him to do. Which seems to be in direct contrast to how *you'd* like to be treated by *him*."

Beth dropped both hands to her lap, fell against the back of her chair and eyed him with weary frustration. "If we were married," she said, "I'd probably kill you the first time we had a fight."

He grinned wickedly. "I don't think so. I'm BPST-trained."

"Who trained?"

"Board of Police Standards and Training. But I might let you wrestle me down just to see what happens."

"You're impossible."

"You're not the first to tell me that."

"I can't marry you."

"Okay."

For all his wily arguments, he made that concession easily and with seemingly little regret. Beth felt a strange pinch of disappointment in the suddenly quiet aftermath of their head-to-head confrontation.

"No hard feelings?" she asked.

"Of course not." He pushed away from the table and picked up his plate and mug. "Come on. I'll give you a ride to the cannery."

She followed him with her dishes. "And I'm paying for the party," she insisted, hoping to take advantage of his amenable mood.

He nodded, putting his things in the sink. "Whatever you want."

"Why?" She put her dishes in after his, then turned to face him suspiciously.

He appeared confused. "Why what?"

She put a hand on her hip. "Why are you suddenly saying yes to everything? To show me what an easygoing husband you'd be?"

"No," he replied, reaching up to button the collar he'd left undone under the loose knot of his tie. "To show you how dull and unfulfilling it would be to have such a husband."

So, he was using reverse psychology on her. She felt warmed and amused. "Ah." She smiled. "The toothless-tiger theory."

"Pardon me?"

"Challenge. Where's the glory in taming a toothless tiger? Is that what you're trying to tell me?"

He considered that a moment, then shook his head. "I don't think so. Generally men don't like to hear the word 'tamed' used in a sentence about them. Some of us can be domesticated but never *tamed*."

"Then what was your point?"

"That you'd be bored in a week by a man who did exactly what you wanted him to do."

She laughed. "That's a myth put forth by men who want everything their *own* way."

"Really?" He shifted his weight and she had the skin-prickling awareness of being hunted. "Do you want me to kiss you?"

She parted her lips to answer, but couldn't decide on yes or no. In her current state of confusion, either answer seemed a lie.

Then with a swiftness that validated her notion of being hunted, his hand went under her hair and caught her nape, gently but firmly. He tilted her head slightly as his came down to block out the sun streaming in through the kitchen window.

And he kissed her. He wasn't forceful, but he wasn't tentative. His lips had the same gentle but confident strength as the hand at her neck, as well as an artful mobility that made her put both hands on his waist to steady herself.

She felt the tip of his tongue against her lips and opened to admit it. But all he did was explore the rim of the inside of her lips. Then he withdrew, ending the kiss with the lightest nip of her bottom lip, effectively erasing any comparison of him to a toothless tiger.

When he raised his head, she felt as though someone had worked her over with a foam bat.

He frowned down at her, looking a little unsettled himself. "I expected you to say no." His voice was quiet, thoughtful. "And because I was sure kissing you would be wonderful, I was going to make the point afterward that you'd have missed the pleasure if I'd done as you asked.'' His frown deepened. ''But you *didn't* say no.''

Still shaken, she pulled his hand from her neck. ''I didn't say yes, either.'' Then because she knew he'd won that one, she admitted with a thin smile, ''But your point was made, anyway.''

He cleared his throat. ''Good. Get your jacket. I'm leaving in five minutes.''

ETHAN FOUND a sales receipt on his desk for a sheet cake. There was a note scrawled on it that said, ''Pick up at three.'' Beside it was a bag that contained paper plates and napkins with *Toy Story* figures on them, as well as a giant package of colorful balloons.

''Your share is seventeen dollars,'' Ebbie called from the outer office, her telephone receiver cradled on her shoulder. ''I'm holding for Chuck. He's rousting a pair of homeless men out of that empty house down the street from your place. I wish that somebody would buy it and restore it, or that the city would condemn it. Between the drifters who break in for a refuge from the rain and the kids who dare each other to go in, the damn thing's on the log every other day. Yeah, Chuck?'' She responded to a question on the other end of the line, logged the call on the computer, then called the shelter to tell them Chuck was bringing them a couple of clients.

At last she hung up the phone and grinned at Ethan, who stood in his doorway. ''I bought Jason a basketball. You think he'll like that?''

''Sure.'' He pulled the right number of bills out of his wallet and put them on Ebbie's desk. ''You made the reservations at Dinosaur?''

"Yes. But I couldn't tell them how many. I guessed twenty, with kids from school. What do you think?"

"Sounds good to me." He patted her graying curls. "Thanks. Even if his grandparents foul up his life, he'll have a party to remember."

Ebbie looked concerned. "I thought you and the mother were getting along when I left. The wedding's off?"

He shrugged, trying to ignore the feeling of something important missed, of two lives destined to entwine, yet somehow evading each other and moving in opposite directions.

But that was ridiculous. This time yesterday he hadn't even known Beth or Jason Richards existed. He'd known Diana a lifetime. He and she had planned on Nikkie for years.

Last night had just been a strangely emotional accident. Jason's fantasies about a father couldn't be safely indulged without completely upsetting four lives.

The hell it couldn't.

"Her last marriage wasn't great," he told Ebbie, then went into his office and stood beside his desk, pretending to study the calendar. "She's determined not to do it again. It was an outrageous idea, anyway."

Ebbie got up from her desk and crossed to his doorway. "Well, *un*determine her. She's afraid of you, that's all."

Ethan looked up from his calendar, eyes narrowed. "What?"

"Afraid of you," she repeated, folding her arms over her matronly bosom. "Because you…light her fire, so to speak. I don't understand it, but I suppose a competent in-charge sort of man could appeal to a woman who was ignored by her first husband.''

He shook his head over her homegrown psychology. "Apparently not. She was very emphatic about it. No wedding."

Ebbie studied him for a moment, then asked, "Disappointed?"

He turned a few pages on his calendar. "No. Nikkie doesn't like Jason and was annoyed that he and Beth spent the night. It was just that..." Ethan abandoned the calendar and sat down in his chair, trying to look busy. "The notion put a little excitement in my life for a few hours, that's all. When you've lived in the same place for thirty-seven years and have nothing in your life but work and a daughter who's trying hard to keep you out of *her* life, there's a certain seduction in a change of pace. Now beat it, all right? I'm busy."

"No, you're not," she said. "I keep your calendar, remember? What does she intend to do about her in-laws?"

He pulled a file toward him. "I'm not sure. I think she intends to tell them the truth at the party this afternoon."

Ebbie looked horrified. "You saw them. You know what they'll do with that bit of information."

Ethan shuffled papers. "It's her decision, Eb. Our job was to find her missing child and we did. The rest of her life is up to her."

"Your job's not over yet," she said.

He looked up at her with strained patience. "Why not?"

She angled her chin with that superior maternal air

she assumed when she thought he was being dense. "Because now *she's* the one who's lost."

Her telephone rang and Ethan shooed her away. "And close the door!" he called.

She did.

Ethan forced his mind from thoughts of Bethany Richards, from the woman who looked at him with eyes that seemed to devour him, then told him she'd vowed never to marry again and was sure they'd only make each other miserable.

He'd see what the musts were on today's schedule, give serious thought to Jason's birthday present— Then it hit him like a bolt out of the blue. A bike! Jason had said he'd bent the wheel on his bike and that it had fallen down the hill. He could use a new one, Ethan was sure.

The bike would need a light, a bell, a water bottle. Jason would need a helmet. He resolved to check out Bike-King on his lunch break.

KELLY SAT on a stool beside Beth and hung over her as she painted a whimsical angel with patchwork wings on a yellow-painted pine board. It was for the door of a little girl's room.

She watched as Beth rimmed the patches with a fine black line and added broken lines to look like stitches.

"You are so clever," Kelly said, propping her elbow on Beth's worktable and resting her cheek in the palm of her hand. "I should order a couple of those for my nieces. The name goes there, right?" She pointed at the expanse of bright empty yellow to the right of the angel.

"Yes. Julia Marie. But I won't let you order any

more stuff from me.'' Beth dropped the brush in the water, then selected a wider one for the lettering. ''You do it just to make work for me so you can pay me. I appreciate it, but *you're* an artist. You can make signs for your nieces yourself.''

''I'm a potter.'' Kelly delved a hand into a bag of microwave popcorn at her elbow. ''And don't tell me what I can and can't buy. I hate painting. It's so tedious.''

''Then I'll paint you a couple gratis.'' Beth dipped an inch-wide brush into bright pink acrylic paint.

Kelly groaned in disgust. ''You know, that's what's wrong with you,'' she said, continuing on a theme she'd begun earlier, before she'd paused to admire the angel. ''You're too generous. You're also too honest.''

Beth concentrated on forming a simple block-letter capital *J*. ''And that's a bad thing?'' she said absently.

''It is when you turn down business, refuse to let a friend rent space in your art mall and decide to come clean about the sheriff to your in-laws when you know they'll probably end up taking you to court over it! That's…*stupid* honesty.''

Beth made a face at her as she dipped the brush in paint again, a perfect *J* executed. ''There's no such thing as stupid honesty. Honesty is always smart.''

''Then why,'' Kelly asked smugly, ''when I asked you if these narrow-legged jeans made my backside look fat, did you say no?''

Beth bit back a smile and concentrated on the lower-case *u*. ''Because they don't.''

''Liar.''

''Diplomat,'' Beth corrected with a grin as she

dipped for more paint. "And anyway, they don't make you look fat. They make you look…lush."

Kelly waited while Beth formed the *l, i* and *a,* then expelled a breath. "Well, I'm not being diplomatic with you. You're insane."

"You don't need to rent space in my mall," Beth said, dipping the brush again. "You have that enormous garage, which you don't have to share with anyone."

"It doesn't have north light."

"You don't need it. You're a potter."

"I want to have a studio in your building!"

"You're just trying to give me money."

"You *need* money."

"Not yours."

Kelly groaned and watched her dot the *i* in Marie with a tiny heart with a patch on it.

"You know," she said, pointing to the heart, "that's your problem right there."

Beth leaned back to get a better perspective. It looked fine to her. "What's wrong with it?"

"Not that one—*your* heart. I swear to God, Beth, sometimes you're such a blonde! Your heart has a patch on it—that's why you won't let me help you and why you've decided against marrying the sheriff."

Beth dropped her brush in a jar of water and snatched the bag of popcorn from Kelly. "My heart does not have a patch on it. I'm heart-whole, and you've helped me too much already. You have to support yourself and your house and studio. My cannery is *my* responsibility. And I'm not marrying the sheriff because…"

Because for a few hours it had been a delicious

notion to share her problems with someone else, to see Jason blossom under the man's attention and to speculate what it would be like to be noticed. Not loved necessarily, just noticed. But thinking she could have that under these circumstances was absurd.

"Because it was a dumb idea. In fact, if you recall, last night when I phoned you to tell you Jason and I were going home with him, *you* told me to be careful. That he was a hunk and all, but the situation was sticky."

Kelly looked her in the eye. "I think you know you need a man, and you're afraid of that."

Beth slid off her stool and reached into the bag of popcorn. "No, I don't. I can live without it."

"It?" Kelly looked smug again. "I wasn't talking about sex. I was talking about the need for companionship, emotional support."

"I have you for that," Beth said with a smile as she crossed to the small refrigerator against the wall. She opened it and took out two bottles of juice.

"Yeah, well, I'm about to withdraw my companionship and emotional support if you don't wise up," Kelly threatened. "Come on. Don't tell your in-laws anything, team up with the sheriff and see what happens. I've asked around. Everyone has nothing but the highest praise for him. Maybe you shouldn't be careful at all. Maybe you should go for it."

"We're talking *marriage,* Kelly. That's a little different from a simple 'teaming up.' And what happens to my son and his daughter when it doesn't work out?"

"Maybe it would."

Beth handed Kelly a bottle of juice and hitched herself back up on the stool. "Yeah, right. You're an artist and you know what happened with *your* marriage. Your husband left you because he was sure you were having an affair with some guy named Art. He couldn't believe you could find a clay pot more interesting than he was.''

''That was my mistake,'' Kelly said after a moment's moody reflection. ''If I'd truly loved him, I *would* have found him more fun than a clay pot. I'd have done my pottery, but I'd have wanted to go home to him.''

Beth shrugged and took a long swig of her cranberry-apple juice. ''Look, the way things are for us now, neither of us is forced to make the choice. That's the safest thing.''

''Is life supposed to be about being safe?''

Beth put her juice down and picked up another brush. ''It's about being able to do what you want to do. And we are.''

''But we're doing it alone.''

''I'm happy about that,'' Beth said, touching up a patch on the angel's wing. ''But if you insist on complicating your life, I've got just the man for you. He's going to be at Jason's party.''

Kelly put her juice down. ''Really? Who?''

''Ethan's brother, Brodie. He owns a garage and he's a great cook. Seems very nice, too.''

''Well.'' Kelly looked interested, then cast a disparaging eye at her jeans. ''Well, you can just bet I'm not wearing these. Lush and fat *are* the same thing.'' She was silent a moment, then said, ''You know, if you married the sheriff, we could double-date.''

Beth pushed the plaque out of her way and put her head in a hand stained with pink acrylic. ''Kelly,'' she pleaded, "if I let you rent a studio, will you leave me alone about the sheriff?"

Kelly's cell phone rang before she could reply. She dug in her big suede backpack for it, pulled up the antenna and pressed the talk button.

Beth glowered at her friend as she addressed her caller. "Gone to Pot. This is Kelly."

Beth left the plaque to dry, then pulled another similarly designed board toward her, the angel already painted, the empty expanse for the name in blue. She dipped a brush in white paint while forming the name Jessica by eye. Now she was preparing stock for the Winter Festival Art Fair.

"Ah...yes," Kelly said hesitantly.

Beth looked up at the odd note in her friend's voice. Kelly pointed to her phone and made a face. Beth raised an eyebrow in question.

"Yes," Kelly said. "Yes, I knew her in Seattle. Why?" She listened, then blinked and shook her head at Beth. "Yes, I know you're asking the questions, but if you expect me to answer them, you'd damn well better tell me what this is about."

Beth dropped the brush back into the water and felt her shoulder muscles tense. Someone was talking to Kelly about *her*.

"Yes. She bought an old cannery to turn it into an art mall." Kelly's voice grew increasingly antagonistic. "Yes, that's a formidable venture, but the woman is very smart, hardworking and a fine artist herself." She paused to listen. "Yes. He's healthy and bright and a real credit to his mother."

Now they were discussing Jason. A little frisson of fear inched up Beth's spine. "Who is it?" she mouthed.

But Kelly was concentrating on another question from whomever was on the other end of the line.

"Rush Weston!" she said in surprise, her eyes widening at Beth. "Yes, I imagine she knows him. He teaches at the college and we've both taken classes there. I believe he'll be renting studio space in her mall when it's ready. No! No, there is nothing romantic between them."

Kelly's mouth worked uncertainly, her eyes rested on Beth in grave concern, then she swallowed and said with singular firmness in her voice and apology to Beth in her eyes. "I don't care who told you that, it isn't true. She's about to be married to Ethan Drum, our sheriff."

Oh, God. Beth put both hands to her face. "And if you want to know any more about them," Kelly continued, "I suggest you call *him* and see how he reacts to your snooping!"

Beth guessed by the sudden silence that the conversation had been terminated. She lowered her hands and asked with a sense of dread, "Who was it?"

"He said he was a reporter for an art magazine, but I'm sure the name he gave me was phony. I subscribe to everything, and I've never heard of it. And why wouldn't he have called you? My guess is he's a private detective hired by Joanne." Kelly looked reluctant to impart that information and she put an arm around Beth's shoulders as they slumped.

"I'm sorry about telling him you were getting married," Kelly continued, "but he seemed to be trying to make something out of your relationship with Rush Weston."

Beth spread her hands helplessly. "But I don't have a relationship with Rush, except as a fellow artist and possibly as his landlord when the building's ready.''

''I know that, but you know what a flamboyant gasbag Rush is. This guy had already spoken to him because he knew about his participation in the art fair. Apparently Rush was indulging his fantasies again and told him that he'd be renting space from you and the two of you would be sharing more than that very soon.''

''Oh, God, oh, *God!*'' Beth paced across her studio, a knot of panic forming in her stomach.

As though reading Beth's mind and her fears, Kelly said, ''Imagine what Joanne could do with that. Jason tells her you're marrying Ethan, Rush tells her detective you're marrying him. She could use you for a hockey puck in court with that!''

Beth put a hand to her chest where terror was building up a full head of steam.

''Do you hate me?'' Kelly asked warily.

They'd done it, Beth thought. They'd actually put a private detective on her with the intention of discrediting her. Or they'd hired an attorney and he'd hired the detective. Either way, the result would be the same.

She couldn't believe it. She'd worried about her in-laws' interference, but she'd never thought they'd go this far.

She was confident they'd find nothing on her that would prove her an unfit mother, but if she fought them, she was looking at probably months of litigation, months that would be even harder on Jason than on her and her efforts to get her art mall going. And that would incur more expense than she could possibly pay for even if she sold the cannery.

"You *do* hate me," Kelly said, her miserable expression reflecting what Beth felt.

Beth went to her friend and put her arms around her. "Of course I don't. You were trying to help."

Kelly hugged her tightly. "You've got to do something about this, Beth."

"Yes," Beth said, dread and fear like a lead ball in her stomach. "I intend to."

CHAPTER SIX

ETHAN PULLED the red-and-silver Blazer into the parking lot of Dinosaur Pizza and drove around the back. He parked beside Ebbie, who was lifting a wide pink bakery box out of the trunk of her old Toyota.

She came around to greet him as he climbed out, then lifted the lid of the box to show him the contents. Buzz Lightyear had been formed in the middle of a cake with green-and-white icing, his features perfectly drawn with piping gel and a little dome of plastic serving as his helmet.

Jason's name was written on the cake with Buzz's highly quoted "To infinity and beyond!" under it.

"Think he'll like it?" she asked.

Ethan nodded. "If he doesn't, it's mine. Good work, Eb. Thanks for doing all the running around this morning and for making the arrangements."

"No problem," she said. "My grandkids are so far away I don't get to do this stuff. See you inside. I've already brought the cups and plates in, and we're going to need your help with the balloons."

He grinned. "I'm ahead of you. I borrowed the helium tank the Red Cross used for the blood drive."

"Clever devil." Ebbie backed away toward the restaurant's rear entrance. "See you inside."

"Right." Ethan opened the Blazer's tailgate and pulled out a blue bike with all the pertinent accessories and a giant silver bow attached to the handlebars. The bike shop had put the helmet in a box, wrapped it in colorful paper and attached another silver bow. With the box on the flat of one hand, Ethan lifted the bike by its frame with the other and was halfway toward the restaurant with it when a little yellow MG convertible came whipping around the corner at a speed that suggested the driver hadn't slowed for the turn. It screeched to a halt inches from him.

He was about to threaten the pretty redhead behind the wheel with arrest for reckless driving when her passenger leaped out of the car and ran into his arms.

Well, not precisely into his arms; both were occupied with Jason's gifts. But Beth caught the front of his tweed jacket in both fists, her blue eyes wide and troubled. He was about to tell her to give him a minute to put the bike down when she said anxiously, "Ethan, I *have* to talk to you."

He sighed. "Is this one of those all-I-get-to-do-is-listen things?"

She didn't seem to mind his sarcasm. "No. Actually your input will be very important. Please. Can we talk before we go in? Brodie just pulled up in front with Jason."

"Want me to take that?" The pretty redhead had backed up and pulled into a parking spot with the same speed and screech of brakes and now stood beside Beth.

She smiled and offered her hand. "Hi. I'm Kelly Braxton, a friend of Beth's. I'm invited to the party. Want me to walk the bike in so you can talk?" Then realizing he didn't have a free hand to shake hers, she said, "Oh, sorry," and took the wrapped box from him.

Ethan shook her hand. "Hi. Ethan Drum."

Her smile was wry. "Yes, I know. Center of the vortex." She handed him back the box.

"Vortex?"

"Beth will explain." She took the bike from him with both hands and set it on the pavement. Then she grasped the handlebars and pushed it toward the restaurant's rear entrance.

Ethan stood face-to-face with Beth, her hands still clutching the lapels of his jacket. She looked a little like she had the night before when Jason told his grandparents she was getting married.

"You want to sit in the Blazer?" he asked, gesturing toward it with the gift-wrapped helmet.

"No," she said. "I need fresh air. Can we just walk up the block?"

"Sure. Let me get rid of this." He sat the gift on the back of his vehicle and closed the tailgate. When he turned to her, she slipped her arm into the crook of his and led him out of the parking lot and up the street. Lined with a print shop, a dog groomer's, a furniture store and a supermarket on one side, and an old brick turn-of-the-century post office on the other, it was surrounded by ancient maple trees, their bare branches like lace against the blue sky.

She leaned into him slightly, her tone quiet but urgent. "I don't have time for small talk, all right?"

He put both hands in the pockets of his gray cords, her arm still looped in his left. Things were looking as though she might have changed her mind about marrying him, after all, but he'd been a cop long enough to guard against too optimistic a view.

He kept walking at a leisurely pace, careful to keep

what he thought to himself. "As I seem to say often when I'm around you—I'm listening."

She sighed. The wind blowing from the direction of the river had a sharp bite. She didn't seem to notice. "While Kelly was visiting my studio today," she said, her breath puffing out ahead of her, "she got a call on her cell phone. Someone was full of questions about me."

"Who?"

She shook her head, her hair moving in loose waves with a gloss and grace that caught his eye. He looked his fill for a moment while she stared ahead, a pleat between her eyebrows, then concentrated on her eyes when she looked up at him. They were filled with fear.

"He said he was an art-magazine reporter, but she thinks he was a private detective. He knew that Kelly and I had known each other in Seattle, and that Jason had run away." She shook her head and added with a mocking twist of her lips, "And he tried to make something out of my relationship with Rush Weston."

He felt instant and profound annoyance, but he kept that, too, to himself. He'd picked up Rush Weston while breaking up a brawl in a waterfront tavern on a Friday night a couple of weeks ago. The man had behaved with scornful superiority, and Ethan had enjoyed pinning him to the bar and cuffing him when he'd resisted arrest.

"What about Rush Weston?" he asked calmly.

"Nothing. Well, you could say we're friends. He's an artist, too, a sculptor, and when he's not being obnoxious, he can be very nice. He's renting a spot in my art mall when I open."

Although Ethan knew his attitude was unwarranted, he resented that she even knew Weston. "That doesn't sound like anything a detective could use against you," he said, sounding mature and magnanimous. What he really wanted to do was warn her to stay away from the guy, but he could imagine how that would go over. And anyway, depending on the point she intended to make with this conversation, he might have very little to do with her life from now on.

They stopped at the corner where the pedestrian light read Don't Walk, and she took the moment to lean her forehead against his upper arm. The wind stirred her hair and strands of it drifted across his chin and throat. He felt a stalling of his brain function. When she lifted her head again, her cheeks were pale and pinched with the cold.

Without giving thought to the action, he reached down to pull the zipper of her red jacket up from between her breasts to her chin.

The light changed. They crossed the street and started back in the direction of Dinosaur Pizza. "You might have guessed by the fact that I'm walking you around like some fraternal organization sergeant-at-arms that there *is* something the detective can use against me."

"And what's that?"

Her grip on his arm tightened. "When the detective spoke to Rush, he implied that there was something between us. He said we'd be sharing studio space and that soon we'd be sharing…more."

That fanned Ethan's annoyance. "How did Rush get that impression?"

Beth stopped walking and looked into his face. She

dropped her arm from his and jammed her hands in the pockets of her jacket. Her eyes were speculative, surprised. She'd detected his irritation and it seemed to have sparked her own.

"I don't know," she said finally, her tone a bit stiff. "He did ask me out a couple of times and I refused. Some men have difficulty taking no for an answer. Certainly a man like you who generally does as he pleases can understand that?"

He narrowed his eyes at her for using his words against him. She looked at him in all innocence.

"I'm acquainted with Rush Weston," he said, then added with relish, "professionally."

Her look of innocence vanished. "What do you mean?"

"It made the paper."

"I don't subscribe," she said impatiently. "It's a way to pinch pennies. I count on gossip. How do you know him professionally?"

"I picked him up in a brawl at a tavern on the waterfront." He provided that information with satisfaction. "If you're trying to present a squeaky-clean image to your in-laws, Weston is not the way to go."

"He and I are not…" she began angrily, a little loudly, then remembering where they were, lowered her voice. "I said he's a fellow artist, that's all. His suggestion that there's something more between us is just a lot of bull. Everybody who knows him understands his tendency to fantasize."

"Your in-laws," he reminded her quietly, "don't know him."

Her lips firmed and she shifted her weight. "You're absolutely right," she said. "That's why I need you to marry me."

Beth spoke the words quickly before she could lose courage, then resisted the impulse to cover her eyes and watch for his reaction between her fingers. Instead, she squared her shoulders, held his seemingly unsurprised gaze and waited for his reaction.

If she'd expected something dramatic, she was disappointed. He simply started walking slowly back toward the restaurant. She had no choice but to follow.

"What exactly did you have in mind?" he asked when she caught up with him.

"I'm desperate," she admitted candidly. "So, I guess, pretty much whatever you want. If you really hate the idea, if you'd just do it for me for now to get us through this week, we can annul it the moment they leave town and I'll find a way to disappear with Jason. Or...something." That wasn't fair to anyone, she knew, but right now her need for a solution was too immediate to allow contemplation of future consequences.

"Or," she continued, trying hard to sell him on the idea, "if you want someone to cook for you and keep house, I'll do it for as long as you want me to. And I'll do my best to help with Nikkie, if she'll let me, provided you do the same for Jason."

He stopped to look down at her with open skepticism. "What about all your denials of domestic competence?"

She nodded, willing to grant him the right to wonder. "I have no domestic competence, but I can do anything I set my mind to. And I'm a damned good mother. I'll do my best for Nikkie."

He moved on again. She kept pace with him.

"Well, so far," he said, "we've talked about your

abilities as a housekeeper and a mother, but not as a wife.''

"In my experience," she said, doing her best to keep up with his long strides, "that's all a wife is. Maybe an answering service, too."

They'd reached the corner opposite the restaurant and another Don't Walk light. He frowned down at her. "What kind of a marriage did you have, anyway?"

She'd been trying to avoid thinking about those days. Cobbler's Crossing was supposed to be a fresh start for her and Jason. But now that opportunity sat squarely in the hands of Ethan Drum. So she answered his question with one of her own—the only one that mattered now.

"What kind of a marriage do you want?"

His dark eyes told her in detail. To her horror she blushed. He noted that and groaned.

The light changed. He caught her arm and pulled her with him across the street and toward the Blazer. They could hear the excited sounds of children's voices and the lower notes of adult laughter coming from the restaurant.

Ethan stood her squarely in front of him against the back of the Blazer, then put a hand to the roof on either side of her. Her heartbeat accelerated and all the air seemed to leave her lungs.

"What I *don't* want in a wife," he said quietly, "is a woman who blushes at the mention of sex."

She tried to fold her arms to put some distance between them, but he was too close. She dropped both arms and flattened her hands against the cold metal of the car behind her. That was steadying somehow.

"You *didn't* mention it," she said, "but I saw it in your eyes. That made it more intimate. I'm sorry."

He seemed annoyed with her apology. "So you hadn't considered intimacy as part of our marriage?"

It was hard, she decided, to allow a fear to surface that she'd suppressed for years. Particularly since it was a fear she'd never shared with anyone except Kelly. She'd borne it for a long time, then when Steve made it clear there was little need to deal with it, she'd simply put it away. And her choice never to marry again allowed her to let it remain hidden.

But her present situation changed all that.

"Frankly…" Her voice came out thin and reedy, and she cleared her throat. "Frankly, I hadn't thought that far. When Kelly repeated what that caller said about Rush Weston, I knew there was only one way out of this, so I came to you. But—" she cleared her throat again, blushed again and closed her eyes when he watched her in obvious confusion "—there's something you should know."

She was hyperventilating and she felt as though she was about to faint. She opened her eyes and found that he still appeared confused, but not angry. He simply waited.

"Do I have to tell you again that I'm listening?" he asked quietly.

He didn't. But a man who listened to her was something new; she suspected that that was why it unsettled her so much. That, and the nature of what he was waiting for her to explain.

"I'm not very good sexually," she said at last.

There was a long moment of silence in the parking lot. Children laughed and shrieked in the restaurant, cars drove by on the street, a siren whined somewhere in the distance. But Beth felt as though she'd been covered with a glass dome, as though she could see out but was isolated.

Ethan studied her for an endless moment, as though that remark might make sense to him if he stared long enough at the woman who'd made it. At last he stepped back, folded his arms and asked, "What do you mean?"

That was the very question she dreaded. She looked at him imploringly. "I mean," she said, her blush draining, pallor replacing it. "I'm not...very skilled at...making love." Her lips twisted in self-deprecation. "I think I'm even worse sexually than I am domestically."

Now that he'd moved away, she could fold her arms, too, but it didn't seem to work as a defense mechanism. She still felt exposed. She dropped her arms and put her hands in her pockets. "It doesn't mean I won't do it," she said, her eyes miserable with humiliation. "It's just a warning that you shouldn't expect...great things."

He studied her another moment, then turned and leaned against the Blazer, too. "What makes you say that?" he asked, his voice filled with disbelief.

When she tipped her head back and looked up at the sky, agonized by the thought of going into detail, he said gently, "I'm sorry. I can see that this is difficult for you, but I want to understand. So tell me. When did you arrive at this conclusion?"

She was asking this man to let her into his life for her own purposes, she reminded herself. She had an obligation to let him into hers. Even into the places she didn't like to go.

"About five years ago," she said, staring at the

toes of her shoes. "I...never found it wonderful, although it was all right the first couple of years of my marriage. But then Steve became very busy and, when he did think about me, sex was always after he'd made some lucrative deal—and then it was sort of quick and triumphant. I sort of...lost interest."

"And it never occurred to you that it was his fault and not yours?"

"I'm not sure it was entirely," she said, remembering the humiliation she'd felt at the time. "I...I'd suggested we try something new. He was disgusted by it and I was embarrassed. Then I realized somewhere along the way I'd lost all appeal for him." She sighed. "And then, I guess, I gave up."

Ethan turned to face her, but she couldn't meet his eyes. "He was disgusted?" he asked incredulously.

She shook her head. "Please don't ask me to tell you what it was."

"I won't." He reached up to catch her chin with his index finger and turn her face toward him. She found his expression gentle and surprisingly easy to look into. "But I want you to know that if you ever want to tell me, I like to consider myself... adventurous."

He pushed away from the Blazer, drew her a short distance from it, then opened the tailgate again. Handing her the gift-wrapped bicycle helmet, he closed and locked the door, put an arm around her shoulders and led her toward the restaurant.

"We'll get married on Saturday," he said. "You can do your art, not worry about the housekeeping, we'll do our best with the kids, and we'll let sex take care of itself."

She stopped him a few feet from the door, her expression serious. "Ethan, I appreciate how well you're taking my news, but...I can't let you get into this if you don't understand that there's a real problem here."

He shook his head, apparently failing to grasp the severity of her warning. He tapped her temple with his index finger. "I think the problem's here, not anywhere else."

She blinked at him, torn between exasperation and admiration. "How could you possibly know that?"

"Because I kissed you this morning," he replied with a grin, "and you kissed me back. The interest is there. Maybe you just need more inspiration than you've had in the past." He pulled the door open. "But some things are better done than analyzed. Come on. Jason's waiting for us."

CHAPTER SEVEN

BETH WATCHED her son surrounded by school friends cheering him on as he maneuvered around monsters in a video game. She guessed there was not a happier child anywhere that sunny afternoon.

A couple of teenage boys in white aprons with triceratops printed on them cleared two long tables of the debris generated by eight large pizzas and four pitchers of soft drinks.

In one corner of the room was a veritable treasure trove of presents. Because of the party's short notice, Jason's friends had not had a chance to buy gifts, but Brodie had arrived with the entire set of *Toy Story* figures down to the barrel of monkeys and the green rubber soldiers. Ebbie had bought a basketball, and Kelly had wrapped several videos in a backpack. Several sheriff's deputies in uniform, whom Ebbie or Ethan had probably commandeered to fill out the party for the sake of the grandparents, appeared with a fleet of toy trucks and a set of Goosebumps books.

The deputies had left early, explaining that they were on a dinner break, and Beth and Ethan had walked with them out to the parking lot.

"Thank you for coming," Beth said sincerely, shaking their hands. "I know you were bullied into this. You really shouldn't have brought gifts."

The taller of the two, whose badge read "Curtis"

shrugged off her thanks. "What's a birthday party without presents?"

The other deputy, shorter, stockier and a few years older, was Billings. "And when Ethan speaks, we obey," he said in a heroic tone. "Right, Chief?"

"Yeah, right." Ethan's tone suggested that wasn't true at all. "Has it been a quiet afternoon?"

Billings nodded. "Yeah. We feel neglected, but we'll adjust."

Ethan put a hand on each man's shoulder. "That's the spirit of the department, gentlemen. Now get out there and make me proud."

"But, Chief," Curtis said gravely, "pride's been your problem all along."

Ethan gave him a shove toward their county car. "Goodbye, Curtis."

As they moved off, Curtis could be heard asking loudly, "Did that shove qualify as boss brutality?"

"No," Billings replied as they separated to walk around opposite sides of the car. "But I'm getting out of here before he does something that does."

Ethan and Beth went back into the restaurant. "Incidentally," Beth said quietly as the boys continued to carry on loudly at the video game, "why did you buy Jason a bike? An expensive bike, at that."

There was scolding in her tone, and he turned just before they reached the tables to fix her with a silencing frown. "His was totaled," he said, "and I wanted to buy him a bike. All right?"

She glanced in the direction of the table and saw that Zachary and Joanne were watching them. Kelly and Brodie seemed completely absorbed in each other, and Ebbie was busy slicing and packaging left-over cake.

"I just don't want you spending a lot of money," she said.

"What *is* it with you and money?" Ethan demanded, keeping his voice low. "Were you frightened by a savings-and-loan bailout or something?"

She gave him a speaking look. "My in-laws are watching," she warned, "and don't get smart with me. I used to have a lot of money and nothing else. Now I have only a little and…and many concerns. But Jason and I do not require much, so there's no point in your indulging every extravagance he—"

She stopped because he'd run a hand over his face as though he'd had about all of her he could take.

"If you play your cards right," he said, smiling—which she was sure he did for Joanne and Zachary's benefit, "you can have everything I have. It's not a lot of money, but usually enough. And you can have everything else—all that was missing in your life before. But not if you keep ragging on me."

"I wasn't ragging, I was—"

"You were ragging."

A glance toward the table told her that her in-laws were still watching. "Now you've probably made them think we're not getting along," she accused him.

"Then maybe," he suggested under his voice, "you should do something to make them think otherwise."

She studied him with suspicion. "Like what?"

"Your call," he said mercilessly. "What comes to mind?"

In view of what she'd explained to him just before they joined the party, her mind was blank. Then she realized that all her in-laws needed to see was a loving touch.

She drew a breath and looped her arms around his neck. His came to her waist. She felt the press of his leg between her thighs, the hardness of his chest against the softness of hers, the hair at the back of his neck against the inside of her wrist.

She smiled in the interest of her performance and asked sotto voce, "How's that?"

Apparently also performing, he returned her smile. "A little lukewarm."

"We're in a pizza parlor."

"I don't think passion has a sense of place. It's as combustible in a downpour on a street corner as it is in the bedroom."

And with that he pulled her against him. She was sure her body's instant clamoring response was only one of surprise.

Then he nuzzled under her hair and kissed the side of her neck, and she knew she was wrong. Her heart jolted and sent what felt like a little stream of lava right down the middle of her being. The pulse of excitement she felt had nothing to do with surprise.

But before she could analyze it further, Ethan said in amused warning, "Uh-oh. Incoming."

She began to step back out of his arms, but Jason collided with them, wrapping an arm around each of them. His face was almost too bright to look at.

He took a fistful of the sleeve of Beth's sweater and pulled her down to his level. "Is Ethan gonna be my dad?" he whispered. "Be real quiet, Mom. Grandma and Grandpa are looking this way, and I think they're trying to listen."

She kissed his cheek. His happiness was infectious,

and it would be easy for the sake of today's performance for her in-laws, to let herself believe as her son did—that her marriage to Ethan was the best thing that could possibly happen.

"Yes," she said, smiling into his hopeful expression. And with that admission, she let go of all the potentially grievous problems the situation presented. If she was going to do this, she would have to do it with certitude and enthusiasm, to be both convincing to her in-laws and fair to the man who was giving her this chance to avoid messy and expensive litigation. "Yes," she said again, "he is."

With a whoop of delight, Jason leaped at Ethan, who bent slightly and caught him in one arm. The boy reached up and gave him a strangling hug.

"I'm gonna really like being your kid," he said in a loud whisper. "And thanks for the bike and the helmet! And the cool party! I've never had so much fun. Never, never, never!"

"Well, good." Ethan straightened and exchanged a wry glance with Beth. "'Cause I think the fun's just starting."

Half a dozen of Jason's friends who were crowded around the video game shouted that it was his turn. Jason raced back to join them.

Ethan wrapped an arm around Beth's shoulders and led her to the table where Brodie, Kelly and the Richardses sat. Ebbie stood at the end of the table, still wrapping up leftovers.

Brodie and Zachary were enthusiastically discussing basketball scores. Ethan joined the men on one side of the table, and Beth sat between Kelly and Joanne on the other.

A young man in a Dinosaur Pizza apron arrived with a tray filled with cups and a pot of coffee.

"We're soft drinked out," Kelly explained, helping the boy distribute cups. "But it doesn't look as though the kids are ready to go yet." She pointed to the knot of little boys cheering excitedly in the corner as Jason turned a wheel with one hand and operated a joystick with the other. His laughter was loud and gleeful.

Kelly laughed just watching them. "Have you ever seen such unbridled delight? Ah, to be eight again!"

"When I was eight," Brodie said, holding his cup out as the waiter poured, "Ethan made me slide down the banister into the basement of our parents' house."

Ethan passed him the cream, his expression unrepentant. "You could have refused."

"You had my Tonka dumptruck and wouldn't give it back."

"Because you had a fear of the basement stairs and wouldn't go down. I was trying to help you deal with your problem. Get past it."

"Sure."

"It worked, didn't it? You no longer have a fear of basements."

"That's true. Now I have a fear of sliding down a banister, falling off and losing my front tooth."

"Lighten up. The implant looks great. Women love your smile." Ethan turned to Kelly. "Don't they?"

"Ah...um..." Kelly stammered. Beth watched with interest as her usually quick-witted friend seemed to lose the power of speech. Beth looked at Brodie, who was giving Kelly the reputed smile, then at Ethan, who also appeared to be studying the action with interest. "Yes," Kelly said, finally pulling herself together. "It's a charming smile."

"See?" Ethan said to Brodie. "Quit whining." Then he turned to Zachary and asked politely, "Did I overhear you say you're having trouble with your car?"

Zachary stirred sugar into his coffee and eagerly launched into a detailed explanation of the Cadillac's behavior.

"When did you meet Ethan?" Joanne asked, her arms folded on the table.

"It's a small town," Beth replied carefully, certain the question was a trap, "everyone gets to know newcomers pretty fast, and Ethan's job requires him to be very involved in the community."

Joanne nodded, her smile suggesting acquiescence, but her eyes suggesting suspicion. "But when exactly? How?"

Aware that a lie of any kind could mean trouble, Beth took a sip of coffee to give herself a moment to think. Had Joanne already asked Ebbie how they'd met? Or Jason? Or Kelly? Was she just waiting for Beth to contradict that information?

Beth suddenly remembered something Jason had told her and decided that a grain of truth in her reply was better than none at all.

"Ethan went to Jason's school to talk to the kids about the sheriff's office. I volunteer there a few hours a week."

She hadn't been there the day Ethan visited the school, but that wasn't what she'd claimed, anyway. She'd simply stated two separate truths.

Joanne glanced across the table at Ethan, who was deep in conversation with Brodie and her husband, then turned back to Beth. "You've only been here three months. That isn't very long to know someone."

"Well," Beth said, thinking fast, "when it's right, it's right."

That, too, was true. Saving herself from litigation over her son was very right.

Joanne's dark eyes focused on her with disapproval. "Can it *be* right when you've just lost Steve?"

"That was a year ago, Jo," Beth replied, thinking that she'd really lost him years before his death. But his mother didn't know that.

"One can't help but wonder," Joanne said, raising her coffee cup, "how deeply you felt about him if you can get over him in a year."

Mercifully Beth was saved from having to respond by Ebbie, who leaned between them and placed a foil-wrapped package in front of Joanne. "There you go," she said. "A little cake to enjoy tonight in your motel room."

Ebbie offered another foil package to Brodie.

He accepted it with a smile, then pursed his lips in imitation of a kiss. "When are you moving in with me, Eb?"

"When Mel gets tired of me," she replied offhandedly.

"Mel?" Brodie asked.

"Gibson," she said, as though it should be obvious. "You didn't know he's been flying in on weekends to see me?"

Brodie made a face. "Ebbie, do you really think a pretty face can make you happy?"

"No, but he's a pretty face with millions."

Brodie looked chagrined. "But…women love my smile."

Ebbie gave a derisive snort. "You can't buy diddly with that, sweetie," she countered. She closed the box, which still contained a third of the cake.

Brodie leaned toward Kelly. "Would you prefer a man with millions, or me and my smile?"

Kelly leaned toward him. "I'm looking for a smile like yours *on* a man with millions. I need someone to support my art habit, but I need him to do it cheerfully so he doesn't inhibit my creativity."

"I thought artists needed to be in pain to work," he said.

She shook her head. "Not me. Pain just makes me miserable. And I can't throw pots when I'm miserable."

"Well—" he seemed to be thinking seriously "—is there anything that'd keep you happy, besides millions?"

"Ah…" She pretended to consider the question seriously, then said firmly, "Nope," and pushed away from the table. She bent down to hug Beth, then went around the table and hugged Ethan, too.

Beth exchanged a surprised look with Ethan, then realized Kelly was pretending she'd known Ethan for some time—something the Richardses would expect of Beth's best friend.

"Great party, guys," she said. "Thanks for inviting me." She pushed Brodie's shoulder as he tried to stand. "Don't get up. Nice to meet you, Brodie. Mr. and Mrs. Richards. See you at the wedding?"

Joanne's manner was cool. "Of course. We'll be there."

"Wonderful. Ebbie, I'll call you about the hors d'oeuvres."

Ebbie looked up from pouring a pitcher of leftover soda into a large carryout cup and covered her momentary surprise with a quick smile. "Thanks. I planned the menu, but left it at the office."

As Kelly waded through the crowd of little boys to find Jason and give him a hug, Joanne said with feigned amiability. "This is a little last minute to be planning a menu, isn't it, four days before the wedding? Or is the entire wedding spur-of-the-moment?"

"The wedding," Ethan said easily, reaching across the table for Beth's hand, "is a tribute to my success in finally convincing Beth I can't live without her." The look in his eyes was intimate and ardent. Beth was ensnared by it and couldn't free herself until he turned to Joanne. "I understand your concern for your grandson and your daughter-in-law, but I promise you I'll take good care of them."

Joanne's mouth worked uncertainly as she obviously struggled with disbelief and the convincing quality of his declaration. Zachary studied Ethan uncertainly, too. Then he exchanged a glance with his wife.

Kelly blew kisses as she passed the table on her way out to the parking lot. Brodie watched her walk away with an interest Beth was thrilled to see. Kelly had sworn off men after her divorce three years before. She'd loved her husband, a football coach at the high school where she taught art. But he'd resented the time she spent on her pottery outside of school and her dedication to the Seattle co-op where Beth had met her.

He'd finally given her an ultimatum—him or her

pottery. It had amazed Beth that he hadn't known better.

Kelly and Beth had commiserated over seafood salads at Pike Place Market the day before Kelly was to leave for Cobbler's Crossing. Most men, they'd concluded, despite their claims of appreciating a woman's skills and talents, still wanted a woman who was traditional, who conformed to their conservative notions of what a wife should be.

Yet those conclusions notwithstanding, here was Kelly now, walking out of the restaurant with her charming derriere being considered with more than casual interest by Brodie Drum, and she, Beth, was about to marry his brother.

What, she wondered, was the world coming to?

The world seemed even a little farther off its axis when the restaurant's front door swung open and five teenagers poured into the shadowy barnlike interior of Dinosaur Pizza.

Nikkie, in a black wool jacket that ended in a band at her tiny waist, an impossibly tight pair of black jeans and boots that looked as though they belonged on a logger, led the way to their table.

Ethan stood up to welcome them, and Nikkie walked into his arms.

"Hi," she said with a shy glance around the table. "Did we miss the party? Hi, Unc. Hi, Beth."

"No," he said, giving her shoulders a squeeze. "We've got cake left, and we'll get you guys some pizza. I thought you had a meeting."

He looked over Nikkie's head to the two girls and two boys who stood behind her. One of the girls was small like Nikkie and had short purple hair with a side part and black lipstick. The other was a tall and glamorous blonde in a long leather coat. Both boys were tall, one gangly with thin-rimmed round glasses and the other thickly built with a blond buzz cut and an earring.

A collective groan rose from the group and Nikkie said morosely, "Mr. Fogarty decided on *Henry V* for our Winter Festival play. We're really bummed out."

Ethan looked surprised. "Why? You love Shakespeare."

"We all love Shakespeare," the buzz cut said, "and it's a play we can get everybody in, but we're looking at Medieval clothes, armor, shields and weapons for twenty."

"On a fifty-dollar budget," the girl with the purple hair said.

"Yeah," the spindly boy concurred. "And he says it's our problem. That learning to mount a production with no money is as important for a drama student to learn as acting."

The blonde sighed. "I wanted to do *Streetcar*. I can do Blanche's lines in my sleep."

The spindly boy turned to her. "Well, you'll have to wake up to do Katharine."

Purple Hair frowned. "*I* want to do Katharine."

The blonde looked down her nose at her. "I have the tiara." Then she spread both arms in a ta-da sort of pose. "And the height to be royalty. You'll have to be happy as my lady-in-waiting."

Nikkie rolled her eyes at her friends, then turned to her father. "And the worst part—besides my cast mates—is that I'm in charge of props *and* I'm playing Isabel, Queen of France."

Ethan smiled sympathetically. "Then you're going to need a really big pizza. First let me introduce you to Jason's grandparents, Mr. and Mrs. Richards. Joanne, Zachary, I'd like you to meet my daughter, Tanika."

The girl smiled and waved. "Nikkie," she said, then introduced her friends. Bradley was the spindly boy, the blonde was Vanessa, Rosalie the one with the purple hair, and the buzz cut was Cameron.

"Guys, you know Brodie," she went on. They all nodded and murmured greetings.

"And you know Beth," she finished casually.

Beth expected instant denial or at least looks of confusion, but Nikkie must have apprised them of the plan—that she and Ethan would appear to be engaged during the birthday party.

It was easy to see why these kids were in the drama club. Their acting skills were excellent. Beth was treated to friendly smiles, a "How's it going?" and a "Love your sweater!"

Nikkie pulled a small gift-wrapped box out of her pocket and looked around. "Where's Jason?"

As though his personal radar had sensed more loot, Jason appeared at Nikkie's side. He looked up at her in astonishment. "You came!"

Beth read annoyance in her eyes, then Nikkie tossed her hair and thrust the gift at him. "I felt like pizza. Here."

He had the wrap off in a matter of seconds and held up a watch with Buzz Lightyear on it. Buzz's arms served as the hands.

"Wow!" Jason's eyes were huge. He turned to Beth. "Mom, look!"

"How did you know?" Beth asked Nikkie. Too late she realized that maybe this was not a question she should ask when trying to convince her in-laws that she, Jason, Ethan and Nikkie spent a lot of time together.

"Because Buzz Lightyear is all he ever talks about," Nikkie said with a laugh. She reached down to push a button on the side of the watch, and a tinny voice said, "Buzz Lightyear to the rescue!"

Jason gasped, beside himself with delight. He raced back to his friends to show off his newest gift.

Ethan patted Nikkie's shoulder. "Come on. We'll get you guys some pizza."

Ethan led Nikkie and her friends to the counter. Jason returned to the table with the announcement that he was out of quarters. Brodie, delving into the pocket of his coveralls for change, went with Jason back to the game.

And Beth found herself alone with her in-laws.

Joanne sighed, gathered up her purse, her coat, the foil-wrapped leftover cake and mumbled crossly, "I feel as though we've been set down in the middle of Paramount Studios!" Then she turned to Beth with a coldly polite, "Thank you. We've enjoyed the party. And thank you for the cake."

"Would you and Zachary like to come back to the house for a while?" Courtesy had forced her to ask. She prayed they'd refuse.

Her prayer was answered. "It's been a long day and Zach's arthritis is acting up." Beth saw Joanne shoot her husband a glance that warned him not to contradict her. Apparently she wanted to get away as much as Beth wanted her to. "We might spend the next few days sightseeing if there's nothing seriously wrong with the car, but we'll be in touch before the…wedding." As usual she applied cool disbelief to the word.

"Good." Beth walked the couple to the door of the restaurant. "I have to get you Ebbie's address."

Ethan appeared suddenly behind Beth. He placed both hands on her shoulders as Joanne climbed into the passenger seat of the Cadillac and Zachary went around to the driver's side.

"You'll have to come over," he said, "and help Jason with the Legos you bought. We have a work-table in the basement where we can really spread out."

Zachary looked interested, but Joanne said only, "We'll be in touch."

Beth and Ethan waved till the white Cadillac was out of sight.

Beth stood on the windy street corner with Ethan behind her and knew her life would never be the same. The first time she'd married she'd been hopeful and in love, yet her life had fallen apart, anyway. This time, she was getting married to a man she hardly knew to avoid a legal battle for custody of her son.

Perhaps, she thought, it was the influence of Nikkie and her drama-club friends, but this moment was like being center stage and having the houselights go out as the curtain came down. Stagehands were about to change the set and move all the pieces of her life around.

It would be interesting to know if she was starring in a comedy or a tragedy.

CHAPTER EIGHT

FOR THE NEXT THREE DAYS, Beth went to her cannery studio in the morning and left for Ethan's house in the evening with a grocery bag or a box in which she'd packed some of her and Jason's clothes and personal items. She did this on the chance that her in-laws' detective was watching her.

She had, in fact, noticed a man sitting in a car not far from the cannery the past two mornings, then noticed the same car parked about a block from Ethan's last evening. Was he taking photos of her comings and goings? It would be difficult to convince her in-laws she'd been living with Ethan for a while if she was photographed with a U-Haul and a group of friends to help her move.

Beth had left the room with the bunk beds to Jason and now occupied the fourth bedroom upstairs. She'd brought her bedspread and curtains from the cannery in a laundry bag. The closet had a small built-in dresser, and Ethan brought up an old wooden desk from the basement to put in an empty corner.

"Diana bought it at a church rummage sale, thinking she'd clean it up and paint it one day, but she was always too busy."

Beth thought she heard a wistful note in his voice and went to sit on the edge of her bed. Ethan knelt

on one knee by the desk and dusted off the legs. It
was a simple maple desk with a spindly-legged chair.

"Are you *sure* you're willing to do this?" Beth
asked. "I mean, if you had a great marriage once, this
might be harder for you than you anticipate."

He turned from the desk, his forearm resting on his
bent knee, the soft chamois in his fingers. His eyes
were quiet, relaxed. "Life is full of surprises. It's entirely possible that *our* marriage could be great."

She nodded, then looked away, occupying herself
with finding pairs in a pile of loose socks in the middle of the bed.

"Are you sure *you* want to do this?" he asked,
pushing to his feet and sitting beside her, leaving only
a small space between them. "Considering how you
feel about marriage? I know how important Jason is
to you, but I really don't think your in-laws could win
a case against you in court."

"I don't think so, either," she admitted, concentrating on folding a pair of woolly blue kneesocks,
"but it would be expensive and nerve-racking to have
to defend myself against them. I also wouldn't want
to put Jason through that. Their threats have frightened him enough already."

Ethan nodded, taking the socks from her and putting them aside. He turned to face her and looked into
her eyes.

"I know. I'm just trying to make it clear that a
halfhearted effort in this marriage won't be good for
any of us. If you're having second thoughts, I'd rather
help you find a good lawyer and lend you the money
to fight Joanne and Zachary. And I'll do my best to
be a friend to Jason, instead of a father."

She sat up stiffly, concern budding in her chest,

then doubling and tripling quickly into a big ugly worry. Did he want out of this? Did *she?*

She tried to examine what she felt, a difficult task under his watchful dark gaze. What she found was an understandable fear of something new, the possibly irrational but very real fear of disappointing Ethan in bed and, under all that, an urgent willingness to try, anyway.

"The wedding's tomorrow afternoon," she reminded him.

"Yes, but you haven't signed a contract. If you want to cancel, just say the word."

"Jason," she said softly, "wants a father more than he wants a friend."

He shook his head at her. "That's familiar ground. I'm asking what *you* want."

She shrugged, reluctant to tell him that she found him attractive and appealing and that just being within sight of him calmed her and made her feel secure. And that the thought of being married to him, of sharing his life and his bed, lit a spark in her she'd been sure had died long ago. She'd bared her soul to Steve so many times and been ignored that she'd put a tight cap on what she felt.

And though she knew Ethan Drum could never be confused with Steve Richards, her defense mechanism remained in place.

"I want what's best for my son," she replied.

Ethan would have taken great satisfaction in shaking her. He saw many emotions cross her face and wished she'd explain them in words. But she was like a mystery without a clue, a case without a lead.

"Fine," he said. "I'm in, as long as you understand that I intend to be a husband, as well as a father.''

She bobbed her head. "I'm in, too, as long as you remember…what I told you."

"Right. Your claim to be sexually inadequate." He got to his feet and offered her a hand to help her to hers. "I don't believe it for a minute."

She held on to his hand when he tried to withdraw it and give the chair one more swipe with the chamois.

She swallowed, put a hand to her hair, then dropped it, high color filling her cheeks. Her control seemed to wobble and she looked up at him, her eyes filled with a curious combination of determination and reluctance.

He tossed the chamois at the desk and gave her his full attention.

"You've been honest with me," she said, nervously tucking her hair behind her ear. "I appreciate that, so I want to be as honest with you. You're a confident virile man and it sounds as though Diana was a devoted and wonderful woman. So you had what it takes for…love to be wonderful."

By love, he knew she meant lovemaking. He listened quietly, wondering what her point was.

She heaved a sigh, as though continuing required great courage. "My experience has been significantly different, and I'm not entirely sure that…you'll be able to change the way I am."

He had every confidence that the problem was not with her but with the man who'd made his business more important than his wife. He opened his mouth to tell her that, but she had more to say.

"So I was thinking—" she looked into his eyes,

then down at her hands, then up into his eyes again "—it would be one thing if we were getting married with the intention of getting an annulment the moment we thought it was safe. But if you want a *real* marriage out of this, you…you might want to make sure, first, that you're not going to regret it later…."

Ethan was blown away by her offer. And guessing by the widening of her eyes, the strong emotion he felt went from him to her through the hand he still held.

He was both touched and angry, and couldn't determine which feeling dominated. He was furious that her self-esteem had been pounded so low she felt obliged to make that suggestion. But it also turned his spine to spaghetti to know that she'd made it because she was trying to be fair to him.

As tempting as her offer was to his longtime celibate body, he knew that accepting it would only strike another blow to the pride her husband had driven into the ground.

He took her face in his hands and kissed her gently and slowly. Her lips were soft, pliable. A bit surprised.

"Thank you," he said when he raised his head, "but that won't be necessary. I'm sure I won't regret anything." He smiled. "Excuse me. I'm going to shower before dinner."

"SHE'S MAKING *frozen* lasagna for dinner," Nikkie said, her voice laced with disdain. She stood in the doorway of Ethan's bathroom, arms folded, shoulder leaning against the doorjamb.

Showered and dressed in jeans and a chambray

shirt, he stood before the mirror over the sink and combed his hair.

"You do that all the time," he said, leaning forward to frown over a spray of three or four gray hairs in his sideburns. Damn. He'd have sworn they weren't there yesterday.

"But she's a mother."

Ethan gave the back of his hair one more swipe with the comb, then tossed it onto the blue-tiled counter and turned to face his daughter.

"Your mother brought home take-out from the deli a couple of nights a week, and we ate fish sticks and tater tots a lot." He leaned a hip against the counter and smiled. "But we didn't love her because she was a great cook. We loved her because she was warm and funny and she loved us."

Nikkie's expression firmed. "You're not expecting me to love *her,* are you?"

"No, I'm not. I'm expecting you to be polite and helpful and understand that she's doing her best in a strange and difficult situation."

"Do you?"

"Do I what?"

"Love her."

"I like her a lot," he answered, the words coming easily. "Liking often turns to love."

Nikkie absorbed that, then straightened away from the doorjamb with an expression of disapproval. "Well, I think it's barbaric." Then she marched off through his room and across the hall to hers.

He followed, stopping in her doorway and watching her yank a silky white blouse off her bed and move to the closet to hang it up.

"Would you find it less barbaric," he asked, "if

she was fixing roast chicken and twice-baked potatoes for dinner?''

She glanced at him over her shoulder with a look he could only describe as parental. ''Please, Daddy. You don't like it when *I'm* snide,'' she said, hooking the hanger on the rod in an angry motion, then closing the closet door.

''Why did you come to Jason's party?'' he asked as she smoothed a bedspread that didn't need smoothing.

''Because our meeting broke up early and I wanted pizza.''

''I think,'' he said carefully, preparing for an explosion, ''that you secretly like the idea of having Beth and Jason around.''

When his daughter gasped and gave him a look that said he was crazy, he raised a silencing hand. ''I know. You're concerned about what it'll do to the life you and I have grown used to. In a way so am I. But deep down, I think you sometimes get a little lonely. I think you're afraid you might like having a stepmother and a brother.''

She glared at him, fists clenched, and he congratulated himself. He knew that look; he saw it regularly. He didn't know if it was the teenager in her or the woman, but she hated it when he read her mind.

''I think you should know,'' she said, her chin angling stubbornly, ''that if she tries to push me around, I'm not going to stand for it.''

''I don't think she's the pushy type.''

''You've only known her five days.''

''It only took me two days with you,'' he said, wandering a few steps into her room, ''to know that *you* were pushy. Had us up all night. Allergic to this, allergic to that. But we kept you, anyway.''

Her shoulders sagged and she appeared on the verge of a smile. "Daddy, I'm half you. You're, like, the motherlode of pushy! Hey!"

Suddenly her expression changed to anger and she rushed past Ethan into the hallway. He followed, wondering what had upset her, and caught up with her halfway to the stairs. She stood glowering at Jason.

The boy had Simba in his arms, the cat's furry legs and tail hanging heavily.

"That's *my* cat," she said, taking the gray bundle from Jason's arms.

"He was on my bed," Jason said, sounding more hurt than defensive. "I was gonna give him some milk."

Nikkie cuddled Simba like a baby. "Milk's bad for cats!" she snapped.

"But everybody gives cats milk."

"It makes old cats sick. Just leave my cats alone and go play with all your new toys."

Jason's voice rose. "Well, excuse me all to hell!"

Nikkie turned to Ethan, the picture of mortification. "Daddy. He said *hell*." She stalked back to her room and closed the door.

Jason looked up at Ethan beseechingly. "He was on my bed. And I thought cats liked milk!"

Ethan put a hand on Jason's head and led him toward the stairs. "They do, but that cat's pretty old and it does make him sick."

"Nikkie hates me."

"No, she doesn't. She's just grumpy because things are changing a little around here."

''She's jealous 'cause I had a birthday and got lots of stuff.''

While that observation did have some truth, Ethan said, ''I don't think so. But she hasn't had to share my attention with anyone else for a long time. Just like you haven't had to share your mom. But Nikkie'll be okay, don't worry.''

They'd reached the stairs and Ethan caught Jason by the shoulder before he could start down. ''No hells and damns around here, okay? No four-letter words.''

Jason appeared confused about that. ''H-e-l?'' he spelled. ''D-a-m?''

''Hell has two *l*s. And damn has an *n*.''

Jason's eyebrows went up. ''It does? Where?''

''On the end. I know it's weird and you don't hear it, but it's there.''

''Oh. Taylor Bridges says that all the time. And I don't usually say hell, but Nikkie was yelling and she's bigger. I wanted her to hear me.''

''Yeah, well, you can say regular words just as loudly as swear words. So don't pollute the conversation with bad language.''

''Okay.'' Jason looked abashed. ''Sorry.''

Halfway down the stairs Ethan caught the acrid smell of something burning. With Jason right behind him, he raced to the kitchen and found it filled with smoke.

Beth had opened the window over the sink, as well as the back door and was waving at the smoke with a dish towel. On the counter was the foil pan of lasagna. It was incinerated.

''God, I can't believe it!'' she said when she saw Ethan. ''I usually prepare frozen meals just fine, but I'd gone down to the basement to put a load of laundry in and got distracted by all the paintable things you have down there—clay flowerpots and wooden boxes and that galvanized tub. I didn't hear the timer.''

She tossed the towel at the counter, opened the refrigerator and pulled out a large white bowl. ''How do you feel about salad *without* lasagna?''

Ethan was not one to be dismayed by small domestic crises when his work showed him repeatedly that the world was filled with such big ones. He could see that Beth was very upset, however, so he dismissed the ruined lasagna with a shake of his head. ''Don't worry about it. Salad's great. Jase and I'll pick up some ribs and chicken to go with it.''

He took his jacket from a hook near the back door and tossed Jason's at him. The boy pulled it on, eager to accompany him.

''Oh, boy!'' Jason's blue eyes shone as he zipped up his jacket. ''I like chicken and ribs better, anyway! I'm *glad* you're a rotten cook, Mom!''

Beth met the amused look in Ethan's eyes and had to smile. ''Thank you, Jason,'' she said, leaning down to kiss her son's cheek. ''It's nice to be appreciated.''

Jason raced through the open door toward the Blazer. Ethan adjusted the collar of his tweed jacket and challenged her with a raised eyebrow. ''Want to practice kissing me goodbye?''

She went toward him, her pace lazy, her heartbeat picking up. Steve had hated it when dinner wasn't ready or not as painstakingly prepared as he preferred. And though he seldom shouted, he'd always shown his disapproval with icy politeness or stiff silences.

And here Ethan was going out with a smile to bring dinner home. Unbelievable.

She stopped within inches of him and asked in surprise. "You're not annoyed?"

"Over food?" he asked. "No. I save annoyance for bad calls by referees or deputies who call in sick on Mondays—stuff like that. Anyway, I seem to remember we'd agreed you don't have to fix meals."

She laughed mirthlessly. "I was trying to make a good impression."

"You could still save it with a kiss."

An unfamiliar sense of well-being made her close the small space between them and tip her face up toward his.

He lowered his head without touching her until their lips met, and the kiss he gave her was sweet but lingering.

Beth unconsciously rose on tiptoe to maintain contact. He responded by parting his lips. She dipped the tip of her tongue into his mouth—and the contact changed suddenly from casual to intense. He wrapped an arm around her waist, pulling her against him. She put both arms around his neck, and the kiss deepened.

She experienced the sensation again of having ingested lava. It shocked her to realize that what she felt was sexual excitement. She pulled her lips from Ethan's and looked into his face, wondering if he could be right about her. Was it possible she *did* possess a strong sexuality?

His eyes were stormy with a decidedly desirous gleam. He drew an uneven breath and grinned. "That kind of a kiss will never send a man on his way," he said, running a hand gently up and down her spine. "It only makes him want to stay."

That sense of sexual well-being seemed to double. "The kids'll be hungry," she said. "You should go."

"I can't."

"Why not?"

"You're standing on my feet." He pointed to his Nikes on which her black flats stood. She must have used them for leverage during the kiss.

She stepped off him, shooed him backward and closed the door behind him, her heart beating like the wings of a hummingbird. She turned toward the counter to find Nikkie, Simba hanging from one hand and Cindy Crawford riding her other shoulder, standing in the middle of the kitchen and glaring at her.

"That was quite a kiss for two people who've just met," the girl said.

Beth knew she wasn't going to get anywhere with Nikkie if she wasn't just as forthright.

"Yes, it was," she admitted. She went to the counter to toss the burned lasagna into the trash. Then she took the plastic container of cat food from the corner and placed it near the empty bowls on the floor. "But sometimes, when two people find themselves in a situation that forces them to make big decisions together...something happens."

"Love?" Nikkie asked sarcastically.

"Closeness," Beth corrected, pulling the lid off the cat-food container as Nikkie put her furry friends down in front of their bowls. "A kind of mutual dependence that means they have to trust each other. And discovering that your trust is well placed inspires a certain...affection that—" Beth stopped abruptly, remembering her promise to herself to be honest.

"It's pretty complex, Nikkie," she said. "I don't entirely understand it myself. I just know that I like your dad a lot—probably for many of the same reasons you do. He's kind, understanding and supportive.

My first husband wasn't like that, so I probably appreciate those qualities more than another woman would."

Nikkie scooped cat food into the bowls. Simba, nudging Nikkie's hand in his eagerness to eat, got sprinkled with the multicolored pellets. Cindy Crawford, far more dignified, sat a small distance from her bowl and when it was full approached with a graceful twitch of her all-black tail. Simba sniffed at Cindy's bowl as though to be certain they shared the same menu. The calico growled, and the gray Persian, satisfied, went back to his meal.

Nikkie leaned against the corner of the counter, watching her cats eat, then swung her gaze to Beth. It was clear she had more on her mind.

"I'm not going to give you a lot of trouble," Nikkie said, "Because Dad seems to want you here. But don't expect me to drool all over you like Jason does with my father. I loved my mother, and Dad and I were doing fine by ourselves."

Beth nodded over the merciless statement of fact. Maybe there was something steadying about knowing exactly where you stood. "I've always thought drool was pretty unattractive," she said quietly. "Perhaps you can just treat me as you would any other friend of your father's."

"His friends don't *live* here."

"Life's full of exceptions. But I'll do my best not to get in your way."

"I'd appreciate that." Nikkie gestured to the back door. "Where was Dad going?"

Beth smiled in self-deprecation, suspecting she was in for more flack. "To get chicken and ribs to go with our salad. I burned the lasagna."

Nikkie made a face. "It was frozen."

"I know," Beth said. "I was doing laundry in the basement and noticed all the neat old pots and things down there. The sort I paint for craft shows. I didn't hear the timer."

Nikkie rolled her eyes. "I can see you're not going to be much help around here."

Beth shook her head. "Probably not. But you and your dad were doing fine. It doesn't sound like you need me for that kind of thing." She turned to open a utensil drawer. "I can set the table, though. So if you'll excuse me, I'll do that."

Nikkie walked away.

Beth put napkins and silverware around the table and replayed their exchange in her mind. It wasn't precisely negative and it certainly wasn't positive. It had simply been a sort of honest declaration of territory—like Simba sniffing Cindy's bowl.

BETH'S FIRST WEDDING had taken place before a justice of the peace in a small town in eastern Washington. She'd worn a simple blue dress and carried a bouquet of carnations and baby's breath bought at a nearby supermarket.

But she'd been excited and in love.

Her second wedding took place in Ebbie Browning's backyard in an elegant canvas tent against which a torrential rain beat unmercifully. She wore a long-sleeved ivory wool dress with a roll-necked collar and a tea-length flared skirt. Kelly and Nikkie stood beside her. Nikkie had not been pleased about being a bridesmaid, but she hadn't refused.

Ethan wore a gray suit, the jacket of which he'd draped over her shoulders in the middle of the brief ceremony when she'd shivered against the rawness of the day. All the guests were prepared for the cold rainy weather, but Beth had had nothing to go over her dress but her bright red parka.

Brodie served as Ethan's best man, and Jason as usher.

The two deputies Beth had met at Jason's party and several other people Ethan had introduced to her from his office stood behind them as they recited their vows.

Joanne and Zachary were there fully expecting, Beth imagined, she would turn to them at any moment and admit it was all a farce. But the ceremony continued and finally concluded with the traditional directive to the groom.

"You may kiss the bride."

Ethan complied gently and briefly with a promise in his eyes for later.

Beth huddled a little deeper into his jacket as they turned to face her in-laws and Ethan's friends.

There were cheers and applause followed by a buffet of hors d'ouevres Kelly had put together.

"Coconut prawns?" Beth said in amazement. "Bacon-wrapped scallops? Crab-stuffed mushrooms and heart-shaped watercress sandwiches?" Beth said to Kelly as she stood between her and Ethan in the small buffet line. "I didn't know you could do this kind of thing. All you ever eat is chicken strips and egg rolls."

Kelly grinned at her astonishment. "My mom was a caterer. I learned to prepare a lot of fancy things. I just don't like to bother—unless, of course, my best friend is getting married."

Behind her Brodie bit a huge coconut-dipped

prawn in half and closed his eyes in ecstasy. "That does it!" he said, piling several more onto his plate. "I have to win the lottery."

"Why?" Kelly asked.

"You're looking for a man with millions, remember?" He reached around her while she remained still and helped himself to two stuffed mushrooms. "And I'm looking for a woman who can cook."

"You missed something, Brodie," she told him, slapping his hand when he reached for another mushroom. "Other people might like them, too. I said I *can* cook, but I don't like to."

"You might want to if you adored the man you were married to."

"I'm not married."

"Only because you don't know me well enough yet."

Kelly sighed dramatically and turned to Ethan, who'd reached the end of the buffet and was pouring coffee for himself and Beth. "What is it with him? He seems bright enough, but he doesn't listen."

"It's a problem he's always had," Ethan explained with a straight face. "Our mother always excused him by saying he was a forceps delivery. I think he's just nuts."

"Go ahead," Brodie said. "Have your fun. But when I win the lottery or become an auto-mechanic mogul—" he pinned Kelly with a glance "—and *you're* begging me to marry you—" his glance went to Ethan "—and you need help IDing tire tracks or repairing the county's dilapidated fleet, I'll tell *you* to take a flying leap. And I'll tell you..." He looked back into Kelly's eyes and something there seemed to stop him and snare his attention. "I'll tell you..."

he said absently as Kelly gazed into his eyes. "I'll tell you that I'll take you under any terms. Any."

Ethan turned to Beth with a whispered, "What's going on there?"

She smiled and whispered back, "Can't you guess?"

He looked at his brother and Kelly again and found they were still gazing at each other. People in the buffet line were beginning to move around them.

"You're kidding!" Ethan said as he held both their coffees carefully in one hand and followed her to the head table, one of four set up to accommodate the guests.

"No, I'm not," she said, putting down her plate. She took the cups of coffee from Ethan's hand and put them down, too. "Don't be shocked. Kelly's wonderful. But she has the same problem I have."

Ethan pushed in Beth's folding chair and sat down beside her. "I think she's great. What problem?"

"She has to do her art. Her first husband wanted her attention exclusively and finally left. At least she wouldn't burn the frozen lasagna."

"In the space of a marriage, how important is that?"

"I suppose it depends on how much you like lasagna."

"Oh, just be quiet and eat," he said, grinning. Then he waved at the Richardses as they left the buffet line. "Joanne! Zach! Come join us."

When everyone had gone back for seconds, Brodie rose to make a toast. "To Bethany and Ethan, who have what it takes to make the perfect life—a man dedicated to protect and a woman who beautifies the world with her art. May your lives be joyful and secure, and may there be just enough smudges and just enough risk to make you appreciate what you've found in each other. Happiness and long life.''

Beth noticed that as her in-laws raised their glasses, they both appeared to be struggling with emotion. She wondered if they were remembering how they'd been forced to miss their son's marriage because of the elopement.

Afterward Ethan and Beth cut the cake and Kelly and Ebbie distributed it. By the time guests began to leave, dusk had fallen.

Ethan and Beth were talking to Curtis and Billings and their wives when there was a scream and a commotion from the driveway of Ebbie's house. The six hurried to investigate and found a group gathered around Zachary, who was on his back near the hydrangea that bordered the side of the house.

''Zach!'' Joanne was on her knees beside him.

He was conscious but groaning. ''My leg,'' he told Ethan as he squatted down next to him. ''Broken, I think. I slipped on the wet grass.''

Curtis pulled out a cell phone and dialed 911. Ebbie brought out a pillow and blankets and an umbrella which Beth held over him. Everyone stood around Zach as protection from the weather until the ambulance arrived.

Joanne rode in the ambulance with Zachary, and Ethan and Beth followed in the Blazer. Brodie took Nikkie and Jason home.

The leg was broken, a simple fracture of the tibia.

''We'll keep him overnight,'' the doctor told Joanne, Beth and Ethan in the waiting room. ''It was a clean break, and I don't foresee any problems, but the pain can be a little hard to deal with and we can take care of that here. If he's doing as well tomorrow, I can send him home with a prescription for a pain-killer, but he'll need crutches for at least three weeks.''

Joanne's brow furrowed in concern. "We were heading home tomorrow. If I lay him down in the back seat of the car, do you think…''

The doctor shook his head before she'd finished. "I wouldn't recommend that. He should stay put a couple of days. He'll be too uncomfortable to move.''

Joanne nodded. "Whatever you say. May I see him now?''

"Of course. Come with me.''

Joanne turned to Beth. "You two can go home.'' For the first time since Beth had known her, the woman looked vulnerable. "I can get a cab back to the motel.''

Beth turned to Ethan, but didn't have to say a word.

"We'll wait for you and take you home with us,'' he said. "You and Zach can stay at our place until he's feeling well enough to go home.''

Joanne looked stunned—also a first in Beth's ex-perience of her. "Thank you,'' she said after a mo-ment. "I'm sure that would be more comfortable for Zach than the motel. I'll try not to be too long, but I won't sleep tonight if I don't see for myself that he's all right.''

"Take your time,'' Beth said. "And give Zach our best.''

Joanne hurried off after the doctor, and Beth and Ethan settled back into the upholstered chairs in the waiting room.

"How did you know,'' Beth asked Ethan, "that was exactly what was on my mind?''

He leaned back in his chair in an attitude of false modesty. "I'm your husband," he said, smoothing his tie. "It's my job to know what you're thinking."

"You've only been my husband—" she glanced at her watch "—three hours and forty minutes."

"I'm a fast learner."

She sat sideways in her chair, resting her elbow on the back and studying him. His long legs were stretched out and crossed at the ankles. He looked pretty wonderful in a suit, she thought.

"Joanne's worried about Zach and so she's subdued right now," Beth warned, reaching over to brush a speck of something off his shoulder. "But it might be difficult to have her around the next few days. She always puts herself in charge of the situation, whatever it is. It was generous of you to offer to let them stay with you…us."

He shrugged, then sent her a questioning glance. "Have you thought about what it'll mean to *you* to have them in the house?"

"Yes," she said dryly. "Constant tension."

"I mean physically."

"Why physically?"

"Because," he explained, "we'll have to give them your room. We can tell them your things are in there because my closet's too small, but you'll have to sleep with me. It won't do for them to see you and me sleeping in separate bedrooms."

Her heart gave a surprised thud. Why hadn't she considered that? There wasn't an extra room for the Richardses.

She did her best to appear at ease as she said, "Well, I thought that was what you'd intended all along."

"I did," he admitted, "but I was willing to give you time to adjust. To come across the hall when you were ready."

"I'll just have to be flexible."

Amusement shone in Ethan's eyes. "Not *that* flexible," he said. "I'm not into anything gymnastic."

She punched his shoulder. "Ethan, I meant—"

"I know what you meant." He laughed, reaching over the arms of the chairs that separated them and cupping her head in his hand to pull her toward him. He kissed her cheek, then settled her against his shoulder. "I was just trying to lighten the mood. You get so serious when we discuss lovemaking."

"I was trying to be casual."

"I know. But your eyes become the color of a bruise and…I get the feeling there are some things I'll have to help you unlearn."

"I'll do my best," she promised.

He squeezed her shoulder. "One of them," he said, "is the notion that the outcome is entirely dependent upon you. It isn't. And anyway, the fact that we're sharing the same bed doesn't mean we have to share anything else until it seems like a good idea to you. But eventually I'm going to show you how mistaken you are about yourself."

Beth's hand rested on his pectoral muscle and she rubbed it gently in silent gratitude for his consideration.

But again she had that feeling of hot lava pouring through her, and she knew they would one day very soon make love. Though her mind and her emotions were confused about her abilities in the bedroom, her body seemed anxious to be proved wrong.

CHAPTER NINE

ETHAN STARED at the glowing numbers on his digital clock: 2:21 a.m. God. He felt as though he was in a sort of time warp where the last three hours had been a week long.

He and Beth had driven Joanne to the Coast Motel, picked up her and Zachary's things and brought her home. Beth had helped her settle into the room, while Ethan had explained to Nikkie and Jason that the Richardses would be staying for a while.

"How long?" Nikkie had asked sullenly.

"I'm not sure," he'd explained. "Maybe a week, maybe two. Depends on how quickly Zachary heals." He'd given Nikkie a significant look. "And that will probably be affected by how comfortable he is in his surroundings."

Nikkie sat in a corner of the sofa, her legs curled under her, a pillow wrapped in her arms, the picture of defensive resistance. "And I suppose we'll be inviting *them* into the family, too?"

"They *are* in the family," Jason said, his tone as aggressive as hers. "They're Grandma and Grandpa." He sat in the middle of the sofa, arms folded, feet not touching the floor. He frowned at Ethan, who was perched on the edge of a hatch-cover on legs that served as a coffee table. "But I don't want them to stay, either. They're gonna start picking on Mom and trying to get me to go home with them.''

"I won't let them pick on your mom," Ethan said firmly, "and your home is right here. Nobody's taking you away."

Jason's frown turned to a fragile smile. "You promise?"

"I promise."

Nikkie got to her feet and threw the pillow onto the sofa. "Well, maybe somebody could take *me* away! If one more person moves in with us, there won't be room for me, anyway!" And she'd stormed off to her room.

Brodie had wandered out of the kitchen, a dish towel over the shoulder of the white shirt he'd worn to the wedding. He'd removed the tie. "I guess I'll have breakfast at the Crossing Café for a while," he said, handing Ethan a mug of coffee. "Looks like you're going to have a full house."

Ethan had hooked an arm around his neck and walked him back into the kitchen. "Bro, if you don't come, there will be no one to cook breakfast. We'll find room for you around the table."

"You mean in front of the stove."

"Yeah."

"Nikkie tells me Beth burned a frozen lasagna."

Ethan smiled. "She was doing laundry and got distracted by all the artistic potential of the junk in my basement. Come on. Weekends are still yours, but save us from toast and peanut butter during the week."

"Okay, okay. I'm such a pushover."

Ethan had put his cup down on the counter and hugged his brother. "Thanks for bringing the kids home and staying with them. And thanks for standing up for me. It wasn't a bad wedding, was it?''

Brodie grabbed his suit coat off the back of a kitchen chair. ''We got rained on, I was pursued by a wacky redhead, and one of your guests broke his leg and is moving in with you. No, not bad.''

Ethan was thinking that, when all was said and done, he had Bethany. And that made the wedding pretty remarkable.

Ethan opened the door for Brodie. ''Ah, about the redhead... Just who was pursuing whom? It looked to me as though *you* were the one hot on Kelly's trail.''

Brodie stepped onto the back porch. The night was dark, and rain continued to hammer the sloping porch roof. He pulled on his coat.

''Okay, I was,'' he said. ''Then...in the buffet line, she gave me that look.''

''What look?''

Staring out at the rain, Brodie shrugged in frustration. ''It's hard to put into words. But I think it means...you're it.''

''It?''

''Him.''

''Who?''

Brodie turned to him, mouth curled in exasperation. ''Think, man. You're not usually this obtuse. I think she might think I could be...you know...''

Ethan shifted his weight and leaned a shoulder against the four-by-four that held up the right side of the porch. He thought he knew what Brodie meant, but he wanted to hear him say it.

''Could you spell it out for me?''

"A lasting love!" Brodie shouted. "Husband material!"

"And that's bad?"

"Very. I'm not interested."

"That's fascinating, because I recall you asking her if she could be interested in you if you had millions."

Brodie continued to stare moodily at the rain. "Yeah, 'cause I don't have millions and have no prospect of getting millions, so I thought I was safe."

"Uh-huh. That's why you were coming on to her all day?"

Brodie sighed and shrugged again. "You know me. That's what I do. Most women understand the game."

"You play this game because of Paulette."

Brodie stiffened. "I don't talk about Paulette."

Ethan shook his head. "Bro, you're getting too old for that game," he said, figuring his love for Brodie gave him permission to dispense with tact. "It's a seventeen-year-old, busting-beer-cans-on-your-head kind of game. And you don't talk about Paulette because if you did, you'd have to admit that you fell in love with her and then got dumped."

Brodie went rigid with anger. "Don't preach to me!"

"Somebody should!" Ethan retorted. "You chase down every woman for miles as some kind of proof of your virility, and then when she stops to let you catch her, you pull back. What is it, exactly? Are you hurting them as some kind of revenge on Paulette, or did Paulette destroy your self-esteem so much that when a woman finally does show some interest, you're afraid she won't find anything in you and she'll leave?"

Brodie swiveled his body toward Ethan and drew

back his fist. As though reliving an old scene from their teenage years, Ethan squared his stance and prepared to block the blow.

But Brodie didn't throw it. After one tense moment he dropped his fist and drew a breath, his eyes still dark with fury. "My life is none of your business," he said flatly. "You'd better go inside and take care of your own. I have a feeling this marriage isn't going to be the walk in the park you had with Diana." Then Brodie's eyes shifted somewhere to the left of Ethan, and his tight angry features seemed to collapse in distress.

Ethan turned to find Beth standing beside him. She'd heard Brodie's remark, he was sure, about his seemingly perfect first marriage.

Ethan put an arm around her and drew her close. The night air was cold. "Hi," he said. "What're you doing out here?"

"I heard the two of you shouting at each other," she said, her eyes going worriedly from him to his brother. "Is something wrong?"

Brodie smiled and shook his head. "You haven't been around long enough to know that we usually end up shouting at each other. It's nothing serious."

Beth studied him skeptically, then changed the subject. "Brodie, thank you for staying with Jason and Nikkie."

"My pleasure." He turned to Ethan, his expression neutral. "You'll have to move the Blazer so I can back out."

Ethan followed him at a run through the rain, but stopped at his truck. "What are you doing?" Brodie demanded as he yanked open his door. "You'll get drenched."

Ethan felt rain soak the shoulders of his shirt, but ignored it. "I want to make sure you understand that Paulette was an idiot, not you. When you're not being psychotic, you're really all right. And I hate to think of you spending a lifetime alone because you can't see that."

Brodie looked back at him, his jaw rigidly set. "Will you get the Blazer out of my way before I back over it?" he asked.

Deciding that any further conversation would be profane and irretrievable, Ethan ran to the Blazer and backed onto the street.

In a move that Ethan thought looked like something out of a slapstick comedy, Brodie backed out with a squeal of tires, raced the twenty feet to his own driveway and turned into it with another squeal of tires and a spray of rainwater, then rocked to a stop. He went into his house without a glance in Ethan's direction.

Ethan pulled into the driveway and ran back into the house. The place was silent as a tomb.

The kitchen clock said it was just after eleven. He shot the bolt on the front door and turned off all the downstairs lights. Upstairs he looked into Nikkie's room and found her asleep, a cat curled up on each side of her. Simba looked up and gave him a faint meow. Ethan pulled the door silently closed.

The door of the room Joanne was using was also closed, and there was silence behind it. He could only conclude that meant everything was fine.

Jason's door was open and Ethan looked in to find that he, too, was fast asleep, one arm hanging over the side of the upper bunk. Ethan tucked it back up and resettled the blankets. The boy expelled a comfortable little sigh and settled more deeply into his pillow.

Ethan walked into his own room to find Beth turning down the bed. She wore a simple blue cotton nightie that skimmed her knees. She looked up at him with a smile he imagined was supposed to assure him that she was quite comfortable with the situation, and if he wanted to make love to her tonight, she was willing.

In her eyes, though, was concern, trepidation. When eventually they did make love, he wanted her to be more than willing. He wanted her eager, confident that she was doing what she wanted to do.

"How was Joanne when she went to bed?" he asked, unbuttoning his shirt.

Beth fluffed a pillow. "Exhausted but fine. Now that she knows Zachary's going to be all right, she'll probably be her old self in the morning. So be prepared to listen to suggested changes for your uniform and possibly even the county code." She smiled as she walked around the bed to the other side and fluffed the other pillow. "Do you sleep by the door or by the window?" she asked, still sounding quite composed.

He knew it was perverse, but he took a certain satisfaction in making her control slip. "I usually sleep in the middle," he said, pulling his shirt off and giving it a hook shot into the hamper by the bathroom. "You can have the two sides."

She tossed the pillow on the bed and looked at him, obviously trying to decide if he was being difficult or funny. Then she smiled. "It's nice to know that even so close to midnight you retain a sense of humor."

It was on the tip of his tongue to tell her there were

moments in a man's life when that was all he had left, but he thought it sounded self-pitying, so he kept the thought to himself.

He pointed to the side of the bed nearest the door. "That side," he said. "You go on to bed. I have to take a shower." He opened the closet door to find that a few of her things had been hung beside his. Seeing her colorful fabrics lined up beside his darker things gave him a weird sense of déjà vu. He remembered when Diana was still alive and his uniforms and sports coats had shared space with silky blouses and pastel linen suits. But the sight also projected him into the future, because he couldn't help but wonder how well this would work, how long those things would be there.

Beth gestured at the closet. "I brought some of my stuff here so I wouldn't have to disturb Joanne in the morning. I hope that's all right."

"Of course." He pulled off his shoes and tossed them into the bottom of the closet.

"She believed me when I said my clothes were in there because your closet was too crowded."

"The best lies are those that have a grain of truth," he said, pushing the closet door closed and heading for the bathroom. But Beth stood squarely in his path, a line of concern between her eyebrows.

"What's wrong?" she asked.

Again he got an unexpected glimpse of Diana, this time in the direct way Beth approached a problem. But at the moment he was tired and would have preferred to forget the whole thing. After all, in just a few short days he'd fallen for and married a woman who was afraid to go to bed with him. And he'd been looking forward to ending what had seemed like an interminable period of celibacy. But he couldn't take what she offered when he knew she'd rather be having an IRS audit or something equally unpleasant. So what could possibly be wrong?

"Nothing," he said, then he leaned down to kiss her cheek and got a disorienting whiff of a spicy rose fragrance. "Go to sleep. Good night." He walked around her and went into the bathroom.

But she followed him and stood in the doorway, preventing him from closing himself in. He saw the rosy tips of small firm breasts under her thin gown and had to tear his eyes away and concentrate on her face. It was pale and anxious.

"You're annoyed with me," she said, "because I'm nervous about...tonight. Is that it?"

"No. I—"

"Well, I'm nervous, but...I want you to make love to me." She looked directly into his eyes, though he could see that took courage.

"Beth," he said patiently, leaning a forearm on the doorway molding, "you say you want to make love with me, but your eyes tell a different story. You don't really want it. And I won't make love with you until you do."

"But I explained." She spoke quietly but urgently. "My feelings are very complex. Part Steve's fault, probably part my fault. But I don't want...the experience diminished for you because of that. I don't want to hurt you—yet there seems no way to avoid it. If you make love to me and I have trouble responding, you'll be hurt. But if we don't make love..." She spread her arms helplessly. "I mean, who *doesn't* make love on their wedding night? I understand that you're annoyed, I just want to make it clear that I—"

He put a hand gently over her mouth to silence her, although he was fascinated by her stream of chatter. The control she always tried so hard to maintain was puddled at her feet. He liked that. And he thought it boded well for their *eventual* liaison.

"Rule number one in this house," he said, lowering his hand when it appeared she'd remain silent, "is that we don't hold ourselves to other people's standards. Each of us does what he or she decides. And if I'm annoyed with anyone, I'm annoyed with myself."

He paused to draw a breath, because being completely honest with a woman, he was just beginning to remember, was harder than it seemed. "I'm used to being in charge of myself and the situation. I thought it would be easy to wait for you to be ready to make love. But I'm discovering that I'm not as strong as I thought. That I'm more vulnerable than I thought. And that's difficult for a man to admit to himself."

A subtle change took place in her eyes. The suggestion that he found her desirable seemed to surprise her. God. He wished he could have had five minutes alone in an interview room with Steve Richards.

She put a hand to his face with a reverence he found humbling. "I hope I can be what you want," she whispered.

He put his hand over hers, turned his lips into her palm and kissed it. "You *are* what I want. That's the problem."

"I meant in bed," she said.

"When two people care about each other," he said, kissing her knuckles now, "they usually have no problem making the other happy—in bed or out.

When that time comes for you, we'll be ready. In the meantime, I really need a shower and you need some sleep.''

"Okay.'' She wrapped her arms around his waist and held him fiercely for so long he was ready to chuck his noble attitude and carry her to the bed. Then she took a step back from him and said with a mystifying disappointment in her eyes that completely confused him, "I usually drop off to sleep the minute my head hits the pillow, so I'll see you at breakfast.''

"Right,'' he replied, and watched her stiff-backed form in the thin cotton walk away before closing the bathroom door.

AND THAT WAS WHY he lay staring at the clock in the wee hours of the morning. He'd taken his time in the shower, grateful to find Beth asleep when he joined her in the bed. She was lying on her back, the fingers of one hand folded against her cheek.

He flipped onto his other side and closed his eyes, thinking how different it was to realize he was married again. Diana's absence had made such a change in his life, and the love they'd had for each other would be with him always. But the image that formed behind his closed eyelids now was Beth's.

As if she'd detected his thoughts, she turned toward him and curled up against his back, her knees tucked up right under his buttocks. His confused libido was confused no longer, and he cursed himself for taking a sympathetic stand with her. They could be making love right now, and he'd have bet everything he owned that he'd have already cured her of her feelings of inadequacy.

But he could tell by the gentle pulse of breath

against his spine that she was still asleep. She hadn't chosen to snuggle against him; she'd done it in an instinctive but unconscious search for warmth and security after a long taxing day.

He tried to clear his mind of thought so that he could get some sleep. That was surprisingly easy. What he couldn't turn off was the reaction of every nerve ending in his body. The part of him in contact with her silky flesh was screaming for him to do something about it. But he'd promised, and she trusted him.

So he lay still even as she snuggled closer. It was character building, he told himself. And he realized he was going to have to be quite some paragon to hold his own in this relationship.

ETHAN AWOKE to the pleasant smell of coffee and…pancakes? French toast? He wasn't sure which, but the aromas wafting upstairs were enough to set his stomach rumbling.

The other side of the bed was empty, but *could* Beth cook anything without burning it? Nikkie was good with eggs, but couldn't seem to get the hang of flipping pancakes, so she never made them. Brodie slept in on Sundays.

Jason appeared in the doorway of Ethan's room, still wearing *Toy Story* pajamas. "Do you smell that?" he asked.

"Yeah." Ethan tossed the blanket back and swung his legs over the side of the bed. "Who's cooking?"

Jason shook his head. "It can't be Mom, and Nikkie's door is closed. It's either Grandma or Uncle Brodie. Come on!" Jason called, then disappeared from view. Ethan could hear his footsteps heading for the stairs.

"Right behind you," he said, going to the closet and pulling on jeans and a sweater. He hadn't fallen asleep until sometime after four, but still he was more ravenous than tired.

And, masochist that he seemed to be, he couldn't wait to see Beth. She should be bright and fresh this morning, all the sleep she'd gotten in direct proportion to all the sleep he'd missed!

Joanne was holding forth at the stove, a pristine counter suggesting that whatever she was preparing had required little effort—or at least none that showed.

It was pancakes. Jason was hard at work on a tall stack drenched in syrup, and Beth sat across from him with two pancakes half-eaten. She wore a red turtleneck and had bundled her hair up in a loose knot. Bangs skimmed her eyebrows when she looked up at him, and silky tendrils of hair had escaped to caress her neck.

The look she gave him was cautious and watchful. He wondered if she'd awakened curled up tightly against him and was embarrassed by it.

Joanne turned away from the stove to see who'd walked into the kitchen. She wished him a pleasant if somewhat haughty good-morning.

He returned the greeting, then went to lean over Beth's chair and give her a kiss. He did it partly for Joanne's benefit, but partly for his own.

"I thought I'd make myself useful," Joanne said, her gaze lingering on him as a new dollop of batter sizzled on the griddle. "I know that cooking isn't one of Beth's strengths."

It annoyed him that she would feel called upon to say so, particularly when she was a guest in what was supposed to be Beth's home.

He gave Beth a calculatedly lascivious look and kissed her again. "She has other qualities that far outweigh cooking in importance."

Beth eyes widened, first in surprise, then in amused appreciation. "Thank you, darling," she said, falling in with his loverlike performance.

"But it's wonderful to have someone around who *can* cook," Ethan said, going to the stove to peer over Joanne's shoulder. He wanted her to know he appreciated her efforts, but he didn't want her picking on Beth. "Anything I can do?"

She stepped aside and pointed to the oven with her spatula. "Your plate's in there."

"Why don't *you* take it?" he suggested. "Since the batter's made, I can probably prepare my own."

"Nonsense." She pulled open the oven door and handed him an oven mitt. "Careful with it. Is your daughter coming down?"

"I don't think so. Sunday's her chance to sleep in."

Joanne nodded. "Well, I'll put a plate in the oven just in case."

Ethan carried his plate to the table. "How's Zachary this morning?" he asked. "Have you called the hospital?"

"Yes, and he had a fairly good night," Joanne replied, expertly flipping a pancake. "The doctor says he can go home this morning if we can pick him up."

"Sure." Ethan reached for the syrup. "We can go as soon as we're finished breakfast."

Joanne turned away from the stove to face him. "We could compensate you for the room and the—"

"No," Ethan said simply. "We're happy to have you here."

"I appreciate that," she said with an upward tilt of her chin that seemed more aggressive than grateful, "but it'll cost you in a dozen little ways. More groceries, more hot water, more laundry, more—"

"No," Ethan said again. And when she opened her mouth to offer further argument, he added quietly, "and that's final."

Her chin went up an extra notch, and she appeared confused, as though receiving generosity and being overruled were foreign experiences for her.

"Zachary might have something to say about that," she persisted.

Ethan cut into his pancakes without looking up. "No, he won't," he returned. "It's my house."

She might have continued to argue, but the smell of something burning turned her back to the stove with a cry of distress. She jabbed the spatula under a smoking pancake and lifted it out, obviously looking for the trash.

"Around the corner of the fridge," Beth told her. "Near the cat food."

The spatula held out in front of her, Joanne followed Beth's directions, then walked back to the stove frowning fiercely.

So Beth wasn't the only one capable of burning food, he thought. He looked up from his plate and caught Beth's eye, then winked and went back to his breakfast.

CHAPTER TEN

ETHAN DROPPED Beth at the cannery on his way to work Monday morning. Their efforts to convince Joanne and Zachary that they were a real family were aided considerably by the built-in stress of getting two adults and two children showered, dressed and fed in order to leave the house at the same time.

Nikkie was carrying a mock-up of a medieval shield she'd made out of cardboard and foil, and therefore she couldn't take the school bus. But she apparently considered arriving at school in a car filled with her new stepmother and stepbrother a severe breach of cool and ignored Beth and Jason completely.

Jason was out of sorts because Ethan had thwarted his plan to ride his bike after school to the old deserted Appleby house in the next block. Ethan had explained that transients often took shelter there, and that though children and teenagers found it fun to dare one another to go in and explore the place, it wasn't safe. Jason had tried wheedling but to no avail.

Beth thought Ethan seemed a little edgy when she suggested he looked as though he hadn't slept well. And by the time the foursome headed for the car, they were all snapping at each other. Beth had a parting glimpse of Joanne and Zachary sitting across from each other in the kitchen. Zachary's leg in its cast was propped on an extra chair, and Beth wondered what they thought of her "happy family."

Nikkie left the Blazer without speaking, and Jason climbed out with only a terse goodbye.

Ethan pulled up to the pier on which the cannery stood and caught Beth's arm when she would have pushed her door open.

"I apologize for my mood this morning," he said with a sincerity that surprised her—apologies had not even been in Steve's makeup. "I haven't been getting much sleep lately."

She turned back, giving him her full attention, wanting to know what was troubling him and to help if she could. "Why not? What's wrong?"

"It's not 'wrong,' precisely," he said with a half smile. "It just keeps me awake."

"What?"

"You," he replied. "You're a cuddler."

Color rose to her cheeks, but she smiled. "That's strange," she said, "because Steve always said that my body up against his made him claustrophobic. So I always stayed on my side of the bed. But—" her color deepened "—when I woke up Sunday morning, I was all wrapped around you. I'm sorry."

"Don't apologize," he said. "It doesn't make me claustrophobic at all. It makes me…" He considered a moment, then apparently changed his mind about telling her. "Never mind. It was no reason to grouse at you. *I'm* sorry. I'll pick you up about six. You said Jason will just walk here from school?"

"Yes. It's not far, so he doesn't have to be picked up. And Nikkie'll get the bus home?"

"She has a drama-club meeting after school, so

she'll get the city bus. That usually gets her home by five.''

''Okay. Do you want me to call and check on her, make sure everything's all right?''

''She'll tell you she's too old to be checked on,'' he warned, ''but I always do, anyway.''

''All right. I'll handle it. Besides, I'll have to check on Joanne and Zachary.''

She pushed open her door again.

''Hey!'' he called.

''Yes?''

''No kiss goodbye? You're forgetting the private detective.''

She leaned toward him. ''Do you really think he's watching?'' she asked, glancing surreptitiously beyond Ethan, then to his left and right.

''I do,'' he replied gravely. ''I imagine he's using binoculars, so you'd better make it good.''

Her smile held amused suspicion. ''You aren't by any chance taking advantage of this situation, are you?''

He tipped his head and closed the few inches that separated his mouth from hers. ''Of course I am,'' he admitted shamelessly, and kissed her until she couldn't breathe or think.

At last he raised his head, and she tried to reestablish a sense of emotional balance, thinking that if he made love with the same artful skill with which he kissed, he might very well be right about teaching her to enjoy it.

She stepped out of the car and blew him one final kiss. He drove away with a tap of the Blazer's horn.

Kelly was perched on a piling by the door to Beth's studio. She was dressed in her studio garb—a ratty denim jacket, old beige cords and a blue sweatshirt stained with clay and glaze. Her short red hair was tumbled, and her eyes were bright with mischief.

"Well, that was quite a kiss," she said, leaping down from the piling as Beth unlocked the studio door.

"We thought the detective might be watching," Beth replied, making her way into the studio, careful not to meet Kelly's eyes.

"Come on," Kelly cajoled. "That was no performance. That was the real thing."

"Well…" Beth flipped light switches, and fluorescent tubes fluttered, then came to life, filling the middle of the cavernous room with a bright glare. Tables around the room were covered with signs and all kinds of hanging wood art that was drying for the Winter Festival Art Fair.

In the middle of the room under another bank of lower hanging lights a large worktable stood, and Beth crossed to it. She dropped her purse under it and pulled off her jacket, hanging it on a nearby coat tree.

"Well, what?" Kelly encouraged, doing the same with her jacket and pulling up a stool without waiting for an invitation.

Beth wondered how to explain to Kelly what she felt for Ethan and decided that she couldn't. It would sound absurd, even to her best friend. "Well, I don't know," she said finally. "He's like a composite of the perfect man. Tough, gentle, firm, kind, funny, warm…" She stopped to grin. "Shall I go on?"

Kelly shook her head and made a gesture Beth interpreted as "Please don't." Then she pulled a circle of pine toward her, one that Beth had yet to decide what to do with, and traced the rings in the grain with the blunt tip of one finger.

"Actually I understand," she said, glancing up at Beth under her lashes. The look in her eyes, Beth noted in surprise, suggested embarrassment. "I've spent quite some time talking to his brother."

Beth wasn't sure what that meant. "You mean he praises Ethan, or you know about Ethan's qualities because you saw them in Brodie?"

Kelly sighed and concentrated on the rings. "If you'd asked me before your wedding, I'd have said it was because Brodie was all those things, too. But on the day of your wedding…" A pleat appeared between her eyebrows. "I don't know. Something changed."

Beth climbed onto her stool and leaned an elbow on the table. She studied Kelly's uncharacteristic frown and put a hand to her friend's knee. "What changed?" she asked. "It looked like the two of you were getting on so well. In fact, in the buffet line, I'd have sworn you made some kind of emotional contact."

Kelly's eyes became unfocused and Beth guessed she was remembering that moment. "Yes. We did. I looked into his laughing face and realized how nice it must be to be fussed over. How much I missed someone laughing about things, rather than finding problems with everything. It came over me as though he'd dropped a net. I was interested. *Very* interested." She sighed and made a face Beth couldn't quite decipher. "But you know what?"

Beth was almost afraid to ask. "What?"

"I think he's one of those men for whom the chase is everything."

"Why?"

"Because the minute I stopped evading him and let him know I could be interested in a relationship, it was as though someone blew up the power station and the lights went out."

"Sometimes," Beth suggested tactfully, "when your emotions are engaged and because you care so much, something that's insignificant can seem bigger than it really is."

Kelly sighed and pushed the pine disk away from her. "I don't think that's the case here," she said, knotting her fingers together and drawing a knee up until her foot was hooked in a rung of the stool. "His ardor cooled considerably the last hour of the reception. When your father-in-law was hurt, I asked Brodie if it would help if I went back to Ethan's with him and the kids, and he told me rather firmly that he'd be fine and that I probably had a lot of cleaning up of food and stuff to do."

That didn't sound good to Beth at all. And suddenly she remembered Ethan and Brodie shouting at each other on the back porch Saturday night.

"Maybe he was just being considerate," she said thinly.

Kelly gave her a look that told her she knew that excuse to be as false as it sounded. "Penny Curtis and Jan Billings were going to help Ebbie clean up so that I could help Brodie. I told him that. But he brushed me off."

Beth tried again. "He might just be a little frightened. You know, the old commitment bugaboo and all that." She smiled. "And you're pretty heady stuff, you know. If he's attracted to you and he thinks you're beginning to notice him, he might just be over-whelmed.''

Kelly considered that grimly for a moment, then tipped her head from side to side as though it could be a possibility about which she remained undecided. ''Well, I'm not going to give him another thought. I was well rid of my ex because he could never under-stand me. I'm not going to get involved with someone else who's going to make me feel unsure of myself. So let's talk about you.'' She caught both feet on the rung of the stool and leaned toward Beth, her eyes gleaming with curiosity. ''How was…the weekend?''

Beth pulled a stack of boards nearer, setting them out in neat rows to prepare them for painting. ''Nik-kie's nose is a little out of joint because not only is she dealing with a stepmother and brother, now there's Joanne and Zachary. Of course, Zachary's stuck in bed for a few days, but Joanne takes a little getting used to. She did make breakfast yester—''

Beth abruptly stopped when she looked up and found Kelly staring at her and shaking her head.

''What?'' Beth asked.

''You know what I want to know,'' Kelly said. ''Did a couple of nights with him spark your interest in sex again?''

Beth sighed and met Kelly's gaze. ''We haven't had sex.''

Kelly blinked. ''You're kidding!''

''I know. I know. I would have, but the day of Jason's party when I asked him to marry me and he agreed, we talked about what each of us wanted out of it, and we agreed that it wouldn't simply be a con-venience thing—''

''So far,'' Kelly said, ''I don't understand.''

"Well, let me finish," Beth returned with mild impatience. Not that even the complete story would clarify anything for Kelly. Beth herself still felt confused. "I told him how it was with Steve and me and how I've…been ever since. He seems to think I'm wrong and that making love with him will be entirely different."

"Well, why didn't you?"

Beth leaned both elbows on the table and rested her chin in her hands. The weekend seemed like something that had happened to someone else—a wedding, a trip to the hospital, a beautiful but suspicious stepdaughter, a man who kissed her with dark-eyed ardor, then gently pushed her away when she said she was willing to make love with him.

"I told him I was willing," she said, running her fingertips over one of her boards. "But he said my eyes told a different story. That he wanted to wait until I was sure it was what I wanted."

"Willing," Kelly said with a wince, "is a pretty insipid word."

Beth straightened and jumped off the stool. "I know it is," she said loudly. The words echoed in the nearly empty room. "But what if I'd behaved otherwise, then he put a hand on me and I froze, sure he'd start telling me at any moment I was cold and unresponsive and completely unappealing? That would have been harder on him than waiting…wouldn't it?"

Kelly slid off her own stool to put an arm around Beth's shoulders. "Steve was a jerk, Beth. And before you get all defensive, I know you had a good thing going in the beginning, but he didn't uphold his end of the relationship. He ignored you when he was busy. He was too ambitious to spend any time with you, to remind you that he cared. Then when he made some big deal, he came home and treated you like...like the spoils of victory. What woman wouldn't conclude that this was no fun and she wanted no more of it?''

Kelly turned Beth to face her and grasped both her shoulders. Her gaze was fierce. ''The thing you have to remember here, Beth, is that you're no longer dealing with Steve. This is Sheriff Ethan Drum—the man who scoured the countryside at night in the rain to find Jason. The man who supported Jason's story so he wouldn't humiliate him in front of your in-laws, who agreed to marry you to help you through this. It's not going to be like it was with Steve. *You're* not going to be like you were with Steve.''

Beth knew that. She just wasn't sure her brain could translate that information to a body that had turned itself off long ago.

''All right, enough about men,'' Kelly declared, hooking an arm in Beth's and leading her toward the door that led into the rest of the cannery. ''Let's talk about something we understand—art. Show me where my studio will be.''

Beth spent the next hour and a half walking Kelly through a series of large separated spaces that would ultimately become the long-dreamed-of art mall. She showed her how each room could be partitioned to make a small showroom in the front and still leave a big working area in the back. There'd be north light from the long series of small-paned windows facing the river and the state of Washington on the other shore.

Kelly chose the space closest to Beth's and insisted on writing her a check. Beth tried to refuse, protesting that it would be another week at least before she had the place painted.

"For a slight reduction in price," Kelly bargained, "I can paint it myself. You've had the building inspector in, so we know the pier and the structure are safe. All I have to do is paint the walls something soft and light, spruce up the showroom area, and pretty soon I can be here working beside you every day and checking on the progress of your love life."

Beth snorted. "Oh, good."

They laughed, then Beth walked Kelly out to her car.

JASON CAME to the cannery from school looking no more cheerful than he had when she and Ethan had dropped him off.

"Taylor Bridges," he said, munching on an apple Beth had brought for him, "doesn't believe Ethan's my dad. He says I'm making it up."

"Maybe you should invite him over sometime," Beth suggested. She knew it wasn't fair to hold a grudge against a child, but the Bridges boy had been a thorn in Jason's side since her son's first day at Cobbler's Crossing Elementary. "Maybe for dinner. Then he can see Ethan for himself."

Jason chewed, swallowed and perked up. "Yeah!" he said. "That'd be cool! Can I do it tomorrow?"

"Let me check to make sure Ethan doesn't have anything scheduled." With a fine-tipped brush dipped in silver paint, she put whiskers on a cat on one of her door plaques. "He has meetings at night sometimes."

"Okay." Jason came up beside her and leaned into

her free left arm as she worked. "You know, coming here's turning out to be a good thing, isn't it?"

Beth wrapped her arm around him and pulled him closer. She dabbed silver dots in the cat's wide green eyes. "You mean because of Ethan?"

"Mostly." As she turned to look at him, he added, "You like him, too, dontcha?"

"Yes, I do," she replied, kissing his forehead.

Jason grinned, his eyes alight with secret information. "You kiss him a lot. I seen you."

There was no denying that. "Uh-huh."

"You're not gonna be having babies, are you?"

"No. No babies."

"Nikkie said you were." He threw the apple core into the wastebasket under her table. It landed with a thunk. "She says if you and Ethan had babies, you wouldn't need us anymore."

Beth stopped in the act of tipping the cat's ears with silver and set down her brush on her palette. She wiped her hands on a rag and gave her son her full attention. "Jason, you know that isn't true. You have always been and will always be the most important thing in my life."

He leaned against the edge of the table. "Yeah, but if you had a baby that was part you and part Ethan, then it really belongs to you. I'm part somebody else and so's Nikkie."

Horrified that he might have been worried about that all day long, she waved him onto the other stool.

"First of all," she said, choosing her words carefully, "all children belong one hundred percent to both their parents."

He frowned, unable to grasp that. "But my dad's dead and so's Nikkie's mom."

"Yes," she said, "but though people die, love doesn't. Your dad and Nikkie's mom still love you from heaven, just like you both love them from down here. Only now you have even more love because you have Ethan."

He considered that and added cautiously. "And Nikkie has you?"

"Yes." She wasn't certain Nikkie would hold the same enthusiasm for the concept that Jason did. "And it doesn't matter to Ethan that he wasn't there when you were born, and it doesn't matter to me that Nikkie was born to another woman. I love her because now we're all a family. And it wouldn't matter if Ethan and I did have a baby, because we wouldn't love it more than we love you and Nikkie."

"So she was wrong." Jason seemed pleased by that possibility.

"She was mistaken," Beth corrected diplomatically. "It's a new situation for all of us, so it's easy to be confused about the way things will work. But I promise you that Ethan and I will always love you and Nikkie, even if we did have a baby."

He smiled, that problem solved. "Can I have a board to work on till Ethan picks us up?"

"Sure." Beth found him a board with a slight irregularity on one edge, and the box of odds and ends paint tubes she'd given him to use when she'd first set up her studio.

On a sudden impulse she drew two cats on a board with a pale yellow background, a fluffy gray Persian and a sleek calico with a black spot above the muzzle. She had the cats painted in an hour or so, then added pink collars on which she carefully printed their names with her fine-tipped brush—Simba and Cindy.

Then she added Nikkie's name in mossy green block letters at the bottom of the board.

She made a few fine-lined flourishes for a border, then pushed the board aside to dry.

"That's cool, Mom!" Jason was her biggest fan. He jumped off his stool. "I'm gonna get my sign. We can put it up at Ethan's, can't we?" He ran across the studio to the small apartment they'd lived in before to retrieve his name plaque from his bedroom door. She saw the yellow kitchen wall through the door Jason had left open; it seemed like an eternity, she thought, since they'd lived there. Their lives had changed so completely.

Remembering her promise to Ethan, Beth called home. Nikkie answered.

"Hi," Beth said cheerfully. "It's Beth. I'm just checking to make sure everything's okay."

"Why wouldn't it be?" Nikkie said rudely.

"Because there's a man there with a broken leg," Beth replied patiently, "a woman who isn't really familiar with the house and a young woman who's helping to plan a play that's in a crisis over props. So my checking to make sure no one needs anything doesn't really seem out of line, does it?"

There was a moment's silence, and Beth could imagine Nikkie sticking her tongue out at the receiver but keeping any further rude remarks to herself because her father had insisted she be polite to her wicked stepmother.

"Zachary is fine," she said with rigid courtesy. "I know because he shouted at me to turn my music down. Joanne is fine. I know that because she told me that chocolate has empty calories and will give me zits."

Beth couldn't help but feel sympathy for the girl at home alone with the Richardses. "And how are you?" she asked, her concern genuine. "Is there anything you need?"

"If you want to help me," Nikkie said with a despondent sigh, "you can find me medieval shields and weapons for twenty. Mr. Fogarty thought my foil-and-cardboard stuff wouldn't be convincing. I'm supposed to try to come up with something else."

"I'll look around the studio," Beth volunteered, "and see if I can find anything that'd help."

There was another silence, then Nikkie said politely but despairingly, "Thanks."

"No problem. See you in an hour or so. We'll bring home something for dinner."

"Don't bother," Nikkie said. "Joanne took a cab to the market and came back with all sorts of stuff. She's making pot roast for dinner."

"See? Everything has an upside."

"If you say so. Bye."

Beth rummaged through a stack of wooden shapes she'd cut out and hadn't had a chance to use. At last she found what she was looking for. It was shield-shaped and full-size. Pleased with herself, she took it to her table and began to trace a shape with pencil.

It was an hour later and she and Jason were admiring each other's work when a cheerful voice shouted from the doorway of her studio. "Bethie! How the hell are you?"

She turned to the studio's entrance to see a tall lanky figure standing there dressed in a white jumpsuit stained with paint. He had graying dark hair pulled back into a long curly ponytail. His eyes were pale blue, his cheekbones angular and his square chin had a cleft in it.

Rush Weston was too attractive for his own good, and he bore the burden with a self-awareness Beth had never seen before in an adult. He was funny, charming, sometimes thoughtful, and always a brilliant sculptor, but he had the ego of a spoiled two-year-old.

"Hello, Rush," she said, meeting in the middle of the room to shake his hand.

He wrapped her into a crushing bear hug, instead. "Bethie, how are ya? Feels like it's been an age! I met Kelly at the coffee bar and she said she'd just rented a studio from you. So I thought I'd better get my deposit in before all the studios are taken."

Beth patted his shoulder, then pushed him firmly away. "No danger of that," she said. "Kelly insisted on giving me money because she thinks I need it. And she's painting her own space so she can get in earlier. Oh, and I've had the building inspector in since you looked around, and everythng's secure."

He nodded. "Good. Good. So if I paint my own space, I can get in early, too?"

"Sure. If you want to. We'll have to see how efficient the furnace is. I might have to get something bigger, which could take a little time. Can you put up with that?"

Rush snaked an arm around her shoulders and squeezed. "I'm unveiling my piece for the county's art association at the festival, and I'd like my studio set up here by then so everyone can come in and look around. And, baby, I can put up with an ice floe in my studio if it means I get to be near you."

Beth looked up at him and said with a certain relish, "Rush, I'm married."

He stared at her a moment, clearly stunned, then dropped his arm.

"I'm married," she repeated. "To Ethan Drum, sheriff of—"

"I know who he is," Rush said with a sharp downturn of his features. "Are you crazy? I thought you didn't want any part of marriage again."

"I didn't. He…changed my mind." That was true. She needed a husband and he was available and willing.

"He's going to let you keep this place?"

"Why wouldn't he?"

Rush wandered around the room, pausing to look at the boards spread out on her table. "I told you I've met the sheriff. Struck me as a hard nose. Doesn't believe in gray areas. Things are black or white. Not the kind of man an artist should tie up with."

"He isn't at all like that," Beth insisted.

"Maybe not now." Rush glanced up, warning in his eyes. "Now that he's landed you, I'll wager he becomes more demanding and possessive."

Beth made a sound of exasperation. "I'm not a fish, Rush. He didn't land me. He decided to spend his life with me—the way I am. He knows how I am about my work and he's willing to live with that."

"So he says."

"So he *is.*"

"We'll see." He waved an index finger above the cat plaque she'd painted for Nikkie, then shook his head over the shield. "When are you going to stop doing this cutesy stuff and concentrate on *real* art?"

Beth bristled. She'd be the first to admit that the

plaques weren't art, but she didn't have the luxury of being an art snob at this point. "They pay the bills, Weston," she said. "And if I'm going to be your landlord, don't pick on my stuff. I might raise your rent."

He turned back to her, his eyes brimming with the passion that always lay just under the surface. It was what made him a brilliant sculptor—and something of a Casanova. "Maybe we could make a deal where you take it out in trade." The lewd suggestion was made quietly and he tried to put his arms around her again.

Beth raised both her arms to block the attempt, so he simply caught her wrists, instead. "There's something between us, Bethie. You know it and I know it."

"You're right, Weston," Ethan's voice said lazily from the doorway. "The something between you is me."

CHAPTER ELEVEN

"I'M SURE that little scene played really well for your in-laws' detective," Ethan said as he pulled the Blazer up to a stoplight. His profile had all the animation of a figure on Mount Rushmore.

Beth was growing tired of explaining. She'd done it once when Ethan walked into her studio to find Rush with his hands on her. She'd done it a second time after Rush had left. And she'd done it a third time while Ethan had helped Jason on with his jacket and walked him out to the Blazer.

"If I explain it all a fourth time," she asked, a weary, slightly antagonistic note in her voice, "do you think you might actually listen?"

He turned to look at her, anger bright in his eyes. Before he swung his gaze back to the road, she saw something else there she found a little thrilling. Jealousy.

The light changed and he accelerated with more speed than necessary. "I heard you all three times," he said as the tires screeched. "It still doesn't make sense."

Swallowing an angry retort, Beth glanced over her shoulder at her son, who was sitting quietly, his eyes uncertain. She gave him a reassuring smile, then turned back to Ethan.

"Can we save this for a more private moment?" she asked stiffly.

"Yes," he said without looking away from the road. "But we *will* get to it."

"Oh, yes," she said, perversely unwilling to let him have the last word. "We will."

He gave her a dark glance, which was soundless but served as the last word, anyway.

As they marched from the driveway to the house, Beth caught Ethan's arm and pulled him to a stop. He turned to her, his eyes glowering with temper and impatience.

"I was just going to suggest," she said calmly, dropping her hand, "that you try not to look quite so much as though you intend to eat us all for dinner. Joanne and Zachary saw the four of us leave the house this morning snarling at each other. If we come home the same way, it might not matter what their detective reports. They'll be sure our marriage is doomed, anyway."

She was right. Which only served to irritate Ethan further.

He'd lain stoically awake beside her for two nights while she'd wrapped herself around him in her sleep and drove him to the brink of insanity. But except for a few moments of general irritability, he hadn't complained.

Then he'd walked into her studio and found her in the arms of a former client of the Butler County Jail. She hadn't appeared to be offering much resistance.

Well. Maybe it was time to stop being patient.

But not in front of her in-laws. Jason was standing between him and Beth now, looking anxiously from one to the other, wondering, Ethan was sure, if his life was going to fall apart. If his mother's three-day marriage was about to end and launch him into the custody of his grandparents, after all.

"You're absolutely right," Ethan said with a forced amiability. Then he pulled the back door open and gestured Jason inside. "Come on, buddy." He continued to hold the door for Beth.

Her expression remained icy for a moment, then with a toss of her head, she swept past him with a smile and a "Thank you, darling."

"There you are," Joanne said, meeting them at the door. She wore a flowered apron over her slacks and shirt and wielded a meat fork. "Potatoes are almost done. You just have time to wash your hands."

The aroma filling the kitchen would have soothed Ethan's mood if he hadn't had to follow Beth's shapely derriere up the stairs and into his bedroom.

While she tossed her jacket onto the bed and went into the bathroom to wash her hands, he hung up his uniform jacket and threw his shirt at the hamper. He pulled on a dark blue sweatshirt and was changing his uniform pants for a pair of jeans when Beth walked out of the bathroom.

"All yours," she said, her tone brittle. She carried her jacket to the closet, and he noted her quick glance at him as he drew up the jeans and zipped them. Her cheeks pinkened, and she looked away.

"You're embarrassed at seeing me dress," he challenged, heading for the bathroom, "yet you can let another man hold you in front of your son and be comfortable with that?"

He concentrated on washing his hands, hearing her firm footsteps come around the bed to the bathroom door. "First of all," she said, her voice breathy with anger, "for explanation number *four*—" this last word was spoken very loudly "—I did not let him hold me. He'd tried to, so I raised both arms to prevent him and he caught my wrists. That was when you walked in."

He glanced at her as he reached for a towel, his eyes rejecting the explanation—for the fourth time.

"And Jason knows Rush. He knows we're... friends, that Rush tends to be physically demonstrative and that it means nothing. I'm sure he didn't give it a thought."

Ethan tossed the towel over the rod without comment and stalked past her into the bedroom and out to the hallway, Beth following. He noticed Zachary's partially open door and went to it, intending to say hello. But Zachary was sound asleep, his leg in the colorful blue cast propped on a pair of pillows, the pajama leg trimmed to midthigh. A sock had been fitted over his partially bare foot.

Ethan pulled the door closed without latching it so that if Zach called out, he would still be heard.

But Ethan didn't want to risk Beth's father-in-law overhearing their argument.

Cooperating, Beth lowered her voice as she trailed Ethan to the stairs. "And I looked away when you were pulling on your jeans," she said as though they hadn't been interrupted, "because it occurred to me that you have nice muscular legs, and I was too angry with you to entertain a complimentary thought."

He stopped in his tracks at that admission and she almost collided with him. He turned to look at her, hands on his hips, torn between anger and pleasure that she found *something* about him appealing.

She stood quietly in front of him, apparently as

ensnared by the moment as he was. Then she angled her chin and added haughtily, "Unfortunately your brain seems to be all muscle, too. Let's move it. Joanne doesn't like to have to wait dinner for anyone."

Ethan could have eaten a mastodon raw—and not because he was hungry. He couldn't remember ever feeling so elementally angry. Even when a perp was resisting arrest and started swinging, he was able to keep his cool and react only in department-approved ways.

But seeing Beth being handled by Rush Weston, then listening to her defensive responses to his questions about the incident, had done something to his equanimity. He didn't have the control over his emotions he usually had—and he didn't like that at all.

During dinner he asked Joanne about Zachary, complimented her on the excellent dinner, asked Nikkie about her day and learned that the drama teacher had been less than enthusiastic about her shield and weapon cardboard prototypes for the Winter Festival play.

"But Beth was going to look for something in her studio," she said with a grudgingly hopeful glance across the table.

"Oh," Beth said, pushing back from the table. "I did bring something home for you to look at. I was so ang—" She stopped, obviously not intending to let her ex-mother-in-law know about her anger at Ethan. She continued with a smile, "I was so anxious for dinner that I forgot it in the car. We could smell the pot roast even in the driveway," she said to Joanne. Then to Nikkie, "I'll go get it. Excuse me a minute."

Jason, seated beside Ethan, paused in his hearty attack on his plate and asked eagerly, "Can we have Taylor Bridges for dinner tomorrow?"

Ethan grinned at him, grateful for the boy's cheerful presence. "You think he'd be good to eat?"

Jason frowned while Nikkie groaned at Ethan's joke. Suddenly the boy caught on and laughed.

"No. I mean can he come over here for dinner. Mom said it was okay, but I should check with you 'cause you might have a meeting."

Tomorrow was Tuesday. That meant a county commissioners' meeting. "I do have to go to the courthouse for a couple of hours, but you can have him over even if I'm not here." He turned to Joanne. "That is, if your grandmother doesn't mind cooking for one more."

Joanne actually smiled. "Of course not."

"No." Jason was adamant. "You *have* to be here. That's why he's coming."

"What do you mean?"

"'Cause he doesn't believe you're my dad now. He thinks I'm lying. So Mom says the best thing to do is show him."

Beth returned with something large wrapped in white paper. Ethan had been so furious when they'd left her studio he hadn't noticed she'd been carrying it.

She'd caught the end of Jason's report and now met Ethan's gaze with an apologetic look. It wasn't quite convincing, because her eyes still snapped with annoyance.

"Taylor's been giving him a hard time for months," she said. "So let's have him come for dinner and see that Jason isn't lying."

"Okay, then let's make it Wednesday," Ethan said. "Is that all right with you, Joanne?"

"Perfectly," she replied, passing platters around the table for seconds.

Ethan half expected Nikkie to react negatively to an attempt to prove he was now Jason's father, too, but she was concentrating on the package Beth was unwrapping.

Shaped like a medieval shield, it had been fashioned out of half-inch-thick board and divided into quarters, the upper left and lower right painted blue with three gold fleurs-de-lis, and the upper right and lower left painted red with three gold lions guardant.

Nikkie's mouth fell open in awe. Ethan's annoyance with Beth was overridden with pleasure and satisfaction at what she'd done. It was a hard-won first step in building a relationship with his daughter.

"Wow," Nikkie breathed, getting up to inspect it.

"I'll have to look up the coat of arms of Henry V to be accurate," Beth said, "but I think it's something like this. And we can check out the coats of arms for Henry's nobles. These are easy enough to make if you think they'll work. I can cut them out, draw the patterns, and you and the drama club can paint them."

Nikkie took the mock-up of a shield in her hands and inspected it in detail, then looked at Beth in astonishment.

"Mr. Fogarty will think this is brilliant!" she said, her usually careful pose of disinterest dissolving in the face of such an impressive solution to her problem of props.

"How would we hold them?"

"Two leather straps on the back, I think," Beth said. "One off to the side to slip an arm through, and

another toward the other side for your hand to grip."
She looked at Ethan. "That's right, isn't it?"

He nodded, guessing she'd consulted him not because she needed to, but because she was feeling generous in her success. "Yes, Madam Armorer. I believe that's right. Of course you could use something
less expensive than leather. Vinyl or some kind of
plastic. No one'll notice from the audience."

"And I have a heavy-duty stapler for putting them
on." Beth touched Nikkie's arm in a manner not intended to be maternal but simply friendly. "You take
it to school and see what the consensus is. If your
drama teacher and the club like it, we'll go into production."

Nikkie was still staring at the shield, touching a
fingertip to the beautifully executed lion guardant. "I
will," she said. "Thanks."

"Sure." Beth pulled out the sign she'd made with
Nikkie's cats on it. "I was making these for the fair
and thought you might like one."

Nikkie studied it wordlessly and Beth asked with a
wince, "Too childish?"

Nikkie shook her head. "No. Not at all. Thanks. I
really like it."

Beth went back to her chair. "I'm sorry," she said
to everyone else around the table. "I didn't mean to
interrupt dinner."

"Can you make me a shield?" Jason asked eagerly. "With Buzz Lightyear on it?"

"A wooden shield," Ethan said, holding the platter
of meat and vegetables for the boy while he forked
more food onto his plate, "is a little primitive for
Buzz. Shouldn't he have a cloaking device or something?"

Before Jason could reply, a deep voice bellowed from upstairs. "Jo! I'm starving!"

Joanne smiled wryly at Beth as she pushed herself away from the table to make a plate for Zachary. "Maybe you could make me one with a wooden spoon on it," she said. "Or a knife and fork. There's a brown Betty in the refrigerator if someone wants to dish it up."

Ethan cleared the table and Beth loaded the dishwasher while Joanne took a plate upstairs to Zachary and remained there. Nikkie and Jason had gone to their own rooms to do homework.

Ethan put the small amount of leftovers into a plastic container and handed Beth the platter. The kitchen had taken on a kind of peaceful ambiance he wouldn't have thought possible, considering his and Beth's anger at each other, his daughter's usual moody defensiveness and Joanne's aggressive personality.

But something had happened at dinner. There'd been an unexpected and surprisingly successful give-and-take that came close to creating a familylike atmosphere.

Joanne had been happy to have people to cook for while she was stranded in Cobbler's Crossing with a temporarily invalid husband, and everyone else had been most appreciative of her meals. Nikkie had been astounded and grateful for the shield Beth had produced to help her with props for the play, not to mention her delight at the sign for her door. Jason had been happy when Ethan agreed to let him invite Taylor Bridges to dinner, and Ethan had been gratified by the boy's obvious pride in having him for a stepfather.

Peace reigned everywhere, but he wasn't going to

be happy until he was sure Beth had no feelings for Rush Weston. And he was going to see that she wasn't happy, either.

"So you're telling me that Weston's in the habit of putting his hands on you," he asked, resuming the argument with a vengeance, "with your consent?"

As he gathered up place mats and tossed them into a hamper in the hallway, he heard the slam of the dishwater door, then the rush of water as Beth started the wash cycle.

When he came back into the kitchen, she was standing in the middle of the floor with an expression that could have ignited fuel. She pointed to the back door. "I'd like to speak to you outside," she said, her voice barely steady.

Even though the subject had really been settled hours ago, he still wasn't ready to give in. He hated Weston and felt outrageously possessive about Beth, and he was spoiling for a fight.

"Certainly." He pulled the back door open for her and followed her onto the back porch.

"I would have thought," she said, turning to face him the moment the door closed behind them, "that a man who'd had such a happy marriage for all those years would understand a little something about trust."

That punched a hole right in the middle of his anger, but it was easy to fill it up again.

"I never found Diana being groped by another man," he said. He knew he was being unfair, but he wanted convincing, damn it.

She put a hand to her forehead and he saw her lips move unsteadily. Regret brimmed in him, fighting the anger for space.

"I know Diana was a paragon," Beth said, lowering her hand to her throat and tugging at the high collar of her red sweater, "and I'm just a woman you think is using you just to hold on to her son. You probably imagine that this isn't really a marriage, and therefore I don't feel called upon to be faithful."

That was precisely the fear he'd experienced when he'd walked into her studio and found Weston there, touching her.

"And I'm sexually repressed," she admitted, looking him in the eye, "which means that after two nights of sleeping alone…well, not alone but apart, you're thinking you can be patient until doomsday and you'll get nothing out of this marriage."

That rankled. He sat on the railing near the porch support and leaned back against it. "I might think that," he said, "if all I wanted out of this marriage was sex. But it isn't. That's why I hated seeing you with Weston."

"I wasn't *with* Weston," she said, a desperate note in her voice. "I mean, I was physically beside him, but there was no 'groping' and no emotional tie that makes me *with* him, except a sort of casual friendship. He came to ask about renting his space early because he'd run into Kelly, and she'd given me a deposit this morning. They both want to be in and set up for visitors by the Winter Festival, so they're doing their own painting."

"Beth," he said, knowing he was the one who had to be conciliatory here, though not about his opinions on Weston. "I told you I picked him up at a brawl on the waterfront. He was drunk and abusive. I don't like the idea of your life entangled with his."

She moved closer and leaned a shoulder against the

post. "I met him when I first arrived here, and you'll notice that I bear no evidence of bodily harm." She looked tired and strained. He thought he could have refuted her claim, but didn't. "I'm sorry you don't like him, but he's an eccentric. I know he drinks sometimes, but that doesn't matter to me because—" the next four words were delivered with slow emphasis "—*we are not involved.* When I first moved here, he gave me a job assisting in his sculpture class and introduced me to other artists, who are now my friends. I promise you that's all he is to me."

"Did you tell him you were married?"

"Yes." She smiled thinly. "You'll be pleased to know he's no fonder of you than you are of him."

"I don't give a rip about him," Ethan said, hooking an arm around her waist and pulling her to him. "You're the one I care about."

She rested a forearm on his shoulder and asked quietly, "If that is true, why won't you trust me?"

"It *is* true," he said, pulling her closer. "And I trust you, but I don't trust him."

"If you trust *me,*" she said quietly, clasping her fingers behind his neck, "you don't have to worry about him. He's going to rent a space from me and that's it. So you can stop yelling at me."

He nuzzled under her hair and kissed the sensitive skin behind her ear. "I'm sorry," he said, planting another kiss, his brain a little muddled by her rose scent. "I'm not usually a man who yells. I'm just…grumpy."

"Hm." She rubbed her cheek against his, then kissed his eyelids, first one, then the other. "Is there a cure for that?"

He groaned with the effort to stop from telling her. "Just…thinking positive, I guess," he said.

Beth knew the answer he withheld and decided it was time she took action. She squeezed him to her and kissed his forehead. "I have a positive thought."

He looked into her eyes with suspicion. "You do?"

"Yes." She leaned her cheek against his forehead and prayed she wouldn't disappoint him. "I want to make love to you tonight."

He didn't move a muscle and she couldn't see his face, but she felt the reaction in him, the punch of one erratic heartbeat, the sudden tension of every muscle.

He drew his head back so he could look into her eyes. "Why?" he asked. She smiled in response, knowing he wasn't interested in lovemaking as a way of making up after a quarrel.

She gave him a quick kiss, thinking what a turn-on kindness was. A curious loosening was taking place within her—strange, she thought, after they'd just had a fairly serious disagreement.

Then she realized it was because he hadn't stalked away from her and left her to absorb the blame. He'd stated his position, fought it out, and when she'd convinced him he was mistaken, he'd apologized.

This was entirely new in her man-woman experience. She felt as though all doors and windows had been thrown open, and she couldn't help the soft laugh that escaped.

"You told me when I was eager to make love with you that I should let you know," she said. "That when it seemed like a really good idea to me that it was time. Well—'' she kissed him again ''—it's time. Except that we have to wait until everyone's asleep.''

He winced and let his head fall back against the post with a thunk. "What time is it?" he asked.

She glanced at her watch. "Seven-thirty-seven."

"Oh, God," he groaned. "Three hours. Maybe more."

"Anticipation should heighten the experience," she said philosophically, giddy with the rush of freedom she felt.

"I vote we sedate everyone, cats included."

This time she kissed him slowly, seductively, letting him know with the deep sensuous exploration of her tongue that she'd never been more serious about anything. "We'll just wait. And think about how it'll be."

The door from the kitchen opened suddenly, and Joanne stood in the doorway. "There you are," she said, then noting their tangled pose, said apologetically, "Never mind. It isn't anything that can't wait."

"What do you need?" Beth asked, thinking talk was cheap. She might try to convince Ethan of her confidence in her ability to be an enthusiastic love partner, and that the three hours or so that would have to pass until then would only heighten the experience, but she knew she would have to have something practical to do in the interim to keep herself from panicking. She did feel a new freedom and knew he'd given it to her. She was just a little concerned about her ability to give back.

Both she and Ethan straightened and headed for the door.

"Zachary's feeling a little better," Joanne said as they walked into the kitchen. "He isn't needing as much pain medication, so he's getting bored. I was wondering if you had books or magazines he could read.''

"How about if I bring the TV and VCR from my room into yours?" Ethan asked.

"But what'll you do?" Joanne asked.

Beth caught the quick amusement in Ethan's eyes and bit her lip. "We're going to bed early," he said. "It's been a rough day."

"But what about tomorrow?" she persisted. "I hate to deprive you of—"

Ethan shook his head. "We hardly ever watch it, anyway. And if there's anything we really want to see, we'll go downstairs."

"Well, if you're sure…"

"I'm sure."

While Ethan moved the TV and VCR and reconnected them in Zachary's room, Beth made a cup of tea to calm her nerves.

Jason appeared with the sign for his bedroom door. "Mom, can you help me hang this?" he asked.

At any other time she might have begged off until she'd finished her tea, but tonight she looked forward to gainful employment. "We need a hammer and a nail," she said, wondering if Ethan kept them in the basement.

"Ethan's got his tools upstairs," Jason informed her. "He brought 'em up to move the television. They're watching a cowboy movie."

Beth walked with him upstairs. "You haven't been bothering Grandpa, have you?"

"They told me to go in," he said, looking offended, "'cause it's a guy movie."

"I see. I'm sorry." She ruffled his hair, enjoying his pleasure in being considered one of the guys.

Beth was pleased and flattered to see that Nikkie had hung up her sign.

The sounds of guns and galloping horses came loudly from the television in Zachary's room. A large metal toolbox stood against the wall just outside the door.

Beth peered around the door and saw Zachary propped up against the pillows, and Ethan sitting in the chair by the bed, his legs stretched out before him.

"There's nobody like the Duke," Zachary said, his eyes riveted to the screen. "Jo always insisted he was going to be her second husband." He grinned, still staring at the screen. "Smart man checked out before it could happen."

Beth waved her hand to claim Ethan's attention.

He walked around the bed and came into the hall, his eyes alight with humor and passion. "Tell me we've moved up the time," he said, catching her hands. Then he noticed Jason standing beside her.

A rueful acceptance replaced the desire in his eyes. The frustration was something they shared, though hers was mixed with more than a little trepidation.

He put a hand to Jason's shoulder. "What's up, Jase?"

"We need a hammer and a nail," the boy said. "I want to put this on my door." He held up his Buzz Lightyear sign. "Mom made it for me before we moved here."

"Ethan," Beth said, "if you can just point me to a hammer and a nail, I can put it up."

Ethan squatted by the toolbox, lifted the top tray,

reached into the bottom and handed up a hammer. "You won't hit your thumb or anything?" he teased.

She pretended to swing the hammer at his head. "I probably use woodworking tools more than you do. At the studio I have saws, sanders, dremels, lathes, you name it, and I have yet to lose a thumbnail or a pinkie finger."

He straightened and waggled an eyebrow. "Ooh. I love it when you talk tough."

"Ethan, come and see this!" Zachary shouted.

Beth pushed him toward the room. "Go. We'll rendezvous later."

He sighed and kissed her again, his eyes lazy with desire. "Words I've longed to hear," he whispered.

Beth hung the plaque with several experienced strokes of the hammer. Jason's pleasure in it made her feel as though it should have required much more effort.

She went into his room to encourage him to get ready for bed and was a little horrified to discover that in less than a week he'd managed to make it look like a warehouse for boy's clothing—one without hangers.

"Jason," she scolded gently, picking up jeans, shirts and underwear off the floor, "you know better than this. Underwear and shirts and dirty jeans go in the hamper. Stuff that's still clean should be hung in the closet."

He followed her as she gathered his things. "But I can't reach the hanger thing."

"The rod," she said, folding clean jeans at the zipper and draping them over a hanger. She was about to suggest he stand on a chair, but a maternal second sense told her that wasn't a good idea. "Then you can put things on your chair and I'll hang them up for you until we can put in a lower rod.''

She collected underwear and carried it to the bathroom hamper. He waited for her in the doorway of his room, a pair of battered tennis shoes in his arms. "Are you happy here, too?" he asked, appearing anxious for the right response. "I mean, you weren't really at first, but you are now, aren't you?"

"I'm happy wherever you are," she said, taking a jacket off the bedpost and hanging it up in the closet.

"I mean you're happy you got married to Ethan," Jason said in exasperation.

A man in the making, she thought wryly, direct and insistent.

But at least she could give him the answer he wanted. "Yes, I'm happy I married Ethan."

"And Nikkie's starting to like you, too."

Beth plucked a pair of pajamas off another bedpost and handed them to him. "We might have to wait a little while for that to really happen. She liked the shield I made, but I'm not sure she likes me yet."

Jason took the pajamas, then wrapped his arms around her waist. "She will 'cause you're a great mom," he said, his eyes alight with a contentment she hadn't seen there in some time. "Aren't we lucky I ran away and all those campers were lost so that the only one who could come and look for me was Ethan?"

He lowered his voice and glanced toward his open bedroom door. "And aren't we lucky I lied to Grandma and Grandpa, and then Ethan helped me?"

Beth almost hated to be reminded of how their situation had come about. It made it seem so fragile, and the possibility that it could all dissolve one day was something she didn't like to contemplate. Particularly tonight.

"We're lucky nobody's caught us," she whispered back conspiratorially.

Jason seemed to like that and ran off giggling to take a shower and get ready for bed.

CHAPTER TWELVE

BY TEN O'CLOCK Jason and Nikkie were asleep, and Zachary had turned down the sounds of battle in deference to the late hour.

Beth piled her hair in a loose knot on top of her head and took a shower, wondering where Ethan was. He'd left Zachary's room a short while ago and she'd heard him go down the stairs, but he had yet to return to their bedroom.

Heart thudding nervously, she spritzed cologne and slipped on a berry-colored silk nightie Kelly had given her years ago but she'd never worn. The color made her flushed cheeks appear to be on fire, and she put her hands over them to cool them.

"You look like you're about to ignite," she told herself with a moan.

"You are," a quiet male voice said from the doorway.

She spun around. Ethan stood there in jeans, bare-chested and barefoot, a tulip glass of something bubbly in each hand. His hair was damp, suggesting he'd showered in the other bathroom. A mild frown creased his brow. "Second thoughts?" he asked.

"No," she denied, moving toward him. "A little nervous, though."

He smiled and handed her a glass. "Me, too," he

said with a sincerity that turned her spine to oatmeal and made her heart swell with love.

He beckoned her out of the bathroom and toward the bed, where he'd turned back the blankets and banked the pillows against the headboard. He held her glass while she climbed into the bed and sat against the comfortable backrest he'd made.

He followed, drawing her into his arm and tipping the rim of his wineglass against hers in a toast. "To learning to communicate."

She drank to that, then leaned against him. His warm shoulder was muscled and smooth under her cheek. She tipped her head back to kiss the underside of his jaw. "That means 'I love you' in…in Romanesque," she said fancifully. His arm around her and his easy manner were beginning to banish her nervousness. She watched his eyes darken at her admission and it was a moment before he whispered, "God, I love you, too." Then he cleared his throat and smiled.

"Romanesque? Really?" He kissed the top of her head. "I thought Romanesque was a style of architecture."

She made an airy gesture with her glass. "It's a mistake everyone makes. It's actually a language."

"Ah. A romance language?"

"No." She turned her face into his chest and kissed his pectoral muscle. She felt his heartbeat accelerate and her own race to match it. "The language of romance. There's a difference."

"I see." He sipped his wine. "And you're fluent in this?"

"Not really," she admitted, leaning her cheek

against him again. "It wasn't spoken where I lived before, so I've had little chance to practice."

"Well." He ran a hand tenderly up and down her bare arm. "I don't want to one-up you, but I happen to be a Romanesque scholar."

She smiled. "I guessed that."

"Yes." She heard the light clink of his glass against the top of the bedside table. "I have a Ph.D. in it. Unfortunately I've also had little chance to practice. But I'd be happy to share what I know." He took her glass from her and placed it beside his. When he turned to her, his eyes were dark with intent. "Together I'll bet we could write the definitive text on it."

She slid down into the bed, her heart thudding, and he leaned sideways over her to rearrange the pillows under her head. Then his eyes met hers and she saw everything he was in them—tough, strong, gentle, funny. And at the moment she held his complete attention, and the realization gave her both profound comfort and unbearable excitement.

She put her hands to his face and rubbed a thumb gently over his upper lip. "I know how to say, 'I'm glad I found you.' Want to hear?"

"Please," he replied softly.

She pulled his head down to her and kissed him with all the tender passion he inspired in her. She parted her lips, he opened his mouth, their tongues met and stroked...and she finally had to draw back to catch her breath.

"Excellent pronunciation," he said, his voice low and a little rough. "What else can you say?"

She traced the line of his jaw with her fingertips,

then trailed her index finger down the middle of his throat to his collarbone.

"I can say, 'You've changed my life,'" she suggested.

"Mm." He ran a hand down her side, over her hip to the top of her thigh. "I'd like to know how to say that, too."

She felt the warmth of his hand through the thin layer of fabric, and a frisson of anticipation arced through her.

She leaned up to kiss the base of his throat, then dropped a series of soft kisses down the middle of his chest. She pushed away from the mattress, forcing him backward until he lay on his back on the bedspread and she kneeled over him.

Ethan felt her lips and her breath at the waistband of his jeans and prayed that his cardiovascular system was up to this. Letting her remain in control so that he didn't frighten her was almost more than he could do.

With the denim blocking her path, she strung kisses across his waist from his left side to his right. He couldn't withhold a groan.

"Do you want," she asked on a whispered breath, "to try to...repeat that after me?"

Everything inside him roared, but his reply was a throaty, "Yes, I would."

He reached under the hem of her gown and moved his hands slowly up the backs of her smooth legs, then down and up again, inching his way to the warm flesh of her bottom.

She eased her weight on top of him, buried her face against the side of his and lay still as he explored her.

Her long sigh fractured as she finally sat up on him

to pull off her gown. The action took the loose clip in her hair with it, and the dark mass tumbled to her shoulders, curly and fragrant.

He reached up to touch it, but she caught his hand and brought it to her breast. The small mound filled his palm, and he felt its tip pearl.

"This means," she said, her voice a little unsteady, "'You've changed *me.*'"

He slipped his hands around her and, sitting up, eased her onto her back among the pillows.

He kissed the slight convexity of her stomach, her hipbones, the juncture of torso and thigh.

Her hands at the waistband of his jeans unzipped them. He sat up to push his jeans down and off, and the instant he was free of them, she reached for his arm to draw him back to her.

He lay beside her and pulled the blankets over them. She pushed herself against him and bent her knee, rubbing it along his thigh as her hands moved down his back and over his hip.

"This means 'I need you,'" she said, her whisper a little feverish. She nipped at his shoulder.

He caught her in the crook of his arm and held her to the mattress when she tried to wriggle against him. She stroked a hand over his belly and downward, but he caught her fingers and stopped her, enfolding her hand in his and carrying it back to her waist.

"Now I have a few things to say," he murmured softly. She settled back with a languorous smile. He stroked a hand down her abdomen and placed it possessively right where she longed for his touch.

Beth was certain she would explode. Her heart couldn't beat this fast, her breath couldn't come in such shallow gasps, her nerves couldn't be stretched this tight without snapping.

He dipped a finger inside her, then found the spot Steve had never believed was there, and said, his lips just above hers, his other arm holding her to him, "This means 'I love you and you're everything to me. Everything.'"

His clever hand began to move, and as she absorbed the wonder of those words, pleasure rushed at her headlong so that the declaration still echoed when fulfillment overtook her.. The sensory impact of the miracle created by love and understanding given and taken pinned her to the mattress with its force. It filled her, bathed her, and just when she thought it might drown her, she rose with a gasp of astonishment, and let it wash over her in breathtaking waves.

She opened her eyes to see Ethan's pleased and slightly self-satisfied expression. Then she closed both hands over him and felt her own satisfaction when his expression turned from smug to seduced, and he grew ready under her touch.

"This means," she said as he moved quickly over her, "'Let me be as generous as you are.'"

Even as he lifted her hips and entered her, she saw his eyes react to her eagerness to please him. She closed her eyes and ran her hands up his arms, hoping that it would be as good for him as it had been for her.

He drove into her and she lost all ability to concentrate. Pleasure rose again all around her, and just as she'd begun to suspect that she'd somehow gotten this wrong, that her intention had been to give Ethan the same delicious pleasure he'd given her, he burst inside her with a cry that he silenced in her hair.

She'd done it. She'd given him pleasure. The past wasn't her fault.

As his body pulsed over her, she came alive again like the molten middle of the earth. In astonishment, she clung to him as they shuddered together for long, long moments.

As the ripples of pleasure cleared, Beth burst into tears.

Ethan cradled her to him, his voice filled with concern. "What?" he demanded. "What?"

How did a woman tell a man, she wondered, that he'd just restored her faith in herself as a sexual being? How did she explain that though she was logical and clear-thinking in every other way, she'd allowed a selfish lover to convince her that the unsatisfying results of his lovemaking had been her fault?

Ethan tried to ease her away to look at her, but she put a hand over her eyes. "Nothing," she said, sniffing. "Nothing. I'm fine."

There was a sharp pain on her left buttock. She yelped and dropped her hand, staring at him in stunned surprise. He'd pinched her!

"In Romanesque," he said gravely, "that's 'Don't lie to me.' What is it? Did I hurt you? Upset you?"

And suddenly the momentous revelation she'd just had about herself seemed to lose all importance in this very sane and comfortable world Ethan had provided. Her tears turned to laughter and she wrapped her arms around his neck.

"Oh, good," he said, turning them so that she lay in the hollow of his shoulder, "I've married a split personality."

She hitched a leg up over his and kissed his throat. "But I'm multilingual. You liked my Romanesque."

"I did indeed. I, however, am single-minded, and I want to know what you were crying about."

"They were good tears," she said, snuggling closer. "Not bad ones."

He drew her arm across his waist. "Great. Then it should be easy to explain to me."

She did. It didn't take very long, and it was like being purged of the past. He listened, understood, commiserated.

"But as of tonight," he said, "it no longer matters. That's over, and I think we proved—" she heard the smile in his voice "—rather forcefully, I might add, that he was wrong and I was right."

"I love you," she said, suddenly exhausted.

"Brilliantly." He stroked her hair, then kissed it. "I love you, too."

"Also brilliantly. Jason said we were lucky."

LIFE WAS IDEAL. For the next week Beth worked like a fiend in her studio and made love with Ethan like a wild woman every night.

The night Taylor Bridges came to dinner, Ethan took the boys to the gym with him afterward, then dropped Taylor at home.

Jason was the picture of self-satisfaction when he and Ethan returned. As Beth tucked Jason in that night, he said that Ethan called him "son" when they were shooting baskets, and that later, when Ethan took them for ice cream and Jason and Taylor went to the bathroom, Taylor told him he was the luckiest kid in the whole world.

Beth thought he probably was.

She wished she was doing as well with Nikkie as Ethan was doing with Jason. Yes, Nikkie was visibly pleased with the shields, but her friends from the drama club, who came nightly to work on them, were warmer to Beth than she was.

Nikkie was polite and no longer overtly hostile, but except when her friends were over, she kept to herself and showed Beth no sign of friendship.

Zachary was comfortable with his crutches by the end of the week, and Joanne declared it was time to return to Seattle.

"You're welcome to stay a few more days," Beth said, "if you think it would—"

"No," Joanne insisted. She looked from Beth to Ethan with a new ease in her manner. "We appreciate your hospitality and your generosity, but you have to get back to your routines and we have to get home. We've enjoyed watching your progress with the props for Nikkie's play, though, Beth. And of course, we'd like to be here for the opening of the cannery over the Winter Festival weekend."

"Please come back for it," Ethan said. "We'll try to get along without your cooking until then."

Joanne tried not to look too pleased, but Beth could see it was an effort.

They left on Sunday morning, and Beth and Ethan made love all afternoon by the fire in the family room. Nikkie and her friends were rehearsing the play at school, and Jason was spending the afternoon at Taylor Bridges's.

On Monday evening the blissful peace was shattered.

Beth had put in a good day at the studio. Ethan had helped her pack up the clay pots in the basement and transport them to the cannery. She'd spent the day washing them and giving them all coats of brightly colored background paint.

She and Ethan and Jason had gone for burgers after work because Nikkie had stayed late at school to rehearse, and Ethan had a Search and Rescue meeting after dinner. Ethan had dropped Beth and Jason at home and given her a lingering kiss goodbye and a whispered promise to be home early.

Jason turned on the television and Beth puttered about the kitchen, making herself a cup of tea and running the dishwasher. The house was quiet without Ethan and Nikkie, she noticed, thinking how quickly and closely their lives had become entwined. Even though Nikkie seemed to do her best to keep her distance, Beth found herself caring and worrying about the girl and wishing she could discover some magic way to bridge the gap between them.

There was a knock at the back door. Beth opened it to find Brodie standing there in a brown tweed sports jacket over a tab-collared denim shirt and casual brown slacks. In one hand he held a rather tousled mixed bouquet of flowers. He looked handsome but angry and stormed past her into the kitchen.

Apparently remembering his manners, he stopped in the middle of the room and said with an apologetic twist of his lips and a thrust of the flowers toward her, "Hi. Are you busy?"

"Not at all," she replied, closing the door. "But Ethan's at a meeting tonight."

He jammed his hands into his pants pockets. "Good. I wanted to talk to you."

"Ah…sure." She looked doubtfully at the flowers. "These are…for me?"

"Why not?" he asked defensively.

Okay. She decided to simply coast until she could figure out what was happening here. She pointed him to the table. "Sit down. Can I make you a cup of tea?"

He looked uncertain for a moment, then nodded. "Okay," he said finally, then held up large-fingered hands permanently stained in the lines and hollows with grease and oil and whatever else mechanics dealt with. "Just don't give it to me in anything delicate."

Beth laughed as she rummaged through the cupboard for something to put the flowers in. She finally decided on a teapot with a chipped spout. She filled it with water and set the flowers in it, wondering what had happened to them. They were beautiful, but crinkled and bruised.

"Not to worry," she said. "We seem to be big on sheriff's-office mugs. Sit down, Brodie. Milk and sugar?"

He pulled out a chair and sat. "I don't know," he admitted. "I've never had tea before."

She stopped in the process of opening a teabag's protective paper envelope. "You're kidding. Well, I can make a pot of coffee if you prefer."

"No." He waved a hand dismissively. "This is my day for doing things I'm not used to."

Beth filled the mug with water and brought it to him.

"That sounds a little ominous," she said, sitting opposite him with her cup. "Do I want to know what you've done today?"

He leaned away from the table, crossed one ankle over the other leg and studied the ceiling tiles overhead. "I called in sick," he said, then quickly added when Beth began to express concern, "I wasn't, I just told my guys I was sick so they wouldn't guess I was being an idiot.''

It was on the tip of her tongue to ask why, but she held off. He seemed to be collecting his thoughts, and judging by the storm in his eyes and the complete absence of his usual good humor, she guessed they weren't pleasant.

"Then I got a haircut," he continued, "went to Buckley's and bought this jacket,"

"Which looks very dapper," she interrupted.

He gave her a glance she found difficult to interpret, then leaned forward over the table and drew the steaming mug toward him. "Thanks. I'm giving it to Ethan. And this shirt with the dumb collar. I feel like I should have a handlebar mustache.''

Beth was beginning to suspect where this was going. She propped her elbow on the table and leaned her chin in the palm of her hand. "I think that's the appeal of those shirts for women. Victorian men wore something like it under those old, stiff celluloid collars. But…I'm guessing Kelly didn't like it.''

He looked momentarily surprised, then took a sip of his tea and shook his head. "Kelly never saw it," he said. "I went by her place tonight to see if she'd like to go to dinner. She was packing up stuff from her studio to move into your cannery. She hardly even looked at me.''

"Well…" Beth struggled between an inherent preference for diplomacy in such matters and the undeniable effectiveness of the plain and simple truth. She did her best to combine both. "I think the night of the wedding, you left her with the impression that…you're not really interested in a relationship.''

He drank more tea, then put the cup down, his expression moody. "I thought I wasn't," he said, leaning back in his chair. He folded his arms over his chest and let his head fall back. "I once had a relationship with this woman I met when she and her father were driving from Portland to their vacation home across the river. He owns Techno-Ware in Portland. Their Rolls-Royce broke down just this side of the bridge. It was only a hose, and I went to them to fix it because, I'm not sure, but I think you'd probably go to mechanics' hell for towing a Rolls."

Beth smiled, but Brodie didn't. He straightened restlessly in his chair, blew out a breath and took another sip of tea.

"Anyway, Paulette—that was her name—looked at me. I looked at her and it was fate. You know, *fate,* in capital letters. Her father was so pleased with me he invited me to their place, she came over a few evenings to see me. I spent a couple of weekends with them. We got along famously, and when it was time for them to go back to Portland, I asked her to marry me."

His eyes seemed to lose focus for a moment, then he rubbed a hand over them, and when he looked at Beth again, his gaze was self-deprecating and sad. He went on as though he could suddenly see it all from a comfortable distance.

"She looked so surprised," he said, shaking his head. "And now I think that's what hurt the most. That I was *so* in love, and all along she hadn't a clue. Then she blinked these velvety brown eyes and said in this husky rich-girl voice, 'But Brodie, you're just a mechanic.'"

Beth reached a hand across the table and covered his, her heart filled with sympathy and anger. "Obviously a zero, Brodie. If she was here, I'd deck her for you."

His thin smile told her he appreciated the offer. "Anyway, it was hard for me to admit I'd been that blind. In fact, I think I've resisted admitting it by deciding that love was never meant to be taken seriously and treating every woman I met that way."

"But you feel something for Kelly?"

"I don't seem to be able to put her out of my mind. Is that the same thing?"

"I'd say so."

"So how do I get her to realize I regret acting like an adolescent and I want to spend time with her?"

"Tell her that."

He blew out another breath. "I did, and I handed her those flowers." He pointed to the ragged bunch in the chipped teapot. "All she did was hit me with them and lock the studio door on me."

Beth went for the teapot to refill her cup. "Want more?" she asked, holding the pot over his.

He shook his head and made a face. "I don't think tea's my thing. But thanks."

Beth laughed and put the kettle back on the burner. "You know," she said, sobering, "I think Kelly feels about marriage the way you feel about tea. She had it once, didn't like the taste, and even though there are other kinds available, she doesn't want another cup."

Brodie frowned at her metaphor. "You mean, she doesn't want *me*."

"No," Beth corrected, leaning toward him. "She doesn't want to risk getting what she had before— which was someone who didn't appreciate her and wouldn't let her be who she is. I think she would want you if she really knew the man under the Don Juan facade.''

He brooded over her words for a moment, then pushed his cup away and stood. He didn't seem any happier than he had when he arrived, but he did seem a little more hopeful. He hugged Beth. "Thanks for listening. I'm glad I've got you for a sister-in-law.''

"Well, you're all right for a brother-in-law, too.'' She smiled, then walked him to the door and opened it for him. "And keep the jacket and shirt. You look great in them, and if you handle this right, you might get to wear them again.''

"Let's hope so," he said.

Just as Brodie went out the door, Nikkie came in, looking flushed. She called a greeting to her uncle, gave Beth a polite hello, then hurried through the kitchen toward the hallway and the stairs, all the while careful to avoid Beth's eyes.

Beth noted that, then dismissed it; her husband's daughter was simply continuing to keep her, Beth, out of her space.

"Have you eaten?" Beth called after Nikkie.

"We had pizza delivered!" Nikkie shouted back.

Ethan phoned at nine o'clock. "This is going on longer than I'd hoped," he said. Then his voice dropped a tone and took on a quality she could almost feel through the electronic connection. "But if you wait up for me, I promise to make it worth your while.''

"I'll be waiting.''

"More than an hour," he said with sudden briskness, "and I'm out of here. I love you.''

"I love you, too,'' she answered, sharply aware of how sincere she was.

She hung up the phone, then turned and almost collided with Nikkie. The girl's eyes were wide and stricken, and Beth presumed she was upset because she'd heard Beth tell Ethan she loved him.

Beth summoned patience and prepared to defend her position. But before she could say a word, Nikkie asked anxiously, "Have you seen Simba?"

Surprised by the question, Beth had to take a moment to think. When Ethan had dropped her and Jason home after dinner, Cindy had been eating, but she couldn't recall seeing Simba.

"No," she said finally. "Why? Is he missing?"

Nikkie made a nervous gesture with one hand. "I think so. Cindy's on my bed, but I've called Simba and looked in all his favorite places and he isn't there."

"Did you check Jason's bunk?"

"Yes."

"Did you ask Jason? He's watching TV."

"Yes. He hasn't seen him, either."

Relieved to find herself in one of the areas of motherhood she understood and in which she felt qualified, Beth was prepared to help Nikkie find her cat. She reached into a utility drawer for the large flashlight Ethan kept there.

"Come on, we'll look around outside," Beth said, going to the hooks by the door for her jacket. "You check the yard and I'll—"

Nikkie stopped Beth with a hand on her arm before she could open the door. Beth looked at her in puzzlement, and saw more than worry in the girl's eyes. Guilt was there, as well.

Jason walked into the kitchen, his expression concerned. "So, we gonna go look for Simba?" he asked.

Instead of snapping an answer at him, Nikkie averted her eyes from Beth and studied her fingernails. "I…I think I know where he might be."

She glanced back at Beth, clearly expecting reproof of some kind.

Beth called on her reserves of calm and good sense. "Where's that?"

Nikkie pointed vaguely west. "In the Appleby house," she said.

"But he never wanders that far. And the house is boarded up."

"You can get in through the basement window," Jason said, apparently pleased to be able to share that information. "The board's loose at the bottom."

"Ethan told you to stay away from there," Beth scolded, missing the connection.

"I have," he said in the voice of the unjustly accused, "but all the kids know you can get in that way."

The light began to dawn for Beth. She turned to Nikkie. "But how would a cat get in there?"

Nikkie met her suspicious gaze and admitted reluctantly but frankly, "He probably followed me. The drama club did have a rehearsal after school like I told you, but Cameron and Bradley thought it would be fun to have it somewhere else, since it was just us. So the club voted and decided on the Appleby house. I ran home to get some Cokes and cookies, and Simba followed me."

At Beth's surprised look she explained, "I know he's a really lazy cat, but when he's been alone all day, he sometimes just wants to be with me, no matter what." Nikkie returned to her story. "Anyway, when we left, it was dark and later than I thought, and I forgot all about him. He probably went to sleep somewhere and..." A big tear slid down her cheek. "All we did was rehearse the play, but Dad'll be really mad."

Beth glanced at the clock over the stove. Nine-ten. "All right." Beth pointed at Jason. "You stay here. Nikkie and I will be right back."

But Jason reached for his coat as Nikkie pulled hers on. "I wanna come," he said.

Beth took the coat from him and returned it to the hook. "No. I want you to stay here. Watch TV until we come back. And Uncle Brodie's right next door." She blew her son a kiss and dashed outside, Nikkie right behind her.

They hurried to the end of the block, looked both ways at the corner, then ran across the street and down another half block until they reached the deserted Appleby house.

Beth headed for the main entrance, but Nikkie caught her arm and pulled her around the house and behind a dormant rhododendron.

The house was a dark rectangle against a moonless sky. The many trees and bushes that surrounded it formed irregular shadows. The wind blew, leaves and branches rustled—and Beth did her best to ignore the gooseflesh on her arms.

"Shine the flashlight down here, Beth!" Nikkie whispered, taking Beth's wrist and pointing it downward.

The beam revealed a piece of plywood that had been nailed over the window. There was graffiti on it and obvious gouges on the bottom edge where a tool had loosened the nails that held it in place.

Nikkie removed the plywood with very little effort. Then Beth hunkered down beside her and peered through the window into the darkness. Even from outside, the place smelled dank and musty and faintly alcoholic.

"Simba!" Nikkie called in a loud whisper. "Simba! Come on, baby!"

No response.

"Simba!" Nikkie tried again.

Still no response. Beth lay on her stomach on the grass and cast the beam of light over what she could see of the basement. There were stacks of dusty boxes, some of them rotting from the dampness. Rusty old gardening tools were propped against an ancient furnace. The concrete floor was littered with the debris left by the occasional transient—paper cups, empty bottles, fast-food wrappers, a filthy jacket.

Nikkie continued to call, and at last they heard a thump. She called again excitedly, but all they heard was silence.

Beth handed her the flashlight. "Hold this for me," she said, taking all her instinctive fears of dark and unknown places and thrusting them away. "If, God forbid, there's a *person* down there, just run to the nearest house and call 911."

"Beth, I should go in," Nikkie argued, trying to push the flashlight back at her.

"No, I will," Beth said firmly. "Just do as I say and stay here."

Nikkie gave in and directed the flashlight beam to the floor just under the window. Beth sat on the window frame, cleared long ago of broken glass by transients, and swung her legs into the basement. Her feet encountered a rusty laundry sink. She stepped into it and squatted down to hold the sides and lower one leg to the floor, then the other. She reached up for the flashlight.

"Be careful, Beth!" Nikkie cautioned with a sincerity Beth would have found touching under other circumstances. Right now all she could think of was finding the cat in good health, getting out of this place and getting home before Ethan did.

She swept the light before her and picked her way across the cluttered floor calling the cat. Things scurried in corners, and it occurred to her that if the cat was alive and well, being in this basement was probably the feline equivalent of a two-for-one day at the Burger Bistro.

She swept the light under and around boxes, tools and broken parts of things she couldn't identify, then went around to the other side of the furnace. She swept all corners with the light first and was relieved to find nothing human crouched in a corner.

"Simba!" she called. "Come on, kitty! Here, kitty!"

A sudden thump behind her caused her to turn with a little scream. The thumper responded with her own scream. It was Nikkie.

"I told you to wait!" Beth whispered.

"Well, I couldn't see you," Nikkie answered defensively. "And I'd feel awful if something happened to you because you were looking for my cat."

"Then next time," Beth said, "don't leave your cat in a haunted basement!"

Nikkie took a step back. "You're yelling," she accused.

"Do you know what your father would be doing if he was here?" Beth asked, turning around again and inching her way forward in the beam of light.

Nikkie grabbed hold of the back of Beth's shirt. "I'm trying not to think about that. Do you see any— There!"

"Where?" Beth asked, and Nikkie caught her wrist and directed the beam to a set of shelves built against the wall. Simba sat between an auto-parts box and a broken light fixture, looking like just another dusty remnant of the past.

"Simba!" Nikkie cried with delight and reached up for him. Her reach was one shelf short.

The cat yawned and watched her straining fingertips with interest, carefully keeping all parts of his body beyond her reach.

"Simba," she said, impatience mingling with her delight at finding him safe. "Come on. I'll give you a can of tuna! *People* tuna!"

A sudden clatter of metal caused Beth and Nikkie to spin around, the beam of light in front of them.

"Jeez!" Jason complained, putting both hands up protectively. "It's just me."

"Jason Richards!" Beth grabbed his arm and pulled him toward her.

"I know, I know," he protested, "but Ethan says a man's got to take care of his family, and he says when he isn't here, it's my job."

"Your *job*," Beth said, leaning over him, "is to listen to your mother!"

Jason looked beyond her shoulder and smiled.

"There's Simba!" he said, pointing. "I can see his eyes!"

"Yes," Beth said wearily. "Nikkie found him. But we're having trouble getting him down."

"Oh." Jason moved around in front of them and studied the predicament. Simba could be heard purring, but he wasn't moving. Jason thumped his chest like Tarzan, and Simba leaped off the shelf and into his arms.

He turned to a surprised Nikkie with a wide smile and handed her the cat. "That's how I get him off my bunk," he said. "I was just playing around one day, and he jumped on me when I did that."

Nikkie held the cat to her cheek and buried her nose in his fur, dust and all. She looked up and said gravely, "Thank you, Jason."

His eyes widened. He glanced at his mother, then back at Nikkie, and replied with another big smile, "Yeah, sure."

"All right, we're out of here," Beth said, urging Jason and Nikkie, with Simba now clinging to her shoulder, before her.

She boosted Jason up onto the laundry sink and pushed on the seat of his jeans until he could wriggle out the window. Nikkie handed up the cat, then followed Jason through.

Beth stepped into the tub, then reached a hand out into the darkness for help as she clambered up. "If we're all very quiet, we might get home without anyone—"

She knew the moment the helping hand clamped her wrist that it didn't belong to Jason or to Nikkie. It pulled her with startling ease and speed through the window to the grass and onto her feet.

On her way up she noticed a familiar pair of boots, uniform pants and jacket. Over the shoulder of the jacket she saw several cars in the middle of the street, their red-and-blue lights illuminating the sheriff's department's logo.

She groaned defeatedly and looked into an angry pair of brown eyes under the low brim of a Stetson hat.

"Hi, Ethan," she said in a very small voice. "You're home early."

CHAPTER THIRTEEN

"ETHAN!" BETH CLUTCHED the bars of the prison cell and shouted at the top of her lungs. "Ethan Drum, you come here this instant!"

Beth heard footsteps hurrying down the hallway from the outer office and into the small bank of holding cells. She could tell by their urgent pace that they didn't belong to her husband.

Deputy Curtis's harassed face appeared on the other side of the bars. "Yes, ma'am?" he asked.

"Where *is* he?" she demanded.

"Um…he's on the phone with the governor's office, Mrs. Drum." Curtis pointed awkwardly behind him. "I'm supposed to ask you to be quiet. You're disturbing the drunk tank."

Beth could not remember ever being so enraged. If she could have gotten her hands on Ethan at that moment, she was certain the seventy-pound difference in their weights would have made no difference.

"The governor?" Beth repeated. "What—is prowling a capital offense? And don't I get a trial first?"

Curtis smiled nervously. "I don't think your case will go to trial, Mrs. Drum. The governor's visiting Butler County in a couple of months. That's what they're talking about."

"You're damned right it isn't going to trial! I haven't done anything!"

"Pardon me, ma'am, but the sheriff's got quite a list of charges," Curtis disputed courteously. "There's breaking and entering, two counts of endangering the safety of a minor, resisting arrest—"

"I did *not* resist arrest!"

"He carried you in, ma'am," Curtis reminded her. "And you were beating on his back."

"Because I hadn't *done* anything!" she shouted.

"You resisted arrest, ma'am," he repeated.

"You tell the sheriff," she said, forcing herself to speak more quietly, "that if I'm not out of this cell and on my way home in five minutes, he's going to be single again. Do you understand me, Curtis?"

"Yes, ma'am." Curtis hurried off to relay her message.

Beth checked her watch. Midnight.

It was twelve-thirty-five when Beth heard another, lazier set of footsteps and identified the tread. Ethan came around the corner, shrugging into his jacket. He gave her one dark look, pressed a button, and her cell door opened electronically.

She snatched up her jacket and stalked past him into the hallway.

"Am I free?" she asked, "or are you taking me down some dark country road where I mysteriously disappear? This is very interesting, you know. I've never seen small-town justice in action before. I always thought *Cool Hand Luke* was an exaggeration."

He pushed the cell door closed and crossed to her, every muscle in his face tight and hard. "I would be happy," he said with a calm that belied the anger in his eyes, "to exaggerate a little justice for you right now, so don't push me."

She would have, but after the past hour and the raging surge of adrenaline brought about by her arrest, resistance and subsequent trip to the car, then from the car to the jail over his shoulder, she was exhausted. She wasn't sure that even her fury could keep her on her feet much longer.

"Where are the children?" she asked coolly.

"At Brodie's," he replied.

"Good." She punched her way into her jacket, adjusted the hem with a yank that should have made her an inch shorter, then zipped it, seriously endangering her trachea. "Then when we get home, we can talk about the divorce!"

ETHAN WASN'T generally a drinking man. He had a beer occasionally, a mixed drink at a party once in a while, but the alcohol he kept around the house was mostly medicinal. When he got home with Beth, he poured himself a third of a barrel glass of Irish whiskey, certain his blood pressure would burst his heart within the hour if he didn't relax.

He was doing his best to *appear* relaxed because Beth was raging like a woman possessed, and he knew his control was making her crazy. It was small satisfaction in light of what she'd put him through tonight, but he was enjoying it.

Still, it would be a long time before he forgot what it had felt like to get a call from Ebbie, who picked up messages whenever he was in a meeting.

She reported that one of his neighbors had called to say she'd been watching the pilot boat through her binoculars and happened to notice several figures by the Appleby house. When he'd asked why she hadn't called the police, Ebbie replied that the woman said she thought one of the figures looked like his daughter.

What particularly troubled the woman was that she'd seen a couple of young men go into the basement that afternoon.

"Well, hell, why didn't she report it then?" he asked.

"Her son had just pulled up to take her to her doctor's appointment, and afterward she forgot. Curtis and Billings are doing back-to-backs tonight. I'll dispatch them for you."

He'd raced to the site, mindless with worry. If there was a transient in the basement, there could be trouble. He knew better than anyone that the homeless weren't necessarily criminal. A certain element was, however, and even for those who weren't, the sudden intrusion of someone else into their sanctum could surprise them into reacting with fear, instead of common sense.

Then he'd arrived. Curtis and Billings behind him, to find Nikkie and Jason on the grass. He'd been giving serious thought to paddling both of them where they stood when he'd heard a voice coming from the basement. Then he'd stared in disbelief when a hand reached out, groping for help. It was wearing the simple gold band he'd put on it a little more than a week ago.

At that moment he'd had no idea what their adventure had been about, but it had sounded as though she'd been suggesting that they conceal it. In view of the fact that he'd forbidden both children to go into the Appleby house, he'd lost all willingness to listen to explanations before he acted.

He'd asked Billings to take the children to Brodie's, then told Beth he was taking her in for questioning.

She'd argued, which he'd expected, but when he'd tried to lead her to the car, she'd kicked him, which he hadn't expected. That was when he hoisted her over his shoulder, carried her past an openmouthed Curtis and put her in the cage in the back of his patrol unit.

Things had gone from bad to worse. Her fury had set off his, and now here they were, two volcanoes about to erupt.

"Would you like a drink?" he asked with strained civility before replacing the bottle in the open kitchen cupboard.

"No," she said, pacing the kitchen like some out-of-control bumper toy. "I want a divorce."

Just as they had when she'd spoken them earlier, the words struck terror into his heart. But he kept his calm facade in place and headed for the hallway to the living room, barely avoiding a collision with her as he interrupted her pacing pattern.

"Okay," he said, and continued into the living room.

He'd called a lot of bluffs in his time, and some of them had even involved weapons aimed at his heart or his temple, but he'd never awaited a reaction with the trepidation with which he awaited this one.

"Okay?" she repeated, right at his heels as he made for the telephone. "Okay? That's all Jason means to you? *Okay?*"

That was a promising response, but he ignored it

and stabbed out Brodie's speed-dial number on the cordless phone.

Brodie answered instantly.

"Hi," Ethan said. "It's me. Everything all right?"

"With me and the kids or with you and Beth?" Brodie asked.

"Not now." Ethan took a pull of whiskey. "The kids all right?"

"They're fine. They're asleep. But they were pretty worried when they got here. They said you went a little Dirty Harry on Beth."

"With good cause," Ethan replied. "So are they okay there for the night?"

"Of course. They wanted to go home, but I figured you had a reason for having them brought here, instead of asking me to go to your place." He paused. "Ethan?"

"Yeah."

"Calm down, okay? If you guys are about to have it out, count to ten or something first. Have a drink. Remember that she and the kids went to the Appleby house to get the cat. They didn't have criminal intentions. And even though you think you know what's best for everybody, that doesn't require them to do it. Kids, sure, but not a woman. Even if you love her."

"I thought you weren't into taking women seriously."

"I've changed my mind."

Ethan laughed mirthlessly. "Do yourself a favor. Change it back. See you in the morning."

He pushed the Off button on the phone and put it back on its base. He took another sip of whiskey and turned to Beth. He felt fractionally calmer.

"Jason means a lot to me," he said in answer to

the question she'd flung at him before he'd called Brodie. "That's why I got just a little upset knowing he'd been in the Appleby place."

"A *little* upset?" she said, her voice reaching a high register. "You didn't even let us explain! You have the kids thinking you're going to kill them in the morning and you *arrested* me."

He pulled the drapes closed and took another sip of whiskey. "I didn't arrest you," he amended. "I only brought you in."

"Just to punish me!" she said angrily. "You had no right to subject me—"

He turned on her, temper boiling despite the whiskey and his best efforts to remain calm. "I had every right!" She stood in the middle of the room and he strode toward her. "I went to a meeting leaving my kids in your care, and what do you do? You take them with you as accomplices to help you break into a private residence. Do you have any idea what it feels like to be the sheriff and arrive at a call only to find that the perpetrators of the crime are your family?"

"The house was empty!"

"It doesn't matter!" he roared. "It's someone else's property! They just don't live here. But that's not the point, anyway. You heard me tell the kids that transients go in and out of there all the time. If some wacko had been in there, you and the kids could be hurt or dead right now!"

She was quiet a moment, assimilating that information. "I had a flashlight," she said defensively.

"Oh, good," he said flatly. "How many rounds does it hold? Or does it just allow you to see the gun before it fires at you?"

She put a hand to her forehead, and he realized

suddenly that she was very pale and that her hand shook a little. Concern for her diminished his anger slightly.

"All right," she admitted in a quieter tone. "I exercised poor judgment. I knew it at the time. But Nikkie was very upset about the cat and she came to me for help."

He guessed she was being carefully nonspecific. He knew how it had all come about, but she didn't know he knew. Nikkie had told him all about it when he'd put her and Jason in Billings's car. She'd assumed all blame and made it clear that Beth had told Jason to stay home and her to stay outside on the grass.

"And you thought to look in the Applebys' basement?" he asked.

She went to the window, drew the curtain back and looked out. "Cats love dark hiding places."

"But the place is boarded up. How did you think he'd gotten in there?"

She turned away from the window and met his gaze, her own direct and suspicious. "If you wanted to interrogate me," she said, "you should have done it when you had me in a jail cell."

"If you'd just told me what happened without a lot of attitude," he countered, "you wouldn't have ended up in a jail cell."

"Oh, I understand." She let the curtain fall back into place and came around the chair to lean against its well-upholstered side. "Your deputies were there and you had to flex your muscles."

"No," he said after counting to ten as Brodie had recommended. "Our children were there, and it was important for them to see that ignoring the rules has consequences. I didn't have all the details, but I figured out what had happened, though I didn't know if it was Nikkie or Jason at fault. I'd have let them believe I was taking you to jail, let them see us drive away, then I'd have taken you for coffee somewhere and chewed you out quietly for not waiting to check on the cat until I got home.''

She arched an eyebrow. "So, it's all right for *you* to disregard the rules and break in?"

"I'm an officer of the law," he replied. "I can go anywhere. And I'm armed." He paused. "Anyway, you wouldn't *let* me handle the situation easily. You turned on all this attitude. What was that about?"

"You were just beginning to convince me that you were different from Steve," she said, "and suddenly you were acting just like him. Full of criticism and accusation, without even bothering to ask for the details.''

Ethan downed the rest of his whiskey and put his glass on the coffee table. "Beth, I'm not Steve. I don't know how many times I have to remind you of that. If I acted at all like him, it's unfortunate, I guess, but I won't apologize. I answered a call in which my entire family was involved, and the knowledge of what could have happened scared the hell out of me. I'm not going to spend a lifetime tiptoeing around you so that nothing reminds you of Steve. I get upset with you, you're going to know it.''

Her jaw remained taut, her chin angled. "I should have stayed with my promise to myself not to get married again. I should have taken Jason and hidden somewhere.''

So. She wasn't tiptoeing around, either. Good. He had a few other things to get off his chest. "You didn't marry me to keep Jason," he said quietly, resting his hands on his hips. "You married me for me. And now that you have me, I don't behave quite the way you expected, so you don't know what to do. Your life was dictated by what Steve wanted for so long that when you were finally free, all you could think about was never having to answer to anybody again. Well, that won't be life with me."

He closed the space between them and took her chin between his thumb and forefinger. "You know me, Beth. You know I'd never hurt you and I'd never stop you from being what you want to be or doing what you want to do, as long as it doesn't endanger you or the kids. But you do something that scares me or worries me, I'll stop you."

She caught his wrist in her hand and pulled it down. "That kind of...paternalism in a husband," she said stiffly, "is so Victorian."

He refused to budge. "So are frivolous women. I don't want to run your life. I just want to keep you safe. If you can't see the difference, maybe you're not mature enough to be married at all. Good night." He left her standing near the chair and went upstairs.

She went to bed in the room she'd used before the wedding. He'd felt sure she would, but he was too angry and too determined to make concessions.

And apparently so was she.

HE SETTLED THINGS with Nikkie and Jason in the morning. Brodie brought them home just after seven and disappeared into the kitchen. They looked terrified, more affected by the events of the previous night than he'd expected.

He took them both in his arms, then sat them on the sofa and listened again to each one's interpretation of what had happened.

Nikkie finished with, "I told you, Daddy. It was all my fault. I went with the kids to rehearse there, and I'm the one who forgot Simba. Beth just went to help me. She told me to wait on the grass."

"Yeah," Jason added. "And she told me to stay home. But you said a man takes care of his family, and you were gone, so I was the man."

In the light of day and after a long and lonely night, Ethan was wondering if he'd made more of the incident than he should have. But then he looked into his daughter's and stepson's trusting faces and remembered how very real his anxiety had been, how important it was that they understood danger and, in that regard at least, obeyed him unconditionally.

He put an arm around Nikkie's shoulders and one around Jason's. "Nikkie," he began, "I appreciate your honesty, and I'm proud of you for not letting Beth take the rap, because she tried to."

Her lip quivered. "She did?"

"Yes, she did. She tried to make me believe you had just decided to look outside for the cat and it was her idea to check the Applebys' basement."

He let that sink in for a moment, then gave her the bad news. "But while I'm proud of you for telling the truth, I'm grounding you for ignoring the rule about the Appleby house in the first place and rehearsing there."

She nodded as though she'd expected as much.

He turned to Jason. "You're grounded, too," he said, "for not listening to your mom."

Jason looked surprised. "I was listening to *you!* You said—"

Ethan cut him off. "—that it's your job to look out for your mom and Nikkie when I'm not here. I know. And I can see where you might have gotten confused, but your mom gave you specific instructions to stay home. Disobeying her isn't the best way to look out for her.''

Jason puzzled over that. Ethan knew that deep down his argument wasn't sound, but he felt obliged to back up Beth's authority. This had all come about because everyone was trying to help everyone else, but he had to hold to the Appleby-house rule.

He looked from one child to the other. "Two weeks. Nothing but drama-club stuff for you, Nik, because I know they're counting on you, but don't try to stretch it. Nothing after dinner.''

"Okay.''

"And, Jase, the bike stays in the garage and you stay in.''

"Okay.''

"Good.'' Ethan stood, pulling the children to their feet. "Let's get some breakfast.''

Beth came down the stairs just as Ethan was urging Nikkie and Jason toward the kitchen.

"Good morning.'' Beth smiled at the children and opened her arms as Jason launched himself at her. She didn't bother to raise her glance to Ethan's.

"Mom!'' Jason held her tightly, then looked up at her, his eyes wide with respect and admiration. "You were in the slammer! What was it like?''

Ethan kept going toward the kitchen, thinking grimly that his point about obeying rules and laws may have fallen short of its mark.

He stopped in the kitchen doorway, turning at the sudden sound of sobs. They were coming from Nikkie, who'd thrown her arms around Beth's neck and was apologizing brokenly for being the reason she'd been taken to jail.

Beth held her and spoke quietly. Ethan couldn't

hear the words but guessed they were something like, *It's all right, Nikkie. It wasn't your fault. Your father's a prehistoric muscle flexer with delusions of power and we're his unfortunate victims.*

In truth, he was happy to see his daughter and his wife finally making an emotional connection. It was just unfortunate that it had to be over what he feared was the death knell of his marriage.

He went to pour a cup of coffee and sat at the table.

"Morning, Cruella," Brodie said. "One egg or two?"

"Two. And lay off me," Ethan advised. "Cruella's a woman, so your sorry little joke doesn't work."

Brodie broke two eggs into a pan and while they cooked placed half a grapefruit in front of Ethan. "I think it does—she's the ultimate villain, man or woman, and only someone who'd collect puppies to make a coat of *their* coats would haul his own wife off to jail for helping his daughter rescue her cat."

Ethan glared at him. "I don't remember asking for your assessment of the situation."

"Too bad," Brodie replied. "It comes with breakfast."

Before Ethan could tell him what to do with breakfast, Beth and the children trooped in and the conversation was terminated.

Beth and the children chatted cheerfully as Ethan drove the Blazer on the now familiar round of elementary school, high school and cannery.

But the cheerful conversation stopped the moment Jason was dropped off and Ethan was left alone with Beth. The vehicle was filled with icy tension for the next two blocks.

Ethan pulled onto the pier and saw two cars parked at the side of the building. One he recognized as

Kelly's MG. The other, a decrepit Volvo station wagon with lumber sticking out of the back, Ethan remembered being there when he'd walked into Beth's studio and found Rush Weston with his hands on her.

He said nothing, simply let the engine idle while Beth shouldered her purse and pushed open her door. She held the door an extra moment and he wondered if communication might be reestablished between them. She seemed to be struggling to put something into words.

"Nikkie asked me if the drama club could come over tonight to work on the shields," she said, her face expressionless. "I told her it was all right."

"It *is* all right." He kept his expression as blank as hers.

"Good." The wind tossed her hair, and a wicked gleam in her eyes marred her attempt to remain completely impassive when she added, "I'd hate to end up in jail for having forgotten to tell you."

She reached back inside for the lunch she'd left on the floor on her side, and he leaned over to catch her wrist. She looked at him in surprise, not frightened but clearly uncertain of what he intended. He liked that.

"Innocent forgetfulness isn't a crime," he said, injecting a warning note into his voice. "But smart sarcasm is a felony, not to mention foolish. You might keep that in mind." He freed her hand. "Have a good day."

She slammed the door.

CHAPTER FOURTEEN

BETH SLIPPED her arms into the two leather handles she'd attached to the back of her prototype shield. She flexed the muscles in her arm and was pleased that the heavy-duty staples she'd used kept the strips in place.

She'd tried vinyl and simple staples earlier, but one flex of Cameron's forearm and a staple popped. Considering Henry V's army would be composed of Cobbler's Crossing's football team, she knew she had to find an alternative. And old leather belts from the thrift shop were an economical alternative to twenty feet of two-inch wide leather from a fabric or craft shop.

Now that she knew the belt worked, she'd run back to the thrift shop in the afternoon for more.

Her studio door opened and she turned around to greet the visitor, the shield still on her arm.

It was Kelly, in black jeans with ripped knees and a man's shirt that had once been white but now looked like a Jackson Pollock canvas. Her red hair was stuffed under a paper painter's cap.

"Whoa," she said, her eyes going to the shield as she walked toward Beth's worktable. "Where's your horned helmet and pointy bra?"

"Lent them to one of the other Valkyries," Beth

said, smiling as she eased her arm out of the straps. "Go away unless you have a caramel-vanilla latte."

Kelly rolled her eyes and leaned over Beth's table to study the coats of arms she'd drawn on the shields. "I brought a bunch of stuff down this morning, but forgot the box with my coffeepot. Brodie came over yesterday while I was packing and I lost track of what I was doing."

Beth showed Kelly the finished product. "I was the recipient of the bouquet you dusted him with," she said.

Kelly admired the shield and said nonchalantly, "I can't imagine why he'd come to see you."

Beth folded her arms. "Why, hoping for a clue to your complicated psyche," she said, then added dryly, "As though I had it."

Kelly gave her a chiding glance and turned the shield over to inspect the back. "You should talk, Ma Barker. I was up late last night and listening to the scanner when I heard about the dustup at the Applebys'. So you're a big bad mama with a record now?"

Beth took the shield away from Kelly and put it aside. "No, I do not have a record. He couldn't arrest me. He just went through the motions to make me pay for having gone down there with Nikkie in the first place. And as my friend, aren't you supposed to be sympathetic to my plight and offer comfort and support?"

Kelly asked seriously, "Is it going to lower my rent?"

"It might forestall eviction."

"Can you evict me if I haven't even moved in yet?"

"We'll ask Ethan," Beth said, taking the shield

from the table and adding it to one of the boxes in which she'd placed the other nineteen wooden discs. "He's good at manipulating the law in his favor."

"I imagine," Kelly ventured, "that he took you to jail to impress upon you and the kids that, as beguiling as a haunted house is, that place can be dangerous at night. And also because you kicked him. He's an officer of the law."

"He's my husband and he was being a jerk."

"At home he's your husband. At the scene of a disturbance he's the sheriff, counted upon by the citizens of Butler County to keep the peace. And you were shouting at him and fighting him, according to what I heard on the scanner."

Beth groaned and went to the open door of the studio to look out at the river beyond the pier. The water was the color of gunmetal and met a sky of the same color. The line of the horizon was almost invisible in the monochromatic world of the wintry Oregon coast.

Seagulls flew around a red-and-black tug pulling a barge mounded with wood chips from the mill on the other side of the bay. Cormorants watched its passing from their perch on old pilings, remnants of other cannery piers.

It occurred to Beth that it was a beautiful setting, but her world felt as sunless as the sky.

Kelly came up beside her. "So what happened to you last night? I saw the two of you shopping after work just a couple of nights ago, and it looked as though you'd found some common ground."

Misery welled up in Beth's chest. "He was shouting at me," she said, her voice dull, "and acccusing me of being foolish…"

"Astute of him, I would say," Kelly offered mercilessly.

Beth leaned a shoulder against her open door, feeling suddenly heavy, burdened. "He was sounding a lot like Steve," she explained, seeing vivid pictures behind her eyes of her and Ethan shouting at each other. "All I could think about was how confining some of those times had been, how demoralizing, and here I'd been beginning to think that with Ethan, those days were gone forever."

Kelly leaned against the other side of the doorway, her hands pressed behind her. "Beth, you're not comparing Steve's selfish claims on you to Ethan's gut reaction when he arrives at a call to find his family in danger, are you?"

Beth put a hand to her head where an ache had been gaining momentum ever since she'd climbed out of the shower that morning.

"I did last night," she admitted.

"He's a man and you scared him," Kelly said simply. "They get really ticked off when they have to admit that to themselves. And it's instinctive to take it out on whoever inspired the fear, whether or not it's entirely justified. It means he cares. I think you should forgive him."

Beth turned to her friend with a disbelieving look. "I have a broken bouquet in my kitchen that says you don't practice what you preach."

"I don't have to." Kelly stared out at the river. "My situation's entirely different."

"How so?"

"Ethan yelled at you because he cares. Brodie backed away from me because I never meant anything to him at all. It was just the sort of hormone-driven game kids play.''

"Not exactly."

Kelly met her eyes with a frown. "What do you mean?"

Beth related the story of Paulette.

Kelly listened. There was a momentary softening of her expression, a small gasp of indignation, then she sighed and turned her gaze out to the river again. "Stupid snot. But it just proves that he's out to pay *her* back by taking it out on every other woman he comes across—get her interested, then drop her."

"He admits he was doing something like that. Until you."

Kelly laughed scornfully. "Right. 'But you're different, Kelly.' I've been around too long to fall for that one, Beth. I'm no different, I just called him on it and he caved, but he can't have any holdouts. He has to make me come around, too—and *then* he'll dump me."

"I don't think so."

"Well, I won't be finding out."

"Fraidy cat."

"Smarty-pants. I'm playing it safe."

Beth caught Kelly by the arm and pulled her back into the studio and across it to a poster hanging over her tool chest. It pictured a tiny boat on a seemingly endless ocean under a vast sky. "What does that say?" Beth demanded.

Kelly shifted her weight and read in a disgruntled monotone, "'A ship in a harbor is safe, but that is not what ships were built for.'"

Kelly turned to Beth and challenged her with a

look. "Okay. If I'm going to stick my neck out, you're going to make things right with Ethan."

Beth offered her hand, secretly pleased to have an excuse to try to rectify things between her and Ethan. "Deal."

Kelly studied her skeptically for a moment, then shook hands to seal the deal. She winced and asked in a small voice, "Doesn't this feel a lot like Butch and Sundance jumping hand in hand off that cliff?"

Beth smiled and tried to think positively. "They lived, didn't they?"

THE KITCHEN was full of laughter and loud music. Beth had spread newspaper all over the table and all over the floor. Nikkie and Vanessa knelt on the chairs and painted the shields' backgrounds while Rosalie, Cameron and Bradley sat cross-legged on the floor and painted in the details, according to the sketches Beth had made.

Jason prowled the room peering over shoulders and admiring their work. Beth was pleased to see that they were tolerant of him and that Nikkie even let him try his hand at stenciling. When his tense hand moved the stencil and created a lion with a lump protruding from its back, she patted his shoulder and told him not to worry, no one would notice.

Then she looked up at Beth when Jason was distracted by something else and made a comically distressed face.

Beth returned a wink and a nod and the unspoken assurance that she would repair the damage.

Ethan kept bowls of popcorn and corn chips filled, soda glasses topped up and the cats out of the paint.

Beth noted worriedly that he made no effort to talk

to her, though she was sure their silence wasn't obvious to Nikkie and her friends. Considering her behavior the past twenty-four hours, she couldn't blame him for ignoring her. But how she was going to fulfill her part of the bargain she'd made with Kelly remained a mystery.

Brodie came over to investigate the source of the noise.

"Jeez," he grumbled theatrically, "do I have to call the sheriff and have this place raided?"

Nikkie and her friends laughed.

Ethan put a glass of soda in his hand and a corn chip in his mouth. "Eat that and be quiet," he said. "We have enough noise around here already."

Brodie took the chip out of his mouth. "I thought maybe you needed help running the roulette wheel or dealing blackjack."

Ethan shook his head and offered a supermarket tub of salsa for Brodie to dip the chip into. "The only gamble around here is whether or not these shields come out right. The guys are talking football, and the girls are talking Brad Pitt. Who knows what we could end up with?"

Rosalie held up the first finished shield. "This!" she said, her voice conveying surprise and awe.

Everyone turned to look, and silence filled the room for a moment. The shield was Henry's. The lions stood out brilliantly against the red paint, and the fleurs-de-lis were beautifully formed on a blue field.

"Beth!" Nikkie breathed, the glow on her face saying everything. "Look at what you did!"

Beth denied the credit with a shake of her head. "You guys did it. All I did was provide the wood and make the stencils. If you act as well as you paint, you're all headed for Hollywood.''

''Oh, I just came from there,'' a female voice said from the back door. ''Unless you're interested in beautiful people, big cars and lots of money, it has nothing for you. That's why I'm *here*.''

The kids laughed. Beth's heartbeat shifted into second gear. Kelly was *here,* she guessed, to keep her part of the bargain.

The kids went back to work, turning their music up a notch to be heard over the adult conversation.

''Can I get you a soda, Kelly?'' Ethan asked. ''Coffee?''

''No, thank you,'' she replied with a smile, then seemed to lose control of it as she turned to Brodie. It narrowed, wavered, then disappeared altogether when Brodie didn't smile back.

Kelly glanced at Beth for support. Wanting desperately for her best friend and her brother-in-law to have at least an opportunity for another go at their relationship, Beth pushed aside her own difficulties and tried to spur Kelly on.

Ethan stood only a foot away from Beth in the corner of the kitchen into which the press of teenagers had forced them, and she reached out to hook her arm in his and lean into him. She gave a smile for Kelly that suggested she, Beth, had already taken her steps in their deal and it was time for Kelly to follow suit or be a welsher.

Ethan didn't move away from Beth, and he didn't remove his arm, but he did nothing positive, either. As she inhaled the fresh rainwater fragrance of him and felt the warm textured wool of his sweater under her cheek, she was very aware that he didn't respond.

She knew precisely how Kelly felt.

Kelly tossed her red hair and refocused her attention on Brodie. "I was hoping," she said in a voice that wasn't at all familiar to Beth, "that I could buy you a cup of coffee."

Beth watched him study her warily a moment, then lift his glass. "Got a root beer."

Kelly put her hands in the pockets of her short leather jacket, her jaw firming perceptibly. "You don't have pie. I could buy you that to go with the coffee."

He considered her another moment, bounced a glance over Beth's head to Ethan, then said to Kelly. "But it's almost ten o'clock. This is Cobbler's Crossing. Nothing's open after ten."

Kelly shrugged. "I'm a caterer, remember?"

The merest trace of a smile pulled at his lips. "I never forget anything."

"Good," she said, drawing the first even breath Beth had seen her take since she'd walked into the room. "I like that in a man. If we take my car, I can have you home in time for Leno."

Brodie put his glass on the counter, slapped Ethan on the back and leaned down to kiss Beth's cheek. "Thanks for the hospitality, guys, but I've got to run." He opened the back door for Kelly. "Can I drive your car?"

She passed through the door before him. "It's very precious to me. Are you a good driver?"

"Nothing special," he replied, "but I'm a good mechanic. I break or dent anything, I can fix it." The door closed behind them and Beth couldn't help her relieved sigh.

"God, that was an ordeal," she said, forgetting for

an instant, in her delight over Kelly's preliminary success, that her own part of the bargain remained undone. She pulled her arm from Ethan's.

Jason brought her an empty plastic bowl, then returned to the table to look over Nikkie's shoulder.

Ethan moved with Beth as she went to the cupboard for the second bag of corn chips. "And what was your stake in that little scene?" he asked.

He didn't look hostile, she noted, just comfortably removed from the situation.

"Kelly's my friend." She poured chips into the bowl and carried it to the table, then went back to the counter and carefully folded the top of the bag. "And Brodie's wonderful. I think they'd be good for each other."

"And you encouraged her to try to straighten out their problems," he speculated, "by letting her think we'd dealt with ours."

She clipped the bag closed and gave him a small friendly smile. "Precisely."

"Artful trickery," he said.

"Everyone should have a skill."

There was a shout from Cameron as he looked at his watch, then a sudden flurry of activity as the young people who'd ridden in with Cameron began to pack up the project.

"Drop the brushes in the water jar," Beth instructed, "and leave all the wet shields side by side on the floor against the wall. I've got something rigged up to protect them. Don't worry about the newspaper. I'll clean that up."

Ethan volunteered to take Rosalie home because everyone else was on Cameron's way. Nikkie went with him.

Beth waved in response to the cries of "Thanks, Mrs. Drum!"

Beth hugged Jason, then shooed him off to bed while she picked up the newspapers and stuffed them into a plastic garbage bag. She covered the painted shields with overturned boxes to keep out the cats, stashed all the paints and supplies in another box and took the brushes down to the laundry sink to wash them.

At last, feeling as though she'd won Henry's Battle of Agincourt single-handedly, Beth left on the back porch light and the kitchen light, then locked up the front of the house and went upstairs to get ready for bed.

ETHAN WALKED into the kitchen with Nikkie and noticed the silence. There was something poignantly familiar about it. It reminded him of all those years when it had been just the two of them, before Jason decided to run away and changed all their lives forever.

Forever. It struck him as a strange word to use in connection with the woman he'd married on an inexplicable impulse, particularly in view of the state of that relationship at this very moment.

Still, he thought fatalistically as he reached behind him to lock the back door and turn off the porch light, the word applied. Even if she left tomorrow, he would still be changed forever. There was a lot of confusion in her, but also so much light, so much spontaneous laughter, so much grace. And so much love.

The shadowy quiet of the house reminded him of the first time he'd made love to her. It surprised him to realize that had been only last week. Every time they'd made love since had expanded and amplified his spirit so that there were moments when it felt too big for his body, as though he would have to live to be four hundred to make use of all he felt.

"Daddy?" Nikkie turned to him from the rack where she'd hung up her jacket. She helped him out of his and put it on a peg. Her eyes were bright from the hectic evening. "Thanks for letting the kids come over and work tonight. We had a great time, and we got a whole lot done."

He nodded, opening his arms in surprise when she leaned into him and stayed there. Over the past few years he'd gotten used to kisses and hugs dealt out sparingly, and usually on the run.

"I'm really sorry about going to the Applebys'," she said, her grip on him tightening "I knew better, but…you know. When you're the sheriff's daughter, everybody thinks you're a Goody Two-shoes."

He held her tightly and kissed the top of her head. "I know that's hard for you sometimes, but let me tell you that Goody Two-shoeses are underrated. They don't usually find themselves in situations where they can get hurt. Try to remember that rules aren't just to make your life uncomfortable. When you're young and enthusiastic about everything, it's hard to recognize potential danger, so I have to do it for you. You have to trust me to know what I'm doing."

"I know." She looked up at him, still holding him, her bright pretty face alight. "I'm just beginning to understand how smart you really are."

His first instinct upon hearing that was to get a tape recorder and have her repeat those words. He was certain there'd be times in the future when he'd desperately need to hear them again.

"And what brought on this revelation?" he asked.

"Beth," she said. Nikkie looked a little mystified, as though an adult truth had invaded her teenage life and confused everything. "I didn't want to like her. I didn't want things to change. But every time I turned around she was being nice to me, trying to do something for me without being pushy like Jason's grandma or sappy like some movie version of the perfect stepmother."

Her voice tightened a little. "When I couldn't find Simba, she was ready to go out in the dark and help me look. Then when I told her where I thought he was, she didn't yell or threaten or anything. I think she probably even might have told you about it when it was all over—or made *me* tell you—but we didn't take time to talk about it. We just went looking for him. And she did tell Jason to stay home, but he thought we were taking too long, so he came to help because you told him—"

"Yeah, I know. A man takes care of his family and I was gone, so he was the man."

She stood up on tiptoe to kiss his cheek. "Anyway, I love you for being so smart," she said. "And I kind of like the way things are turning out around here. Good night, Daddy."

"Good night, Nik."

Ethan turned off the kitchen light and headed for the stairs, resolved to end the standoff with Beth. He couldn't change his position on the Appleby house, but he could certainly concede that, though his entire family had ignored his instructions, they'd done it for reasons that had everything to do with responsibility and generosity, however misguided.

Nikkie's door was already closed, and the only

light in the hallway came from the night-light in the bathroom. Ethan peered into the room Beth had used the night before, expecting to find her curled up under the covers, asleep.

She wasn't. The bed was undisturbed.

She'd gone to his room? He took a few steps into the room, but his bed, too, was undisturbed, the coverlet carelessly thrown across it, just as he'd left it that morning.

Where was she? Feeling that same familiar but unwelcome silence he'd recognized just a little while ago in the empty kitchen, he suppressed any notion that she might have left.

She needed him. Even if she was angry, she was too responsible to leave in a fit of pique.

Just to be certain, he went to check on the one thing she'd never leave behind. Jason was there, fast asleep in the top bunk in the room at the end of the hall, one arm hanging over the side. Simba was curled up in a ball on Jason's pillow, his head against the boy's.

Ethan felt great relief, and then a swelling of the deep affection Jason's straightforward ways inspired. He tucked the arm up onto the bunk, then stroked the cat, who'd awakened with a start.

Simba purred and went back to sleep.

Ethan walked into his bedroom and over to the window, wondering if Beth could have gone to Brodie's. But Brodie's house was dark. Of course. He'd left with Kelly.

"Ethan."

Beth's voice came from a corner of the darkened room. He turned away from the window, his heart giving an erratic lurch. "Beth." He spoke quietly, hoping to calm himself. "What are you doing in the dark?"

"I was sitting in the chair, thinking about things," she said. She was wearing his white terry-cloth robe. It fell almost to her ankles, and her face and throat gleamed above it, her dark hair disappearing in the shadows. He felt weak with the need to touch her.

She lifted her chin. "I still think your tactics last night were uncalled for," she said, her chin coming down as she spoke, the line of her shoulders softening under the big robe. "But in all fairness, so were mine. And you did have good reason, I guess, to get a little out of control. I, on the other hand, was reacting to the past, instead of the present and…"

She expelled a breath, tried to put her hands in the pockets of the robe, but they were too low for her to do more than slip her fingertips in. She folded her arms and said, "I'm sorry."

He crossed the distance between them in two strides and took her in his arms. "*I'm* sorry," he said, absorbing the rightness of holding her against him after a separation that had seemed interminable, though it had been only a day. "I was beside myself with worry when I saw all of you there, but I should have handled things differently. I should have understood. But I was feeling, rather than thinking."

She nuzzled his throat, her hands gently exploring his waist. "Me, too." She tipped her head back and asked, her voice dropping an octave, "Why don't we shower yesterday away—together? Water is a sort of dialect of Romanesque."

He didn't say anything for an instant, and Beth experienced the panicky fear that she'd overstepped.

She'd often done that with Steve, offending or embarrassing him.

Then she saw Ethan's white smile in the dark and he wrapped an arm around her, and walked with her into the bathroom, stopping at the shower stall. He hooked a finger into the belt of the robe and pulled until it was undone. Then he slipped it off her shoulders.

His eyes shone with the same expression she'd seen in them the first time he'd made love to her. A very male appreciation of her body, coupled with a kind of disarming humility.

She reached her fingers under his sweater and T-shirt and pulled them up and off. Unbuckling his belt and unzipping his jeans, she slipped her hands between his briefs and his warm flesh and pushed the briefs down to his ankles. He toed them the rest of the way off.

He opened the shower, pulled her in with him and backed her into the cold tile corner to protect her from the onslaught of water until he had the temperature adjusted.

Then he brought her in front of him under the spray. It was a warm and comfortable drumming on her shoulders, and it seemed to create an answering beat within her. She put her hands to Ethan's chest. "Want me to soap you?" she asked.

He leaned down to kiss her greedily. "Later," he said, and lifted her into his arms, encouraging her to wrap her legs around him.

She complied, holding tightly to his neck, and felt a small jolt of surprise when his fingers parted her and slipped inside.

He tipped his head back to look into her face. "I won't drop you," he promised, humor in his voice.

She shook her head, his fingers distracting her. "That isn't…it."

"What, then?" he asked, kissing her lightly. "Is making love in the shower new to you?"

"Yes. Remember…I told you I wanted to…try something with…with, um…"

"Steve?"

"Yeah, Steve. And he…"

"Right. He was disgusted by it. This? Making love in the shower?"

"And standing up. He…said it…wouldn't work. That the shower was for hygiene, and the only way to have sex was…in bed. Ethan!"

"All right. I'm with you. And I'm about to prove to you that he was wrong about that, too."

Her body caught in the tight spiral that was the prelude to fulfillment, Beth held on to him in an agony of waiting. He propped a foot against the tile and entered her surely, making a seat for her with his hands as he leaned his shoulders back against the wall in the small space.

She cried out at her sudden release. It shot through her like fireworks, hot and colorful and lighting up the night.

She clung to Ethan as he erupted inside her at the same moment.

He clung to her, his hands stroking her hips and her back until the celebration finished and the sky cleared.

They soaped each other's bodies and washed each other's hair. When they got out and dried off, they sat in the middle of the bed while he rubbed her hair with a towel. Then they pulled the blankets up over them and, arms and legs entangled, drifted off to sleep.

Beth's last thought before she drifted off to sleep was that she felt sure she'd never doubt Ethan's opinion on anything again.

CHAPTER FIFTEEN

HENRY V'S ARMY lined up backstage in three tight rows, their shields held out before them, and smiled as though war was the last thing on their minds. Beth imagined that after the roaring success of their opening night and the cast party ahead of them at a waterfront restaurant, it would be the restaurant staff who would need the shields.

Ethan photographed them for posterity, and then the army tried to break ranks. But Ethan pointed them back into place and posed Nikkie and her friends in front of them, then pushed Beth into their mix. She tried to protest, but Bradley and Cameron brought her physically into the middle of the front row.

"Thanks, guys," Ethan said finally. "I'm finished." The cast exploded from their tidy rows into a moving knot of excitement. Parents and teachers milled around them, offering their congratulations and their parting instructions for the night ahead.

Nikkie rushed to where Ethan stood with Beth and Jason, and Brodie and Kelly. "The football team's going to the cast party on the rooter bus, but Mr. Fogarty's taking the drama club to the party in his van, and he says to tell you he'll have us home by eleven. My curfew's ten, so I thought I'd better make sure."

"Eleven's fine." Ethan flicked her chin and

grinned. "Just remember that you're the queen of France and act accordingly."

She struck a haughty pose. "*Mais, oui.* I have several beheadings scheduled for zee morning."

"Good. I'm glad to see you have an enlightened legal system in place."

Beth gave Nikkie a hug. "You're aware, of course, that your father's system is about as enlightened, so watch yourself. His spies are everywhere."

Nikkie looked heavenward. "Be sure to watch *your*selves, too. You're going to that dance-and-dessert thing with Uncle Brodie and Kelly. That sounds like trouble to me."

"We resent that!" Kelly said with feigned offense as she hugged Nikkie. "You were wonderful, sweetie. And all your props looked perfect from the audience."

Brodie took Nikkie from Kelly and hugged her in turn. "You were brilliant, Nik. Genius is unpredictable, isn't it? I mean, I have it, you have it, yet it managed to skip your father altogether!"

Ethan gave his brother a mock punch on the arm. "Careful," he warned. "This room is full of weapons."

"Duh! They're all phony."

Ethan gave him a cold smile. "The way you irritate me, Bro, I could run you through with a paper sword."

Brodie kept an arm around his niece. "This could prove to be a troublesome evening, Nik. We'll call you if we need bail money."

Ethan laughed. "The way she saves, we'd rot in jail. No, I think we have to count on graft and corruption if we get arrested."

"Oh, good. The job's going to be fun again." Curtis appeared beside Ethan. "I'll look the other way for a pickup."

His wife, a plump blonde in a bright pink suit, elbowed him in the gut. "Are we talking trucks or women?"

"Trucks, Penny," Billings assured her. He and his wife, a gorgeous brunette half a head taller than he was, came up on Ethan's other side. "He's been off women ever since that gorgeous little DUI rabbited in the middle of her field sobriety test and he had to chase her down the riverbank and into the water."

"Nikkie, you did a wonderful job!" This praise came from Joanne. She and Zachary had approached the group. They'd arrived that afternoon for the Winter Festival weekend.

Zachary patted Nikkie's shoulder. "Good work, young lady." He appeared quite well, though he leaned on a brass-handled cane. "Your shields, by the way, looked very authentic."

"Beth's responsible for that," she said with a smile in Beth's direction. "We're going to sell them at the Parents' Club auction at the end of the school year to make money for the drama club *next* year."

"Wonderful idea." Joanne leaned toward Beth to be heard in the crush of people. "Would you mind if Zach and I go home rather than on to the dance? We're pretty beat."

Jason's grandparents were staying at Beth's and Ethan's for the weekend. Beth shook her head. "Of course not. I laid in some snacks, so help yourselves."

The conversation ended abruptly when the announcement was made that the rooter bus was leaving in fifteen minutes. With costumes to change and determined to be on time, the "army" cut a wide swath through parents and friends.

The friendly insanity, however, went on well into the evening. Ethan, Beth and Jason, Brodie and Kelly, and Curtis and Billings and their wives shared a table in the fairground hall for the after-theater dance and dessert.

Ethan and the deputies recounted stories of their more humorous cases, with Brodie, as the man who repaired their vehicles, making a few contributions. Jason sat beside Ethan, leaning over his arm, laughing with the men and absorbing every word. The women talked children and jobs and men, remembering wryly what it was like worrying about them when they were late.

"Who'd have guessed," Penny Curtis asked, indicating with a jut of her chin the laughing men, "that they were late because they were having such a good time?"

Jan Billings shook her head. "Bert could have fun at the dentist. What do you do with a man like that?"

"Thank God for him every day," Kelly advised.

Beth had to agree.

"All right, what'll you have for dessert?" Ebbie suddenly materialized at their table wearing an apron with the Ladies of Law Enforcement logo. The group had provided and was serving desserts as a fund-raiser for the county's new women's crisis center. "And make it snappy. Don't think that because I work with most of you that I'll take any guff. Now. We have double chocolate torte, blackberry cobbler with vanilla ice cream, or crème caramel with whipped cream. No substitutions."

She studied each face in turn. "It would help me a lot if you'd all have the same thing and then consider seconds. It's been a long day, and this is a good cause."

Beth saw the mutiny brewing as the men from Ebbie's office exchanged glances.

"Cake," Ethan said with a straight face, "and I'd like that à la mode."

"Only the cobbler comes with—" Ebbie began.

"I'll have the crème caramel with ice cream," Curtis said.

"You can't—"

"I'll have the cobbler with whipped cream." This from Billings, who turned to his wife.

Picking up the game, Jan asked, "Is there a sampler plate with a little bit of everything?"

"Cake with whipped cream," Penny ordered briskly.

"Cake with crème caramel," Brodie said. "And the same for Kelly."

"I'll have the cobbler with ice cream." Beth gave her companions a scolding look, then when Ebbie offered her a smile for her cooperation, she added, "But I'd like my ice cream on the bottom, please. And could I have a raspberry vanilla latte to go with that, with nonfat milk but real whipped cream? Dusted with cinnamon."

Everyone laughed heartily and Ethan pulled Beth into his arms and kissed her temple in congratulations. Then they all awaited Ebbie's reaction.

She drew a breath so deep that the bib of her apron rose and fell, and she looked around the table again, desire for retribution just barely masking the laughter in her eyes. "Eight chocolate cakes," she said, scribbling on her pad, "and eight regular coffees. Jason?"

She leaned over the child whose head rested on Ethan's arm, apparently willing to give *him* a choice. But he was fast asleep.

"If he wakes up," Ethan said, "I'll share with him."

Ebbie nodded, then looked around the table one more time. "The tip," she said, her voice soft with significance, "had better be worth my while."

Curtis looked up innocently. "I didn't know you tipped at charity functions."

Ebbie patted his head. "Then you're going to be our first registration at the new home for battered *men*."

The men groaned and booed at her threat, and she blew them a kiss as she returned to the kitchen.

Conversation and laughter began again, and Beth leaned comfortably into Ethan, his arm still around her. He eased his other arm out from under Jason's cheek and let the boy's head fall to his chest. Jason stirred restlessly, found a comfortable spot on the wool of Ethan's jacket, tucked his hand under his chin and didn't move for the next hour.

Beth couldn't remember ever being more content in her life.

SATURDAY DAWNED cold but sunny. Beth looked out the kitchen window with gratitude, knowing that even though the art-fair organizers had put up tents to protect the artwork in the event of rain, people would be far more likely to walk around—and to linger and look—if the weather was fair.

Brodie and Joanne prepared breakfast, and Beth

and Kelly tried to skip it in the interest of a little extra time to set out their wares on the pier where all the tenants of the Cannery Art Mall—as Beth had named it—would be showing their work. The rest of the artists would be strung out under tents along the river.

"You have to eat something," Ethan insisted. "It's going to be a long day. You might not get any lunch." He pressed a glass of orange juice into Beth's hand as she tried to dodge him to get to her jacket.

She took several swallows and then handed it to Kelly, who finished it. "Thanks. But there'll be vendors all over the pla—"

"It's ready." Brodie carried two steaming plates of omelettes and toast to the table. "Sit down. You could have this eaten in the time you spend arguing with us."

Ethan took their jackets from them and returned them to the pegs. Brodie pulled out chairs.

Kelly sighed at Beth and, resigned, moved to the table. "I remember now why we made that pact about men and marriage."

"What pact?" Joanne asked from the stove.

Aware of the potential danger in that line of conversation, Beth tried to warn Kelly off with a severe look, but Kelly, her mind no doubt on other things, had apparently forgotten Joanne's connection to Steve on this sunny morning.

"Never to fall for another one," Kelly answered, reaching for the pepper. "My husband wanted everything his way, and Beth's usually forgot she was alive. He—"

Kelly stopped abruptly, awareness dawning on her face.

Joanne frowned and put the spatula down on the

stove. Her expression changed from the almost convivial cheer they'd grown used to to that of the woman Beth remembered all too well from the old days—defensive, judgmental, argumentative.

"What do you mean?" Joanne demanded.

Beth closed her eyes, thinking that the last thing in the world she wanted to discuss this morning was her relationship with Steve. But maybe it was time to set the issue straight. Not the ideal time, certainly, but time all the same.

"I didn't mean anything, Joanne," Kelly said, apology in her eyes when she looked at Beth. "I was talking out of turn."

Joanne moved to the table, pulled out a chair at a right angle to Beth's and sat. The smell of something burning came from the stove. Brodie picked up the spatula and turned the charring omelette. Then Ethan moved to the table, as well, and took the chair opposite Joanne. He leaned back in it as though in the role of observer, but Beth knew better now. He was making himself available if she needed him.

"Kelly was my confidant in Seattle, Joanne," Beth said with courtesy but no apology, "and she listened to my problems when Steve wouldn't. She knows what I went through the last couple of years with Steve."

Joanne went pale. "Steve gave you everything."

Beth nodded. "Everything he could buy, yes."

"He was a wonderful father."

"On the five or six times a year he actually came home before Jason went to bed, yes, he was."

"He was working for *you!*"

Beth sighed. Old pain tried to resurrect itself but failed because there was so much new love. "Joanne, he was working for himself, because some inner demon made him always want to do more, make more, get more. I don't know if he was trying to prove something to you and Zachary or just to himself, but it controlled his whole life.''

"You had that wonderful house on the sound that everyone envied!''

"That's why we had it,'' Beth said. "Not because I wanted it, but so it could be envied. So everyone who visited would want what it contained, and Steve could make more sales, open more stores. I was the answering machine. My job was to make everyone who called Steve at home feel as though he was getting special treatment. I was a business tactic, Joanne, not a wife.''

"Then why did you stay?''

Beth had thought about that often in the year since he'd been gone. Especially lately, knowing what marriage *could* be like.

"Because Jason loved him,'' she said, "and I'd made a vow.''

Joanne's lips pinched closed and she looked away a moment, her eyes welling with tears. "So you're glad he's gone?''

"Joanne.'' Zachary had come into the room. His tone was reproachful.

Joanne looked up at her husband defensively. "Well, she was miserable. She hated him. She *must* be glad.''

"I *was* miserable,'' Beth said candidly. "But it was because I'd loved him so much in the beginning and then it all disintegrated from inattention. Even in my worst moments, I never hated him, never wished him dead. I was just so…disappointed.''

She reached blindly for Ethan's hand. He caught hers and squeezed it.

Joanne excused herself and left the room. With a moody glance around, Zachary shook his head and turned to follow her. Kelly put both hands over her face and burst into tears.

Beth's mouth trembled dangerously. "Kelly, stop it!" she ordered. "It wasn't your fault. That conversation was long overdue."

Ethan used Beth's hand to pull her out of her chair and into his lap as she sniffed back tears of her own.

"It isn't grief for Steve," she said. "It's...I think it's..."

"I know." He rubbed her back and pressed his cheek to her hair. "Grief for how it should have been. But I don't want you to be unhappy." He snatched a napkin from the holder on the table and gave it to her.

She dried her eyes and drew a breath. "I'm not unhappy. I just hate confrontation."

He grinned skeptically. "Really? I've never noticed that."

She laughed and kissed his temple. Then she turned to her friend, who still had tears streaming down her cheeks. "Kelly, it's okay."

Brodie dropped the spatula and crossed to the table. He leaned over Kelly and put his arms around her, then glanced at Ethan, humor glinting in his eyes. "Didn't we make a pact about staying away from women?"

Ethan held fast to Beth. "No," he replied. "As I remember, we made a pact to seek them out."

Brodie looked from the weeping woman in his

arms to Beth, dabbing at her eyes with a napkin.
"You mean...we're doing well?"

Ethan grinned. "Damned if I know."

PEOPLE THRONGED the art fair. The colorful tents set
up along the water made Cobbler's Crossing look like
some medieval encampment. Musicians had been
hired to stroll among the exhibits, and the sound of
their instruments floated through the air as though
sent from another time.

But it was the aroma of waffle cones that was driving Beth crazy. After her set-to with Joanne, she
hadn't had time to eat her omelette, and she and Kelly
had hurried to the pier on empty stomachs, after all.

Rush Weston had already arrived and, in high spir-
its at the prospect of the day ahead, had helped them
haul out tables and set up their work. All the while
he'd boasted of the special project he would unveil
at one o'clock, the sculpture that would grace the
lawn of the art association's newly acquired permanent home near the maritime museum.

"I beat out fourteen other artists for the commis-
sion, you know," he said several times.

Appreciating his help, Beth and Kelly agreed he
was wonderful, winking at each other across the long
table the three of them had carried out of Kelly's studio.

Rush was set up around the corner of the cannery
building, and the tall sculpture stood under what appeared to be several bedsheets sewn together. The
sheets protruded with something pointy out the top
and out the back, causing Kelly to speculate.

"Knowing him," she said to Beth sotto voce as
they dutifully admired his setup of sculpture and

bronzes, then returned to their own areas, "it's probably a giant breast! But I'm still anxious to see it. The guy's a genius."

Beth nodded. "I'm with you. And it was nice of him to help us."

"Mm. Only, it makes me wonder what he's up to."

Ethan, with Nikkie, Jason and Taylor Bridges in tow, arrived shortly after the opening with a wonderfully aromatic bag of food from a local takeout place.

"I'll sit for you," Nikkie offered, "so you can have breakfast."

"Brodie brought breakfast for Kelly, too," Ethan said, catching Beth's hand and pulling her aside while Nikkie took her place behind the table. "So why don't the two of you take a little time to relax and look around before the midmorning crush?" He put a hand to her cheek and looked into her eyes, his own gentle but searching. "You all right?"

She nodded. Her disagreement with Joanne had put a bit of a pall over the day. But if things went well, the exposure would help her as an artist and present the Cannery Art Mall to everyone who visited as the place for unique fine art and the more commercial but one-of-a-kind handicrafts.

She turned her lips into his hand. "I'm fine," she said. "I can't believe that deep down Joanne and Zachary weren't aware of all that about Steve, but I thought it was time to say it. I'm sorry it had to be in your kitchen."

"It's *our* kitchen," he corrected with a sweet smile. It turned wicked as he added, "I just don't want you cooking in it very much. Go find Kelly and a quiet place to have your breakfasts. I promised the boys I'd take them to the carnival." He pointed to the Ferris wheel a couple of hundred yards farther down the waterfront. "Nikkie'll watch your table until you're finished."

Beth put the take-out bag down and looped her arms around Ethan's neck. His warmth and his calm seeped into her, and she kissed him lingeringly, trying to tell him how truly happy he'd made her and how much she loved him.

"Yeah," he said, his voice ragged as she finally drew her mouth away. "Me, too."

"Dad, come on!" Jason said impatiently. He caught Ethan's hand and tugged. "You guys can do that later. Me and Taylor want to ride the moon jet!"

"All right, all right." Ethan kissed Beth one more time, then strode after the boys as they ran up the pier to the waterfront path.

Only as Beth replayed the scene in her mind did she realize Jason had called Ethan "Dad." It brought a lump to her throat and seemed to seal her life in place.

"I THINK I'M DEAD," Kelly said, nibbling on a sausage roll as she and Beth wandered slowly through a Peg-Board setup of small scenic paintings done in the impressionist style.

Beth sipped at a paper cup of tea as she stepped back to study a painting of mountains and a meandering stream. "That's funny. You look very much alive to me."

"I mean dead as a single woman," Kelly said.

They were now on opposite sides of the Peg-Board setup, and Beth leaned around it to look into Kelly's face. "I know that being a potter makes your *brain* go to pot, but try to be clearer. Are you trying to tell me we're going to be sisters-in-law?'' Kelly and Brodie had wandered off together the night before in the middle of a dance and hadn't been seen again until they'd appeared in Ethan's kitchen that morning.

Kelly's expression was both terrified and excited. ''Will it mean a reduction in rent?''

''No,'' Beth said. ''If I'm going to have to put up with you day in and day out, it means I'll need *more* money. Will you please speak plainly?''

Kelly came around the Peg-Board, chewing and swallowing her last bite of biscuit. Her cheeks were flushed. ''Brodie asked me to marry him last night.''

Beth squealed and caught her in a hug. She couldn't think of anything more wonderful than having her best friend become a part of her family.

''Brodie's wonderful,'' Beth said. ''You're going to be so happy!''

Kelly took a step back, still holding Beth's arms. Her eyes were filled with amazement. ''Who'd have thought just a year ago,'' she asked softly, ''that we'd both end up in love with and marrying the kind of men most women only dream about?''

As they hugged each other again, Beth realized it would never have occurred to *her*.

BETH SOLD six door plaques to an older woman who was thrilled to find the names of all her grandchildren. After a trip to her car with those, the woman returned to buy four painted flowerpots for gifts, then wandered over to Kelly's table and picked up several bowls.

Beth had just secured the morning's take in a locked box in her studio and intended to take advantage of the lull to tidy up her table when Kelly strode over and took her by the arm.

"Come on," she said. "Let's go see Rush's grand unveiling."

Beth glanced at her watch. It was three minutes to one.

"You go ahead," she said. "I should haul out some more things. These people are in a buying frenzy, and I don't want to miss one patron with an impulse to overspend."

Kelly rolled her eyes. "Jeez, Louise, lighten up. All our customers are collecting at Rush's, anyway. See. Our end of the pier is empty."

Beth looked up from rearranging a pair of children's chairs she'd painted with whimsical mice to find that Kelly was right. A few people were headed for the carnival, but everyone else was formed in a large semicircle, half-a-dozen people deep, around Rush's display tables.

"All right." Beth followed Kelly to Rush's area and discovered her friend had an ulterior motive in insisting they go. Brodie and Ethan were there, too.

Kelly went right into Brodie's arms and into a kiss that made everyone nearby smile and look away. Except Beth. She watched them, feeling as though, in a life filled with miracles, she'd been given yet another.

Then Ethan wrapped his arms around her from behind and found a spot for them in the crowd where she could see. The local radio station was broadcasting remote, and the *Crossings Crusader* had sent a reporter and a photographer.

Beth leaned her head back against Ethan's shoulder. "Did you know," she asked, "that Brodie and Kelly are getting married?"

Ethan smiled. "He just told me. Well, actually he stammered around a lot and I figured it out for myself."

Beth laughed. "Ebbie'll be thrilled to do another wedding." She gasped. "Uh-oh."

"What?"

She widened her eyes in mock alarm. "Kelly catered for us. Does that mean I have to cater for her?"

"No," he replied, kissing her cheek. "I think it means Kelly'll do it and ask you to serve."

Beth pretended hurt feelings. "That's mean."

His arms around her squeezed. "I'll make it up to you later," he whispered in her ear.

Rush cleared his throat, and the broadcaster who'd attached a microphone to the pocket of the artist's chambray shirt stepped out of his way.

Beth leaned back again into Ethan. "Where's Jason?" she asked.

"I sold him to the carnival," Ethan replied.

"Did you get a good price?"

"I threw in Nikkie. She's so good at the midway games she'll bankrupt them in a month, and then they'll be home again. But we can do some high living in the meantime."

"Oh, good."

The strolling musicians had stopped behind Rush and now played a little flourish. Rush began to speak. He talked about what a beautiful spot Cobbler's Crossing was and how the area was a source of inspiration for artists, himself particularly.

"Everything's about 'himself particularly,'" Ethan grumbled softly in Beth's ear.

She jabbed him gently with an elbow, then turned her attention back to Rush, hoping the sculpture would give him the fame his ego seemed to need so desperately.

He went on to talk about himself, giving a rather lengthy history of his career, then said that everything changed for him when he moved to Cobbler's Crossing.

"I found friends here," he said dramatically, his strong profile tipped upward, "and my particular inspiration." He swept a hand toward the shrouded sculpture. "This piece, entitled *Water Woman,* is the culmination of a four-month labor of love. My heart and my soul have gone into it, and I now present it to you, the people of Cobbler's Crossing."

Rush yanked on the sheet and it fell into his arms, revealing a life-size bronze of a nude female figure. A collective cry of approval rose from the crowd.

As Beth admired the statue from the base on which it stood on tiptoe on one foot, the other leg raised and bent at the knee as though the woman had been caught midstride, she thought she noticed a slight change in sound in the common cry of approval.

But the artist in her was too busy appreciating the "movement" in the bronze. The body was poised in an upward stretch, as if toward something just beyond reach. The thighs were long and slender, the hips rounded, the waist slender, the breasts uptilted and generous, the reaching arms graceful.

And then Beth saw the face.

With a little gasp she fell back against Ethan, and that was when she noticed that the arms around her were now like rock and the tension coming from him almost palpable.

She heard someone else gasp and knew the sound had come from Kelly.

The face on the sculpture...was Beth's.

CHAPTER SIXTEEN

THERE WAS A SMATTERING of applause among the other artists assembled, enthusiastic cheers from some men in appreciation of the female form, and startled glances at Beth from acquaintances who thought she must be embarrassed. There were also the disapproving frowns of those who would never understand that nude modeling did not suggest a morally bankrupt character.

The almost painful grip of the arms around her indicated that her husband was among that group. Beth pushed her way out of his embrace and turned, thinking that if she explained calmly and carefully, he might understand.

But she knew the moment she looked into his eyes that that wasn't going to happen. He was wearing the same expression he'd worn the night he'd hauled her out of the Applebys' basement and taken her to jail.

A cold knot formed in her midsection. They weren't going to be able to come together on this. She could hear his argument now. *Do you know what it's like to be present at the unveiling of a nude sculpture and have everyone identify it as your wife?*

Beth saw her in-laws standing in the front row of spectators across the semicircle. Their expressions could only be described as horrified shock.

Embarrassment, frustration, anger and disappointment became a turbulent combination in Beth's chest. She wanted to hide, she wanted to throw things, she wanted to be sick, and then she wanted to die.

But before she did any of those things, she wanted to kill Rush Weston.

But that was self-indulgence, she told herself, and something for which she had no time at the moment. Beth Warner Richards Drum had had it with everybody.

As Rush invited people closer to study the sculpture, Beth realized she was tired of being threatened with the loss of her child, tired of having to be on the watch for her in-laws' detective, tired of having to remind Rush Weston that he didn't love her and she didn't love him, tired of having to remind her husband of the same thing.

Feeling as though she should slip an arm into one of the shields she'd made for Henry V's army, she turned to Ethan and said into his furious dark eyes, "I'll deal with you later. Excuse me."

She knew that genuine shock was the only thing that prevented him from grabbing her and telling her what he thought of her then and there.

She marched through the crowd to where Joanne and Zachary continued to stand gasping at the sculpture. She collected congratulations and pats on the back for being Rush's model and "inspiration," as well as several glares, as she crossed the pier.

She stopped in front of Joanne, arms folded with resolution. "Where is he?" she asked with the air of royal command she'd learned from Joanne.

Joanne met Beth's gaze, her own imperiousness in place. "Who?"

"The detective," Beth replied. "Where is he?"

She saw embarrassment in Joanne's eyes for an instant, then it was gone. "What detective?" she asked innocently.

"The one you hired to check me out," Beth said, shifting her weight, her voice rising a trifle. "The one who's been following me and photographing me. Tell me where he is, or I'll have you arrested for harassment."

"Really?" The imperious look now became scornful. "You're threatening me after you posed naked for that…"

Zachary suddenly pointed his cane at a youngish man in a trench coat who stood several yards away, even now taking photographs. "Right there," Zachary said. "That's Frank Bowker."

Beth pointed to the spot where she and the Richardses stood. "You stay right here or I'll come after you, I swear it."

She turned in the direction of Bowker and was on him even as he took a final photo of her. Then he was preparing to run, backing away and trying to secure his camera over his shoulder. But she had him by the lapels before he could get away.

He was several inches taller than she was, and he appeared to be fairly substantial under the coat. Nevertheless there was no Mike Hammer toughness about him. In fact, she thought she saw fear leap in his eyes when she grabbed him.

"You're coming with me," she said, giving him her best Ethan-in-a-temper look. "And I don't want to hear one complaint or feel the least resistance, do you hear me?"

He seemed to try to pull himself together. "Who do you think you are?" he asked with false bravado.

While he was posturing, she snatched his camera from him. "The woman whose privacy you've been invading," she replied.

"Following you and taking pictures is not a crime," he said, his voice faltering.

She got right into his face. "When your husband is the bad-tempered sheriff of a small town, it is," she said, disregarding the distinct possibility that Ethan wasn't going to be her husband for much longer. "And I'm also holding this…what? Six-, seven-hundred-dollar piece of equipment?"

He sighed. "Nine," he said.

She looped the camera strap over her shoulder. "Then you'd better follow me."

Beth strode back to her in-laws as the rest of the crowd dispersed to the food stands and the other tents. They stood alone, a man and a woman who suddenly looked old and rather frail. But Beth refused to let her resolution slip.

"I'd like you to come with me, please," she said. "And, Zachary, be careful with your cane—those spaces between the planks." Then she marched off toward her studio as though completely confident that her in-laws and their detective were following.

Beth saw that Nikkie was manning her table. "That's quite a bod for a stepmother," Nikkie said under her breath, then giggled. "Are you back? Where's Dad?"

"Would you mind watching the table for a little longer?" Beth asked. Sad, she thought, that it was all falling apart when she and Nikkie were finally becoming friends. "I think your father's…still looking around."

"Sure, no problem. Take your time."

"Thanks, Nikkie." Beth ushered Zachary, Joanne and Bowker into her studio and closed the door. She flipped on all the lights she had, but the cavernous space was still dimly lit everywhere but under the fluorescent bulb above the worktable. So she gathered everyone there.

She pulled a stool up for Joanne. "You might want to sit down, Jo," she said.

"I'll stand," Joanne insisted. "You don't frighten me."

"It isn't my intention to frighten you." Beth made herself speak calmly. "It's my intention to explain a few things to you, then make it clear that there is no way in hell you will ever get Jason from me."

"Beth—" Zachary began.

Beth silenced him with a raised index finger. "I know you're a judge, Zachary, and I know you have influential friends, but even you can't make a case where there is none."

"But there's a statue of your naked body!" Joanne exclaimed.

"Joanne, it's art!" Beth said slowly, carefully. "I posed for Rush's sculpture class when I first moved here to make extra money. I didn't know Rush had sculpted me, but now that he has, I'm flattered to grace the lawn of the art association's new building." That wasn't true, but it wouldn't hurt to let Joanne think it was. "And that is not against the law."

"It's—" Joanne made a face "—disgusting."

And for the very first time Beth had an insight into Steve's sexual reactions to her. Was that what Joanne had taught him? That the body was disgusting?

"It isn't disgusting at all," Zachary said quietly. He used his cane to hike himself up on the stool, then rubbed at his cast as though the leg inside it ached. He gave Beth a thin smile. "I thought it was quite beautiful."

"Zach!" Joanne's eyes widened.

He sighed. "Don't be such a priss, Jo," he said mildly. "You looked like that once, and I enjoyed looking at you. But when I was made a judge, you changed. You became full of self-importance and you assumed a dictatorial code of behavior, which you inflicted on Steve—until he became just as stiff and self-absorbed. You did it to me, too."

Beth stood paralyzed in complete surprise, afraid to breathe for fear she'd be noticed.

"Zachary!" Joanne gasped, leaning against the table for support.

"It's true, Jo," he said heavily. "We used to be fun, you and I, and now you've turned us into caricatures of stuffy old folks. And you turned a boy who was already too serious for his own good into a man consumed with status, with wanting more."

"Are you saying…?" Joanne's mouth quivered, unable to say the words.

"That the adult he became is your fault?" Zachary shook his head. "We all get to a point where we have to look the past in the eye and decide what we want for our own future. Apparently he grew blind to his wife and son, and all he saw was getting and owning. But he did that to himself."

Zachary sighed and ran a hand over his face, then he turned to Beth. "I admit I was a little worried when I first saw your apartment in this place." He looked around, nodding as he noted the fresh coat of paint and the refinements she'd made. "Steve was always telling us that your art took so much time away from him, and I believed him. I was worried for Jason. But now that we've spent time with you and I've seen you with him and with Ethan and the girl, I don't think there was every anything wrong with you. I realize now the problem was with Steve.''

Beth was still afraid to breathe.

Joanne looked even more shocked than she'd been by the statue.

''I didn't want the detective, either,'' Zachary continued. ''But Jo thought it would give us something concrete to go on, and I've found it's often easier to take the line of least resistance when her mind's made up. But no more. Give her the film, Bowker. All of it.''

Bowker backed up a few steps, prepared to resist.

''Now,'' Zachary said more loudly. He took the wallet out of his jacket pocket. ''Hand the cartridges to Beth, you'll get paid in full, and this will be over.''

Beth's heart began to thump erratically. Over? The threat of losing Jason finally over? She'd talked a good line about the solidity of their case, but she didn't believe for a minute that she was invincible where the law was concerned. After all, she'd gone to jail for looking for a cat!

Bowker vacillated a moment, then apparently decided that immediate payment was more appealing than cartridges of film that would have no value to anyone else. He delved into his camera bag, produced six cartridges and placed them on the table.

Beth handed him his camera. ''And I want the one that's in there now.''

Bowker took it out and handed it to her. Zachary wrote him a check, which he quickly pocketed, and then he left.

Joanne put a hand to her heart. "Oh, my God," she moaned.

Beth turned to her in concern.

"Don't fall for it, Beth," Zachary said, easing himself off the stool. "She always has palpitations when she doesn't get what she wants. She'll be fine. I want to thank you and Ethan for your hospitality. We're going back to the house now to collect our things, then we'll head for home."

Beth steadied him as he braced against the cane and regained his footing. "I have to tell you something else before you go," she said.

He raised an eyebrow. "What's that?"

She heard herself speak as though it were someone else's voice. "That I did marry Ethan to stop you from taking me to court."

Zachary smiled. "I don't think you did. I think you married him because you saw in him everything you missed with Steve. I like that boy. I loved my son, but I didn't always *like* him."

Joanne now had both hands over her face.

"Neither did you, Jo," he said, slowly closing the few feet that separated them, the thump of his cane echoing in the big room. "How many times did you tell me he should make more time for Jason? You were willing to believe him about Beth because you were jealous of her, but you worried about Jason all the time. I think you wanted the boy just so you could make up to him what Steve didn't give him."

Joanne lowered her hands. Beth could see the lines that bitter disappointment had etched in her face.

"I wanted Steve to be better than he was," she said, her voice thin. "I told him Jason needed him. But he said...he said Beth wanted more."

"Jo, you knew that wasn't true." Zachary cupped his wife's cheek. "You wanted it to be true so you wouldn't have to blame him, but it wasn't. He became selfish and small. Admit it."

Joanne shook her head against the words, and Zachary pulled her into his arms. "He was such a cute little kid," he said to Beth, his own grief visible in his eyes. "It's hard to let go of that when they grow up and turn into someone else."

Tears welling in her eyes, Beth put a hand on Joanne's back. "Zachary, don't leave for Seattle like this. Why don't you spend the night and leave tomorrow? Come on, I'll walk you to your car."

Beth hugged Joanne before helping her into the Cadillac. "Steve and I had a good couple of years in the beginning. I like to remember that. I wish you would, too."

Joanne held her for a moment, then leaned back to look into her eyes. "You weren't ever as happy with him as you are with Ethan."

Beth was glad that had been phrased as a statement rather than a question, considering that Rush's grand unveiling had seriously endangered what she had with Ethan.

"I'll see you at home," she said.

Beth stood in the middle of the parking area that fronted the river and watched them drive away. She felt as though a heavy burden lay suspended in her chest. Much of it had been lifted by Zachary's words, but she'd come to care about her in-laws in the past few weeks more than she ever had when she'd been married to their son. She hated to think of them lonely and in pain.

Her worries had been relocated, not relieved.

She headed back toward the pier at a determined pace, scanning the crowd for Ethan or for Rush. She'd take on whomever she found first.

Then she stopped in her tracks. The pier was empty; the crowd was gone. Tables and booths had been abandoned. Where was everyone?

Then she heard shouts coming from the other side of the cannery. She followed them, picking up her pace until she was running. Had something terrible happened? It must have. What else would have made the artists leave their work unattended?

Then, as she rounded the corner of the building and saw the knot of about a hundred people gathered at the pier's railing, she realized that their shouts were cheers.

She stared in shock as Brodie and several other men hauled Ethan out of the water with a rope. Rush Weston's arms were wrapped around his neck.

Rush was peeled from Ethan's back and laid on the pier, coughing and spitting up water. Jan Billings kneeled over him as the crowd gathered around.

Ethan, drenched and perched on the railing, swung his legs onto the pier and leaped nimbly down as Beth approached. Kelly threw a blanket around him. "Ambulance is on its way," she said. "Sorry about the musty smell. I keep it in the trunk of my car. Are you okay?"

"Fine," he replied tersely.

"Daddy!" Nikkie tried to embrace the bulk of him under the blanket.

He allowed her one moment, then kissed her temple and took a step back. "I'm okay, Nik. I don't want you to get wet."

"What happened?" Beth asked. Concern for him,

despite her anger and helpless frustration over the way this day had gone, made her voice and her manner sharp. "Did it make you feel better to throw Rush in the water?"

Ethan dried his face with a corner of the blanket. When he lowered the rough brown wool to look at her, she saw instantly that he wasn't at all hypothermic. A man couldn't be on the brink of freezing and still have eyes that hotly angry.

"Beth, he—" Brodie began, but Ethan silenced him with a look.

"When I can't speak for myself," he said, his tone deadly, "I'll let you know."

"My mistake." Brodie, probably also concerned about Ethan's dunking, snarled back at him. "Second one today. The first one was pulling you out of the water."

Ethan glared at his brother for a moment, then a smile curved his lips. "Did I forget to thank you for that? *My* mistake."

"I suggest everyone calm down," Kelly said diplomatically. "Here, Ethan. A vendor brought you this cup of coffee. Ah. There's the ambulance."

Kelly pulled Beth and Nikkie aside as Ethan moved over to Rush, who was now sitting up. Jan was rubbing circulation into his shoulders and arms.

Rush looked up as the crowd parted to let the EMTs through with their gurney. He focused on Ethan and even from a small distance Beth heard him say clearly, "Thanks. I'm not sure I'd have jumped in after *you*."

Ethan accepted that with a nod. "I just wanted to make sure you lived to serve your thirty days for swinging at me."

Beth heard the exchange with an awful sense of
having been impulsive and wrong once again. Oddly
it made her feel more defensive than penitent. She put
her fingertips to the throbbing that had begun at her
right temple.

"Yes," Kelly said wryly, "stupidity does give you
a headache, doesn't it? Rush was telling a group of
guys that the model had been his lover. Ethan suggested he tell the truth. Rush swung at Ethan, not the
other way around. Ethan dodged him and Rush landed
in the river. He can't swim."

Rush was in the ambulance in a matter of minutes.
The EMTs apparently tried to convince Ethan to go
along to be checked over, but he refused.

The ambulance drove off. Jan Billings railed at
Ethan about getting out of the cold air and into a hot
shower and dry clothes even as she lent him the cell
phone in her purse to call the office.

"I'm on my way home," he told Jan when he
handed back the phone. "I appreciate your concern,
but I'm fine. Beth!"

The note in his voice was authoritative. Considering Beth had intended to make the afternoon about
taking charge of her own life, she didn't respond well
to the sound of it. Now that she was sure he was all
right, she became furious all over again for the way
he'd reacted to the unveiling of Rush's bronze.

"Yes?" she asked frostily.

He whipped the blanket off, balled it in his hands
and handed it to Kelly. "Thanks, Kelly," he said,
then to Beth again, "You're coming with me. Nikkie,
will you go back and watch her table?"

Beth tried to protest. "I can't just—"

Ethan ignored her and turned to his brother. "Will

Bridges has Jason and Taylor at the carnival. He's bringing Jason back at two-thirty. Can you bring him home?''

"Sure."

"Nikkie is supposed to meet her friends at three at the taco booth," Beth informed him. "We can't just ignore her plans."

"That's all right," Kelly said traitorously. "At three o'clock, we'll move your table up against mine and I'll watch both of them. We'll get the kids home afterward, don't worry."

War was in the wind, and while Beth had been eager to confront it earlier, she'd felt completely in the right then. Now she was guilty of having accused Ethan of a petty act, when it had really been an heroic one. And she didn't want to walk into a fight at such a disadvantage.

"Joanne and Zachary are at home," she told him. "You go home and shower and I'll be along later."

Kelly pointed to the cannery. "Beth's old apartment is still there. It's tiny, but there is a shower and…you know, room to argue."

Ethan shook his head. "This is going to be a loud argument. We need privacy."

"You need the shower and dry clothes first," Jan insisted, her arms folded resolutely. "And I'm going to hang around until you do it, or I'll call the EMTs back and make them take you to the ER."

Brodie gave Ethan a push in the direction of the cannery. "Go shower. It'll take me five minutes to run home and get you a change of clothes."

Beth showed a stiff-backed Ethan to the shower in her small apartment. She handed him a towel, which he took with a terse thank-you and closed the door on her.

Fuming, she went back outside to help Nikkie as a crowd began to form around her table. It occurred to her that there was something to be said for notoriety.

True to his word, Brodie was back in a very short time with a bag, which he carried into the cannery. Ethan came out shortly afterward in a dark blue sweater and cords. He caught Beth's wrist in the middle of a transaction.

"Ethan, I was—"

But he interrupted her to speak to Nikkie. "Thanks, Nik. Uncle Brodie'll take you home."

"Where are you going?" Nikkie asked, wrapping a clay pot in newspaper. She looked worriedly from her father to Beth.

"We'll be home by dinner," he replied. Then he hauled Beth up the pier toward the parking lot.

Beth dragged her feet and pulled against him. "Ethan, my purse is—"

He threw an arm around her waist, anchored her to his side and kept walking. "You're not going to need your purse."

Beth pulled at the fingers biting into her side. "Every woman in this town is going to vote against you in the next election if you keep acting like a Neanderthal!"

The possibility apparently didn't concern him. He strode across the parking lot with her held close to his side. When he reached the Blazer, he put her in, then locked and closed her door.

He was behind the wheel in an instant and turned the key in the ignition. He switched off the radio, switched on the heater and whipped out of the parking lot and onto the fortunately empty highway with the speed of a competitor at Le Mans.

"You have a bad habit," she said coolly, "of letting your temper affect your driving."

"Don't worry about it," he replied. "I've had pursuit training. But it'd help me if you didn't distract me with conversation."

She leaned her head back against the headrest and closed her eyes. "Another one of those arguments where only *you* get to talk?"

"Yeah. Right. Whose voice are *you* hearing?"

Beth didn't respond, partly because he was right, and partly because she was trying to save her reserves of wit for what was coming. She was going to need them. He was a worthy if completely unreasonable adversary.

She had no idea where he was going. He followed the main road through town to the far end of the waterfront. There he turned off onto another road that led down a slope to a little cove sheltering a long-deserted yacht club. The old frame building had fallen into disrepair, and most of the windows were broken.

There wasn't a soul around.

The parking lot and boat ramp stood empty under a weakening afternoon sun. Clouds massed on the western horizon and began moving toward Cobbler's Crossing. The grass along the riverbank bent with the wind.

Beth looked away from the clouds as Ethan stopped in the middle of the parking lot, turned off the ignition with an angry jerk and rested his wrist on top of the steering wheel.

He stared angrily through the windshield, apparently collecting his thoughts for an attack on Rush's sculpture.

On the theory that the best defense was a good offense, Beth launched her own attack. She yanked off her seat belt and turned toward him.

"I'll save you the trouble, Ethan," she said, sad and disappointed that it had to turn out this way. "I've been through this with you once before, remember? I know exactly what you're about to say."

He turned to her, the anger in his eyes momentarily diluted by confusion.

"At the Appleby house," she said. "This is a slight variation on the theme. 'Do you have any idea,'" she said, her tone deepening as she mimicked his voice, "'what it's like to attend the unveiling of a nude statue in front of most of the town and discover that your wife posed for it?'"

She resumed her natural voice. "You were embarrassed, and like almost everyone else, you think that because someone models in the nude, there has to be lewd and lascivious behavior involved. That modeling was done in a sculpture class Rush was teaching in the presence of eighteen students, many of them other women. I had no idea Rush was planning me for the art association's front lawn, but I'm tired of defending myself to you. It's clear you're not going to have the tolerance for living with an artist that you claimed you would."

"The only thing that's clear," he returned, "is that *you're* the one who's completely misunderstood the situation. Sure, I was surprised to see that the sculpture was you, but I was not embarrassed. My initial anger was not that you'd posed nude for another artist, but that I dislike the man particularly, and I felt a very natural male inclination to kill him because he'd seen the very image I revere.''

Her angry indignation severely dented, Beth tried hard to firm it up. ''Because you thought—''

She'd been prepared to accuse him of presuming Rush had made sexual overtures, but Ethan interrupted her. ''Don't tell me what I thought. You're not inside my head. In fact, I wonder if you've even been anywhere near me for the past month and a half if you can so misread me.''

''Well, if you're not angry about Rush, what's the problem?''

''The problem is you,'' he said brutally. ''I was raving inside that Weston had seen…you. But that was my gut reaction, and I was telling myself that I had to work on that, that what I was feeling wasn't reasonable and I had to get a grip on common sense and see that image of you for what it was— very…beautiful.'' His eyes grew turbulent and grave with that admission, then anger took over again. ''Until you turned around to me and I saw you do it again.''

''Do *what* again?''

''Mistake me for Steve.'' He said the words quietly, but the confines of the car amplified them and seemed to cause them to hang there long after they'd been said.

Beth opened her mouth to defend herself, but he went on, ''Just like you presumed I threw Rush in the river. In the six weeks we've been together, I've proved Steve wrong about you over and over, but that still doesn't seem to separate me from him in your mind.''

Beth watched the clouds move in over the water,

heavy and dark and blotting out the sun. The interior of the car seemed suddenly darker, too.

"Maybe *you're* confusing *me* with Diana," she retorted. "I warned you once that we could never have what you had with Diana."

"I don't *want* what I had with Diana!" he roared. "It was great but that was *her!* I want *you!*"

"Then if you want me, you have to put up with a woman who poses for life-drawing classes! Or who might want to take a class herself! Do you want to go through this emotional struggle every time the subject arises or every time someone teases you because that's me on the front lawn of the art association's building?"

Ethan wondered how it was possible for a man to love a woman and want to murder her at the same time. But that was precisely how he felt.

"You know," he said, "I think you're the one who can't make the adjustment here. This isn't about modeling or not modeling. You're the one who still thinks you can't have your art and a relationship, too, but it isn't because of me. I think you've just decided it's easier to live day and night in your studio doing your thing and not having to worry about working someone else's needs into your life."

Somewhere deep down she recognized a grain of truth in that and closed it off. Assuming an air of feigned surprise was easier than assuming guilt.

"Gee," she said, "when I disagree with you, I end up in a jail cell. Do you think that notion could have anything to do with it?"

"No," he replied evenly. "I think your behaving like a brat has a lot to do with it. Did you really think you could take on another marriage—even one that was just intended for your own purposes—and never have to consult me on anything or explain yourself when necessary?''

She met his gaze, her own unflinching. ''I didn't expect to have to do it at every turn. I guess I thought that at home you'd be my husband and not the sheriff.''

The radio crackled. Then, ''500, come in.''

The voice was Ebbie's, and Ethan yanked the microphone off its hook. ''500. Go ahead.''

''Ethan, we have to transport a juvenile to Portland.'' Her voice sounded apologetic. ''I know it's your day off, but there's no one else available.''

The last thing Ethan wanted to do at that moment was transport a sullen juvenile a hundred miles and drive home in the dark on the winding highway.

Then he glanced at Beth, who looked cold and distant and even less appealing than the long drive in the dark.

''I'm on my way,'' he said, then replaced the mike on its hook and turned the key in the ignition. ''We'll have to finish this later.''

He expected a sharp retort, but she said nothing, folding her arms and leaning as far away from him as she could while he turned around and headed out of the parking lot.

CHAPTER SEVENTEEN

BETH STOOD for a long time under a lukewarm shower, trying hard to revive herself after a brief three hours of sleep. Ethan hadn't come home until just before midnight, and he'd never come upstairs.

She'd heard subtle sounds in the kitchen and lay tensely on her side of the bed, waiting for him to come up. By then her anger had abated somewhat and she'd been willing to have it out with him, to state her case again and listen to his.

But the opportunity never arose.

She'd finally fallen asleep shortly after four in the morning, and when she'd awakened at seven-thirty, he'd already left for the office.

She took that to mean he didn't want to talk. Maybe he no longer considered their relationship worth the argument required to keep it together.

Sadness weighted her limbs and burned in the pit of her stomach. She went downstairs, desperate for a cup of coffee, and found Jason and Nikkie whispering over breakfast cereal. They stopped guiltily when she walked into the room.

"Hi." She smiled from one to the other, trying to force cheer into her voice. The effort failed. "Didn't your uncle Brodie come over this morning?"

Nikkie studied her worriedly. "He isn't home. I made the coffee. How come Daddy left so early?"

Beth poured half a mug of the thick black brew and took a sip before answering. It was strong enough to generate sound when it hit her stomach. She withheld a wince. "I don't know, Nik. You'll have to ask him." She went to Jason, leaned over and kissed his cheek. "Guess you and I have to take a cab to school and to work."

"Cameron's coming to pick me up in his dad's van," Nikkie said. "The drama club's having a field trip today to the Coaster Theater in Cannon Beach. We can drop you and Jason on the way."

"Great." Beth headed for the basement stairs. "Do you think he'd have room for a few boxes, too?"

Nikkie looked surprised. "Boxes?"

"Yes. I have to take a few things back to the cannery."

ETHAN STARED at the coffee and pecan roll Ebbie had placed on his desk. After no sleep and enough caffeine to keep six people awake for forty-eight hours, he imagined that putting that much sugar into his system would be like dropping a match into a can of gasoline.

He felt too incendiary as it was. He pushed the roll away and tried to force himself to focus on the paperwork before him.

But Ebbie appeared in his office doorway looking uncharacteristically apprehensive. He felt himself tense.

"What?" he demanded.

She pointed vaguely in the direction of town. "There's a...a riot. On Ashley and Ninth."

He stared at her. "A riot. In Cobbler's Crossing."

"Yes."

"Well, aren't there two police units on this morning?"

She shifted her weight. "Yes. They're the ones who called for you."

"Curtis and Billings are patrolling."

"They're already there."

"God." Wishing now that he'd eaten the roll, Ethan ran out to his car and made Ashley and Ninth in just under four minutes. The sidewalk was choked with people, but not the type usually associated with a riot.

There were no professional agitators and no angry youths, just men in business suits standing in front of the bakery, older women with shopping bags, younger women with small children by the hand and pushing strollers. A pair of homeless men, one in a trench coat, one in a tattered paisley silk jogging suit, stood on a bench on the sidewalk across the street for a better look.

As Ethan left his car and pushed his way to the core of the crowd, he was grateful to see that there were no apparent injuries and the mood seemed more confused than hostile. Good. The situation was redeemable.

His thoughts on that changed when he finally reached the source of the disturbance and found every single member of his family involved and most of their friends.

He stared, unable to believe his eyes. Nikkie had Curtis by the arm and seemed to be giving him some elaborate explanation that had the vocal support of the entire drama club, whose members were gathered around her.

Zachary and Joanne were bending the ear of one

of two young police officers in the middle of the fray, while Brodie spoke to another.

Beth and Kelly and Portia Pintoretto had Billings cornered. Mrs. Pintoretto owned Gifts Galore, which Ethan noticed had a gaping hole where a display window had been. As he watched, Kelly and Mrs. Pintoretto grabbed each other's arms, apparently prepared to duke it out, but Billings stepped between them, looking desperate.

Just to add interest to the picture, a half-dozen medieval shields—the ones Beth had helped Nikkie and her friends make—were scattered about the sidewalk, two of them in the gift-shop window.

Trying to imagine how all this had come about, Ethan stepped intrepidly into the middle of it.

Jason was the first to notice his presence. "Dad!" he shouted, and raced toward him as though Ethan were God himself.

Ethan opened his arms and Jason flung himself into them. Nikkie was right behind him.

"Daddy, you've got to help us. It's all a big mistake, and…and…" She began to cry. "It's all my fault again, but Mrs. Pintoretto wants them to arrest Beth and Kelly, but they didn't really do it. Well, they did it, but they didn't do it on purpose!"

"Ethan!" Zachary joined them, leaning on his cane. "Thank God you're here. Please try to make them understand that Brodie says he can fix all of them without charge. I'll pay him of course, once he—"

"All what?" Ethan asked reluctantly, holding the children to him.

"The cars."

"What cars?"

"The ones I smashed into when I tried to stop the van."

"What van?"

"King Henry's van. You know. Cameron's."

Ethan remained quiet for a moment, trying to decide if it was him or the situation that simply refused to make sense. He searched his mind for a logical question.

"Why did you have to stop the van?"

"Because Beth was in it," Zachary said. "She was moving back to the cannery."

For an instant the sheriff in Ethan turned off, and the man in him felt a sudden and powerful onslaught of temper. She'd been leaving? While he was gone?

He looked for her face in the crowd, but couldn't find it. Billings had both arms out straight, holding Mrs. Pintoretto off with one hand and preventing a swinging Kelly from getting to her with the other.

"She *wasn't* leaving," Nikkie said, sobbing. "I told her Cameron would take her to work and Jason to school 'cause he was picking me up for our field trip—remember you signed the slip?" When he nodded, she went on, "Well, she asked me if there'd be room in the van for a couple of boxes, and when I asked her why, she said because she had to move some things back to the cannery. Jason and I thought she was moving her stuff back because you guys were gonna get a divorce. I know you had a big fight yesterday."

"So Nikkie called Kelly, and Uncle Brodie was there," Jason said. "And we thought they could come to the cannery and talk Mom out of leaving."

"But Grandma and Grandpa..." Nikkie began,

then corrected herself. "I mean, Zachary and Joanne…"

Zachary smiled. "You were right the first time, Nikkie."

"Well, they overheard me telling Kelly on the phone, and they followed us and made Cameron stop the van so Mom couldn't leave until you got a chance to talk to her."

Ethan managed to assimilate all that, but he still had questions. "How did the window get broken?"

Joanne appeared. "Kelly did that," she said with a wide smile. "When Leadfoot Richards here got the van stopped—" she hooked a thumb at Zachary, who smiled proudly "—Kelly and Brodie were right behind us, and Kelly jumped out and started taking Beth's boxes out of the van, yelling that nobody was leaving anybody."

"Then Mom tried to get the boxes back," Jason said, his eyes shining with the excitement of the drama, "and they were fighting over them, and when Kelly pulled really hard, all the shields flew out and a couple of them went through that mean lady's window. Boy! They fly just like Frisbees!"

"The shields," Ethan asked, just to make sure he was keeping up, "were in the boxes?"

"Yeah," Nikkie said. "She wasn't moving out. She was just taking the shields to the cannery for storage until the Parents' Club auction."

Ethan felt such relief at that news that he gained a new confidence in himself and the situation. He looked around for Beth, but still couldn't spot her.

Billings was listening patiently while Mrs. Pintoretto chewed him out and Brodie was forcibly dragging Kelly away. He brought her toward Ethan and the group gathered around him.

"That woman needs a lobotomy!" Kelly declared, yanking herself out of Brodie's hold. "And you didn't have to take her side!"

"I didn't take her side," Brodie argued. "I just thought you could have been a little more conciliatory about breaking her window."

"I tried. I explained to her that I'd have to repay her for her window in installments and she called me something rude in Italian."

"Do you speak Italian?"

"No."

"Then how do you know it was rude?"

"Because a universal gesture went with the word! And it's going to cost me everything I made at the fair and what's left of my savings, which I was going to use to buy a sign for the front of my studio."

Brodie looked smug. "No, it's not. I paid her."

Kelly's anger fell away and her expression softened. "You did?"

"I did. So you've got yourself a man who is more than a pretty face. Though I'm not a millionaire, I *am* able to take care of your damages."

She giggled and threw her arms around him. "My hero!" she exclaimed.

The drama club cheered. Joanne and Zachary nodded approvingly.

Curtis, Billings and the two police officers approached Ethan.

"Take Jason," Ethan directed Nikkie, "and see if you can find Beth."

"Right."

"Mrs. Pintoretto's willing to drop all charges,"

Billings said, "now that your brother's paid for the window."

"All right. And the owners of the cars?"

Curtis nodded. "Same. Damage isn't serious. A crunched bumper, a couple of lights and a bent mirror. Brodie says he can repair all of it. Believe it or not, everybody's happy."

"It's a miracle," one of the cops said. "When we walked into this, I thought we were going to have to call for hats and bats, just like in 'NYPD Blue.'"

The other cop grinned. "Fortunately for us, Drum, they're all your family. You think maybe you could put an electric fence around your house or something? Possibly post a warning when you guys are coming to town?"

"Hilarious, gentlemen." Ethan looked around at the dispersing crowd. "So we're finished here? No charges, no formal complaints, no tickets, no fines?"

"All clear. Except for you, who has to go home to this crime wave. Just to show you our hearts are in the right place, we'll sweep up the glass for you."

"Appreciate it."

"Daddy!" Ethan turned to find Nikkie and Jason looking concerned. The drama-club members were clustered around them, also worried. "Beth's in your car. In the cage."

He looked up and saw her seated in the back of his unit behind the metal screen that served to isolate the perpetrator. She had a hand to her forehead.

"You're not going to put her in jail again, are you?" Jason asked.

"No." He glanced up at Cameron. "How's your dad's van? Do you need to call him?"

Cameron shook his head. "Nope. It's cool. Not a scratch. We can still take Jason to school."

"I missed him when I went into the spin," Zachary called out. He and Joanne stood out of the way near a parking meter with Brodie and Kelly. "And got the car in front of me with my tail."

Joanne rolled her eyes. "Keep him out of the Grand Prix."

For the first time in about twenty-four hours, Ethan felt like laughing.

"Chinese food at Ming Ha's," he said to his newly adopted in-laws and to his brother and Kelly, who were picking up the shields. "Six-thirty? My treat."

"Sure," Brodie replied. "But why?"

Ethan couldn't think of a good reason, except that now that all their lives were interwoven, they didn't need one. "It's Monday. Family night."

He turned to the drama club, his daughter's eccentric but loyal support. "How about you guys? Chinese food tonight on me? Lots of old folks, though."

Heads nodded and their reply was unanimous. "Cool!"

"All right. See you tonight." He kissed Nikkie and Jason, then headed for his patrol car.

He opened the back door and leaned in to pull Beth out. She looked exhausted and upset and very fragile. "You need a lift somewhere?" he asked gently. "You can ride in the front."

Heavy-lidded blue eyes studied him suspiciously. "You mean we caused this whole—" she waved a hand at the barricades still up on the street, at the damaged cars just now being driven away, at the police sweeping glass off the street "—mess, and you're letting everybody off?"

God, he'd made quite an impression on her over the Appleby-house incident if she thought he could take this mini-riot, which was the result of everyone's love and concern for everyone else, and make them pay for it.

And then, because he felt guilty, he took off his hat and leaned down to kiss her slowly in apology. When he raised his head, he saw confusion in her eyes.

"What was that for?" she breathed.

"Because I'm sorry for ever bearing any resemblance to Steve, for not understanding instantly about the sculpture, for making you believe that anytime we disagreed about anything you were going to end up in jail."

The confusion in her eyes cleared and the love he'd grown used to seeing there shone brightly. She wrapped her arms around his waist and leaned into him with a little groan of contentment. "Oh, Ethan. I didn't think that. But what you said yesterday did make sense. When Steve died, I was so drunk with freedom that I did want to maintain it in a way, even after you married me. I was being selfish. So today I wanted to turn over a new leaf. I figured you'd have to take me in or something, and I was going to go quietly and wait for my chance to explain."

He walked her around the car and put her into the front seat. Then he got in behind the wheel. "You don't have to explain," he said. "Everyone's done it for you. The kids went nuts when they thought you were leaving. Zachary, Joanne, Kelly and Brodie were determined to stop you. And I think the drama club was just happy to be involved. They're all meeting us for dinner tonight, by the way. Chinese food."

She smiled. "How come?"

"Family night," he explained. "I'm taking you home. You're exhausted."

She looked at him across all the gear that sat between the two front seats, her expression disarmingly hopeful. "You don't have a coffee break coming or something, do you?"

"You hungry?"

She sighed. "Last night was horrid and I really really missed you."

Her words fell on him like a caress and made him curse the half mile between them and home.

He snatched the radio mike off its mounting even as he started the motor. "500," he said.

"500," Ebbie answered. "Go ahead."

"I'm code seven, Eb. For a couple of hours."

"It's early for lunch, Ethan."

"I'm not going to lunch, Ebbie. I'm taking Beth home."

"For two...? Oh. Oh! Right. Right. Two hours. Gotcha. Take your time. It's quiet, except for the riot you just cleaned up, and the rioters are all yours, aren't they? See you when I see you."

Ethan replaced the mike. All his. Despite the morning's events, he found great happiness in that knowledge.

"So how did it feel to arrive at the scene of a riot," Beth asked, laughter in her voice, "and discover that the rioters were your family?"

He laughed softly and accelerated. "Routine, my love. Routine."